WHOA!

With the trail juncture in sight and full of milling horses, Dun Lady's Jess broke into a startled canter. "O-oh no," Arlen said, his teeth clicking as he bounced; he yanked on her mane, the only thing at hand. "Whoa!"

And then Lady caught wind of *others* in the woods around them, closing in on them. With the sudden downwind rustle of brush, a figure emerged from camouflage of leaves and dull brush almost at her feet.

"Whoa!" Arlen cried again, completely unaware of those *others*, clenching her barrel with his long legs and hauling on her mane. Metal slashed at them, gleamed dully along an astonishingly long blade—and quite abruptly Lady did just as she'd been told, tucking her butt and dropping her head so Arlen flew neatly over her withers, rolling onward and out of reach. The blade flashed down to score her shoulder and she kicked out wildly. Ramble screamed, a stallion's challenge, and knocked her aside, knocked her *down*—

She wrenched herself away, trying to avoid Arlen's sprawling figure, well aware that more agents converged upon them.

Armed men and women, ready to turn the hunt into a kill.

BAEN BOOKS by Doranna Durgin

Dun Lady's Jess
Changespell
Changespell Legacy
Barrenlands

Touched by Magic
Wolf Justice

Wolverine's Daughter

Seer's Blood

A Feral Darkness

Other Books
Star Trek: The Next Generation—Tooth and Claw
Earth: Final Conflict—Heritage

Changespell Legacy

Doranna Durgin

CHANGESPELL LEGACY

Copyright © 2002 by Doranna Durgin

A Baen Books Original

Baen Publishing Enterprises
P.O. Box 1403
Riverdale, NY 10471
www.baen.com

ISBN: 0-7434-3544-3

Cover art by Carol Heyer

First printing, June 2002

Distributed by Simon & Schuster
1230 Avenue of the Americas
New York, NY 10020

Production by Windhaven Press
Printed in the United States of America

To Alan—our Bookhound—and
all the people who loved him.

Many thanks to suspects usual and new: to Barbara Gampt for things Ohio, to Judith, who always catches the things no one else does, to Jennifer for the missing scene, to the SFF gang who cheered me on, and to Jenni McPhail for trusting me with Phoenix Fire—who believes she should have her own book but finally, after many food bribes, accepted that I couldn't change Lady from a courier-bred dun to a grey Arabian in the middle of a series.

(And you may blame this book on Lucienne, who quite wickedly said "What if . . . ?")

Chapter 1

Arlen meant to be home before now.

With the Lorakan Mountains looming on the western skyline to remind him just how much land lay between here and Anfeald, he calculated the distance to the nearest travel booth versus the time before Jaime's next visit.

He wasn't going to make it.

From one world to another she would come, from Ohio on Earth to Anfeald in Camolen, and she'd find him . . .

Absent.

Not that anyone would be able to tell her why—not Carey, his close friend and head courier, who thought Arlen attended the special field calling of the Council of Wizards in Siccawei. Not his two apprentices, who thought the same. Not the Council itself, with a renewed emphasis on confidentiality after the

1

events of the previous summer, the rogue wizards and their mage lure-enhanced powers run amok in Camolen with far too many people chatting about the particulars.

They'd overcome that trial—Arlen and Jaime, Carey and Jess, and Dayna, ever twiddling with her forbidden raw magic on the sly. It had been more the others than Arlen himself, who'd first been hampered by Council strictures and then by recovery from a long-distance blow dealt by an enhanced and vengeful wizard.

The thought of it made him wince. Without the mage lure, Willand would never have been able to touch him. And even knowing she'd had it . . .

Well, he'd underestimated her.

But his friends—armed more with determination and wits than conventional magic—had taught the Council a lesson about acting instead of reacting. About shaking off the strictures of their endless debates to choose *action*—even to the point of taking to a trail in Siccawei without him.

So here Arlen stood, gazing at the moonrise over the mountains with three layers of heartland jackets over his Jaime-gifted silken long underwear and OSU sweatshirt, and a blanket from the road inn wrapped tightly around his shoulders on top of it, his breath frosting the air and riming his thick grey-shot mustache. A porch board creaked under his foot, reminding him of the need for quiet with an inn full of grouchy winter travelers at his back.

He could send Jaime a spell message through the Mage Dispatch service, but that would only reveal his location to the alert and nervous mage lure-runners he'd come here to thwart. They had reason for their nerves—the old border guard spells against them had worked once, and with the study he'd done this past week, the spells'd soon work again.

But not until he made it home. Back to warmer Anfeald in south-central Camolen, to the winter-burnt pastures and hills, the turned-over garden fields, the deep-honed respect for his wizard's power from Anfeald's landers and the casual irreverence from Carey in spite of it. And Jaime. Commuting between worlds, rearranging her life to spend nearly half her time here with him. In another day she'd be sitting in the rocker by the thick-silled open window of his personal rooms, one spell heating the room and another keeping the heat from escaping. She'd have the old black and white cat on her lap while the young calico male tried to impress her with his antics and headstands.

But she'd be waiting for *him*. Wondering, perhaps worrying, probably annoyed on top of it all.

Like most powerful wizards, Arlen rarely pulled himself up into a saddle. Town coaches, shoe leather, mage travel with transfer booths . . . they all came more easily. Even so . . . in the morning, he'd see about securing a horse, one to get him to the nearest transfer booth three townlets down the road in Amses.

Jaime would be waiting. And for once, Camolen rested quietly around him.

❧

Branches warp and ooze, merging into one another. Winter-flattened ground cover of fall leaves compresses into a blanket over the earth and melts into the roots of the tree, swirling old golds and dulled crimsons into silvery bark to obscure the small den-hole there.

An uneasy ground squirrel bolts for that hole.

Half the squirrel makes it home. Rich brown fur merges into the red-gold-silver patch where its life ends, following twisted eddies of matter.

Hoofbeats sound in the cold winter air. Dun mare, deep buckskin with black points, a black line down her spine, and wiser eyes than most. Alone, unhindered save for the padded leather girth and chest band holding a courier's pouch over her withers, she prances to a stop, sampling the air with widened nostrils and the raised neck of a wary posture, alert for movement, for scent, for something on which to pin her attention. To define the *wrongness* she feels here.

After a moment, she snorts and moves on, her equine vision unable to perceive the frozen patch of distortion by the side of the trail. Too still, too close for her to see out of that eye at that angle.

With a flick of her tail, Dun Lady's Jess leaves the birth of death and destruction behind her, never knowing it's there at all.

Chapter 2

Suliya swept the main aisle of Anfeald Stables, spending more energy on resentment than she did on the chore itself. She should have been out on a courier run today, burn it all, and here she was doing clean-up chores instead. Inspecting stalls, rewrapping bandages, mixing a warm winter mash . . . and sweeping up the inevitable clots of mud, melting ice chunks, and wasted hay. Half the day's horses were still out, slowed by the roads despite seasonal spells meant to clear them. No doubt their riders were wind-chilled and stiff and more than ready to return home, but Suliya longed to have been one of them. The only rider making fewer runs out of Anfeald than she was Carey—and everyone knew he had to keep his schedule light because of the wizard-inflicted damage he'd taken a year and a half earlier.

Suliya was the last of the couriers hired to rebuild

the stable after that summer, and initially she'd counted it a rare opportunity. Anfeald's reputation was spotless, their horses impeccably bred and trained. Working here meant the opportunity to watch Jaime Cabot apply her unique Earth riding theory—and to watch others take lessons under her, a bonus earned by the top-performing couriers. Working here meant being in Arlen's hold, and Arlen's reputation as a man of power had risen considerably these past few years. Working here meant being one of the best.

If she ever got the chance.

Her father hadn't believed she would . . . that she could. "Try one of the smaller barns," he'd advised her, even upon showing her the trail. "Someplace they might tolerate your lack of discipline." She hadn't believed it of him—that he'd truly reach the end of his patience. That he'd truly withdraw his support. Not the SpellForge head chair, so full of his public image.

At three years old, she'd wandered his giant work suite unchecked. At ten, she sat in on meetings, met her tutor's requirements, took riding lessons, and charmed everyone she met. By sixteen she was bored and jaded and knew that the best way to reclaim her family's distant attention was to push boundaries in all ways.

And at nineteen her father overrode her mother's wishes and did what she'd never believed possible.

He kicked her out.

Not without money in her pocket, but without direction, without—other than the ability to ride—discernible worldly skills.

But with a goal. She'd show him he was wrong. She could find her own success, make her own way. *If she ever got the chance.* If Carey ever took her seriously.

She shoved the broom over the cobbled floors—spelled so the horses wouldn't slip, just as spells kept the under-mountain stables supplied with constantly circulating air and made sure the cistern-stored water stayed fresh—and considered the reason she was sweeping and not riding. Sweeping and not proving her worth to Anfeald and Carey.

Carey's girlfriend, that was why.

Carey's girlfriend, who'd decided to move from Kymmet Stables to Anfeald, arriving only a moon's span after Suliya herself and yet automatically slotted as a senior rider, with authority over Suliya and almost everyone else there. If it weren't for Jess, Suliya was certain she'd have been moved up from her starter position to something more meaningful, maybe even to a junior courier. But Jess had arrived, taking on the training of the young horses, taking on the occasional run, making Suliya more of a backup rider than anything else.

And leaving her sweeping the aisles.

The sound of raucous laughter echoed down the hall from the job room at the back of the stall aisle; four of the couriers were back for the day, drinking hot tea and warming themselves over exaggerations of their past exploits. Envy tugged at Suliya, but she couldn't blame them for her situation. They'd all been here before her, some of them since the summer Carey was hurt and everyone else had been killed. Still . . .

She wished she didn't feel so left out. Or that she even knew how to join in.

At that choice moment, one of the massive front doors eased open, making way before the rising night wind. "Ay!" Suliya exclaimed, jumping to get her broom placed over the pile of sweepings—but not quickly enough. As a dun mare walked into the stable, the swept hay scattered along the length of the aisle and settled back into the corners from which it had come. A lone dun mare, elegant even in her winter coat, ice on her whiskers and fetlocks, ice weighting the end of her tail, and a unique harness carrying a bulging courier's pouch just behind her withers.

Carey's girlfriend.

Suliya glared at the mare unnoticed as she ran to shut the door, securing it with its own weight behind the slight bump in the floor. The dun—Lady, they called her, when she was her horse self—stopped in the middle of the aisle, shook vigorously, and lifted her head with perked ears to scent the air.

"He's not here," Suliya said brusquely, taking a hank of the dun's mane up behind her ears and giving a slight tug. Lady's spellstones clinked dully there, sewn into several braids. With them, she could return to the woman Jess, but not here in the middle of the aisle. There was a special stall set aside, where Jess kept a change of clothes and which Anfeald used as a mid-aisle storage stall.

Lady hesitated—not surprisingly, since they'd moved the stall only days earlier, swapping it out with another to separate two horses who'd taken to kicking at each other. But Suliya tugged again, perhaps not as gently as she might have, and Lady followed her—right into the wrong stall.

Suliya realized it immediately. But something wicked spoke within her, something tied to her resentments and envy. She slid the stall door closed without latching it and went back to her sweeping. Let Lady change to Jess and ask for clothing—when Suliya brought it, maybe Jess would notice that Suliya existed in the first place.

After a moment, Lady sorted out the situation—wrong stall, no clothing waiting here—and gave a short, sharp snort of annoyed objection. In another moment, she changed. Suliya couldn't feel the magic—few of the couriers had that kind of sensitivity—but she heard a difference in the way the stall bedding rustled, and knew it had been done. She dumped her recaptured hay sweepings into the waste bin, listening, ready to grab up some clothes.

After a long, considering silence, the door slid open; Suliya turned to see Jess step out into the aisle without a stitch of clothing, the courier harness dangling from one hand. Barefooted on the cold cobbles, she gave no sign of discomfort—or embarrassment—as she headed for the correct door, two stalls down. She appeared not to notice Suliya's near-gaping consternation, nor the appearance and startled reaction of two grooms from a stall at the far end where they'd been releveling the floor.

She carried herself with absent dignity, and she was beautiful—long lean legs and flanks, erect carriage, masses of dark sand hair spilling down her back with a strikingly black centerline the longest section of all and echoed in a faint dark line down her spine. Suliya was struck by the feeling that this was the first time she'd actually—truly—seen the woman. Seen that she was so human . . . and so obviously not.

As Suliya stood frozen with the broom in her hands, she heard Carey's cheerfully teasing call to the two grooms—coming from within the hold, he could see nothing but their stupefied expressions. He walked around the corner into the aisle just in time to see Jess disappear into her stall. Even from the middle of the aisle, Suliya could see his eyebrows shoot up to disappear behind the uncontrolled fall of his dark blond forelock. Without hesitation, he came on.

For a moment, Suliya held out the hope that he'd aimed himself for Jess . . . but a few strides told her otherwise. Slightly uneven strides, another leftover from the summer that had torn through these stables, but otherwise the perfect image of a courier rider. Tall enough and substantial enough to hold the strength for rough, long rides, lean enough to keep unnecessary weight off the horses' backs. And experienced enough to run Anfeald Stables in spite of his relative youth— Morley, head of the Siccawei Stables, was nearly fifty. Carey struck Suliya as a hard thirty.

Suliya, at just under twenty, intended to be running her own stable by his age as well. Or earlier.

But as he approached, she winced inside; thinking of his reputation, the things that had gained him this post several years earlier. Uncompromising standards. An eye for detail. And the willingness to do what had to be done, no matter what it was, to accomplish the job before him—be it delivering a message or saving Arlen's life.

He wasn't likely to offer quarter to the lowliest of his couriers.

Then again, she'd only made a mistake.

"What," he said, bemused as he nodded at Jess's stall, "was that all about?"

Poot! Fess up. Fess up now. "I must have put Lady in the wrong stall. We just changed them—"

He gave her a look, one that expressed his protective annoyance—but he didn't berate her for leaving Jess to walk naked from one stall to another. Then again, he knew Jess best. Maybe *he* would have anticipated her decision to stroll from one stall to the other. Suliya certainly hadn't.

Carey turned for the stall, but stopped as Jess emerged from it, clothed from head to toe in winter layers—a deep green tall-neck weave under a brilliant turquoise, magic-hued sweater, the color offsetting the natural permanently tanned shade of her skin to perfection. Her hair was still wind-tossed, her cheeks still flushed, and the courier harness now settled over her shoulder like a natural extension of her clothes. She stopped once to wriggle a foot more comfortably into its ankle boot; she often fussed with her shoes, and just as often went barefoot within the warmth of the hold itself.

"What happened to that famous horse's memory of yours?" Carey said, his voice teasing as he held out a hand for the harness. "And how was the run?"

Jess shrugged the harness off her shoulder and handed it to him. "This is my first time since the stalls changed," she said, glancing at Suliya with larger-than-normal walnut brown eyes. More perceptive than normal, too, it seemed to Suliya at that moment. She tossed her head in a minute gesture, one Suliya had seen often in the mares at paddock. "You," she said, "will not take advantage of my nature as Lady."

"I don't understand," Suliya said, afraid that she did. She abruptly and sincerely regretted the wicked impulse that had allowed her to close the wrong stall door and walk away, for she wasn't accustomed to any of it— the envy, the bitterness, the impulses—if she had been, she'd have had a quick covering comment at the ready.

Suliya didn't. For Suliya was simply too accustomed to doing as she pleased without being called on it— or caring if she was.

"You *do* understand," Jess said. Despite almost two years of human experience, she still handled the junction of vowel and consonant with an awkwardness of tongue—never quite stumbling over the words, but often giving the impression she might. "Going to the stall may have been a mistake. Closing the door wasn't. If I had been human, I could have hesitated at the stall without breaking rules. I could have refused to go in. I could have pushed my way out before you closed the door. When I am a horse, Carey's people trust me to do none of those things. And I trust them to treat me honestly." Her eye flashed annoyance. "If you cannot do that, you will not handle me as Lady again."

Carey's hands paused at the courier pouch fastener. "Braveheart—it was a mistake."

Jess didn't reply . . . but she didn't remove her gaze from Suliya's.

It wasn't a gaze Suliya could hold, not when she realized she'd done more with her simple impulse than put a woman in the position of asking for her clothes. She'd broken a trust. And from a horse's point of view, trust was everything. She dropped her gaze to the gleam of the cobbles. "I'll make sure it never happens again," she said, struggling with unfamiliar capitulation.

In response, Jess merely said, "Yes," and somehow managed to encompass a plethora of unsaid words.

Carey cleared his throat, taking Jess's unwavering gaze from Suliya; Suliya couldn't stop a sigh of relief. "And how," Carey said, "was the run?"

Jess said, "You are changing the subject."

He grinned, unrepentant; he had a lean face and a long jaw, prone to intensity and sternness of expression; the grin turned it light, turned him from someone who often intimidated Suliya into the man with whom she often saw the other couriers joking. "I'm changing the subject," he agreed, his words no more repentant than his grin.

Jess lifted a shoulder, dropped it in the slightest shrug. "Siccawei was right—part of the riverbank caved in. I couldn't have made it with a rider on my back." *Neither could any other horse*, she meant.

Burnin' poot wrong. Suliya clamped her mouth down on the words. If *she'd* been the rider—and she would have been, had Jess not intervened—she was certain she could have made it. The run to Siccawei was a tough one in bad weather, but most of the couriers made more of it than it was. And in this case, the run had been to a small new sub-hold that Sherra had established to let some of her apprentices explore—

carefully—the use of raw magic. Out between Siccawei Hold and Anfeald, making the run shorter than normal; easier than normal. Carey often used it as a drop-off for less time-dependent documents.

"That bad?" Carey said, flipping through the papers from the pouch. He glanced at Suliya and she pulled her thoughts from her face.

"Bad," Jess said. "Arlen should tell Sherra we can't make any more runs until a road team fixes it."

"Bad, then," Carey agreed.

"If a road team goes out there, maybe they can do something spellin' about the whole thing," Suliya said, referring to the dangerous part of the dry riverbank, where it narrowed to a rough path skirting the river. "Some kind of bridge or something, so we don't have to go around."

Jess looked at her with honest shock. "That would take away the fun of it!"

"Fun?" Carey said, and grinned again. "Don't know that I'd call it *that*, Jess. Not for the rest of us. But there is a certain . . . challenge. A nice change of pace."

Suliya looked away, wishing she'd just kept silent . . . and thinking it still seemed like a good idea.

"Dayna is well," Jess said suddenly, and smiled. "She is rolling her eyes about how timid the others are."

Carey snorted. "I think they're just there to slow her down—Sherra's no dummy. Dayna doesn't have the advantage of growing up with her parents whispering the horrors of raw magic in her ears."

"Disadvantage?" Jess said, frowning.

"Advantage," Carey said firmly. "She's never been frightened away from using it." He jammed the papers back into the pouch and tucked the tangle of leather under his arm to hold the other hand out to Jess. "C'mon. Natt and Cesna are waiting for these, as little as they'll be able to do with them until Arlen gets back from the Council gathering. And Jaime's coming early tomorrow—you wanted to make sure the housekeeper had things set to rights in Arlen's rooms, didn't you?"

Jess stood visibly straighter at the mention of Jaime's arrival, brushing hay off her sweater as though Jaime were arriving any moment. One hand found her hair; she made a face. "Groom this?"

Carey laughed. "C'mon. You might just talk me into it." His open hand still waited; he wiggled the fingers.

Jess took the hand, and bumped her hip against his in a teasing way—but gently, as if ever aware of his old injuries. Carey lifted their joined hands to Suliya by way of a parting gesture, and she stood in the middle of the aisle with her broom, watching them head for the job room, heads tipping slightly closer as Jess murmured something that made Carey laugh out loud. "Later," he said, as if he'd grown used to and easy with some of the outrageous things Jess could say.

Suliya and her burnin' broom and her bitter envy. She could have made that run, she knew it; she was rife with knowing it. She could be one of them. But she wasn't sure they'd ever give her the chance.

❧

In a northern precinct of Camolen, frigid water lapping the edge of a lake suddenly becomes solid, and then grows tiny, brittle stalagmites that weave together and spire toward the sky. Just over the Lorakans, along an ancient trade road into Solvany, solid rock dribbles down along the side of the craggy mountain, revealing a hibernating burrowdog just long enough for melting rock above to impale and merge with it, killing it in its sleep.

South of Anfeald, a road team scout heads for the unexpected mud slide by the dry riverbed and never makes it. His partner returns with a babbled story

about swirling leaves, melting trees, the hind parts of
a ground squirrel sticking out of solid once-dirt, and
of a man lost to the astonishing explosion of a nearby
bush, wood turned to sharp-edged metallic shrapnel.

She bears the wounds to back up her story. Wounds
with shrapnel made of twisted metal hazel bush bark.

⮜⮞

"He's not *here*?" Jaime said, sounding every bit as
unhappy as she looked, as well as slightly disoriented
after her distinctly magical journey from one world to
another.

"*I'm* here," Jess pointed out. She stood by the door
of the special world transfer chamber in the lower level
of Arlen's stone-carved hold. Jaime looked good to her
eyes, but then Jaime always looked good to her eyes,
even when she had an unusual haircut that made her
look like she'd just gotten out of bed, short and mussed
and almost certainly on purpose, since she'd never
failed to groom herself before. The first glimmers of
grey showed among the dark strands, silver peeking out
from her bangs.

Jess had never known Jaime's age . . . the oldest of
the friends she had met in her first days as a woman,
all of them from the same small area on Earth. Older
than Dayna, younger than Arlen—whom she'd always
known, if not always as a woman. And Arlen's hair was
older than the rest of him, greyed like a grey horse,
starting early and heading steadily for silver-white. Jess
had always thought it a shame that the wizard lacked
dapples.

"And I'm glad to see you," Jaime said to Jess, running a hand through her hair, ruffling it even more.
"But if you were expecting Carey and you got *me*, you'd
be disappointed, too—"

"Teasing," Jess interrupted, and grinned.

Taken aback, Jaime just looked at her a moment.

Then a smile crept in at the corners of her mouth. "You've gotten better at that."

"Yes." Jess, her grin down to an amused twist of mouth, held out her hand to take the overnight bag hanging from Jaime's grip. "Carey says Arlen is out doing Council business, and Natt says the Council just called a rush field meeting to investigate something strange."

"They *have* changed from last year," Jaime said, giving up the bag and emerging from the booth. "Used to be they'd take reports and consider their actions for at least a month or two when something strange happened. Now they're actually out on a field trip?"

Jess remembered the look on Natt's rounded face when he'd relayed the news; her amusement at teasing Jaime faded altogether. "Things have not changed all *that* much."

Jaime caught her meaning right away. "So this is something pretty alarming." She followed Jess out into the main hall of the first floor, an asymmetrical floor plan that had never confused Jess as it did everyone else who first arrived here; her sense of direction wasn't easy to fool, and she found the several floors of the hold with their branching, seldom-square rooms fit Anfeald's nature perfectly. Carved from one of Anfeald's characteristic thin-soiled eruptions of rock with the entrance at the bottom and Arlen's private rooms built to rise just above the natural surface, the hold was solid, dependable, and just a little bit quirky. Like Arlen himself, Jess thought.

Carey waited for them by the stairs, close enough to have caught Jaime's words. "Alarming," he agreed, "but whatever's up is new enough that no one seems to know anything about it. Even news-mongering Aashara isn't spreading gossip—although she's been pretty careful about Council matters since last summer."

Jaime sighed. "I suppose it's been quiet for a while now. Too much to hope it could last forever."

Giving in to impulse, Jess petted the ruffled and deliberate disarray of Jaime's hair, a soothing gesture she remembered being on the receiving end of in her days of early training. "It *is* quiet. Dayna has not panicked Sherra for days now. Did you bring new pictures of Sabre? Is Mark happy bossing the barn while you're gone?"

"Happier than I thought he could be," Jaime admitted as they headed up the stairs. They were stone, like the rest of the hold, climbing with angled flights that didn't match in length or direction—also like the rest of the hold. Large windows lit the stairwell with soft skewed shadows, spelled with an invisible barrier to keep the cold out and the clumsy in. "He's really settled into the role . . . I'm not sure Dayna would recognize him. He's grown up a lot in the last year . . . and he's not that skinny guy anymore, either."

"Then you should bring pictures of him, too," Jess said wistfully. It had been a long time since she and Carey traveled to Ohio, to Jaime's barn on her family's old dairy farm property, the Dancing Equine. World-travel spells were strictly controlled, with two layers of fail-safe checkspells erected at all times. Jaime was the only one with dispensation to move between worlds, and had a special spell that allowed for her travel— and her travel only. Had the Council not owed her so much—and owed Arlen so much—Jess had no doubt they would have told the couple to choose a world and stick to it.

As it was, Jaime split her time in what she'd called the universe's longest commute. And Jess could well understand why she was unhappy to find Arlen gone.

"We asked the cook for that black deer venison you like so much," Carey offered as they topped the last of the stairs and headed down the hall—past the apprentice studies, past Arlen's five-walled workroom with its giant picture window overseeing the gardens and pastures of his domain—to Arlen's personal rooms.

"Quit trying to cheer me up," Jaime said. "I intend to pout for a while longer. Maybe until Arlen gets back."

"Oh," Jess said, disappointed. She led the way into Arlen's common room, a welcoming place of layered rugs over stone floor, bookshelves, and a sitting area that often disappeared under his various needlework projects. She left Jaime's bag by the end of an overstuffed couch and sighed. "Maybe I should go work on my reading, then."

Carey laughed out loud, and Jaime said gently, "That's one of those things people say when they *don't* want you to quit doing something, Jess. I *am* sad that Arlen's not here . . . dammit, I'm annoyed, too—but it doesn't mean I don't want to spend time with you. How about we try a lesson, after dinner? Is that new covered ring still heated?"

"Natt's keeping it warm for us," Carey said, even as Jess said, "Yes!" in response to both questions.

"Good," Jaime said. "I hope you planned for an early dinner . . . Ohio timing doesn't quite match up, as usual. I'm starved, and now that you've teased me with that venison—"

"No tease," Carey said, helping himself to the rocking chair by the window and stretching his bad leg out with a wince that made Jess frown—though she'd learned to hide it, to keep such faces on the inside. Winters were hard on him, and she knew it by the grateful way he accepted warm packs and liniment rubs in the evening—but this was not evening, and it was not private. So she looked away, and thus managed to catch the astonished delight on Jaime's face as she peered into the room that had once been a guest room and now held some of Jaime's things from Ohio—her custom-made, adjustable-width dressage saddle, which she forbore to keep in the tack room while she was gone; a full wardrobe that didn't fit in a bedroom closet Arlen had never made for two; a collection of books by Camolen's riding masters, past and present . . .

"There's a light in here!" Jaime said. "It almost looks like a fluorescent bulb!"

Carey absently kneaded his thigh. "I can't speak for that, but I can tell you you're one of the few in the hold to have one of SpellForge's permalights."

"Permalights," Jaime mused. "Someone on Earth could have come up with that name."

"Invoke the thing, and it stays lit, even when the wizard walks away, falls asleep, whatever. Thousands of starter spells in the same stone, too—right there at the base of it."

"Wow," Jaime said. "All those hours I put into learning how to keep a glow going when I wasn't really giving it my full attention." She looked back to give Carey a wry look. "Or maybe I should say, *trying* to learn how."

"Oh, the old-school wizards are scandalized." Carey pushed the calico cat from his lap, guiding the demanding creature toward Jess where it repeatedly bumped its head against her leg. She sat cross-legged on the thick carpets and tugged gently at its tail until it stood foolishly on its head, purring. Carey snorted at them both and turned his attention back to Jaime. "They think allowing such a thing will ruin the next generation of wizards—that children won't learn the proper discipline to hold glowspells, and that they'll learn them late in the first place. Using glowspells has always been the first indication of a child's talent."

"Hmm," Jaime said. "Well, they may have a point.

Now the parent can trigger the spell and walk away. But you know, even with parents plunking kids down in front of televisions, the kids who enjoy reading still start before anyone thinks they can."

"Pretty much a summary of the opposing arguments I've heard, minus all the blustering," Carey said. "In any event, Arlen thought you'd like it."

"He would have liked to see your face when you noticed it," Jess said. "But I saw, and I'll tell him."

"I wouldn't worry about it," Jaime said. "I'm sure I can find a way to express my appreciation when I see him." She left the guest room, tossed her bag inside the bedroom, and said, "One nice thing about spell travel . . . no need to freshen up. Now, what about that dinner?"

Carey pushed himself up from the rocker as Jess stood in one smooth motion, not bothering to uncross her legs until she was up. She followed them from the room, but couldn't help a glance back over her shoulder. The hold seemed empty without Arlen; she would be just as glad as Jaime when he came back.

Chapter 3

South of Anfeald, midway between Siccawei's new sub-hold and the dry riverbed, the ground heaves like thick molasses going into a boil—and then settles, as solid as it has ever been. Sherra stands off to the side, looking for signs of the exploding hazel bush. It has melted into something else.

Tied at a distance, her palomino mount rattles air through its nose; it is as wary as she, and cannot seem to decide whether to watch before or behind itself. It lifts its head to call to the empty woods, a stallion's cry.

"Hush," Sherra says absently, thinking it anxious. She knows only as much of horses as she must, and in this place she has other things on her mind. Keeping an eye on the quiescent earth, she gathers her concentration for the spell that will tag this spot for the Council wizards, allowing them to accomplish the tricky business of transporting without a formally established booth.

The horse calls out again, craning his head against the halter lead; this time he sounds less demanding, more welcoming—a lower call, more musical. Sherra ignores him, finishing her spell, unaware of the subtle creep of earth before her.

Almost immediately the Council begins to arrive. Seventeen of them altogether, the very best of Camolen's best . . . everyone but Arlen, who is too far away to accomplish free transport. The wizards who oversee all of Camolen's magic, policing their own, protecting everyone else.

None of them have ever seen anything like this growing miasma in northern Siccawei's woods. None of them know what has caused it. They throw a tentative identifier spell at it, the most basic of spells that identifies only intent—benign or malignant. They don't expect it to work.

It doesn't—but the ground heaves at the offense, and a tree trunk spits out what was once a bird.

They eye each other in alarm, and Sherra steps forward to invoke the most gentle of healing spells, the most benign of magic. All seventeen of them stumble backwards in alarm as pebbles spurt up from the muddied, melted patch of woods, ducking as the missiles rain down through the trees.

The palomino snorts alarm.

There will be no more magic used here; they will bring in null wards to contain this spot while they try to understand it—although even Camolen's finest find themselves uncertain it can be understood at all. They congratulate themselves on acting so quickly, on keeping news of this strange area so confidential so they can respond to it without inciting panic.

The palomino nickers; even Sherra recognizes it as a greeting.

But they see nothing. No one.

And then they feel the magic.

It is not of their making.

Raw magic, magic without control, without signature. It brings the disturbed woods to sudden, violent life. The ground reaches for them—

☙❧

Carey shifted his weight, gave his leg a subtle stretch, and leaned over the rails of the indoor ring to watch the growing frustration on Jess's face—an interesting contrast to Jaime's slightly distracted patience. She knew as well as Carey that Jess's biggest challenge as a riding student was that she expected too much of herself—expected to understand new things right away, expected to do them right the first time, expected to figure things out before she was told.

Just because her every gesture, every expression, spoke so loudly of who—and what—she was. Because she had an insight no one else could match.

Carey knew, and Jaime knew, that there was such a thing as expecting too much, even from a riding student who had started life as a horse. But Jess hadn't yet accepted that philosophy.

Carey glanced behind him as someone entered the long, wood-sided structure; this end held what was meant to be a large viewing area separated from the riding area by wooden fence rails and a wide gate. But Anfeald held more individual training sessions than it did schooling clinics, and inevitably the generous viewing space did double duty as storage, with hay overflow, training rails, rakes and shovels and wheelbarrows nibbling away at its edges.

Sliding the door closed he found not Arlen—only a day into Jaime's visit, and she already had them looking to every open door in sympathetic anticipation—but Suliya, her riotously curly, deep-mahogany hair spilling free from its binding. She went to rummage among the manure forks.

He hadn't failed to notice that she often turned up when Jaime gave lessons, or that she tended to lurk in his own shadow. And he suspected she thought she hid her feelings better than she did—that it didn't show when she disagreed with Jaime, or that she'd hidden her resentment at her starter position in Anfeald. Or her resentment when she saw Jess going out on a run, whether or not it had been meant for Suliya.

An odd one, all right, her expensive wardrobe and demeanor clashing with her lack of experience and her need for a job in the first place. She'd hoped for more when she'd arrived here, that much was plain. But she'd overstated her qualifications, and the vague responses of her references hadn't revealed the exaggerations—exaggerations Carey had the feeling she actually believed. She had yet to learn just how much she had to learn; she was a young woman in the process of discovering herself—if she looked hard enough. But it was her journey, not his. Carey hoped that if she kept watching, kept dogging his heels, maybe she'd figure it out.

If not, she wouldn't last much longer. But she was good with the horses and meticulous about finishing those jobs she'd been assigned, so she'd earned some forbearance and a little more time. And Carey had no doubt she'd taken every year of lessons she laid claim to—just as he was certain she'd ignored half of what she'd been told because she felt she already knew better. Now she winced, watching as Jaime walked up to Jess and her green young mount and widened Jess's outside hand. "Give him a little more room to move into that rein," she said, audible enough in a ring that had been spelled for clinic acoustics. "Remember how green he is—with a horse like this, on the trail, giving him this room can be the difference between a minor shy and a panicked runaway."

"You don't agree?" Carey asked Suliya, not concerned that Jaime would hear; the acoustics spell included a damper on this end of the ring. Jaime herself had often proclaimed envy, wishing for a similar system at the Dancing Equine.

Suliya started slightly, taking a few unconscious steps toward him so she could keep her voice low even though it was unnecessary. "I didn't say that—"

"Sure you did," Carey told her. "Not out loud, but you said it."

Suliya flushed; not even her sepia skin could obscure her deepened complexion. She flushed often and easily, and Carey had learned to take it as a sign of those moments when she thought she was right about something but didn't feel she could say so. Frustration more than embarrassment.

"You've never taken a lesson with Jaime, have you?"

"No," Suliya said, glancing first at Jess and Jaime, and then at the packed dirt floor. "I haven't been here long enough to earn them."

Carey gave her a mildly surprised look. "Who told you that?"

"I—" she said, looking startled, then having to think about it. "I assumed I just wasn't allowed yet—"

Mildly—more mildly than he felt—he said, "All the information and sign-up is on the job room wall, next to the assignments."

"I—" she said again, and even bundled as she was in scarf, thick feather-stuffed jacket and bulky gloves, Carey could see the difference in her posture. "May I, then?"

"Maybe not this time," he said. "She's scheduled in. But I'll put you on the list for next time she visits. There's a catch, though—"

Suspicion shuttered her dark brown eyes. Carey swallowed his annoyance and said, "Relax. You just have to listen to her. Do what she says, whether you agree with it or not." He knew from experience . . . sometimes the pieces of riding theory didn't make sense until you had a certain number of them in hand. "Make an honest effort. If you have differences, you can consider them later on. Right now, you do it her way." It was a test of sorts, and he let it show in his voice, even as she nodded slowly, thinking hard behind a face she was trying to keep blank. Watching her, he added more casually, "If you think we won't be able to tell . . . well, maybe we won't. But the horses will."

He didn't add that they, in turn, would be able to tell from the horses . . . if she didn't know that, then she had more to learn than he thought.

"I can do that," she said without hesitation, although he'd have preferred it had she taken a moment to think. "Please . . . I'd like to be on the list from now on."

"I'll see to it," he said. He turned back to the conversation in the ring, aware of Suliya's departure with her manure fork but no longer heeding her. Suliya would work out . . . or she wouldn't.

"Hold yourself in position even if he does drop on the outside," Jaime was saying. "He's an exceptionally shifty little guy—not of your breeding, is he?"

Jess laughed out loud. "Only you would ask that!"

Jaime shrugged, gave a self-deprecating grin Carey could imagine more than he could see. She looked great this visit; she'd always been the down-to-earth, cut-to-the-heart-of-the-matter member of those who had been involved in his first, unplanned trip to Ohio—the first to believe Jess in her struggle to convince Dayna, Mark, and Eric she'd been a horse, the one who shepherded Jess through the steps of learning to become human. Now Jaime looked softer, happier . . .

And it wasn't just the haircut.

It was Arlen, and how he'd made her welcome here, made Anfeald as much her place as his ... given it to her. Given of himself to her.

Too bad he couldn't get his butt back here to see her.

Jess corrected herself, "Only you would ask that and *mean* it the way you do. No, he is not my younger brother, or even a nephew. Carey brought him in last fall from Shibaii. I think he's too ... *shifty* ... for courier runs, but we thought to give him another year."

"He might grow steadier," Jaime agreed. "But I wouldn't be surprised if he didn't."

Jess gave the chunky bay gelding a pat. "I wonder what it would be like if I *did* breed."

Carey stiffened. He wanted children ... Jess wanted children. But Jess's human body had never settled into cycles, even though she'd started to recognize when, if she shifted to her Lady self, her mare form would be in heat.

It made for an interesting personal life. But it meant, he thought, that children would remain out of their reach. And yet ... he knew Jess hadn't given up. And he remembered that it was her stubborn persistence that had finally given her the key to triggering the changespell from Lady form, when everyone in Camolen had told her—repeatedly—it couldn't be done.

"Do you want to?" Jaime asked Jess in surprise— apparently forgetting about the acoustics spell she admired so much. "Does Carey want to?"

Hell, yes. Never as a young man, full of goals and battles and a young man's selfishness. But with Jess in his life ... with his eyes newly opened to the pride of the cook when his family grew by yet another child, at the way his own eyes strayed to the few hold children playing outside the gardens ...

He'd helped them build a snowman this winter. With a snowhorse.

"Yes," Jess said to both, smoothing the bay's sparse mane. "Arlen says . . . Arlen says maybe it's for the best if we don't. We can't be sure what will happen."

"But you want to anyway," Jaime said, her voice soft and understanding. Much more than Carey had expected, with her own decision to devote her life to her riding and not a family.

He saw the sudden catch in Jess's shoulders; he heard the cut-off sound she made. It took a moment for his brain to catch up with his eyes and ears, and to realize she fought unexpected emotion. By then he heard it in her voice, in those perfect acoustics; even her tight whisper reached him with clarity. "Yes," she said. "I see the foals . . . they call to me." It was all there in her strained voice—the longing, the doubt . . . the fear. Fear of success and fear of failure both . . . and what fear of what she was might do to her.

Damn the acoustics, anyway.

❧❧

The sky bends around them, the air turns into snowflakes of solidified gases, suffocating three of them instantly. No direction is safe; the others stand their ground, trying to mute the magic flowing around them. Ice-edged dirt shoots from the ground, slicing two of them in half; their bodies melt back into the tangle of roots and rock now roiling at their feet.

No more are they wizards, no more are they Camolen's finest. Now they are but terrified men and women, panicking, screaming . . .

Dying.

❧❧

"I'm sorry," Jaime said, putting a hand on Jess's calf where it rested against the gelding. "I wish I could do something."

"You listen," Jess said, licking a tear from her upper lip and feeling the trembling flare of her nostrils, her equine expression of emotion. She sighed and patted the gelding. "I am glad enough to have Carey. Maybe it is too much to ask for more."

"I don't know that I believe that." Jaime let her hand drop from Jess's leg, her attention wandering inward while she hunted words. Finally she shrugged and said, "I think you just can't stop living your life in the meanwhile."

"Okay," Jess said, one of the colloquialisms that she'd brought with her from Ohio and had seen spread through Kymmet before she came here. "Tomorrow, I should be Lady, and you ride. Show me the things we talked about today."

Jaime grinned. "Only if we get to do some of the fun stuff, too. You been practicing?"

Jess made a face. "Canter pirouettes . . . I need help. I need a rider to help me balance. But Carey won't."

"Not yet?" Jaime glanced over her shoulder without raising her voice. "Get over it, Carey."

He leaned into the ring so they could hear his reply and said pleasantly, "Mind your own trail."

❧

The palomino hits a frenzy of panic. Eyes rolling, ears flattened, he coils his powerful body and fights the lead rope. The branch cracks; the leaves tremble as though buffeted by a great wind. The distorting world closes in on him—

—and his lead rope goes *through* the melting branch, freeing him to gallop as hard and fast as he can, spurning the path for a direct route between trees, ducking and dodging and more than half blind with fear. To his last stable he runs, death flickering on his heels.

❧

Jaime, as dignified as Jess had ever seen her, looked over at Carey and said, "Make me."

"You know," Carey said, "just because once I set off one little bad spell inside your barn doesn't mean you get to boot me around forever."

"Yes," Jaime said, "it does."

Jess felt a flash of worry—but then she caught the sly look in Carey's eye and the humor lurking at the corner of Jaime's mouth and she laughed out loud instead, swinging a leg over the gelding's rump to dismount. The extra-wide ring door slid open with a bang that startled both Jess and the gelding; he jumped one way and she, looking after her toes, jumped the other. Carey jerked around with a frown at the ready— everyone in Anfeald knew better than to slam doors in the horse areas, or to leave them open when they'd been found closed—

But his admonishment went unspoken, and Jess knew why as soon as she saw the expression on Cesna's face. Grim and shocked, with her mouth working in a hunt for words, her chin trembling . . . Cesna was the youngest of Arlen's two apprentices, an often impulsive girl still in her late teens who had been born to the scholar's life. She carried her weight in her hips and her feelings on her face, and Jess had never seen her so beside herself. "I've been looking for you," she finally blurted, stumbling to a stop before them while the gelding tilted his head to snort at her jerky, alarming movement.

Carey put a hand on Cesna's shoulder, kneading slightly—a gesture Jess had never seen him make with anyone but her, and one that was Cesna's undoing. She threw her arms around Carey's neck and sobbed, leaving him as startled as any of them. With awkward uncertainty, he patted her back, looking over her head to Jaime with a plea in his eyes.

Jaime, mystified along with her concern, came

alongside Cesna to rub a gentle circle on her back; Jess soothed the gelding with a pat, and then gave a slight jiggle of the reins to tell him he still had to mind his manners—along with her toes. She said nothing; she had seen Cesna upset before, but this time . . . this time, a strange, unfamiliar clenching in her stomach told her this was not the same. This was more. This was . . . profound.

After a moment during which Cesna's sobs only grew in intensity, Jaime said, "Maybe we should find Natt?"

Cesna shook her head emphatically enough that Carey had to withdraw or take a hit to his jaw, and then she said into his shoulder, "Natt's talking to Siccawei. He's trying to find out what happened—"

"Cesna," Carey said, a hint of frustration, of *needing to know* behind his concern for her, "what *did* happen?"

She looked up at him, revealing a face Jess found to be alarmingly red with emotion. "We all felt it," she said. "So many of them . . . all the apprentices felt it."

"Cesna," Jaime said, exchanging a glance of trepidation with Carey, "*what*?"

"They're dead," Cesna said, clenching Carey's lightly padded jacket; it wasn't enough to keep her from sliding to her knees, and he went down with her, gripping both arms in an attempt to slow them. "They're all *dead*."

The shock of it hit Jess like a buffeting wave of air, making everything else distant and remote. Cesna's sobs faded away; Jaime's stunned comprehension barely touched her. Even Carey's grim and obvious denial meant nothing to her. *The apprentices felt it. They're all dead.*

The Council, that's who she meant. It's who she had to mean. The untouchable, the powerful, the core of all of Camolen's magical protection. The Council.

The Council and *Arlen*.

Chapter 4

Death.

Arlen reeled on his horse. He could not feel the form of death nor the details in the sickening wave of weakness that swept over him; he clutched the saddle pommel, fumbling the reins.

The horse plodded onward. It felt not death or weakness, only the desire to reach the next home barn of the livery ring.

Death. Arlen found himself shaking, as if a myriad cold tendrils worked their way through his jacket layers and wrapped themselves around the heart of him. He swayed; his thoughts went grey and distant.

But he clutched the saddle and he didn't fall; the horse kept moving, lurching slightly with each step as it broke a path through the snow.

Everyone else knew enough to wait out the morning chill before heading the short distance between one settlement and another . . . but Arlen had planned to reach the travel booth in Amses this morning, and from there to warmer Anfeald and Jaime—

The Council.

Only with the Council did he have such close ties, forged by years of personal communication over distance, years of arguing and working together.

Death . . .

Had it been all of them?

He loved none of them, he respected most of them, he on occasion wanted to slap some sense into one or two of them. Eighteen Council wizards including himself, seven with precinct holds like his own . . . and then there were those touchy western provinces over the Lorakans whose senior wizards kept to themselves.

Sherra? he thought, reaching for her, reaching despite this distance from which she was unlikely to respond or even hear him unless expecting him. *Darius? Tyrla?* Even less likely to respond, without the history of casual chatting he had with his close neighbor Sherra.

And respond, no one did.

Their silences didn't mean anything . . . or so he told himself. *Not at this distance.*

Arlen took a steadying breath, watched it plume out in the air before him, and gathered his reins; one had looped almost to the horse's knee, but it hadn't appeared to notice as it lowered its head to navigate the snow, its single-minded intent carrying it closer to an accustomed herd and freshly forked hay.

Single-minded. He, too, had to be single-minded.

Arlen shut out the cold and his fears and the dark shout of denial buried deep within him, and focused himself on his own goals. Reach Amses. Pull every bit of rank and influence to jump the travel booth line.

Get home to Anfeald and—

For good or bad, find out what the silence meant.

☙·❧

"Arlen's rooms," Carey snapped, to no one in particular—and to everyone. Jess, Cesna, Jaime . . . all caught in a stasis of stunned reaction. Carey wished he felt the same, instead of this grim, overwhelming and familiar weight that settled on his shoulders. *Make it happen.* Whatever it was, make it happen. Fix something, deliver something, save something . . . no giving up, no matter what. Arlen would be depending on him. Carey didn't waste any more time, not in thought or regret or even consideration. "Go there. *Now.* Have someone else put that gelding up, Jess, and don't say anything about this. Jaime, can you make it on your own?"

Jaime struggled to respond, her throat bobbing; she swallowed hard and then the words burst out of her. "Hell, yes! I need to know what Cesna's talking about. Get her up there and sedate her into a zombie if you have to, but I *need to know.*"

"Sedation might not be such a bad idea at that," Carey muttered, climbing to his feet and, by dint of his grip on Cesna's arms, bringing her up with him. *Hauling* her up. "Pull it together, Cesna. There's more to this than spilling a few words—because if what you're saying is true, losing the Council won't be the end of it."

If what she was saying was true. As overwrought as she was . . .

Maybe she was wrong.

He saw the same thought reflected on Jaime's face as she grabbed Cesna from the other side, and between the two of them they kept her on her feet between the indoor ring and the tunnel-like rear entrance of the hold itself. Carey took them up a back way, one that was spelled to stay locked for anyone besides Arlen, Carey, and—recently—Natt. Testament to her mindset, Jaime didn't question Carey about it, not when they took the first turn she probably hadn't even known was there, not when they spilled out of a stairway into Arlen's workroom.

He'd broken all the rules to show it to either of them—but Cesna would hardly remember, Jaime could be trusted, and it was far better than revealing Cesna's state to everyone they passed. Far better than starting a panic until he could confirm what had happened . . . and what they needed to do next.

He deposited Cesna on the stool in Arlen's workroom and glanced at Jaime—*stay with her*—and even as he strode from the room he heard her low, urgent voice. *"Who's dead, Cesna—and how?"*

He found Natt standing by the side of a long, box-topped desk in the corner of the apprentices' room—the dispatch desk. A grey-haired woman sat at the desk itself, her hands moving reflexively as she sorted messages still visible only in her mind. Some she'd transported, printed in the hand of the sender and on the original paper; half of those were on thick red-bordered confidential sheets, and the printing wouldn't show until the right person touched them. Auntie Pib, her name was, and she'd come to know Carey very well during the time Jess was at Kymmet—and he, her. Well enough to spot immediately that her normally chocolate skin bore an undertone of grey, and the habitual, ever-present tremble of her hands had worsened considerably.

Natt—a chunky, round-faced man given to understated sartorial finery—turned to Carey with the gravest of expressions. "She's overloaded," he murmured. "We need to get relief here, and keep them on short rotating shifts."

"Can you call someone?" Carey asked. With Arlen, it would have been a given; he'd handed out summons

rings—like Carey's courier ring—to his crucial hold
service people.

"Yes," Natt said, embarrassment spreading over his
face. "It didn't even occur—"

"Do it," Carey said abruptly, and Natt frowned—
frowned as though he hadn't expected Carey to come
in and take over, Carey who was Arlen's closest friend
and who had been working in this hold since he was
in his early teens. But Natt's hesitation was short; it
evolved into relief. Into realization . . . *someone else
would make the decisions*.

Carey wished he could say the same. He gave Natt
a moment of concentration to make the summons—just
about the time Jaime appeared in the doorway, only
glancing at the crowded interior—two work desks, bookshelves lining every wall but the dispatch desk corner,
and a long pastoral mural painted on the wall where a
window might have gone. Jaime said, "She's useless. She
just keeps repeating that the Council is dead."

"That's all she knows," Natt said. He pulled his hands
down his face, briefly stretching his features out of
place. "It's all *we* know—we felt it happen. And we
have this." He handed a scrawled, red-bordered note
to Carey. "It came—to me—from Siccawei's secondary hold. They don't have a regular dispatch service
there; it was probably all they could do to send this
as confidential. And they're clearly not going to say
anything more through dispatch at all. We need to send
someone . . ."

He trailed off as Carey took the paper; Jaime
crowded in close. The note was addressed to the
Secondary Council, and to the first apprentice for each
Council wizard. "Council ambushed," he said out loud,
although Jaime could read it, just as she spoke
Camolen's common dialect; the world-travel spell
prepared its travelers well. "Send contact," she finished.

"Cesna's sensitive to interpersonal communication," Natt said, apology in his strained voice. "It hit her hard. I think it was probably all she could do to get to you in the first place. It's all she *needed* to do; I'll deal with the rest of it for now."

"Send contact?" Jaime repeated.

"It means they're not willing to transfer any more information through even the secure dispatch methods," Natt told her.

Carey glowered, albeit at no one in particular. "Or it means they don't know anything else."

Dayna had felt the start of it. Less sensitive than some to magic-driven interpersonal communications, she had the dubious honor of being the first to feel the raw magic. Outside the Council, no one outstripped her ability to detect it, and no one outstripped her ability to wield it—when she was allowed to use it in the first place.

This surge had been unshaped magic, without so much as will or intent behind it. Just a careless wave of power, one that somehow entirely lacked backlash. And yet—

Look what it had done.

She sat on a little bay horse named Fahrvegnügen—dubbed courtesy of Jaime's brother Mark and his questionable wit—and glanced at Trent, wishing she hadn't. Wishing she hadn't been one of the few who'd taken this ride to find Sherra when the palomino stallion had returned alone to Second Siccawei. And wishing most of all that she wasn't standing on the edge of a warped, diseased section of woods that looked like nothing more than a particularly disturbed Dali painting, a scene of carnage so beyond her imagination that she could barely comprehend it.

She should have known things had been too quiet.

Going too well. Camolen didn't have that kind of track record with her. On the surface it was a quieter, much more peaceful place than Earth, but when things went wrong with magic, they spiraled almost instantly into crisis and past the cold war stage—usually before almost anybody even knew there was trouble in the first place.

She couldn't imagine it going much wronger than *this*.

Slowly, Trent dismounted. The palomino had been his, lent to Sherra when her own horse threw a shoe on the way from Siccawei, and initially he'd blamed himself for giving her a mount more difficult than she was used to. Initially he'd thought the palomino, with its trailing lead rope, had simply pulled away from her grasp and left her afoot. Initially, he'd simply mounted up to go find her.

And then Dayna had come rushing out of the hold, having already detected the raw magic, and having brought Iri, a more advanced wizard, from her sudden faint to whisper nothing more than *dead*. So with Iri's wails building inside the small, two-story hold and no one currently more in charge of this small, two-story log facility than Dayna, she'd put her cold hand on the palomino's bridle to stop Trent from mounting up, and told him to wait for her. And for Katrie, one of Sherra's strongarms who'd worked with Dayna in the past and who'd come with her to this experimental little wizard's hold.

Katrie, tall, strong, hardened Katrie, now came out of the snow-covered bushes wiping her mouth; she pulled the bota from her gear and rinsed her mouth, spitting. "Sorry," she said, swiping fingers through her short pale blonde hair; there was hardly enough of it to be in disarray, but it looked as ruffled as Dayna had ever seen it.

"No problem," Dayna told her tightly. "I only wish I'd done the same." Instead, all the horror sat in her stomach like a cold poisoned rock. She shivered, drawing her fur-lined hat down over her ears.

Of the wizards who'd come here, there was very little sign. The area sat quiescent, an unnatural mix of colors, heaving ground, and distorted trees. Maybe an acre of it, with a central blot of bright red that had once probably been a bird.

A grasping hand jutted from one of the trunks, dripping skin. A scrap of someone's perfectly preserved scarf rippled in the frigid breeze, pinned by metallic leaves. Dayna thought she saw someone's bottom protruding from the ground, but couldn't tell without a closer look . . . and wasn't about to take it.

Trent turned a circle, the fidgety palomino's reins in his hand as he searched the woods, putting his hands around his mouth to bellow, "Sher-ra!"

Katrie and Dayna exchanged a dark glance; Katrie shook her head. She rewrapped her scarf around her ears, a combination headband and neck scarf, and shook her head again.

"It doesn't matter," Dayna said, as Trent moved off the trail to repeat the call in a different direction. "Let him look. Just don't let him get too close to . . . *that*."

"No," Katrie said, direct and immutable disobedience; she had no intention of going to Trent. "I'm staying here, with you."

Dayna looked at her in surprise, and abruptly understood. With the others dead, she'd suddenly become more valuable to Camolen. She was the only one with a working understanding of raw magic, which somehow played a role in the tragedy before her. She was one of a very few taken for schooling within a wizard's hold, even though the circumstances were so mitigating as to make her actual aptitude meaningless—as an offworlder with a feel for forbidden raw magic, where *else* would she have been placed but under expert supervision? But because of that supervision, she'd learned in leaps and bounds. Because of her experience with conventional magic used at the highest levels and because she was gifted with an innate talent that had thrived under expert tutelage, Katrie in her stubborn loyalty had the right of it.

Dayna was of value. If not among the vocationally oriented wizards who made up the Secondary Council and kept Camolen running, she was among the few remaining wizards with the skill and mindset to *find out what happened*.

And to keep it from happening again.

If they could.

But for all her experience—unwanted, unasked for experience—Dayna had never taken action alone. Even assigned to the changespell team last summer, she'd been nothing more than a cog in someone else's wheel. No, when she got outrageous, when she made terrifying make-a-difference decisions, she'd always had her friends there as a catalyst.

So when she got back to Second Siccawei, she sent a message out to Carey, Jess and Jaime . . . and she even wished for Mark.

We need to talk, she said, hoping that between them, they could make some sense of this tragedy, untangle the threads that needed to be tugged and followed and eventually cut.

But it occurred to her, too . . .

Maybe she just didn't want to be alone.

The tingle of the courier ring against Suliya's left forefinger came as such a surprise that she absently scratched the finger twice before realizing she'd been summoned. She left her satisfied thoughts about her forthcoming lessons—along with the tack she'd been cleaning and her certainties that she could play by the rules despite her disagreements with riding theory. That young gelding Jess had been on today, for instance . . . she mused about it on the way up the stairs. She'd have held the rein closer to his shoulder, not further out, giving him firm restriction instead of more room. But it didn't matter; she'd just do as Jaime said in lessons, and Carey would soon understand that Suliya had ambitions.

Her confident thoughts came to a stuttering halt at the top of the stairs; she faced the long hallway—apprentice rooms off to the right, Arlen's workroom to the left, and his personal rooms at the end—for the first time since her arrival here. And she hadn't been expecting the soft sounds of crying from the workroom.

Across the hall, sounds of conversation drifted out—a brief exchange of raised voices, Carey's included. With hesitation, she approached the apprentice room—a peek into the workroom showed her nothing, although someone *was* there . . . somewhere . . . crying.

A glance into the apprentice room stopped her short. An older woman with darker skin than hers whom she'd seen but didn't know, Arlen's older apprentice, Carey, Jess, Jaime . . . they all gathered near the dispatch desk, making the room seem small. Jaime had her arms clenched around herself so tightly it was a wonder she could breathe; her eyes were red-rimmed and haunted. Jess looked for the world like she wanted to be holding Carey's hand, but he was busy gesturing, a sheet of dispatch paper in his grip, so she did what Suliya occasionally saw of her—she crowded in close, touching Carey now with her shoulder, now with her thigh, and the next moment briefly connecting along the length of their bodies. If she'd been a horse, Suliya realized with a blink, Jess would have been hanging her head over Carey's shoulder.

Strange to realize how often she had probably done just that, and long before she was ever human.

Burnin' hells, Suliya'd never seen any single one of them so obviously upset.

Jess noticed her first—somehow—twisting around to look at the doorway, nostrils slightly flared and head raised; they *all* looked at her after that. With the sudden feeling she wasn't supposed to be there at all, Suliya raised her hand. "Ay," she said, unable to keep a defensive note from her voice. "Summons. I thought maybe Arlen was back."

"No," Carey said grimly.

Natt shook his head. "It was me."

Suliya took a step inside the room, more confident. "What's going on?"

Carey gave a slight shake of his head. "Couriers receive assignments, not explanations." But he waved her off when she would have responded. "In this case, you're going to find out sooner than later anyway." He seemed to notice for the first time how Jess crowded him; finally he took her hand.

Suliya took another step into the room, now flanked by a work desk on either side; she looked from Carey to Jaime to Natt, and at last to the dispatch wizard at the desk. The woman looked exhausted; she wouldn't meet Suliya's eyes.

For a moment, no one would meet her eyes.

Suliya felt the first trickle of fear.

"There's been some kind of . . . incident with the Council," Natt said. "It . . . *appears* as though they may all be dead."

"The *Council*?" Suliya said, openly skeptical because of the shock of the idea. But she looked at their faces again—she looked at Jaime, at her anguish and denial, then at Carey's determination. She'd heard about him . . . his high standards, his resolve to do what had to be done when things got grim . . . his willingness to drive himself to the limit to accomplish those same things. His own body was living proof.

He'd drive her to the limit too, she suddenly realized. And that meant this might be her chance to prove to him—

"Arlen," Carey said distinctly, watching her as though she didn't get it, "was with the Council."

"What are you going to do?" Suliya asked. "What do you want me to do?"

Jaime turned on her. "Don't you even want to know what happened?"

Carey closed his eyes a brief moment, softening his reaction with visible effort. "It's not like we have the answers, Jay. But we'll get them. And *you*," he said to Suliya, "are going along for the ride."

"I don't understand." With all the high emotion in the room, Suliya thought a quietly wary answer was best. She still didn't quite grasp what had happened and raced ahead without her, although she was apparently about to be part of it. Not necessarily a bad thing.

"I am going to the new hold in Siccawei," Jess said, speaking up for the first time, her words thicker than usual. "Dayna has asked for us—"

"I can't leave," Carey said. "Not now. And Jaime needs to be here; if Arlen—well, if he tries to make contact"— *if he's somehow not dead,* unspoken words that came through loudly enough for Suliya to hear even without practice in reading him—"it'll be here."

"So it's me," Jess said. "But not alone. Though I *could*." She directed the last straight at Carey, no little annoyance or defiance in her voice.

"Of course you could," Carey said impatiently. "That's

not the point. The point is, I don't want you to do it that way. I wouldn't want *anyone* to go alone on that route right now."

Jess didn't look entirely convinced.

Neither was Suliya. "I'm not going on a run?" she said. "I'm just—" and she stopped herself from saying *tagging along with Jess*, hearing just in time how petulant it would sound. She didn't mean it that way . . . she'd only wanted the chance—

Carey jerked his head at the doorway, his meaning clear enough; Suliya, with a glance at Jess, left the room. Carey followed her—Carey alone.

He took her to the end of the hall, with the stairs at her heels and the light from the stairwell window splashing against his face and sparking the bright green flecks in his hazel eyes. Not quite angry . . . but looking at her as intently as anyone ever had. She opened her mouth without words in mind, anything to forestall the lecture she saw coming.

He got there first. "Just listen," he said, catching her gaze and holding it, holding it even when she would have looked away. "Listen well. You may be looking for something more important, but there *is* nothing more important to me than making sure Jess makes it safely to Second Siccawei."

Trouble-ride, that look of his. She tried to turn her words around, unspoken as they'd been. "I just didn't understand why you picked someone she doesn't really know."

"Because we have a burning lot of messages going out, and they all have to get there *right now*. You know some of the routes, but you don't know any of the shortcuts. And today," he raised a meaningful eyebrow at her, "is a shortcut day."

She'd know the shortcuts if she'd had the chance to make more runs before this . . . but she didn't say it. Honestly puzzled, she did say, "Why so many messages? Why can't Mage Dispatch handle some of it? If things are really bad, people could use the transport booths to carry messages. Those shortcuts . . . they're rough. The horses will pay for using them."

He gave her a grim little smile, one that should have warned her. "Takes a while to map it all, doesn't it? The Secondary Council is in a panic; the first thing they did was shut down the transfer booths—they're trying to contain whoever did this. Frankly, I'm not sure they could keep the whole system running during a crisis of this magnitude. They're only prepared to replace Council members one at a time."

She blinked at him, brushing one fat mahogany corkscrew curl away from her face. "They shut down the whole burnin' *system*?"

His wry grin looked a little predatory. "Now you're hearing me. The Council is *dead*, Suliya. And they died between *here and Second Siccawei*."

Definitely predatory. As if he'd let herself follow her ambition right into a job she might have otherwise refused. *He'd drive her to the limit, too. . . .*

But it might truly be the chance she'd been looking for. If she did well, Carey would know. He'd depend on her again, and she'd have the start she'd been looking for. And then she wouldn't need her family's good will at all—

Carey looked at her with suddenly narrowed eyes. "Jess was right, wasn't she? You *did* put her in the wrong stall on purpose."

"What?" Suliya said, totally taken off guard. "Why—"

"Never mind." He cut her off with a sharp gesture, though his lean features had hardened. He eased a little closer; despite herself, Suliya took a step back, and therefore a step down. "Never mind that," he said again, this time as though more to convince himself than her. "You handle yourself with this run, and I'll forget it. But let that kind of thing happen on this run—even a whisper of it—and you're through here." He looked at her, at the dismay she was unable to conceal. "Or didn't it ever occur to you that I have to be able to count on you in *all* ways, whether that means mucking out the stalls on an off day, or being someone my other couriers can trust—just like you can always trust Jess to take the runs no one else can manage safely."

She hadn't thought at all, actually. Not at the moment she'd acted. She hadn't thought about anything more than her resentment, and how unfair it was that Jess had walked in and taken away her rides. At the time—and now she did look down, down at her clenched hands and the worn stone step at her toe—the farthest thing from her mind was that Jess had taken that ride to protect her. Now it suddenly seemed obvious—Lady's assignments were often the fast, hard runs; the other couriers always seemed grateful. And this time she'd handled the mudslide for Suliya.

Not that Suliya was the least convinced it would have been necessary, but—

"I won't let you down," she said.

"No," Carey said. "Don't."

Jaime didn't believe it. Couldn't. Just as when she'd been a girl. "Your mother's dead," they'd said, and she never believed it. Had waited for years for her mother's return.

She'd been wrong, then. She wouldn't be wrong now.

Chapter 5

Jess came down from Arlen's rooms, barefooted and silent on the stairs; dim late-night glows invoked by the housekeeping staff made quiet light in the corners.

She heard no one else. They'd all retreated, like Jaime, to their nighttime quarters. To their families and friends, to huddle and worry and bolster each others' belief that it really wasn't true after all.

Jess believed it. And Jaime didn't, not truly—and didn't *want* to—so she threw herself into the chore of keeping the practical aspects of the hold functioning even though the housekeepers—wizards and physical workers alike—were long used to functioning on their own. It was thanks to Stenna, the evening maintenance warder, that Jaime was finally asleep; it was she who had mildly spelled Jaime's spiced wine, a thoughtfulness she was well prepared to offer after years of evening rounds to discover overexcited or fretful staff children and their frustrated families. "It only works if you're already truly tired," she'd told Jess when Jess had reacted with alarm at the thought of spelling children to sleep on a whim, and since Jaime had been exhausted . . .

Now, finally, she slept.

While Jess, wide awake, thought of tomorrow's ride and what she might find at the end of it, fully aware that she'd be responsible for reporting every nuance to Carey and Jaime. And Natt and Cesna, of course, but despite her casual fondness for them, it was not they whom she worried about.

Arlen.

She quite abruptly sat on the steps and cried.

In some ways, being a horse was so much easier.

After a while she stopped, and a while after that she scrubbed the hem of her thick, soft, cotton shirt over her face, sighed, and continued down the stairs.

Their rooms—hers and Carey's—were a luxury, a gift of the friend she now mourned. He'd given her the room next to Carey's and then cut a door into the stone wall, adding a lightweight wooden door carved with relief images of running horses. Hand-carved, too, and not done with easier copying magic. Jess's room held her things from Ohio and from Kymmet—her photos, her horse show ribbons, an old pair of Carey's saddlebags that had given her such comfort when she had been newly human and hunting for the man she had depended on as a horse . . . Carey's things were slowly migrating over from what now served as their bedroom, and it was there that she found him. For a long moment she stood in the doorway between the rooms and watched him staring out the big window that made his such a nice room to have in this hill-held structure.

With no glass between the room and the cold winter air, the unobstructed view had an intimacy that Jess never felt looking out of a window in Ohio. Full moonlight reflected off the snow beyond the hold, making it easy to pick out a late-arriving rider.

"I should be down there," Carey said. "In the stable."

"Why?"

He lifted one shoulder; it had an irritable look from behind. "It's my job. I shouldn't be up here about to climb into bed while my riders are still working themselves to exhaustion."

"They are proud to ride for you," Jess said. "And we are all tired." They would be more tired before this was over; a year and a half of living through crises as a human had taught her that much.

Come to think of it, things had been little different when she was a horse. But then, at least, she had not fully understood what was at stake.

"Doesn't mean I shouldn't be down there," he muttered, sounding every bit as tired as she expected. "If only Calandre hadn't tried to turn me into a garbage heap—"

"We are *all* tired," Jess repeated. Calandre hadn't actually tried to turn him into a garbage heap, but the spells were similar and when he was feeling bitter he said it that way. "You cannot do everything, Carey. None of us can."

"So sayeth the horse who learned to be a woman and then, when we all said it couldn't be done, taught her horse-self to use spellstones."

"Just a few of them," Jess said.

"Just a few," he repeated in a dry murmur, resting his forehead against the edge of the window.

"And I still do not understand so many things about being human . . ." It might distract him. It sometimes did.

Not this time.

"Carey," she said, and he didn't answer. She

glanced at the bed—rumpled, unmade—and at Carey—bare-chested, light sleeping pants tied at his hips. He'd tried to sleep, then, and couldn't. Too bad Jess hadn't brought Stenna here to work her sleep spell on Carey. She gathered her thick hair and shoved it down her shirt so it wouldn't tangle when she pulled off the shirt. "Carey," she said again. "I feel you being far from me, and I need you. Come back."

He shook his head slightly, still staring out the window. Yet another rider came into view, riding a horse that stumbled and almost fell. "Somehow," he murmured. Not much of an answer, but one she understood anyway. *Somehow*, he had to make it all right.

Except this time, possibly for the first time, he didn't think he could do it. She could see the internal war of it in every tense line of his body. She left the shirt at the foot of the bed, and walked quietly up behind him, putting her arms around his waist and resting her chin on his shoulder. She said, "Come back to me."

He tipped his head so it rested against hers, and they stood that way together, watching the riders come in.

Chapter 6

Twisted magic blooms to life across Camolen like frost coming up on a cold surface . . . strange, obscure morphing corners and isolated crannies, gully bottoms and tree tops. Hissing darkness, wayward odors . . . glanced at, they are dismissed. Inhaled, they are politely ignored.

A madness of reality takes note, unnoticed.

❧

Dayna uncrumpled the dispatch Bendi had managed to pull in off the system—it was all she could do to keep up with the urgent messages, and Dayna was certain Bendi missed at least half of the ones aimed at Second Siccawei. Sometimes the Siccawei dispatch wizards fielded one for them and sent it again, giving Bendi a second chance.

But Bendi was only one person, working within a secondary hold established for retreat work. None of them were prepared to have Second Siccawei as ground zero.

Not that the others knew what ground zero even meant, or had done anything but cast her strange glances when she muttered it. But Dayna knew . . . and she knew they'd soon be overrun by Secondary Council wizards trying to determine what had happened. The ill-used paper in her hand told her as much, along with its listing of immediate restrictions on basic travel and transport services. Well enough for them—given an anchor point, most of them could free-travel. Certainly they could communicate with each other over considerable distances; their own efforts and convenience would hardly be affected.

But there were those who commuted to work via the travel booths—and some of those people provided basic services. And there were those who were isolated and depended on basic dispatch communication for their needs.

And there were those like Dayna, who'd seen ground zero the day the Council died and who now had little choice but to sit idly by and watch the Secondary Council close down Camolen in their belated search for the cause.

And then there was Dayna unlike anyone else, Dayna alone who had felt the undirected magic sweep through the area, leaving no backlash.

She already knew they wouldn't believe her. Didn't believe her. Undirected, raw magic left backlash. Always. Therefore she was wrong.

Dayna knew she wasn't.

She just didn't know what it *meant*. Or if she'd get a chance to find out.

Do something.

Anything.

Make it better.

Right. Stuck here in little Second Siccawei with no one listening to her and no grand ideas about how to *make it better*, not any of it. How could you make the death of your friends *better*?

So she sat cross-legged in the wide-silled first floor window of Second Siccawei, watching for Jess to arrive while crumpling the dispatch from the Secondary—no, not anymore. Just the Council, now. Or as close as Camolen had to one. Crumpling the dispatch and thinking of Sherra. Dignified Sherra, full of calm and somehow always able to share it with others. Sherra who had given Dayna so much—healing her upon her first arrival here, taking her in as apprentice when it became clear that Dayna's combination of ignorance and talent was a danger to everyone around her . . . and then allowing her to stay. On Earth, Dayna had been just another drone, working in a small hotel, a petite woman with life closing in around her.

Here, she had purpose. Here, she had a kind of power she'd never imagined on Earth. Here, she thought she'd found a semblance of control over life . . . though with Sherra's death, with Arlen's death, she now suddenly realized that control was nothing more than illusion, here *or* on Earth.

Sherra. Arlen. If anyone had enough power to claim control, it would have been them.

But they hadn't. They'd died.

She smoothed the paper over her knee, coming one step closer to hating the crabbed handwriting of whoever had sent it. Around her, the small hold offered unusual silence; it was a hold in mourning—and one in waiting, shackled and unable to act. Muted noise came from the kitchen . . . everything else might stop short, but the people always needed to eat.

Finally, Dayna caught a glimpse of movement at the splotchily snow-covered edges of the hold clearing.

Stables were on one side of the clearing, the hold on the other, and a path leading back to the main route between Anfeald and Siccawei. Jess emerged first, in her characteristic Baltimore Orioles baseball cap—Mark had given her a new one for Christmas—her scarf flapping loosely and her winter coat unfastened almost to the waist, an indication of the exertion of the ride. Dayna didn't recognize the woman behind her, and as she slid from the window sill she craned her neck to keep a view of the yard, waiting for Carey or Jaime . . .

But there was no one else.

Dayna ran to the door, grabbing a jacket from the hook there—way too big, so not her jacket, but who cared. Hadn't they taken her seriously? They'd sent only Jess and this woman Dayna didn't know.

And then she was out the door, getting a good look at Jess's face—tired from the run, grim from what she'd seen along the way . . . from whatever had gone on in Anfeald before she even left. They'd taken Dayna seriously, all right—or no one would be here at all.

Jess met her in the middle of the yard, her horse's winter coat curly wet but cool enough from the final walk in so it no longer steamed. "He needs a cooling blanket," Jess said. "Do you have someone in the barn?"

Dayna hesitated, looking at the second rider. Her horse was still steaming, and although she was flushed and tired from the run, she lacked the haunted expression underlying Jess's exotic features. Whoever she was, she didn't have a personal stake. She didn't even look like she fully understood the situation. She sat her horse awaiting some signal from Jess, her clothes beautifully made and imbued with scintillating magical color, her face a dark cinnamon-tinted tone with features that made Dayna think of Asian and African-American blood—her leftover Earth thinking coming to the fore again—and the most astonishing hair springing from behind her exquisitely knitted ear and scarf wrap.

"This is Suliya," Jess said. "New with Carey. The others couldn't come, but no one takes this route alone for now."

"No one *ought* to take it at all after this," Dayna said, grasping at her normal composure again. Sardonic. Maybe not what someone else would strive for, but Dayna found it a comfortable place. "We do have some people working the barn—Siccawei sent us a couple of horses and someone to organize the place, but we're not nearly up to speed for what we'll need."

"It's a small hold," Suliya observed.

"Yeah," Dayna said, giving her a second look. "A small hold that just became the center of Camolen's biggest magical goof-up since the Barrenlands blew up three hundred years ago, and with limited dispatch service available to anyone while we try to deal with the mess. Believe me, we're going to need all the couriers we can get."

Jess swung down from the horse, straightening the snug, leather-seated quilted riding pants she wore. Suliya, bedecked in similar but sleeker, tailored pants, took the hint and dismounted as well; Jess pulled her saddlebags from the horse and the smaller courier's bags from atop them, and handed over the reins to her mount as she collected Suliya's bags.

"You might want to take a look in the barn yourself," Dayna said, only just now realizing it. Jess gave her a *why* expression, eyebrows raised. Dayna shrugged, pulling the oversized borrowed coat more tightly around herself as the wind picked up slightly. "Trent's palomino," she said. "He survived whatever happened there."

"Not hurt?" Jess asked, arranging the saddlebags over her shoulders and taking in Dayna's confirming gesture;

in another moment she glanced at Suliya and led the way.

The barn showed all the signs of descending chaos—newly arrived feed stacked in the way, debris and gear and equipment boxes clogging the short aisle. Only one stall had an occupant.

"The others are working," Dayna said. "We don't know how many will actually be back for the night, or if we'll have enough stalls—or enough teams fit to work tomorrow. We're just a small, brand-new hold . . . most of our communication has been handled by chatting to Sherra person to *person*, for pete's sake. The only thing the couriers handle are the long documents we want her to see."

Suliya appropriated two stalls and went to find cooling blankets, mesh-lined wool that would keep the horses warm but wick the sweat away. Jess dumped the saddlebags over the door of an empty stall and paced down the aisle to the palomino—an end stall with a reinforced wall between it and the neighboring stall. "Light?" she said to Dayna.

Light flared in the corner of the stall in response—a cool, even permalight. Jess hesitated at the stallion's door as she retrieved his halter from the hook there. "Ramble," she said after a moment. "His name is Ramble."

Of course she'd remember.

She lifted the halter from the stallion's door and slipped in the door, closing it most of but not all of the way. Dayna moved closer—cautiously, because she'd already learned the hard way that this one would bite—and got there in time to see the two exchange a greeting, the palomino a little suspicious to be greeted in such a horsey manner as Jess went to his head and exchanged breath with him, first one nostril and then the other.

He didn't let the introduction last long; he swung his head in posturing threat and pushed at her, teeth bared. Jess wheeled and kicked him in the chest. The stallion flung his head back in dramatic alarm, lunging away from her. Jess glanced up at Dayna in embarrassment. "I still forget," she said, chagrined. "I do it the horse way." She looked at the halter hanging on her arm, lifting it slightly. "The human way," she said, "for a horse as rude as this one. I don't think he grew up with mares the way he should have. They would have taught him better than this."

Even as she spoke she had the horse haltered, the chain shank of the lead threaded around the noseband. "You shouldn't need this," she said sternly to the horse, and although Dayna was no horsewoman, she could see that Jess unconsciously matched every body movement the stallion made, all the small gestures he used to claim her body space. When he bobbed his head and snorted in wet disgust, she could only assume that Jess had stood her ground. The stallion made one last halfhearted attempt to close his teeth on Jess's shoulder and she rattled the chain lightly in warning; he turned away, sulking. "Here," Jess said, handing the lead to Dayna through the barely open door. "Hold him. Has anyone checked him since he came without Sherra?"

"Trent rode him back out again," Dayna said, gingerly holding the lead. The stallion eyed her and she knew right then that it had her number. "He likes this horse—don't ask me why—so I figured the horse was okay."

But Jess ran her hands across his back and quarters and then down each leg, following the line of his sloping shoulders across his chest and up his neck. Touching as well as looking, and eventually ruffling her hands through his long pale mane. "Handsome," she said. "And strong. Too big for a courier's horse, but . . . nice."

Dayna snorted. "Says who, Jess or Lady?"

Jess gave her a sly glimmer of a look. "Both of us." But then she frowned, moving around toward the back of the horse. In another moment she'd dug out a small pocket knife, but Dayna didn't see why; she was too busy giving the horse her best evil eye as he opened his mouth in what he must have thought was a cunning manner, his lips twitching toward her hand.

"Stop it," Dayna hissed at him. "You brat." She shoved his head away and he carefully watched something in the corner of the stall a moment, but his lips twitched again, betraying his intent.

Tucking the knife away and preoccupied by whatever she'd gathered, Jess nonetheless gave him a pinch on the neck. He flared his nostrils and flattened his ears and refused to look at either of them.

"Your face is going to freeze that way," Dayna informed him.

"I . . . *bit* him," Jess said. "He's sulking." She came out of the stall, slid the halter off one-handed, and replaced it on the door. She held out her other hand. "Look."

"Big chunk of horsetail hair," Dayna said. "Trent won't thank you for that."

Suliya returned, alone but hauling an overwhelming armful of blankets. "Couldn't find anyone," she said loudly from the other end of the barn. "But I've got the coolers."

"Good," Jess said, and nothing else, to which Suliya frowned and went to work in the stalls. But Jess was looking at the horsehair, holding it out again to Dayna. "More than hair," she said. "Hair and . . . I think a leaf, but part of it is metal and part of it is . . ." She shook her head sharply, at a loss for words.

Dayna saw it, then. A leaf, transformed and tangled in the horsehair—no, made *part* of the horsehair. A simple leaf, caught in the tail of a fleeing horse and damaging only hair with its final distorted spasm. She took in a deep breath of air, let it out slowly. Very slowly.

"We saw this spot," Jess said. "We cut through the woods to go around it. This is what killed the Council, isn't it? Not this leaf, but . . . this strangeness."

"Yes," Dayna said. "But we don't know what it is, or why it happened." And they weren't likely to find out, not while those in power refused to listen to those who had been there. She frowned, and waved Jess's head-tilted response away. "Not you," she said, letting the frown turn into something more weary and more determined at the same time. "Let's talk inside, where it's warm."

"Ay," Suliya said from the other end of the barn, faint petulance in her voice as she startled Dayna with the southern Camolen colloquialism. "I could use some help down here."

Jess rolled her eyes, a very human expression Dayna hadn't seen her use before, and she had to bite her lip to keep from laughing out loud for Suliya's sake. But then Jess was just as much horse as human again, with the little toss of her head that meant irritation. She said, "Go be warm, Dayna. Suliya and I will come when the horses are settled."

"No real rush," Dayna said, still amused. "You can't start home until tomorrow, anyway."

Jess gave her a somber look. "Anfeald without Arlen," she said, "isn't really home."

Arlen accepted a fine glass goblet from his host and raised it in a gesture of appreciation he was too distracted to truly feel—too full of frustration, chafing to find himself still *here* at all.

Guides dammit, anyway. Jaime. Anfeald. The Council. He still had no idea what had happened. What was *happening*—without him.

Instead, he waited out his second day in Amses, long enough to find this small family restaurant tucked away at the edge of the town's residential area. Beautifully presented tables, privacy, and personal service—all a stiff contrast to his first meal in the town, and all of which he noted in only the most absent way. Amses was a mining town—small, family mines delving not only for silver, but for the rarer specialty spellstone material, the ones that could hold the most complex of spells.

Ironically, Arlen the wizard had done quite a bit of business with some of these mines. But Arlen the traveler didn't purport to know anything about them— for Arlen, uncertain of events, had gone as incognito as an eccentric wizard could get.

Probably not far enough. And it was nothing with which he'd had any experience.

He abruptly realized that his host—and chef—still hovered by the table. "It was a truly excellent meal," he told the man, someone who obviously knew how to fling a number of spells himself—although in an establishment of this quality, he no doubt had his own spellcook to handle the details of preserving food, heating cooking tops, and sanitizing the dishes. "Only the ability to digest it in my own house this evening could possibly improve the experience."

An understatement of the most severe nature.

The server, a young man whose resemblance to the chef left no doubt about family ties, gave him a sympathetic look. "We have several business travelers caught here in Amses until the travel system is working again."

"I haven't been able to get any news at all," Arlen said, lacing it with the amount of complaint he thought appropriate for a businessman who was used to the best. Burning hells, he was a *wizard* used to the best;

there couldn't be much difference. "No public dispatch at all, and the news pedestals are empty. Have you heard anything about how long things will be down?" He took a sip of the wine—definitely a good vintage—and glanced from his small, round table to see that no one else was paying attention to the conversation. It was simply his turn to speak with the chef.

"Nothing," the young man said. "No word about what's happened, either. It had to have been pretty big, to have affected all of Camolen—"

The chef cleared his throat. "Plenty of warnings not to panic being distributed," he said. "No good can come of panic. We've enough service wizards to keep Amses going for a few days. The break from dispatch news might even do us all a little good."

"Sit back and enjoy the sunsets while you can," Arlen suggested, trying not to think of the fact that the break from dispatch news had been caused by the deaths of people he cared about. *I should have been there, should have tried to stop it—*

And then you'd be dead, too.

"Exactly," the chef said, entirely unaware of Arlen's inner struggle. "I hope your meal here has helped to make your stay pleasant whether you intended to be here or not."

"It's gone a long way," Arlen said, meaning it. "If you could direct me to an equally pleasant overnighter, I'd be grateful."

That, they were glad to do, although the chef returned to his kitchen and left the younger man doling out directions. Arlen paid for the meal with Anfeald scrip—all he had, and worth a remark from the server.

He'd hardly been prepared to keep himself inconspicuous. And, arriving in his newly assigned rooms at the recommended establishment, he thought again that doing so was his only course of action. Until he found out what happened to the Council. Until he found out why he was the only one left. For while he hadn't been able to confirm anything—hadn't been able to reach anyone at all, either on the Council or the Secondary Council—there was a deep part of him that *knew* the others were dead—all of them. And of anyone in Camolen, he knew only a tragedy of that magnitude would provoke the service shutdown he was witnessing.

Do something.

Anything.

Make it better.

He was a senior wizard. The only surviving wizard. If anyone could do something, it was him.

But not from here. Not without more information. Not without something to act *against.*

Meanwhile, if the other Council members had been killed, then he, too, was a likely target. No one knew he was here . . . but if someone were looking for him . . .

He tossed his bags on the bed, a solid creation of beautifully worked stripewood head and footboard, and peered out one of the room's two windows; the overnighter held only four customer rooms, and this one looked out onto the property's vast back lot. Snow-covered arbors, walkways, and benches hinted of summertime beauty. For now, it lay abandoned, and offered him the privacy he wanted. As did most overnighters, this one offered breakfast; it would be midday before he needed to venture forth. Enough time, he hoped, to get over the surprise of arriving to a non-functional travel booth and finding his travel time expanded from a day to—

He didn't even know. He'd never traveled a distance such as this without the benefit of wizardry. Coach travel would probably be the most efficient . . . perhaps interspersed with rental horses to cross coach lines and make himself less predictable.

He glanced into the bathroom—all of the usual
fixtures there, along with soap and towels and a discreet basket of potpourri, all of which he'd paid extra
for; the other rooms in the oversized house shared a
common bath. Along the wall next to the bathroom was
a full-length mirror set into a burnished metal frame
with a local-artist look to it. Here, he hesitated, realizing for the first time the extent of his folly.

The man he looked at was Arlen the wizard. Who
else wore such a thing as a university sweatshirt given
to him by his lover? Beyond such eccentric items, his
wardrobe held habitual dark blues and blacks, fine
materials magicked so as never to fade, their sheen
never dulled by pilling or fuzz.

*Dump it all at a secondhand store and take up new
clothes in trade.*

There was nothing he could do about his
height . . . taller than most was taller than most, on
horseback or trying to fold his legs inside a coach. But
his hair was as distinctive as the rest of him—full and
shaggy and never much attended.

Cut it. Dye the steel grey to a darker color.

The mustache. He ran a finger across the brushy
abundance of it, watching himself do it in the mirror.
He'd had this mustache all his adult life, and he
couldn't imagine anyone would immediately recognize
him without it—especially once the pale skin beneath
it colored up a little.

Shave the mustache.

Nothing he could do about the overbite . . .
something that should have been attended to in his
youth and had not. But it wasn't a bad one, not bad
at all—not enough so people would remember him just
because of it . . .

At least, he didn't think so. He hadn't had a good
look at it since the mustache first grew in.

"The problem is," he told his reflection, "you are so blatantly . . . *you*."

Arlen the wizard. Mild until circumstances called for otherwise, good with a needle, full of hidden humor. Easy enough to say he was usually absorbed in work. Of late, often absorbed in Jaime.

Jaime.

She was here, now, and had been. Who knows what she thought of his absence. The general impression he'd left was that he'd gone off on Council business—

She'd think him dead.

Jaime. She was the one person he might manage to contact. She had no skill with magic, but she had what everyone in the Council lacked . . . his love. She had his intimate trust. And of late, she did indeed respond to casual direct communication within the hold, the kind of magic that held only a whisper of a signature, closer to raw magic than anything else a wizard might do.

He took a deep breath, still watching himself in the mirror. The mustache removal could wait, he decided. It was evening, and quiet; a time Jaime often used to read. She'd be the most receptive now. Then the mustache, and tomorrow the clothes. "Good-bye, you," he told his image, and turned away from it. Tomorrow he would become someone else.

Tonight, he reached for Jaime. And tomorrow night, and the night after . . . until he was close enough to touch her.

Carey rubbed his fingers across both eyes, trying and failing to wipe out the gritty feel of fatigue at the end of a day that wasn't even over yet. Lowering himself onto Arlen's couch next to Jaime's suddenly and miserably curled-up form, he hunted for words—*Are you all right? Do you feel any better? Can I do anything?*—

and couldn't find any to which the answers weren't resoundingly obvious. *No, no, and no.*

He settled for resting a hand on her arm, but even that made her wince. He sat back against the far-too-comfortable pillow softening the arm of the couch and took a deep breath, trying to put things in perspective, trying not to worry too much about this one more thing. It was a winter illness, probably; everyone got them.

Except there wasn't anything going around right now.

Just plain grief and stress, then, giving her a sick headache that the hold's healer hadn't yet been able to touch.

Except she'd never reacted this way to grief and stress before . . . and the guides knew they'd seen each other through plenty of it.

Arlen dead, the Council gone, Camolen shut down, his couriers riding way too many miles a day, his horses starting to show the strain, and the ache of missing Jess after only a day so strong he felt it in his very bones . . .

Do something.

Anything.

Make it better.

Arlen had always counted on him to fill that role, to be the one who acted when acting became necessary.

But this time, he didn't know what to fight for. He didn't know *how* to win, or what it meant accomplishing . . . or if given their losses, it was even possible to win at all.

Chapter 7

Jess sat cross-legged in Second Siccawei's first-floor window seat, staying out of the flurry of hold activity while she waited for Suliya to present herself as ready to go and for Dayna to be sure she'd said all she wanted to say in the letter she was sending back to Anfeald. Unlike yesterday, the rest of the hold bustled in preparation for the arrival of several new Council members—wizards who were skilled enough to use the new anchor point positioned by Second Siccawei's advanced apprentices to spell themselves here.

In fact, from the general tenor of conversation in those who rushed through this main sitting room, Jess thought they'd recently arrived. Upstairs somewhere. She wasn't concerned with them and she was sure they weren't concerned with her. She was just a courier, even if she happened to be one who counted slain Council members among her close friends.

She twisted around to watch the yard as another courier left, trotting out at a smart pace with bags bulging. She'd be surprised if they had any more horses left to go out, though she hadn't seen Garvin, the head rider, leave yet. She'd be just as glad not to encounter him again; they'd met him last night over the dinner meal and he'd been brusque and unpleasant, a bandy-legged and barrel-bodied older man that Dayna admitted had been the only adequately experienced person available after the sudden demand for couriers.

From her seat Jess could watch not only the yard, but the stairs to the second level that ran along the side wall; even as her gaze lingered on the departing rider, she caught movement from the corner of her eye and found Suliya descending the steps, her corkscrew hair caught back in two tight braids and her winter gear and saddle-bags slung over her arm. She looked decently refreshed after the night's sleep; Jess herself had been up early, unable to rest and equally unable to find anything on which to act; normally drawn to the stable, she hadn't found solace in the thought of sharing space with Garvin. Breakfast turned out to be a grab-it-yourself occasion full of eggs and chunky pepper sauce and thinly sliced salted steaks, none of which Jess had ever been inclined to eat. She'd found one of last fall's apples and gotten the cook to remove the preservation on it, but now her stomach growled in hollow resentment.

"Nice place," Suliya said, encompassing in her praise the room they'd shared the night before, the breakfast-scented sitting room and, Jess thought, the cook who had been so accommodating to her requests for more thoroughly warmed eggs. She shrugged on her thin silken underjacket and said, "Ready to go?" although Jess hadn't made any move to get up.

"I'm waiting for Dayna," Jess said.

"She still wants to ride out as far as the,

er . . . problem spot?" Suliya said, and at Jess's nod, frowned slightly. "Are you sure you want to wait? They might need us at Anfeald."

Jess didn't hide her surprise. "Dayna is a wizard," she said. "She asked to ride out with us. We wait."

Suliya shrugged, a large gesture. "You've got the say."

"Yes," Jess said, looking steadily at her, not sure but that some human behavior of Suliya's eluded her.

After all that, the wait was short; Dayna came pounding down the stairs, still pulling on a dark brown sweater that only made her look grim in nature.

Or maybe, Jess thought with a second look at her face, she was grim all on her own.

"Damned wizards," Dayna muttered, only confirming the thought.

Suliya raised an eyebrow at Jess, who ignored it to eye Dayna warily and say, "What—"

"They don't believe me," Dayna said, not even giving Jess the chance to finish asking the question. "I thought maybe to my face they'd at least be more polite about it, but they don't believe me. They think that spot in the woods is the result of some sort of spell, and they intend to figure out what it was, and who cast it. Idiots."

Jess tried to understand what was wrong with that way of thinking. "And you think . . . what you felt . . ."

"It's a reaction, not a result," Dayna snapped, then closed her eyes, took a visibly deep breath, and said, "I felt the raw magic sweep through here; I know it wasn't directed. But there was no backlash, so the energy had to go somewhere. If whatever happened in the woods reacted to that magic, it may well have sucked it up. *Voila*, no backlash, because there's no loose energy whipping around."

"So that would mean there was no one out there casting spells at the Council," Suliya said. "But that doesn't make sense. Where does the disturbed area come from? Do you think it's *coincidence* that the entire Council was wiped out?"

"I think," Dayna said, narrowing her eyes in a particularly dangerous-looking expression, "that the Council could have been attacked one way as well as the other, if the person behind the magic knew what the reaction would be. I *think*," and she added dark weight to her tone, enough so Suliya winced, "that the new Council won't be able to figure out who did *what* if they aren't starting at the right place."

"But you're the only one here who knows the feel of raw magic so well," Jess said. "Why—"

"Don't ask that one, Jess," Dayna interrupted. "The answer isn't something I should say out loud."

Silence fell between them, with Suliya looking like she might want to offer commiseration but too uncertain to follow through, and Jess thinking about what Dayna had said. Finally, looking at the jacket in Dayna's hand, Jess asked, "Do you still want to come with us as far as the . . . spot?"

"Are you kidding?" Dayna snorted. "I'm coming *with* you, period."

"Ay, *what*?" Suliya said, as though it had been startled out of her, but Jess only nodded.

Dayna glanced at Suliya, but her reply was reasonably mild in tone in spite of her obvious agitation. "They've made it clear they're not interested in my help here. What's the point of staying? If I'm at Anfeald, Carey will find some way to make me useful. Cesna is still in shock, from what I hear; I can at least take over her duties. And we'll be together."

Together . . . Jaime and Dayna. The two outsiders. And Jess and Carey, who had always taken Dayna seriously. Jess understood that much unspoken, even

as she knew Dayna made herself trouble to leave here
unbidden.

"It's so stupid," Dayna said, jamming her arms into
the coat sleeves. "No one knows what happened, and
they're not going to figure it out as long as they keep
ignoring what I've told them."

Jess tilted her head, an inquisitive equine gesture
indicating something that didn't make sense. "But . . ."
she said, waiting for Dayna's attention, for the look in
her eye that meant she was truly listening, "Ramble
was there. He knows."

Understanding turned to impatience. "He can hardly
tell us, can he?"

Suliya stiffened, raising her head—a movement that
had nothing at all to do with the conversation, and one
to which Jess felt an immediate start of alarm; no horse
reacted so without something to be alarmed about.
"Ay!" she said. "The horses!"

Jess whirled to the window, puzzled, but Dayna
understood immediately, snarling, *"Garvin!"* and making
the name into a curse.

In an instant Jess understood why, recognizing the
departing hindquarters of the gelding she'd ridden from
Anfeald. While Suliya stood in astonishment, mouth
open, Jess bounded from the window sill, stuffed her
bare feet into her padded winter riding boots without
tightening the side laces, and bolted out to the barn
without her coat.

There she found Suliya's horse also missing from its
stall and the palomino—the only remaining mount—
snorting with interest at her sudden arrival; Garvin
looked up from the wheelbarrow he had just positioned
in front of an empty stall. Human words escaped her;
Jess let her body language speak for her, tall and
offended, chin lifted to lay back her phantom equine
ears and her glare dark and steady upon him.

"Be of some use," he said, ignoring the belated arrival of both Dayna and Suliya behind him. "There are stalls to clean."

"You had no right—" Suliya started, crowding close behind Jess, close enough to make Jess shift her weight, one leg aching to kick behind as would any tense, crowded mare—until Dayna pulled Suliya back, hissing words with an undertone of warning.

"We are not yours to order," Jess said. "The horses were not yours to assign."

He shrugged; his heavy features, starting to sag with age, offered no apology. He looked—and Jess was not sure, but the sight of his expression made her eyes narrow and her nostrils flare, a mix of human and equine responses—*pleased* with himself. "We're in emergency conditions," he said. "I'm serving my hold. And I outrank you, so I suggest you do as you're told and keep your complaints to yourself."

Suliya moved up beside Jess, more carefully this time; Jess felt the difference in her, that they were standing together, not simply making way for Suliya—who now said in the coolest of tones, "We're not the ones you have to answer to. Carey is expecting those horses back today. He's expecting *us* back today, and back at work. Since you're inclined to throw rank around, I'm sure you realize the influence Carey has within both the courier barns and the Council. Or had you *intended* for this to be the last job you ever worked?" A different Suliya, one apparently used to playing games of rank and influence, and one Jess was grateful to have beside her.

"Carey," Dayna added, much menace in her voice, "isn't the only one with a louder voice than Garvin's. Courier shortage or not, none of the holds can afford to retain a man who makes a bad situation worse."

"Get off," Garvin scoffed, not looking quite so smug

as he had a moment ago but not convinced, either. "I'm getting results; I'm getting the messages out. You can be useful here as well as anywhere, whether it's cleaning stalls or running messages. If you *really* want to get back to Anfeald, then *you*," he gestured impolitely at Jess, "can play at being a horse and carry your friend home."

Jess went cold-angry, her eyes widened and head lifted. *Play* at being a horse?

Suliya's hand landed gently on her shoulder, enough of a surprise to distract Jess; Suliya raised her other hand, cutting off Dayna's hot response to Garvin. When Suliya spoke, her voice remained calm and cool, but with a cutting edge. "Your mistake," she said, "is that like most small people who have overstepped their authority, you think you can intimidate us out of recognizing it, or anger us enough so we respond personally instead of intellectually. But I've been watching my father run planning meetings for SpellForge since I was old enough to sit on a booster pillow without sliding off."

Behind them, Dayna made a noise; to Jess, still seethingly speechless, her response meant nothing.

But Garvin hesitated, appreciably taken aback. "This has nothing to do with SpellForge—"

"No," Suliya said. "It doesn't. But the experience allows me to recognize when a career is ending, right on the spot. I've seen it often enough. And I'm very, very good at weighing clout. And, ay, you know what? You *don't have any*."

"I'm serving my hold," Garvin said again, although this time the words held less aggression and even a hint of worry. "The horses won't be back until the end of the day. You can weigh clout all you want; I've done my job."

"You've done far more than that," Suliya said. She

glanced at Jess and, with the first signs of hesitation, gestured at the end of the barn.

She wanted to talk in private. Fine by Jess, who had no desire to be next to this man and who was thoroughly irritated with her own inability to understand the undercurrents of the conversation, not to mention with things human in general. She gave the man a warning glance; he wouldn't meet her eye, but he looked far from cowed. He looked like a man quite certain he could figure out a way to make himself look right.

When they reached the end of the barn—not all that far—Jess kept her voice to a mutter that didn't mask her anger. "I want to kick him from here to—" But she stopped, took a deep breath, and found solace in Dayna's sympathetic expression. "Against the rules. Even human ones. So I won't."

"That doesn't mean you can't feel like it," Dayna said. "*I* feel like making his nose hairs grow down to his chin."

"Can you?" Jess said, somehow instantly comforted at this image.

Dayna shrugged. "Sure. Lots of hair growth spells floating around. But . . . rules and all. I won't."

Suliya's mood had gone from cool to grim. "Sorry if I overstepped," she said. "I just thought . . . he was so insufferably—"

"Is it true?" Dayna asked her. "About sitting in on SpellForge meetings?"

Uncomfortably, Suliya said, "Yes. But I don't want people to know it. And I don't want to answer questions about why I'm *here*. Besides, the important thing right now is that he's *right*. We can change his attitude, but we can't change the fact that we're stuck here without horses. Even if you—" She looked at Jess, hesitated, and said, "Even if you agreed to change to a horse, you can't carry two of us over that terrain. And we don't even know if there's another saddle here."

"The palomino's . . ." Jess said, but with doubt in her voice. Her horse-self was an athletic creature, sturdy in size and build and well sprung in the ribs. The tall, rangy stallion had a leaner build and sharper withers and probably wore a saddle that would pinch her back even without a rider's weight in it.

"The palomino," Dayna repeated. "We could take him. That would make two horses."

"He belongs to Trent," Jess said.

Suliya glanced over her shoulder at the erstwhile head courier for Second Siccawei. "Let Garvin deal with that."

Jess shook her head, short and sharp. "He belongs to Trent. We will not take him without asking."

Suliya said, "But—" and Dayna stopped her.

"Jess makes the call on that one," she said. "I can talk to Trent. The question is, can you ride Lady without a saddle if they don't have one here?" Then she stopped, her expression going wry. "Or maybe *I* should try that, because I'm not sure I can handle that stud under saddle."

"He will be easier, following me," Jess said, shivering as the cold bit through her sweater. She looked at the younger courier, trying to keep her misgivings from her face. "Only Carey and Jaime," she started, and then stopped, hunting for words that could express the depth of her misgivings without insulting Suliya.

Suliya didn't give her the chance. "Don't worry," she said, but too glibly to be of any real comfort. "We won't have any trouble. And we both know the way."

"I'm going to go find Trent," Dayna said. "I'll leave you two to settle things with our good friend Garvin." She peeled off her coat and gave it to Jess. "It won't really fit, but it'll help. I'll bring your coat and saddle-bags when I come back out."

Jess took the coat gratefully, although the stretch of it across her shoulders was a laughable thing. As Dayna dashed out the barn and back to the log-walled hold, Jess strode down the aisle, Suliya on her heels. She stopped before Garvin, finding sullen defiance stamped in every heavy feature of his face, his thick, greying brows dominating with their frown. He said, "Don't think you can make trouble for me—"

"You have made your own trouble," Jess said, no longer interested in him, but only in getting on the road. In returning to Carey, the solid and dependable part of a world fracturing around her. "We need the gear for the palomino, and I need to see your extra bridles. A sidepull, if you have it."

"This isn't a training facility—we've got a couple of extra bridles, but no sidepulls. And that palomino's not going anywhere—"

"That's our concern," Suliya said, but Jess said nothing, just looked at the man. After a long moment, he cursed and flung himself gracelessly down the aisle toward the tack room.

Jess didn't care. She'd already put the man behind her, and Anfeald ahead of her.

Chapter 8

Lady smelled the death long before they reached it.

Smelled it and tasted it and felt the fear of it trickle through her withers and stiffen her back. Not death precisely . . . a wrongness with death twisted in. She tensed, jigging along the path with her neck raising, very little of the Jess-self present. A better understanding of speech, without the conceptual ability to process its complexity. A memory of her goals—*return to Carey*. An awareness of her alter-life, and an ability to return to it when she was ready. But for now . . . she was Lady. A smart, honest horse, straightforward in thought and action and just as wary of *wrongness* as any other horse, just as concerned. Just as needy for her rider's support.

Suliya, feeling Lady's gaits shorten, clamped down on the reins, tightening her thighs around Lady's barrel. Lady knew better, she knew she wasn't trapped by those reins, by the unpleasant pressure on her tongue from this thick, unfamiliar bit . . . but anxiety tumbled in on top of wary tension. Ramble, his deep gold color hidden beneath a lighter winter coat, pale mane and tail floating in pampered thickness, tread close on her heels—crowding her, scenting her . . . occasionally snaking his neck as if to herd her, just as often nickering an invitation to admire his magnificence. Too preoccupied with Lady's presence to care about the inexperienced rider clinging to his saddle, and not yet caring about the wrongness they approached.

A small covey of wood grouse burst into flight from the path-side brush; already anxious, Lady startled— not nearly as much as she wanted to, ever aware of her bareback rider. Still the bit jerked in her mouth— *run from it*—legs clamped around her barrel—*run from it*—and her rider's fearful stiffness pervaded Lady— *run from it!*

She didn't. Legs spraddled, head flung high . . . she didn't.

Bolting was against Carey's Rules.

After a long moment, Suliya began to breathe again, probably never supposing that Lady could tell she wasn't, and that her failure to do so frightened Lady as much as anything. Her head still flung up against the pull of the reins, Lady nevertheless relaxed a fraction.

Dayna said dryly, "Maybe we should walk the rest of the way to the damaged area."

"She knows better," Suliya said, frustration pushing the breathless tension in her voice.

"I've never," Dayna said, dismounting the palomino with a little stagger, "seen anyone pull on her mouth like that before. I don't mean the staying on part, I mean before it. And after. Don't think Jess won't remember when she changes back. Hell, that's why I'm not riding her in the first place."

"She—" Suliya said, and stopped; after a moment, the discomfort of the bit eased, and Lady, reassured by Dayna's matter-of-fact behavior, lowered her head to huff a breath at the bush where the grouse had been.

"They're gone," Dayna said, and gave her a pat on the neck. Suliya threw a leg over Lady's rump and slid down to land beside her, and Lady lowered her head far enough to give a relieved, mane-flapping shake.

But she didn't relax completely. Not with the *wrongness* ahead, and Dayna leading the palomino toward it.

Then Dayna, too, stopped short. "Burning hells," she said, her voice full of intricate human feeling. Surprise and fear and awe; Lady recognized them all, and her ears flicked forward and back in independent succession, listening to Dayna, listening for danger.

"What is it?" Suliya flipped the reins over Lady's head, giving them an absent tug before Lady had a chance to step out politely on her own, not noticing Lady's offended hard, round chin. Oh, yes, she would remember.

"It's outside the null wards," Dayna said. "It got through the null wards!" She stopped short, the palomino snorting wariness behind her shoulder.

"Maybe they missed a spot," Suliya said, coming up beside Dayna and the stud and at the last minute thinking to put herself between them, creating plenty of personal space for both horses. Lady, too, snorted at the ground before them, bringing her head up in an attempt to focus on it, to make sense of it; the offensive and alarming smell was stronger than ever.

"Not *they*," Dayna said pointedly. "I was one of two wizards who set these wards. I know damn well we had this area contained. There's no way—"

But she stopped short, and after a moment said more quietly, "I guess there *is* a way, whatever it is.

The damage either cropped up outside the original area, or it came right through the ward. I could probably tell, if I got close enough—"

"No!" Suliya said, and Lady backed up at the volume of it, too unsettled by sights she literally couldn't comprehend and smells that meant *danger* to any animal on hooves.

Dayna laughed with no amusement whatsoever. "No kidding. It's not worth the risk, not when the Council wizards will see it tomorrow anyway. I say let's give this whole . . . *meltdown* . . . a very wide detour. The horses don't want anything to do with it, and I don't want to be on either of them when they're acting this way."

Suliya glanced at Lady's bare back, giving it a rueful pat. "Not bareback on this one. She's . . . more sensitive than other horses I've ridden."

"She warned you," Dayna said, most practical as she turned the palomino around, hunting the woods for something to stand on just so she could reach the stirrup. "Carey's a head courier with the reputation for the best training stable in Camolen, and Jaime rides the highest levels of competition at home. You might be good—it's not like I know enough to really tell— but you're not *that* good."

Suliya said nothing . . . but Lady knew resistant body language when she saw it.

Arlen, bedecked in a faded orange knit sweater that made him wince even though his jackets obscured it from the public eye, his hair shorn close to the nape of his neck and the short thickness of it absurdly refusing to lie flat at a forehead cowlick he'd forgotten he had, tucked his new luggage—bulging saddlebags—under his knees and tried to keep those knees from straying into the seat space of the tired-looking man opposite him.

Anything to get home.

They'd grunted acknowledgment of one another upon embarking, and muttered a few polite words about the weather (sparkling clear); the roads (not as kept as a coach route should be); and the inconvenience of the service failures.

"Family expected me home two days ago," the man said, annoyed but resigned. "The Council never thinks of the inconvenience to the rest of us when it pulls something like this. Insignificant, that's us."

Fool! Arlen wanted to say. *Can't you tell something horrible has happened? Is* happening? Instead he rubbed a finger over the smooth and sensitive area his mustache used to cover and said, "Mmm."

"My sister is probably worried spelless," said the tidily arrayed woman sitting beside Arlen. She shifted slightly, and the coach's permalight caught the glint of her hand jewels; she fussed at one of them in a fitful gesture. "But surely she'll figure out I had to take a road coach."

And then there was Jaime, who must believe that Arlen had been in the middle of whatever conflagration had taken place—especially after so long with no word. He'd almost reached her the evening before, he was sure of it. And as careful as he'd have to be about using magic—about splashing his signature around where other sensitives could recognize it, revealing his presence before he'd figured out what had happened, what was happening, and how to respond to it—he knew he'd try again this evening. He'd try, and he'd keep on trying until he was close enough to cross the distance between them, or until she somehow recognized his far-off touch and made the hint of response of which she was able—and which would make all the difference in the world.

"How about you?" the woman asked him, her raised

voice indicating it hadn't been the first time she'd tried to get his attention. "Do you have family expecting you?"

"Hmm?" he said, coming back from his thoughts. Jaime. Carey. Jess. *His family*. The people most associated with Arlen the wizard. He gave her a vague smile and a short, disinterested shake of his head. "No," he said. "No one."

I'm on my way, Jaime. Whatever's happening, hold on.

◈

On a small farm in eastern Camolen, beyond the boundaries of Sallatier Precinct and within a craggy area so sparsely populated its namesake wizard hasn't the skills to earn a place on primary or secondary councils, reality twists. A young boy hunts his family's hardy wool-producing goats . . . and eventually, he finds them.

What's left of them.

◈

Suliya slid from Lady's warm back with a groan, shoving open the heavy stable door at Anfeald. Dayna, too, dismounted, although the doors were plenty tall enough to encompass a horse and rider without threatening the rider's head.

Dayna and the palomino were definitely ready to part ways. Even as Suliya leaned her shoulder into the door, she caught the sly movement of the stallion's lips, and managed to convey the short and weary warning of "Teeth!" before things went too far.

Bless the warmth of the stable, its cobbled aisle and big square stalls. Not indoors-warm, but out of the wind and heated with the welcoming scent of horseflesh. Suliya directed Dayna to an empty guest stall—"Just throw him in there. Pull the bridle if you can, and I'll come grab his saddle"—and hesitated before Jess's changing stall, easing the bit from the mare's mouth and giving her an automatic pat on the neck.

She'd never have thought it would take so long to get here, not even using the ride-around for both the damaged area and the mudslide along the riverbank. But then, she'd never considered just how much she relied on her stirrups to ride such terrain. It had been just as hard on the mare, she knew—not that she'd ever admit just how many times Lady had made a sudden shift of weight or speed to keep Suliya on her back. She didn't even have the energy left to note which horses were out, which couriers had returned. Carey wasn't in evidence, but she expected he'd show up quickly enough. Word spread fast when riders he'd been waiting for returned, and the wheelbarrow sitting in the aisle was indication enough that someone had already left his or her job to do just that.

She looped the borrowed bridle over her shoulder and grabbed a halter to use with the stallion; with another horse, especially a tired horse, she might unsaddle the animal loose in the stall, but obviously not even the day's ride had taken the wander out of the palomino's lips.

Dayna waited outside the stall with the bridle, holding it with a puzzled look on her face—as well she might, for she'd unbuckled it in the wrong places and now it was only a tangle of leather pieces. She accepted Lady's bridle without a word, leaving Suliya's hands as free as possible. Suliya tied the stallion short, and left him that way until she was ready to leave, the double saddlebags—hers and Jess's—piled outside the door and the saddle balancing on her hip. "We need to make sure he gets a good grooming," she said. "And we need to get an orange lock spelled in his mane as soon as possible. Can you—?"

Dayna lifted a questioning eyebrow, her face badly wind-flushed, her layered sandy hair pulling out of its tieback.

"It means he bites," Suliya said wryly, pulling the halter off and slipping out the door with no time lost.

Dayna shook her head. "Specialty spell," she said. "Probably one of those easy ones that doesn't take a wizard—you just have to know the spell. I don't."

Jess came up the aisle toward them, moving at somewhat less than her usual energetic pace, her hair in need of a brushing. She stopped next to Dayna and turned her rich brown, too-large eyes on Suliya for a long moment.

Suliya, flushing, felt the sudden urge to say, *I wouldn't have pulled if you hadn't been bouncing around like a three-year-old!* and somehow found the necessary restraint to *not.* Right or wrong, protesting would only bring the incident to Carey's attention. Then Jess released a long sigh, fluttering it slightly through her lips just as a horse might do. She said, "I know the spell," and went into the stall. She hesitated a moment an arm's length from the horse, waiting for some invisible—to Suliya—signal accepting her approach, and laid four quiet fingers on the horse's crest.

After a moment, bright orange color crept down the flaxen mane, a streak for each finger.

"Four streaks," Dayna said. "I take it that's pretty bad."

Jess retreated from the stall and latched the sliding door closed behind her. "It means to always watch, yes." She bent to retrieve the saddlebags, and abandoned them just as quickly, straightening to head for the cross-aisle at the back of the stable with most of her usual spring returned to her step.

"Carey," Dayna said with satisfaction, just before Carey rounded the corner.

"How'd she—" Suliya started.

"His step, I think." Dayna watched with a small, tired smile as Jess reached him, but it faded when Carey opened his arms and wrapped Jess up in a long embrace, pulling back to wipe some imagined smudge from her cheek and smooth her wayward dun hair. He had a habit of trailing his hand down the dark central stripe of it; he did it now.

"What's wrong?" Suliya asked as Dayna's expression changed. She was more used to seeing Jess as the emotive one, Jess taking Carey's hand or moving in close to him, but Dayna's concern seemed out of place.

Or maybe not. "It's just . . ." Dayna muttered, watching the two more closely, "He's not like that. I mean, something's wrong." And then she snorted, loud enough to draw Carey's brief gaze even as he and Jess exchanged quick words. "Well, *obviously* something's wrong. But I mean . . . something since he last saw her."

"You know them that well then, ay?" Suliya said, giving Dayna herself a closer look. A small woman, lightly boned, slightly built. Close to boyish in figure—she'd have made a good courier, if she'd had a little more strength. Though from what Suliya had gathered at Second Siccawei, Dayna had strength aplenty when it came to magic—even if there was something not quite right about it, making people acquire the same kind of expression they might when talking about one of her own bastard step-siblings.

Dayna snorted again. Small she might be, but subtle she was not. "You learn a lot about people when you go through hell with them."

At that, Jess cast an anxious look back at them—or maybe at the palomino, Suliya wasn't sure—and then, surprisingly, took off down the hall that led into the hold. Suliya and Dayna exchanged a glance, and then as Suliya shifted the saddle to a better hold, Dayna moved up to meet Carey as he came toward them.

"Dayna," he said, a greeting full of unspoken words that Suliya couldn't decipher. None of the tenderness he showed with Jess, but a certain kind of respect.

"What's happening?" Dayna asked, also bypassing normal greetings as she nodded at the spot where Jess had been.

"Jaime's sick," Carey said. "Yesterday evening, too. I think . . . well, Simney can't tell what's going on, but says it's not anything dire. But Jaime's pretty miserable, and you know Jess . . ."

Dayna nodded. "I'll wait," she said. "See if she feels better later."

"She did, last night," Carey said by way of agreement. He reached for Suliya, who gave him a moment of blank-faced confusion before handing over the saddle and collecting the saddlebags. Carey gave Dayna a somewhat grimmer look. "We've got a lot to talk about."

"We certainly do," Dayna said. "I take it Jess mentioned that the new Council is blowing off my observations about the . . . incident."

He gave her a fleeting grin as they headed for the tack room. "Blowing off. Expression left over from Ohio?"

"Yes. And did she mention the stallion? Why we brought him?"

He led the way into the tack room, settling the saddle over the top of another on its rack and dropping the saddle cloth into a hamper of similarly dirty horse blankets; rows of empty saddle racks lined the wall, and he took the bridle from Dayna to place it on an unassigned bridle hook on the adjoining wall. Thigh-high equipment trunks lined each wall beneath the racks and hooks of carefully cleaned leather accouterments—cruppers, chest bands, courier bags, hobbles—although as with the saddles and bridles, most of the spots were empty, the walls bare. "Why you brought him?" Seemingly without even looking, he took Jess's saddlebags from Suliya, leaving her her own. "It was the only way for you to get here, she said—something Garvin and I will deal with later—"

Impatiently, Dayna said, "I'd have waited another day to catch a different ride, if that was the only reason. But Jess said it best—he's the only one who saw what happened to the Council. The only one who lived through it. The only one who can tell us—"

"*Tell* you!" Suliya said, drawing both their startled attentions her way. She shifted under Dayna's sky blue gaze and Carey's appraising expression, but Dayna quickly picked up the conversation where she'd left it. "If we can use a changespell . . ."

Carey gave a quick shake of his head. "It's checkspelled. You know that. You burning well ought to, after last summer!"

She shrugged. "There's raw magic—"

"That's crazy!" Suliya said. In her mind's eye she saw the development wizards at SpellForge, testing spell formulas, going over every element; more times than she could remember, they'd given her derisive warnings about the use of raw magic. How dangerous it was, how unpredictable, how horrible the consequences.

Dayna gave her a wicked little grin; Suliya hadn't seen that gleam in her eye before, and she wasn't sure she liked it now. "What do you think I do?" she said. "What do you think Second Siccawei is all about?"

"I grew *up* wandering the halls of SpellForge," Suliya said, taking a step back from Dayna but shaking her head with each word. "Raw magic is a fool's tool—and anyone who sticks around to watch is a fool, too!"

"You two get along well together, I see," Carey said dryly. "Ease off, Suliya. As it happens, I agree with you

in this case—but it just might be that there's more to
the world than you know."

"You don't think I can do it," Dayna said to him.
"I expected more of you, after what you've seen."

"I've got an entire hold to think about," Carey said,
and Suliya realized to her horror that he was truly
tempted to let Dayna try. "And what I *think* is that
we have too much at stake to make the wrong decision right now."

Dayna took his words in silence, a narrow-eyed kind
of silence that looked like a thoughtful marshalling of
more argument.

A sudden clap of sound rocked the stable; as one,
they ducked, crouching close to the floor. Carey
recovered first, bolting for the stalls; Dayna muttered
a nonsensical phrase that sounded like, "Good God,"
and then very definitely, "Does this sort of thing *always*
go on, or is it only when I'm here?" and then she, too,
was out the door.

Suliya followed, but at the head of the long stall
aisle, stopped to gape. Snow floated in the air, more
thickly over the middle section, snow from nowhere.
The air bit at her lungs and nose with a singed dry-
ness, completely at odds with the existence of snow.

Carey glanced at the falling flakes, raked his gaze
along the stalls, and finally snapped, "Report!" in a
voice loud enough to make it down to the big double
doors and back again. Suliya brushed futilely at the
snow buildup on her sleeve. Snow that didn't melt,
snow that wasn't quite white—*not snow*. Wood shavings. Wood shavings that ought to have been in one
of these stalls.

Halfway down the aisle, a groom staggered out of
a stall, cleaning fork in hand, completely covered with
shavings—but looking more bemused than alarmed or
injured.

"What happened?" Carey said, meeting the young woman halfway. Klia, the niece of one of the senior riders and a cheerful girl with a middling work ethic and not much in the way of goals for her life ... not someone Suliya could understand in the least, though she liked her well enough. "Are you all right?"

Klia swiped an ineffective hand over her short curly hair. "I'm not sure," she said, looking dazed enough that she probably wasn't sure what time of day it was, never mind what had happened a moment earlier. She stuck a finger in her ear and wiggled it, making a face. "You sound a precinct away."

"What," Carey said, trying for patience and almost making it, "were you doing?"

That, the girl could answer; her face cleared with relief. "I just finished this row of stalls, and since we've got so many horses out, I thought it would be a good day to run a drying spell on them all."

Suliya nodded to herself; no matter how clean they tried to keep the stalls, in the winter there seemed to remain an underlying dampness. The drying spells took care of that, but couldn't be done when the stall was occupied. Made sense. More initiative than the girl usually showed, in truth.

"Interesting drying spell," Dayna said, mild amusement in her eyes as the floating wood chips thinned. "More like a recipe for sweeping practice."

Hurt protest showed in the girl's face. "But I run that spell all the time. This has never happened before."

"Does it always work?" Dayna went down to the stall in question, peered inside, and shook her head. "I suppose it worked in a way, this time. It sure is dry in here. Easy to tell, too, with all the shavings out of it."

"Always." Klia tried again to clear her hair, and finally bent over to shake her head like a dog, sending wood shavings flying.

"That's not true," Suliya said, gaining Carey's sharply attentive gaze. "Sometimes she has to invoke it a couple of times before it works." She'd heard the muttering often enough; Klia was like that with all her small personal spells.

Dayna returned to them. "There's your answer," she said, as though it were self-evident. Carey lifted an expressive brow, amazingly similar to the expression Suliya felt on her own face. Dayna looked at them both—looked *up* at them both, by far the shortest of all three of them—and said, "Oh, come *on*. When it doesn't work, she's introduced a wrong element."

For her impatience, she got only blank stares, but Suliya saw a surprising gleam of humor in Carey's eye at the whole situation—one which made her think perhaps he understood after all, and was actually teasing Dayna. For one so focused, she'd expected anger, not humor, at such a mishap.

But no one had been hurt. The cleanup was simple enough—push brooms, hand brooms, perhaps a dusting spell or two, and in that moment she was struck by the potential of what his friends saw in him, what *Jess* saw in him . . . someone other than the head courier doing his job.

Whatever humor he'd gotten out of the situation, it vanished with Dayna's impatient next words. "She introduces a common wrong element, one there's a checkspell against because *this* is the result. But the Secondary Council is responsible for overseeing checkspell management, and all of a sudden they're filling the role of the Council . . . the checkspell has failed. Carey, it *won't be the only one*."

And Carey's hazel eyes grew darker as his eyes narrowed; he seemed to have forgotten that Klia and Suliya were there as he matched Dayna's intensity, staring back at her. "The changespell," he said, his voice low. "We could find out what happened to Arlen . . ."

She nodded. "It's worth a try, don't you think?"

Suliya blurted, "The penalties—"

Carey gave her a startled look—not as if he'd forgotten her, but as if he were surprised anyone thought the penalties mattered with the stakes at hand. "I'll deal with the penalties," he said. "Klia, if you're sure you're all right, get a start on cleaning up this mess. Suliya will help you. And Dayna . . . you were there when Jess was first changed. I want to know what to expect." He gestured at the back of the hall—no doubt meaning his small office off the job room.

"She didn't have language at first." Dayna kept pace with him, almost two strides to his one. "She learned damned fast, though."

Suliya, standing in a waning storm of wood shavings at the end of a long day, opened her mouth to ask if someone else might not help clean up the mess Klia had made, although a small inner voice reminded her that they were *all* tired, all overworked.

But it occurred to her that this was where things would be happening. Maybe not right away, maybe not even tonight—she had no idea of the preparations needed for what they planned. Even so, sooner or later, this stable would turn into the nexus of action . . . would maybe even provide the crucial information that allowed the new Council to understand what had happened to the old.

Suliya intended to be part of it.

Chapter 9

Not far from Anfeald the City, on one of the abrupt rocky hills thrusting so boldly from the soil, snow melts off the south side and becomes firmly entrenched in the crannies of the north side—until late in the day, when the hill . . . shimmers. Dissolves. Turns to a flat puddle of stone.

The astonished deer sunning itself on the southern hump of the hill gives a startled bleat and leaps for safety.

Not soon enough.

✦✦✦

Jess stood outside Arlen's rooms, ignoring the morning bustle from the dispatch desk inside the apprentice room; there were few messages coming through now, but they'd become harder to retrieve, requiring Natt and a backup dispatcher to be on hand at all times. The last several, for all the trouble they'd taken, had been little more than "stay calm, no further developments, couriers on the way" notes. The couriers, upon arrival, brought large quantities of family messages traveling from precinct to precinct across Camolen, and a few crucial bits of information—which of the wizards were being chosen to fill the new Secondary Council, which services were considered nonessential, an update of known checkspells now temporarily suspended—but nothing that Jess really wanted to hear. *What had happened to the Council.* Or even better, *it's all a terrible mistake, everyone's fine.*

Rather than admit she still hoped for that last, it was easier to pretend she didn't care about any of it.

But she cared about Jaime, who waved her in to the sitting room where Jess was promptly accosted by the young male calico cat. It jumped to the arm of a chair to paw the air and demand attention, and she absently scratched her way down its back as she eyed Jaime, who sat on the couch lined up against the window. With circles under her eyes and an entirely uncharacteristic jittery presence, Jaime looked years older in just the few days since they'd seen each other.

But she gave Jess a wry smile at the assessment she obviously knew she'd gotten, and passed a hand over her hair. "The good thing about this cut," she said, "is that no one can tell when you *haven't* styled it."

"You were asleep when I got here last night. Carey said you were sick."

Jaime rubbed the bump on her once-broken nose, the one she'd acquired not long after meeting Jess . . . and not long before meeting Arlen. "I'm okay in the mornings," she said. "It's the strangest thing . . . the last two evenings . . ." She let out a gusty breath and shook her head. "I'd say it was a migraine of the worst order, except I've never had them. It comes on, it lasts the evening, and it goes away. By then I'm not good for much, though."

"Are you good for much now?" Jess asked, meaning it as a simple question and not realizing until after she'd spoken how the words might sound.

But Jaime only smiled. "Not as much as usual," she admitted. "Though I'm not sure it matters. I'm nothing but a guest at the moment—people aren't exactly interested in lessons right now, and Carey's already using his horses to capacity. He doesn't need another rider."

"No," Jess said, "but the hold needs a rider." It wasn't the right word, she knew it wasn't. But it was the right concept, and Jaime as much as Carey understood her occasional need for shortcuts and had the ability to follow them.

Jaime did. In that instant, her already reddened eyes teared up, her cheeks flushed. Resolutely, even if in a voice that threatened to fail her, she said, "That should be Arlen. I keep thinking—" *He'll be back.* Even though she couldn't say the words, Jess saw the fierce hope flare briefly in her eyes. But it faded, and she said simply, "I don't even *live* here."

"You care enough to leave your world to come be with him. And he loved you. That makes you important to Anfeald . . . it makes you someone they can . . ." She gestured for a futile moment, and finally said, " . . . come together around. Do things for."

"I should have spent more time here," Jaime said, as if she hadn't been listening. She turned her head to the window beside her and closed her eyes, but not before Jess saw the self-recrimination there.

Jess came to her, knelt by the couch. "*Dayna* could stay here. Dayna had no family in Ohio, no people who meant anything to her. For you, things are different." By *people* she meant Jaime's horses as much as her brother. "We cannot make yesterday's decisions today."

Jaime still didn't look at her. She whispered, "But I miss him. I miss him more than I thought—" She stopped, took a deep breath, and looked back to Jess with overbright eyes. "He was so certain that this time he could teach me that little spell to protect leather from rain. I just can't seem to get it, but he was so sure—" Another deep breath, a long pause, and she said, "I suppose he'd want the place to keep going. Eventually another wizard will be assigned to the precinct . . . Arlen would want it in the kind of shape he could be proud of."

Jess nodded. "He likes things to be right." Then she frowned. "Should I say it that way? Or should I say that he *liked* things to be right?"

Jaime blindly shook her head. "You say it however you like. Let's see what's up with Dayna, shall we? Surely we've had at least one furious dispatch from Second Siccawei demanding that she return."

Rising to her feet, Jess said, "She got a private message. She threw it away. I don't think she likes the way the new Council is looking at things."

"Dayna and authority," Jaime said, following Jess out the door and leaving the calico to pace the magically-imposed cat boundary behind her. "Never a good mix."

Carey scrawled a last-minute assignment on the day's job sheet, trading one of his more experienced couriers for Suliya—a short run, one that would soothe her frustration and give the other courier a much needed break—and pinned it to the job board under the permalight.

Half of the runs were already in progress; the usually tidy job room spoke of the stress on his riders. Several half-filled mugs on the communal desk, someone's jotted notes on the floor—he bent to pick the paper up, leaving it on the desk where whoever dropped it might see it—losing himself in the details of running Anfeald Stables, his mind a muddle of the need to act and an unexpected wariness of doing the wrong thing.

In the past, his willingness to act—his *determination* to act—had helped spur a small group of friends to surprising victories. Victories that those in charge had said couldn't be won—especially not Carey's way. Carey's way had always started out as the *wrong* way . . .

Starting out wrong doesn't mean ending up wrong.

Using a changespell was wrong—wrong for any number of reasons. Because the Council said so, but also because of the way it imposed human will on animals, irrevocably changing them in ways they often literally couldn't accept. And not always changing them for the better . . . Jess would say that to him if she knew what he was thinking, and she would be right. She often was. She'd softened him, taught him to see he couldn't go through this life alone, living on the strength of his goals. Taught him that sometimes the price of those goals on the people around him wasn't worth it.

Starting out wrong doesn't mean ending up wrong.

But people had died in the past as a result of his actions. In the end he'd gotten what he'd gone after— Arlen's freedom, imprisonment of rogue wizards, safety for Camolen—but people had *died*.

They would have died anyway.

Maybe.

Or maybe no one would have died, or fewer people, or their deaths would have been of an easier nature, or—

He closed his eyes—tightly—trying to squeeze the conflict right out of his mind.

It didn't work.

Practical afterthought struck him; he crossed the room to the courier boxes mounted on the wall and slipped the reassigned packet out of its current box and into Suliya's. A tight twinge from his leg reminded him that he, too, had paid for his decisions. Time to see the healer, he thought. Once every seven or ten days . . . longer than that and even Jess's massages couldn't keep him going. On the bad days—and he did have them—he felt as if his body had been wrung out like a rag head to toe, every muscle aching, every joint creaking. On the not-so-bad days his leg took over the job—aching, tiring easily, his tendons like creaky, rusted cables.

Dayna peeked into the room, hesitating until she saw that he was alone and then entering much too casually, scrubbing her hands through her straight, sandy, shoulder-length hair. Dayna on the prowl, just as willing as Carey to do things the wrong way if she thought the alternatives were even worse.

He said, "I've still got four more riders coming in," just in case she thought they had privacy.

She shrugged. "We can talk until then. Are we going to do this today?"

"You mean, are we going to *try*?"

She shrugged again. "I'm not really worried about it. There are a number of subtle variations on that spell—and I know them all. I *ought* to, after last summer. One or the other of them will get through."

"And then what?" Carey sat down on the edge of the desk, legs thrust out with one ankle over the other. "How long did it take before Jess could put a meaningful sentence together? How long before we actually *learn* something—and will it be worth what we put that stallion through?"

She dropped her hands from her hair to her boyish hips; the Camolen-style tunic and trousers combinations she'd taken to wearing were always just the right colors to suit her, but they never did anything but emphasize her adolescent shape. He was beginning to understand that she liked it that way—that it somehow made her feel safer. Ironically enough, being here on Camolen had made a difference, too—given her a skill, enough power so she could relax, mellowing from blunt and abrasive to merely blunt. Blunt like now, staring at him in disbelief. "Last time I talked to you, you *wanted* to do this. You wanted to know what happened to Arlen. What's happening to Camolen *now*."

"And maybe I still do." Guides, yes. Until he did, how would he know what to do *next*? He shoved his forelock out of his eyes, not quailing before her annoyance as she'd have obviously preferred. "I'm just thinking it through."

"There's a first," she muttered, but she came to sit next to him at the edge of the desk—or would have, but she was too short and ended up leaning against it instead. "Look . . . I'm not saying it'll be easy. The easiest part is actually making the change, unless I'm totally off base about the checkspells."

"But you don't think you are." His arms crossed again, he stared absently at his knees while he pondered her words.

"I spent some time thinking about it last night, running through a few of the preliminary phrases. No, I don't think I'm wrong. But you're not wrong, either—it'll take some time before Ramble can tell us anything, assuming he's capable of making the transition. But Carey—" She shifted, putting the side of her hip against the desk so she could aim a dreadfully earnest stare at him, one he could feel even if he didn't look over to meet it, "Jess was right. He was *there*. He's the only one alive who *knows* what happened. He's Custer's horse all over again, only the U.S. Army didn't have the chance to ask what happened. *We* do. And I'm telling you, the new Council isn't on the right track.

They're still trying to trace signatures and figure out what kind of spell was used so they can counter it and checkspell it."

Bemused, Carey said, "Custer's horse?"

Dayna waved an impatient hand. "The only survivor of one side of a pivotal battle in my country's history. It's not important. Listen up . . . even if you don't think about Arlen and Sherra—"

How could he not?

"—The thing is, as long as the Council's going off on the wrong track, we not only don't catch the bad guys, we aren't protected from whatever happened. It could happen again, any time—it could happen to the new Council as easily as it happened to the old, if someone really wants to ruin this country."

Carey made a quick face. "Camolen's on the western end of a small continent. We may annoy some people with our isolationism, but not to *that* extent."

"You're being obscure," Dayna said. "And evasive. Just make up your mind, okay? Do you want to do this or not? If you do, then we need a place for it—a private one."

"I think we have to assume we'd get caught," Carey said; it was the least of his worries. The peacekeepers had their hands full; Anfeald might still be quiet—not yet aware of their loss—but the glut of messages going from one peacekeeper station to another was enough to tell him not every precinct had responded to the service crisis with calm. Even Anfeald the City had experienced some opportunistic looting.

"Fine, but not until we accomplish something. That means having a place to stash whoever the palomino turns into—"

Out of time. The murmur of voices in the hall made Carey raise his glance from knees to doorway, and Dayna cut her words short just as Jess came through the door. She was dressed for barn work in a patched, drawstring-waist tunic and tough pants worn so thin across her bottom he couldn't help but stare when the opportunity presented itself; she obviously didn't expect to ride today. At her side, Jaime wore the stretch breeches that gave away her other-worldly origins; he had no intention of sending her out on a run, but she might well have decided to work with one of the young horses for which no one else had the time.

Jess grinned to see him there. "Carey," she said, a greeting she somehow used to encompass everything from a casual hello to the unmistakable invitation she'd given him late the evening before. "Dayna," she added, a simpler word restricted mostly to the meaning of *hello*. She would have walked up to him, stood with him for a moment with her cheek just touching his, breathing in his scent the way she was wont to do, but she visibly checked herself and headed for the courier boxes.

Carey ducked his head to hide a rueful smile. They'd had a discussion or two about the need to keep close contact out of the job room, but just this once . . .

He would have welcomed her.

"Lady's not going out today?" she asked, poking her hand into the empty box assigned to her horse-self.

He shook his head. "Thought I'd hold you back in case something comes up. Everything else today is pretty routine, as much as there is of it."

"Suliya is going out," she observed, nowhere near a criticism.

"Do I know her?" Jaime said. "Pretty young woman, not as dark as Auntie Pib? Hasn't taken any lessons yet?"

"That's her," Dayna said, and then, a more personal aside, "You doing okay, Jaime?"

Jaime took a quick breath, like someone had slapped

her, and Dayna immediately said, "Never mind. Not here."

"No," Jaime said. "Not here."

But Jess had ignored this exchange, her attention on Carey and her expression . . . concerned. Hesitant. Hunting for words. He broke his own rules and took her hand. She said, "Suliya . . ." frowned, and then glanced at Dayna. Carey didn't understand why, not at first.

Dayna snorted and filled him in, brusque where Jess was trying to learn tact. "She's hardly on the same level as the rest of your riders."

Carey ran a thumb absently along Jess's long fingers. "She rode Lady yesterday, didn't she?"

"Yes," Jess said, watching his face, making sure he understood. "I would not let her do so again."

"Not to worry, Jess," he said. "I never would have put her on Lady in the first place. She's going out on old Bristen today, on the pasture-side run to the little peacekeeper station."

Her anxiety eased away. "You *do* know."

He grinned at her. "I know."

"She *could* be good . . ."

He rubbed at the corner of his mouth, trying to keep the grin from getting bigger. "I know that, too."

"Good." And for Jess, that was enough—to know he knew. She trusted him in this, as she trusted him in everything.

If she found out about the changespell . . . *when* she found out . . .

Best by far to have it a done deal before she learned of it. A done deal, and a successful one. And even so . . .

He gave her hand a gentle squeeze and she smiled at him, unaware there was anything behind the gesture besides the spontaneous expression of his feeling for her.

Somehow that made it worse.

༄࿐

Despite the pall hanging over the stable the day after Jess returned from Second Siccawei, Jess found solace in the indoor ring, introducing and refining basic ground manners in the youngsters and pretending not to notice the unusual quiet—so many riders out, Carey preoccupied, Jaime vacillating between hope and despair. . . .

She and Jaime laughed fondly over the yearlings' indignant expressions, their astonishment that anyone should require them to do anything but bumble around as they wished, regardless of whose heels they stepped on and whose space they invaded. Quivering noses, flared nostrils, and hard, offended, little chins ruled the day. And then when each of them was through, Jess scratched their shoulders and along their thick manes until their lips quivered with delight instead of righteous offense. She spent extra time with the dark dun yearling she would have recognized as her brother even without the pedigree she'd read in Carey's office, and tried not to wonder what her own progeny would be like.

Or what they'd be like *if* . . .

No point in *ifs*. Not now, when there was so much else to think about anyway. Jess put her forehead to her brother's for a moment, raising his curiosity; his winter-furry ears perked forward to the utmost. And then she gave him a purely human kiss on the nose and said to Jaime, "The last one."

Jaime's smile immediately faded. "Let's go see if there's any news, then. And I want to talk to Simney, see if there's anything she can do for these . . . events I'm having in the evening."

"You think it will come back tonight?" Jess fastened the toggle flap of her coat, preparing to lead the yearling back into the crisp day and to his paddock behind the hold-hill.

Jaime said fervently, "I sure as hell hope not. But if it does, I'd like to be ready. Even if it means putting me straight to sleep for the night." She shook her head at the thought of it. "Go put that kiddo back in the paddock; I'll wait for you in the job room, where it's nice and warm."

Jess stuck her tongue out in a recently acquired gesture that seemed to span both worlds and led the yearling outside, tromping across the crusty ground— snow made rough and hard by cycles of melting and freezing under use—to the closest paddock where the young horses had a small herd of their own, overseen by a retired mare who made sure they kept their equine manners. Cold bit at the threadbare seat of her pants, and she ran back to the small rear entrance of the stables in a slippy-slidey rush.

She would have headed straight for the job room, releasing jacket toggles on the way, if she hadn't heard Dayna's briefly raised voice from down the aisle. Dayna, in the stable? Over supper the night before, she'd thought she'd heard Natt murmur something about getting help with some of the hold's defense spells, along with mutters about hoping they wouldn't need the spells anyway. And she was certain Dayna had agreed.

Not that she'd expect to find her friend in the stables under anything but unusual circumstances, anyway. Without the little bay Fahrvegnügen, Dayna was lost when it came to horses.

So Jess followed the voices to one of the foaling stalls at the end of the aisle—bigger than usual, more private, set up for easy use of surveillance and environmental spells. Unused at this time of year, they were usually bare and cold. But as she walked closer, head tipping with the curiosity of it and phantom ears flicking back and forth in search of clues, Dayna's voice rose again and she had no doubt. Dayna and . . . Carey, in a frustrated-sounding reply.

Jess hesitated outside the nearly closed sliding door, making no attempt to conceal herself as she looked through the bars comprising the upper half and too startled at what she saw to interrupt. Dayna, as she'd heard. Carey. The stall, fully bedded on one half and in the back, a pile of blankets and . . . clothes?

And the palomino stallion, standing at the end of the lead in Carey's hand and munching carelessly at a small chunk of pressed, dried hay at his feet. Had Carey been paying attention, the set of the stallion's ears would have told him to look for someone in the aisle.

He wasn't.

"It *ought* to have worked," Dayna said, anger tinging her voice. "That last one really ought to have done it. I can't believe no one's dropped the ball on it, not with things the way they are."

Carey rubbed a hand along his jaw; he had that tired look that Jess knew so well from these past few days, and something more besides. The frustration she'd heard. Worry—a *new* kind of worry. "They're all pretty recent spells," he said. "Maybe the Council wizards aren't prioritizing yet; maybe they're just handling the standard checkspells and using a timeline for the more obscure ones. Anything within a year . . . two years . . ."

Dayna's anger turned to gloom. "A system like that would make sense to start off with," she said. "Once they get a little more settled, they'll probably ease up on the more obscure variations."

"Maybe that's it, then," Carey said. "Maybe we wait."

Wait for what? Jess moved closer, right up to the narrow slice of open door, her mouth open to ask the question, hesitating until they noticed she was there.

Dayna gestured vehemently at the horse. "*Wait?*

With who knows *what* out there going dangerous, the new Council on the wrong track, and the only answers within this annoying horse?"

They wanted answers from the horse.

"Wait," Carey repeated, sounding like he didn't like it any better than she. "You had another option to consider? You've been through every variation of the spell you know, and you said it yourself—no one knows this spell better than you."

"Changespell!" Jess blurted.

The stallion whipped his head up, alarmed more by Dayna and Carey's startled reaction than by Jess's seemingly sudden presence; he'd known she was there from the start. Dayna scowled, threw up her arms, and muttered an obscenity she hadn't learned on Earth—

But it was Carey to whom Jess looked. Carey, with his expression cycling from surprised to aghast to . . . guilty.

"Changespell," Jess said again, only this time she whispered it. "Carey—"

"Jess—" he interrupted, taking a step toward her, looking at the lead rope in annoyance, and handing it off to Dayna—much to Dayna's consternation. "It's all we could think of. We *had* to try—"

"No." Jess said it firmly and decisively; she shook her head once, her chin lifting. "Not this."

"You said it yourself, Jess, he *saw* what happened." Dayna would have put her hands on her hips with impatience, but she realized the stallion was eyeing her, lips twitching, and she took a wary step away from him. "He can *tell* us—"

"No." Jess stood in the door, not backing away when Carey reached it and would have come out to talk to her in the aisle. "No," she said in rising anger, "he *can not.*"

Dayna said, "If he was human . . ." and let the implication stand on its own.

"What do you think, if *he was human?* He would have no words, he would have no knowledge of himself. He would be scared and angry. He would be of no use to you, and you have *no right!*" Behind her, Jaime's questioning hail made her flick one of those phantom ears back, but only for a moment; Dayna and Carey had all her attention.

"He might be able to tell us plenty, eventually," Carey said grimly. "We won't know until we try."

Jaime came up softly beside Jess, sliding the door open another foot and looking from face to face, taking in Dayna's stubborn expression, Carey's conflict of guilt and determination, and Jess's outright anger. "My God," she said. "Tell me this isn't what I think it is."

"It's exactly what you think it is," Dayna said. "And for darned good reason."

Jaime just looked at her a moment, a sad contrast to the anger and betrayal coursing through Jess. And then Jaime shook her head, and said, "If the reasons had been good *enough*, you wouldn't have tried to do this behind our backs."

Carey was silent, watching Jess; trying, she thought, to say something with his eyes—hazel eyes gone dark in the lighting of the stall and the tilt of his head, full of pleading words behind his determination.

She was in no mood to listen.

Dayna gave the lead shank a desperate-looking yank as the stallion lifted his head from his hay to eye her arm, chewing the fodder with twitching lips that gave away his wicked thoughts. Her voice held a hint of that same desperation. "We did it this way to avoid this kind of confrontation. It's a waste of time!"

"Only if you think you get to make decisions for the rest of us," Jaime said, placing a quiet hand on Jess's arm.

"Jaime," Carey said, his voice low. "Jess. We haven't

made decisions for anyone but this horse. And yes . . . when it comes to that, I do get to make those kinds of decisions here in this stable."

This horse.

"Trent might disagree," Jaime said.

"This *horse*?" Jess said, feeling the sting of it.

"Trent might," Carey admitted. "I'll accept the consequences for that."

Jess couldn't stop it; added to the flare of her nostrils came the slight tremble of her chin. She felt it and she hated it, because it meant she suddenly wasn't so much angry as she was hurt, and angry was so much easier. She said in a low voice, "And me?"

"Ah, Jess," he said. "Braveheart, I need you to understand—we've got an enemy out there, and we don't know anything about him. Her. *Them*. We don't know what happened to Arlen, to *any* of them. This is our only chance to find out more. What choice do we have?"

"You remember seeing the other animals who changed," she said in that same low tone. "What it did to them. You know even if you change him, you may learn nothing."

He gave the briefest of nods, quelling Dayna with a look when she would have interjected with argument. Somehow this was between Carey and Jess now. "I know those things," he told her. "The risk of *not* doing this if it can help us is just too great to ignore."

She eyed him; a moment ago she would have trusted him with her life, with her heart . . . now she didn't know, and it hurt.

Then he glanced at Dayna and said quite practically, "It doesn't really matter, if we can't manage the spell."

"I'll find a way," Dayna muttered, as much to herself as anyone else. She jerked her hand back just in time. "Burning hells, Carey, take this lead rope. This horse must be carnivorous."

"No," Jess said. "He's a stallion who's spent too much time in a stall with no one bothering to teach him manners or give him things to think about besides what his nature tells him to do. He's playing with you."

"If he really wanted to bite you," Jaime added dryly, "your arm would be broken by now."

Jess gave Dayna a long, even look. "He won't be any different, as a human. Just like I was Lady, when you found me. I had Lady's manners and habits." She thought about the things that she and Lady shared, from their basic natures right down to her sly practice of stepping on the feet of fools who offended her without any awareness of their transgressions. She *still* had Lady's manners and habits. She *was* Lady.

"He'll bite, you mean," Dayna said in flat distaste.

"All that and more, I would imagine," Carey agreed. "I never said it would be easy to manage him. Nothing like the experience you had when you took Jess in."

Dayna gave Jess a sudden narrow-eyed stare, a piercing look that made Jess shift uneasily. "You ended up in the park because Carey used the world-travel spell, and a glitch in the part that was supposed to help the traveler adapt changed you. The *first* world-travel spell, the one Arlen's refined a dozen times over; it's a whole year older than the changespell. If I can't circumvent the changespell problems . . . that's our answer!"

"You want to hit Ohio with a human version of *that*?" Jaime said with a skeptical twist of face, nodding at the stallion. Bored, the horse started pawing at the bedding, digging himself a hole; Carey moved him to the side of the stall and deftly looped and tied the lead rope to the wall-mounted ring there. "Yeah, that makes a *whole* lotta sense."

Carey took the suggestion more seriously, but ended up frowning anyway. "Leave Anfeald?"

"I'm not exactly keen on going back, either," Dayna said. "No matter *how* much I miss McDonalds' fries. But it's an alternative." She looked at Jess again, in a way that gave Jess the sudden impulse to turn around and leave. "We'd need me, to keep a solid lifeline with magic. And Carey, just because I know he'd never let anyone else run off and have all the fun. Someone has to be the boss. And . . . Jess. To handle the stallion. To help him."

Jess wished she'd followed that impulse. That she'd gone off to mix a special mash for the horses who would start returning any time now. That she'd gone upstairs to meet the silly demands of Arlen's calico.

Anywhere but here, to hear the choice Dayna had given her.

Help them do the thing she hated the very thought of by helping the stallion survive the transition to humanity. Or don't help them, and let the stallion suffer a harder, maybe impossible transition.

The anger came back.

Dayna, startled at the sudden glare Jess aimed at her, took a step back, all but bumped into the stallion, and scooted immediately forward again.

It might have turned into a standoff of glares if Natt hadn't come rushing down the aisle, his threadbare but always worn dresscoat flapping with the breeze of his movement. "Jaime! Jess—have you seen Carey?"

Jess stepped back so Carey could come out of the stall, not quite leaving him the space to do it gracefully. He glanced at her; he knew aggressive equine posture when he saw it, even passive-aggressive. "Natt," he said and, as Jess had, took in the apprentice's flustered expression. "Not again. Don't tell me—"

"Not like last time," Natt assured him quickly. "But

maybe just as serious in the end. The . . . event . . . that killed the Council, the damage . . . there's a new spot."

"That's no surprise," Dayna said, slipping easily by Jess to join the conversation outside the stall and visibly glad for the excuse to do it. "I already reported yesterday that the meltdown was spreading."

"More than *spreading*," Natt said. "It's shown up somewhere else entirely. Out in Sallatier, near Lander Chesba's hold."

"An entirely new spot?" Jaime said, doubt on her face, along with the unmistakable desire for someone to tell her she was wrong.

But Natt said, "Yes. Completely unrelated. With no signs of spellwork anywhere in the vicinity."

Carey stiffened. "Was anyone hurt?"

Natt shook his head with reassuring confidence. "No. One of Chesba's couriers found it—apparently a day or so ago. It's just taken this long to spread the word."

"Then I'm right," Dayna said, not looking pleased about it. "It's not just a matter of figuring out who killed the Council. It's bigger than that, and we're *all* in danger until someone puts a check on whoever's behind this."

"Maybe now the new Council will be more interested in what you felt," Natt offered.

Dayna snorted. "Maybe," she said, unconvincingly. "I've already told them everything I know, anyway. They don't need me back there."

"They do if you're the only one who can feel—" Natt started, but cut himself off at Dayna's look. Not the glare she might have given him once; even Jess was aware that her time here had changed her, given her moderation. Just an even look, and the slight shake of her head.

"I tried it their way," she said. "Let *them* keep trying it their way. More power to them if they open their eyes and manage to make any headway. Me . . . I'm going back to doing things my way."

Watching Jess, his back straightening with a tired kind of resolve, Carey said, "I don't think we truly have a choice any more."

But Jess didn't meet his gaze, as much as she felt the weight of it. She looked at the stallion, instead— starting to doze now, his sheath relaxed, sex organ exposed. Jess—unlike Dayna—was under no illusions about what it would be like to deal with this horse as a man. He would be earthy, unruly, and not interested in human rules. Although he was far from mean, he had too many years of displacement and coping behaviors gone uncorrected, and they would carry right over to his human form.

She should know.

Chapter 10

Arlen shifted, hunting for a more comfortable position in the front corner seat of the long-bodied coach. Only the second full day of coach travel, and already—despite the well-padded seats and coach stabilizing spells—he was beginning to rue his bony posterior, an anatomical feature that until now had always seemed perfectly adequate. Until now, with another small town behind him and yet another batch of passengers in this modestly but comfortably appointed coach.

He hadn't become used to the exposed skin between his nose and upper lip, or to sitting through hours of travel, unable even to refine his spellwork lest someone recognize his signature . . . but Arlen had already perfected the evasive smile and nod procedure. The businessman with dubious taste in clothing and not much to say, but amiable whenever he said it. Never offering any indication of his

111

desperate need to reach home, or the privileged knowledge that drove him there.

He'd had no luck reaching Jaime, uncovered no information regarding whatever disaster had befallen the Council—and, in fact, his fellow travelers still seemed to lack any awareness a disaster had occurred at all. Most of them crabbed about the service disruptions in a good-natured way; a few were rude and intemperate. None appeared to realize that the problem went far, far beyond their inconvenience.

Arlen's first attempt to eavesdrop on the wizard dispatch had met with a blocking shield of profound strength. He'd had no doubt he could bypass it . . . but not without revealing his presence in the process. So he remained as ignorant as the rest of the populace— or nearly so—and sat here in this coach—eight passengers on a side, drawn by a six-horse hitch in a comfort- and safety-spelled coach body with the driver in a separate, enclosed compartment in the front with a door between the sections—exchanging the occasional murmur of conversation, reading a book on the history of needlework techniques and patterns . . . and determined to vary the strain on his anatomy by renting out a horse for the next leg of the journey. A fast horse.

The coach jolted, instantly grabbing his attention— the way these long-bodied road coaches were spelled, the passengers shouldn't have been able to feel the biggest of road holes. Another jolt, and he heard the driver's curse right through the door against which he sat; the other passengers lifted their heads from their reading or their naps, showing the alarm that Arlen was trying to hide. Fifteen other people, all of them trying to get home after being stranded on unexpectedly one-way travel booth trips, suddenly more intimate with each other than ever intended as they jostled back and forth, grabbing seat arms and muttering apologies.

A third jolt and the long coach suddenly slewed around, trying to make a turn for which it was never meant; the driver shouted to his horses, panic in his voice, and the wheels lifted beneath Arlen, tossing him upward to the accompaniment of screams—

As swift as that, he ran through a quick spell to bleed inertia, sending the energy opposite to the coach's slewing motion. As swift as that, the coach settled back to the ground and came to a halt, jerking slightly as the horses hit the end of the suddenly motionless harness.

Men and women looked around, dazed, untangling themselves from each other and their belongings, and as their hushed conversation changed from inquiries about each others' conditions to the first demands of "What the burning hells was *that*?" the driver called back for them to stay calm and stay in the coach.

Arlen was already calm, but he had no intention of staying in the coach. He dropped his book on his saddlebags—he hadn't even lost his place—and slid the door open just wide enough to exit as unobtrusively as possible, knowing the others would soon follow suit regardless. Skipping the step-up to hop straight to the ground, he glanced back over the road—a main coach road, packed dirt heavily maintained by a conglomeration of coach service wizards—and found the cause of the initial jolts. Misshapen, discolored areas potted the road like deformed cow patties, gleaming with a sheen he'd never seen in nature. No coach was designed to navigate such obstacles; no coach service wizard would have allowed the obstacles—whatever they were—to remain, not for an instant. They were enough to cause what would have happened here had he not—

Used magic. Flung his signature around for the world to perceive.

Small magic. Someone would have to be looking for him, or be very nearby, to have detected it at all. Not much chance of either, given that he was probably presumed dead.

He found the driver, a small pot-bellied man with a cap covering his obvious baldness and a seamed face that had been on the road for a lifetime, ostensibly checking the near-side lead horse, still visibly trembling in reaction, and with his attention wandering inexorably back to the road ahead.

Or what was left of it.

The road ran through the snow-covered rough northwest country, pastures and farmland nestled between rugged rock formations on which the dark stone of southern exposures had drawn the sun and left stark patterns of black with white-filled and shadowed crannies. Sparsely populated between towns, the land remained undisturbed by man during all but the most temperate times of the year, the brown ribbon of road the only sign that people came this way at all.

Now, in truth, that road twisted back on itself like a ribbon, crumpled into a ball and thrown to the ground to settle slowly down upon itself. The snow-covered rock formations lurched in gravity-defying angles, pocked with randomly melted areas that had nothing to do with sun and shadow.

Arlen stood by the driver a moment, neither of them saying anything; the horses had stopped only a length or two before the road, sheening with unnatural swirls of color, turned inside out on itself. Arlen squinted at it, trying to make sense of what he saw to no avail; his gaze skipped away, repelled by the foreign nature of the elements before him. He glanced at the driver and found the short man staring with such open-mouthed bafflement that there was no question about his own difficulties.

And while every whit of common sense Arlen possessed shrieked *danger!* at top volume, he took a step closer, and another, focusing on not the whole inde-scribable scene, but only that small part of it closest to him. A gyration of earthy colors in slick but uneven surfaces. Dirt and rock caught in a roiling boil and solidified in the moment.

But *how*? And *why*? The wizard in him immediately began sifting through spells, wondering what to com-bine with what to achieve this horrifying effect—while the very sensible man in him fought not to turn on his heel and run as far and fast—

To the side, the road burbled. It twisted, it warped . . . it slid toward him like oil slicking across downhill ice.

"Burn it right *off*," the driver gasped as Arlen skipped backwards, all thoughts of wizardry vanishing and nothing left but the wisdom of escape. The spot subsided even as Arlen retreated out of danger, but from the corner of his eye he spotted another dark bubble of activity.

He didn't know what it was, he didn't know what had caused it . . . but he knew it was growing. And he knew, watching the process corrupt yet another pre-cious few inches toward the front hooves of the snort-ing coach team leaders, that nothing living would survive that process. "Turn these horses around," he told the driver. "Get us back to the last connector."

Wide-eyed, the man said, "Look at this team—look at the coach! It's not *made* to turn around on road this width. It *can't*."

"It can," Arlen said grimly. "It *will*, unless you want to be stranded out here on foot with . . . *this*." He waved his hand at the miasmic scene before them.

"I'll unhitch the horses," the man said. Behind them, the other passengers had disembarked and were milling uncertainly, all in one piece and apparently not will-ing to move as close to the oddity of the road ahead as Arlen. "We can take turns riding them back to town—"

"The coach can turn," Arlen repeated, calling on the authority of his Council voice for the first time since this trip had started, pinning the frightened man with a gaze full of certainty.

Realization crossed the man's tense features. "It was you," he said. "We should have tipped over . . . we didn't. That was you."

Arlen wasn't willing to say that much out loud. "The coach can turn," he said, imbuing his words with as much meaning as he could.

This time the man nodded, the lines of his face deepening with the difficulty of the situation. He said, "Sit up front with me for a while, be easier for you to work that way," and gave the near-side leader a pat; the horse was no happier than they to be so close to the unnatural remains of the countryside. Then he turned, reluctantly wading into the group of passengers to explain that the couch wouldn't be going any further, asking them to load up again so they could get themselves away from here. . . .

Arlen only half heard the querulous and frightened replies as he stood by the team of pretty matched bays, their snorts and bit-jingling as much a part of the background as his fellow passengers. None of it could compete for his attention, not with this strange magic in front of him. Magic, because nothing else could have caused these disruptive and surrealistic changes. Strange, because . . .

He hadn't felt it. There was no signature, no surge of magic. Just the stuttering creep and crawl of growing damage.

He wasn't yet sure just what had happened to the Council. But he suddenly knew where to start looking.

Strings of spellstones clattered softly against one another, dangling from Dayna's hand so thickly she could barely hold them all as she headed for the third floor meeting room where the travel team had quietly gathered supplies. Stones so Jaime—who planned to stay in Camolen—could trigger the message board she and Arlen had devised for quick information dumps between worlds, stones so each of them could return to Camolen, stones of protection, stones for every little thing Dayna could think of—and that she thought had the slightest chance of working when their strongest ties to Camolen's magic would come through her.

She'd gotten quite good at making spellstones in her year and a half of intensively tutored time here . . . and she'd gotten even better at it in the last day—especially when it came to choosing the right stones for the job. Even now she glanced at her collection of glimmering, active stones and gave silent thanks to Arlen for keeping such a complete stock of quality materials. Hard stones, crystals and gems—some of them drilled for chains, some of them set into wire harnesses. Small enough to be inconspicuous, light enough so carrying them was no great hardship.

The others, too, had been preparing. Jaime would stay behind to keep Anfeald running, and to supervise the stables; she'd been cribbing notes since the day before, at least until evening came and she found refuge from her strange new nightly malady in a heavily dosed goblet of wine. Jess had been gathering clothing for the palomino's use as a man, and for her own immediate use upon arriving in Ohio—for she, too, was starting the journey as a horse. And Carey . . .

Carey had spent his time communing with Jaime and Natt and Cesna, all of them talking as fast as they could to try to address all the necessary details to keep Anfeald running smoothly under any contingency—right up to the very possible arrival of a new master or mistress for the hold. Both Anfeald and Siccawei were prized precincts, and the new Council wouldn't let them go without wizards for long.

Dayna closed her eyes and shuddered off rising goosebumps at the thought of anyone but Sherra running Siccawei. The hold, the city . . . the very precinct had been infused with her quiet habits of celebrating life. Not so surprising, given her interest in healing . . . in providing people with a place *to* heal.

Like Dayna, newly arrived in Camolen, full of rogue magic and anger and self-defensive defiance.

It was all still there, of course—a year and a half was nothing on a lifetime's habits. But she liked to think some of her edges had softened.

Maybe.

Stones in one hand, a small personal duffle in the other—she wouldn't need to take much, not with a number of her things in storage at Jaime's farmhouse— she navigated the turn in the doglegged hallway and found the door to the room already open.

Not that they'd been trying to keep their plans especially secret—Natt and Cesna knew, had both seemed too exhausted to argue about it; Cesna, in particular, looked about ready to drop, and seemed more grateful than concerned about their intent to gather information from the palomino. But with Suliya in the mix, Dayna wasn't making assumptions about how quickly their attempts to be quiet would shift to indiscreetly loud protests about this, that . . . and whatever.

To her initial relief, she found the room empty but for Jess, bent over the table with her long hair falling forward to obscure her features. And then on second thought, and at the heavyhearted look she found on Jess's face when Jess brushed her hair back and looked up to greet her, the relief fled.

Jess was, after all, the only one of them dead-set against this plan. Even Suliya thought it was a good idea; she just didn't see why she was part of it. But Jess . . . Jess came not to help them, but in spite of them. Because she couldn't stand the thought of the palomino facing the world as a human without someone who truly understood him.

Who knew exactly what he was going through.

"Ay, Jess," Dayna said in greeting, as cheerfully as circumstances allowed.

Jess hesitated, hands pausing as she folded a pair of loosely tailored pants they hoped would fit the palomino as a man. "You sound like Suliya."

Dayna wrinkled her nose. "It's catching, I guess." She spread the spellstone strings out on the table that took up half the room—it was already covered with clothing, letters from both Dayna and Jaime to people in Ohio—and as much gold as they thought they could safely and easily carry. They had no intention of being distracted by lack of funds, and with the slight difference in the value of gold on the two worlds, Arlen's petty cash easily covered what they felt comfortable taking. "Got some stones for you, Jess. Nothing heavy duty—just if you need to send a message back, or need to reach one of us in an emergency . . . that sort of thing."

Jess glanced at them, neatly placing the folded pants into the duffle assigned to the palomino. "I think I'll need another braid." She currently bore two—small, tightly braided sections of coarse sandy dun hair behind her left ear, holding the spellstones with her special personalized changespells along with the courier recall stone, the protection from hostile magic in use directly against her, the friend-foe spell . . .

Dayna didn't think any of them would be of much use in Ohio. She'd kept them as simple as possible,

going on faith and the knowledge that previous stones
had maintained at least a tenuous connection with
Camolen.

She separated the stones into smaller bundles, leaving a bundle at each of the seats around the table.
"Carey's, Jaime's, mine, yours . . . Suliya's." Then she
looked up at Jess, who was stuffing thick socks into a
pair of nearly shapeless lace-up shoes. "Tell me again
just *why* Suliya's coming? She obviously doesn't want
to."

Jess gave her a flat look, her dark-rimmed brown
eyes so expressionless that Dayna should have seen her
reply coming. "*I* don't want to go. The palomino will
say he did not want to go, when he is able. Suliya is
like the rest of us . . . doing as events have said we
must."

Dayna stopped in the act of untangling Carey's
spellstones, opened her mouth—and closed it again,
mustering her willpower to stem the words crowding
on her tongue—words to underscore the potential
danger Camolen faced, that they were the only ones
who could travel to Ohio and hope for the slightest
chance of success, that they were cut off from everyone else with no opportunity to convince the new
Council that the travel was necessary in the first
place—at least, not in time.

But she didn't say any of it, because Jess already
knew it. She simply disagreed with it.

That she *could*, that she'd grown enough from her
first moments of being human to this complex woman
who could examine a multifaceted situation, come to
her own conclusions, and stand by them—

As far as Dayna was concerned, it was merely evidence that they were doing the right thing—that the
palomino would adapt, and without the handicap Jess
carried for her first weeks in Ohio—when no one knew

who or what she was—would quickly be able to tell them what they needed to know.

But she didn't think she'd make points with Jess by bringing that up now. Instead, she said, "I meant, why *Suliya*. She obviously doesn't want to come; she'd rather stay here and ride for Anfeald. And she's not the easiest person to work with." Honesty compelled her to stop and add, "Of course, neither am I."

The smallest of smiles tugged at the corner of Jess's mouth. She said, "I thought about asking Ander, but with no dispatch and no travel booths, Kymmet is too far away. And they probably need him."

Ander. Tall, gorgeously blond, a little too certain of himself—but good in a pinch. Dependable. He'd saved Jaime's life the summer before, lost his heart to Jess in the process . . . and still counted her among the people he'd go far, far out of his way to help.

If he'd known she needed him. If he could get here.

Dayna shook her head. "You're right. I wish we could reach him . . . but he's too far away. But—"

Jess looked over at the door, as if reassuring herself that Suliya wasn't standing right there, then looked down at her hands. "We can't spare the others," she said. "They all know the shortcuts; they know the horses and the roads. And the palomino . . . I will need the help. Besides," and she gave Dayna a shrewd look, more shrewd than Dayna expected from this woman who started life as an honest and willing horse, "you saw her with Garvin. She has . . . a confidence. She'll need it."

"She has *a confidence* because she doesn't know how much she doesn't know," Dayna said by way of a grumble. "Including, I think, that sometimes life isn't fair—or should I say, sometimes it won't be fair to *her*."

Jess gave her a questioning look at that last, picking up the strung spellstones Dayna had brought her and running them through her fingers in an absent, explorative way. She'd almost broken herself of the habit of investigating new things with her sense of smell and so didn't raise the stones to check their scent, but Dayna often saw her nostrils flare upon meeting some- one new . . . and often caught Carey smiling at the impulse, an affectionate smile he'd only recently allowed himself.

It struck her then how well she understood and liked these people, and that with their world already turned upside down, maybe it was time to make other changes, to settle closer to them. After all, she had no idea who would take Sherra's place at Siccawei. Or Arlen's . . . or any of them. She hadn't known half of the deceased Council members, and although she'd caught some quick scuttlebutt before leaving Second Siccawei, she certainly didn't know the new Council members.

Or whether any of them would be the least inter- ested in mentoring a woman from another world with a penchant for raw magic and an odd mix of skills— struggling with basics on some levels, soaring above most of her peers on others.

Jess, unaware of Dayna's wandering thoughts, said with honest curiosity, "How can you tell? You only met her days ago."

Dayna dragged her thoughts back to the conversa- tion. Suliya. "Let's just say I know the type."

Jess made a noise to show she was thinking about that and tucked the spellstones into a small pouch.

"You really should wear those," Dayna said, sorting through her own, making swift decisions about how to restring and reorganize them.

With a slight shake of her head, Jess looked down at herself. "I start as Lady," she said. "When we get there, then I'll put them on." She looked abruptly at the door, and Dayna knew to expect someone; she wasn't surprised when Carey entered the doorway, stopping there to lean against the frame in a deceptively lazy way that let Dayna know he was actually good and ready to go.

"Jaime'll be here in a moment," he said. "Suliya's supposed to be here already. We're as prepared as we're ever going to be . . . let's get this thing started."

"Time to lock and load," Dayna said, rolling her eyes when Jess and Carey turned identically baffled expressions her way—although Carey almost immediately realized she was using an Earth expression, and dismissed it as not important enough to follow up on. His gaze fell on Jess for a long moment, and he said, "You just about ready?"

"There is no *ready*," Jess said. "There is waiting, and then there is making the change. But I will never be *ready* to do this to him."

"I know," he said, watching her with a wistfulness Dayna rarely saw on the long angles of his face. "But you might try being ready to do it *for* me. For us. For Arlen."

Jess looked at him then, but it was a look full of thought, and far from conclusion.

Chapter 11

Suliya finally showed up with two heavy bags slung over her shoulder, eliciting much dry amusement from Carey. Just shy of a shouting match later, they'd whittled her supplies down to one bag—"It's *spring* there," Carey said more than once, eyeing the extra sweater she wanted to bring, "and we can get anything you need!"—and gathered up all the gear to head for the foaling stall from which they planned to depart, the barn almost entirely cleared of witnesses. Two horses and three people, all holding hands and clinging to lead ropes with the plan to avoid the separation Carey and Jess had experienced on their first journey.

Then again, Jess thought as she trailed the group down the aisle, on that first journey she and Carey had just pitched over the edge of a steep, vertical, dry riverbed, with Carey already flung from the saddle by the impact of an arrow. Since then they'd used more refined spells for the handful of visits to Earth they'd made, and had no way of knowing how much of the separation had been caused by the spell, and how much caused by the circumstances under which Carey had triggered it to save their lives.

Jess set her saddlebags down next to her changing stall; she intended to wear her harness with her bags—and clothes—firmly attached; she knew for certain her gear would come with her even if the travelers became separated, and if nothing else she wasn't going to end up in Ohio—off-trail in one of the area's nature parks, to be precise—without clothing to pull on. Nakedness had never bothered her in the least . . . but she'd learned to avoid the reactions from others when they had to deal with it.

She waited for Tenlia, one of Carey's couriers and tired-looking at that, to lead her second horse of the day down toward the door, lifting a hand in greeting to Jess on the way by; the woman didn't even notice the occupants of the foaling stall, although the travelers would wait for the barn to clear before acting. No wonder Jaime had been left with instructions to recruit riders if she could, to scour Anfeald for suitable horses, and to streamline the ride assignments—although Jess still harbored hopes that Jaime would decide to travel with them. Jaime, the one person who seemed to understand the depth of Jess's reluctance over their decisions for the palomino, the one who saw the goods and the bads of their plans clearly in spite of what she wanted or wished things would be.

Jaime, who was coming down the aisle to see them off.

Jess lingered by the door of the changing stall, wanting a few last human moments. "Are you sure—" she started as Jaime reached her—but Jaime shook her head before Jess could even finish.

"I know this might be my last chance to get home," she said. "Believe me, I know that. There's no telling how things are going to go on this end—or if the new Council will even allow the travel spell at all without Arlen—" She stopped, closed her eyes, took a deep breath, and then met Jess's gaze with a sad, almost self-mocking look. "It's just that I can't believe it yet." *Arlen's death.* "And until I can believe it, I can't leave. I can't . . . I mean, what if he shows up tomorrow? No one ever *saw* him dead . . . and if he did—show up, I mean—then I have to—"

"Jaime," Jess said, cutting her off with that single low word; Jaime looked surprised, as if suddenly realizing she'd been babbling. Jess said, "Do you remember how hard I looked for Carey when Dayna and Eric first found me? When no one believed I was a horse—*Carey's* horse—or that he was even real?"

Jaime gave her a hesitant nod.

"Stay here," Jess said. "Wait for Arlen."

Jaime seemed to stop breathing for a moment, and when she started again it was in an uncertain fashion. But then she turned to the matters at hand and said, "Anyway, I can do some good here for both Carey and Arlen, at least when I'm not drugged into oblivion. And Mark ought to be expecting you; I spelled him a message last night. The only question is whether he'll read it in time—he doesn't seem to check the thing regularly."

"We have his phone number," Jess said, Ohio words that felt strange in her mouth after so many months without a visit. "And Simney is working on the thing that happens to you in the evening?"

Jaime gave her a wry grin. "Yes, Simney is working on *the thing*. And Cesna, too; it's giving her something to think about that has nothing to do with Arlen, and she's good at little mysteries like that. They both agree it has something to do with magic. They'll figure it out. I can afford to be a little more patient as long as I have the spelled wine."

Carey and Suliya came down the aisle leading the stallion. Carey peeled off from her side then hesitated by Jess and Jaime. "You all right?" he asked Jaime. "You want to make any last-minute changes?"

Jaime shook her head, resolute despite the delicacy she seemed to have taken on over the last few days. Jess had never imagined looking at Jaime's strong rider's body and thinking the word *delicate* at the same moment, but here she'd done it, and not for the first time. But Jaime just said, "I wish you'd rethink this plan, but I'm through arguing about it. I'll stay here and do what I need to. I hope I'm wrong, and this turns out to be the right thing." She hesitated, but didn't offer him a parting hug even though it hung between them. She and he had started off too much on the wrong foot, and Jess had long ago accepted that the history between them meant they would never be close friends, no matter how well they knew one another.

"Thank you," Carey said, holding Jaime's gaze a beat longer than necessary—saying those things they could never say. And then he turned to Jess and repeated his question. "You all right? Last-minute changes?"

Jess, too, shook her head. The changes she wanted would never happen, and it would bother her too much to ask and be denied . . . again. She still mourned the loss of something between them. Something she hadn't yet quite identified, but felt as keenly as any clumsy hand on the rein . . . and something that Carey only now seemed to notice.

"Jess," he said—and stopped, at a loss. "Jess, I—"

Jess said softly, "Choices matter," and left it at that. He rubbed his thumb over his lower lip, looked at her another contemplative moment, and then, torn, looked away, failing her and knowing it. Making choices. "See you on the other side of the spell," he said, hesitated again, and then headed for the foaling stall.

"Yes," Jess said, still softly, watching after him. "The other side of the spell."

"Don't worry," Jaime said, keeping her voice low. "You know how he gets when it comes to doing his best for Arlen. The man practically brought him up. He'll get through this."

"Through being a man-brained mule's butt?" Jess asked, not quite able to put the asperity in her voice that she'd intended.

Jaime laughed anyway, and gave her a quick hug. "Come back soon," she said. "I'll keep a stall bedded for you."

And Jess had to laugh too, no doubt what Jaime had intended. She ducked into the changing stall, centering herself so she'd fit as Lady; closing her eyes, she triggered one of the sapphire stones dangling from her long, thin, spellstone braid.

The magic swept through her, blinding her to everything but the changing sensations of her world; she threw her head back, embracing the essence of the Lady shape she loved so well. Four strong hooves, nostrils flared to catch the sudden renewed strength of the scents around her, the awareness of her own strength, her speed, her power . . .

Her willingness to harness them all for the people around her.

Fully, solidly equine, Lady lowered her head and shook like a dog, black mane flapping . . . a changing-time ritual. Then she took careful stock of herself, sorting out what remained of her human feelings and intentions, finding her own conflicts anew, recognizing the imperative the Jess-self had left for her—to

stand while harnessed and then join the others at the
foaling stall even though some part of her—Jess parts
too complex for her to think about in Lady form—
didn't want to do it.

It was a new dilemma for Lady . . . *do this* and *don't
do this* directions at the same time. She ducked her
head, scratching her nose along the inside of her fore-
leg, black forelock falling into her eyes. She was as dun
as dun got, Lady was—not a sooty dun like her brother,
but a fine clear-coated buckskin dun, thick black line
down her back, tiger striping ghosting up her legs, black
points all around. Striking color on solid conformation,
good sloping angles, strong loin, and a sweet arching
neck . . . she raised her head, a dry-boned, clean-cut
head unlike the coarser features of the palomino, who
now stuck his head from the open foaling stall door
as he puzzled about suddenly scenting a new and yet
somehow familiar mare.

Suliya gave his lead a futile tug and that put Lady
in motion. She nudged open the unlatched stall door
and waited with ill-concealed impatience while Jaime
buckled up her special courier harness—saddlebags,
clothes, and all—her head bobbing, ears pricked in
complete attention at the foaling stall. But when Jaime
gave her a pat and said, "You're all set," she flicked
an ear back in her version of a thoughtful frown,
turning her head to nuzzle her friend. Worried.

"It's okay," Jaime said softly. "Go ahead."

So Lady blew a gentle snort and headed for the stall
with long, free strides that were entirely reflected in
the way she moved as Jess. By the time she got there,
Suliya had convinced the stallion to move to the back
of the stall, but she couldn't stop his posturing; he met
Lady with his neck arched high, prancing in place and
offering a courtly series of grunting nickers.

Lady flattened her ears, informing him that he was

far too forward, and Suliya eyed her with alarm. "Carey—"

"We're going," Carey said, placing a hand on Lady's harness, holding tight.

And Lady's world wrenched itself inside out . . . and despite the sudden inner cry of Jess's despair in her mind, jerked her right along with it.

Chapter 12

The spring ground was wet against Carey's face, the strong humus smell of it unmistakable in his nose. He lifted his head, watched the woods spin around his field of view in response, and quickly closed his eyes. "Burning hells," he whispered to himself, only now realizing how much improvement Arlen had made in the refined versions of the changespell. He clenched his jaw on the bile in his throat, told himself *don't throw up, don't throw up, don't*—

Someone beside him threw up.

That would be Suliya, her first introduction to world travel full of turbulence and a rocky landing, and he ought to say something reassuring like *it gets better* but just at that moment his jaw was clenched even harder—

He swallowed, took a breath, swallowed again . . . and cautiously lifted his head to the steady drizzling rain that silvered the young, brightly green leaves around them.

We're all here. Not separated, not flung to the
winds . . . Dayna, sprawled on her stomach much as
he'd been, groaning imprecations at the world; Suliya,
dazed and clinging to the lead rope of an empty
halter—a halter draped carelessly over the lanky form
of a man with an odd gold-tan sheen to his completely
exposed skin and orange stripes in his flaxen hair.
Unlike the others, he hadn't arrived spilled over on his
stomach; he looked more like a puppet for which
someone had suddenly cut the strings, ungainly and
awkward. And not yet conscious . . . the best time they'd
ever have to get clothes on him.

"Suliya," Carey said, or meant to; it sounded more
like a croak. He worked his too-dry mouth until he had
enough spit to try again, and said, "You have to get
him dressed . . . now . . . *before* he wakes up—"

She apparently found the thought of wrestling with
the palomino man alarming enough to get her moving past her discomfort; Dayna dragged herself through
wet leaf layers to lend a hand.

And Carey found Jess. As unconscious as the palomino, taking the change hard . . . curled into a shivering
ball, her head lolling with a slackness that sent a skin-
tightening moment of dread through Carey even though
he knew better; he could easily see the movement of
her goosebumped ribs with her breath. "Clothes, Jess,"
he muttered, making it to her on hands and knees and
gently disentangling her from her harness. Limp-
limbed, she gave no sign of rousing; he couldn't recall
ever seeing her so affected.

Then again, he hadn't been there the first time it
had happened, her first experience with these parkland
trees and paths and the entirely new world that greeted
her opening eyes.

Stifling a curse and a shock of guilt—*I did this to
you*—he dug through her carefully packed saddlebags

and pulled out her underlayers, an Earth-made sweatshirt with a horsey design and a pair of Wrangler jeans. With Suliya and Dayna exchanging snatches of directions at each other—"Move his leg" and "Lift his butt" and one short, mortified, "Watch out for his— the zipper!" in the background, he dressed Jess on his own. Dressed her as though she were a child, hands gentle on her long limbs, confidently intimate as he arranged her underlayers and carefully eased her hair out from within the sweatshirt.

As he snapped the jeans together, her breathing went from slow and shallow to a quick fearful stutter, and he leaned over to meet her confused gaze as her eyes fluttered open—not successfully at first, not all the way, but when finally she looked out from behind them, she found him waiting.

"You all right?" he asked, a strange echo of his words from the barn.

She frowned slightly, looking at the canopy of trees above them, glancing at her own rain-beaded hand as if she weren't sure that's what she'd find at the end of her arm. Then she said, "Hard," in one of her single-word sentences that always made perfect sense to him.

"Yeah," he agreed, running a hand down her arm. "Take your time. All we have to do for now is find the path. No hurry."

"*Some* hurry," Dayna said from behind him. "If we get caught off trail, we're going to draw a lot of attention. The rangers here aren't police officers per se, but they won't hesitate to call them in if they think something off-spell is going on."

"Something off-spell *is* going on," Suliya muttered.

"That's the point," Dayna said. "Hand me that shoe, will you?"

"I think he's starting to come around—" Suliya's voice rose a little in trepidation; Carey glanced over his shoulder to find Dayna struggling with the last shoe and the palomino—the *man*—on his back after their ministrations, his arm twitching.

Jess rolled to her side, struggling to make it at least to her knees. "He will be so scared—"

"Take it easy, Jess. We can handle it."

"But you don't *know*—" she cried, more anguish than volume, and too wobbly to do anything but fold back to the ground and rest her head on her arms despite her best effort.

Carey stroked the back of her head, following her long hair down her spine, as aware as she that these next few moments were crucial, and would likely set the tone for the rest of their time with this newly changed man. "No, we don't know. But we'll do our best. Be easy, Jess."

He didn't think she had a choice, not to judge by the soft whimper that escaped from her. But he'd hoped the man would be slower than she to recover; she, at least, was accustomed to changing.

"His name," she said, muffled and indistinct, "is Ramble."

He'd never even asked.

Dammit.

The Ohio woods of Highbanks Metropark looped and swirled around Jess, defeating her every attempt to rise; utter frustration released a tear; it followed the upper curve of her cheek and then dropped to the already wet ground just inches from her face. She'd wanted to be here to *help* Ramble, to make these moments as easy as possible for him.

She'd never expected to find herself as weak as a newborn foal.

Memories came rushing back, the way it had been that first change—memories nearly buried by the intensity of her confusion at the time, and by the number of seamless changes she'd made since then, both on her own and while traveling here.

Arlen had indeed improved the spell from that first hesitant version. Or something else had gone very wrong—

Arlen, she thought, focusing on the image of him. They were here for Arlen, and for the rest of Camolen. And *she* was here for Ramble, to help him adjust. Not to swoon dizzily in the leaf humus, not to get lost in the enormity of her own first change. Not to churn inside over how badly she wanted to lean into Carey's hand on her back at the same time she was so deeply, coldly angry at him.

"Carey," Dayna said uncertainly from the other side of Carey, from where Jess had managed to get a brief glimpse of the man Ramble had become before the weight of her own limbs dragged her back to the ground. Bigger than any of them, with a ranginess that perfectly reflected the palomino's own.

If he gave them trouble, they'd be no match for him.

"Carey," Dayna repeated, more uncertainly yet.

Carey brought his head down to hers. "Be easy, Jess," he said, and she couldn't tell if he kept invoking one of his old Words with her out of habit, or because he thought it might truly have some influence that sat deeper than her wariness of the needs that drove him.

If so, he was right. She couldn't help it, couldn't help but listen to him crooning *easy* and respond with the trust that he'd trained into her as a foal, then a yearling, then a young mare under saddle. She sighed deeply, losing the edge of her anxiety. "Go help," she told him.

Her back was cold where his hand had been.

Her attention drifted; she didn't know for how long.

Long enough for some of the strength to seep back into her muscles. The world steadied; she became more aware of the rain dampening her sweatshirt, of the birds boldly ignoring them to flutter in the surrounding underbrush, of Carey murmuring not far away—using the same kinds of words he gave Lady but slightly firmer. More authority than reassurance, but not pushing.

Ramble needed more than that. He needed to hear a language he could understand. *His* language.

Her language.

She jerked her head up at a sudden explosion of activity—Ramble in action, Dayna just trying to get out of the way, Suliya tugging at his arm, Carey simply placing himself in Ramble's way, giving him a quick push and then giving him the time to think about it.

Jess remembered the impossible effort of trying to make her new arms and legs work. As had been Lady's nature, she'd been thoughtful about the process even through her fear. Ramble, she thought, was more likely to get mad—and then, without a halter, without restraints, they would lose him to the woods.

She got to her knees where he could see her, the trees tipping only mildly around her now . . . and she lifted her head to give him a throaty nicker.

He froze, distracted from human antics; he perked his ears and arched his neck and—

No. So strange, how she could look at this human form and know exactly what the horse in him meant to do. But the human form merely tipped his head slightly, straightening almost imperceptibly, focusing sharply on her.

She remembered that, too. Sudden binocular perception over her entire field of vision. And color. Intensive color, for the first time, and the assault of it on her mind. How grateful she'd been when she realized she could trust Dayna and her friend Eric even if she closed her eyes, how relieved to retreat to the interior of Dayna's house and its muted color scheme. Now, still on her knees, she moved a little closer, calling to him again. More quietly this time. Reassuring instead of attention-grabbing.

He softened a little, taking cues in that most horsey of ways . . . if she wasn't running, then he didn't need to run, either. If her posture was soft and relaxed, she perceived no threat to either of them. She lifted her chin a little, stretching her neck, eyes wide and curious. A mare inviting a stallion to say hello.

"There you go," Carey breathed, easing aside so he could move with Ramble, maintaining the connection he'd established.

"We're spellin', then, ay?" Suliya said, as quietly as Carey.

"I think we'll be all right," he said. "Just give him some time. Let him tell us when it's all right to get a little closer."

Jess shifted a little, putting her shoulder to the man, taking away any sign of aggression from her stance and giving him the chance to make the approach. Clumsily, still on his knees, still dropping a hand to the ground for balance now and then, freezing and tilting his head in warning when Suliya once moved too suddenly, hesitating to watch Dayna when she murmured something about finding the nature trail and then eased away to do it, he approached.

Ramble came to within arm's length of Jess and then stopped, apparently simply unable to process what he should do next, without a long neck with which to stretch out his head and greet her, carefully tasting of her breath while she inspected him in turn. She gave him a little nicker, a gentle exhalation. Encouragement, all the while watching him for any signs of sudden fear

or aggression—hard to tell when he might explode, with
the tension underlying his movements and filling his
burnished features—hard-boned features, with a curved
nose reflecting the mild arch of his horse's face, his
cheeks and jaw less refined than Jess's. His eyes flick-
ered between worry and interest and downright annoyance, and she knew they had been right not to push
him, knew they needed to stay soft and relaxed and
quiet—

Dayna's panicked reappearance shattered their careful peace into irretrievable shards. She startled Jess,
she startled Carey and Suliya, and her gritted-teeth hiss
of warning—"Park naturalist on the trail, we *don't* want
to be caught here—" turned Ramble's alarm into action.
Boxed in on three sides by Jess, Carey and Suliya, he
whipped around, surging to his feet to bolt away in the
fourth—and colliding solidly with Dayna. Carey and
Suliya were on him in an instant, even while Jess made
it to her own feet, hesitating to join the fray when one
more person could turn Ramble's resistance into utter
panic and escape.

For she had no doubt he could escape, and *would*—
if they drove him to it.

"Easy," Carey said, his arms spread wide to make
himself imposing without actually grabbing for the man,
but Suliya latched on to Ramble's arm and suddenly
found herself facing his teeth, spared a serious bite only
because Ramble's neck didn't reach nearly as long as
he thought it should. Far outmatched, Dayna ended
up on the ground practically under his feet, and her
attempts to disentangle herself only made it worse; Jess
groaned in dismay as the scene turned to chaos, and
then whirled at the barely audible scuff of a hard-soled
boot against rock.

They couldn't be caught here—and here they were,
making noise, being visible, being as obvious as any

small group of people could get. Off trail, breaking rules, with none of the identification of which this world was so fond, and a whirlwind melee centered around a man who until just a short while ago knew only of being a horse. A stallion.

Jess hesitated, frozen with indecision—but just for an instant. Then she sprinted for the nature trail from which Dayna had come, wobbly but intent, ignoring Carey's surprised, "Jess!" and his curse as, with another spurt of noisy struggle, Ramble reclaimed everyone's attention.

She veered as she ran, dodging trees and avoiding roots and sending the birds in all directions—something else that ought to grab the park naturalist's attention— aiming to hit the trail behind the naturalist, to draw attention back down the trail and away from her friends. She, like Dayna, knew this park; she knew the spot where they'd arrived, and in what direction the nature center and parking lots lay. But still uncertain on her feet, she tripped—a vine, a root, a rock, she couldn't tell—and went sprawling, smearing herself with wet leaves and dirt.

A woman's alto voice, full of authority, rang through the air. "Hello, in the woods! Come back out to the trail!"

Jess rubbed her dirt-covered cheek on the inside of her wrist and climbed to her feet. The fall, at least, had gotten the naturalist's attention. No running, not anymore—and just as well, for her brief spurt of activity had cost her. Stumbling more than before, she did as directed—she headed for the trail, still aiming to hit it closer to the nature center than if she'd followed the woman's voice.

Within a few moments, she saw the movement of the tan-and-brown-clad naturalist through the trees; the woman had accurately pinpointed Jess's location and she was waiting on the trail when Jess arrived, hopping one-footed onto the packed dirt trail as she disentangled her bare ankle from one last encounter with a thorn-studded green vine.

They regarded one another for a moment, but a moment was all the naturalist took. "These woods are protected," the woman said. "What were you doing out there?"

Jess needed another moment yet, taking in the woman's unyieldingly stern face, her short dark hair slicked back under a Metroparks cap, her water-beaded raincoat crinkling audibly with the movement of her hands going to her hips. She looked Jaime's age, with more sun lines and smile lines that weren't the least bit in use at the moment.

She looked like someone who expected answers.

Jess had thought only of drawing attention, and not what she'd do when she *had* it . . . and lying had never been something at which she was convincing. Before she could come up with one, the woman's eyes narrowed, flicking from Jess's odd dun hair with its black center stripe to her larger than normal irises, and then to her damp, dirt-smeared clothing.

And her bare feet, one ankle dripping blood from the vine.

"Looking for my friend's brother!" Jess blurted, only the truth after all and a desperate attempt to draw attention from her tough-soled feet. Her phantom ears flicked back and forth, attending the woman, listening for the sounds of the struggle she'd left behind her. Nothing so far . . . either she'd given them enough distance, or they'd gotten the palomino under control.

"He's off the trail, too?" the woman said sharply.

"I got lost." That one was a lie, but her awkwardness in telling it looked as much like embarrassment at being lost as anything.

"In more ways than one, I think," the woman muttered. "Do you live here? In the Columbus area?"

Jess cocked her head, trying to understand the relevance of the question . . . trying to decide how to answer it.

"You sound like you might be from . . . out of town," the woman said, not unkindly despite her obvious remaining disapproval at Jess's presence in the woods.

"Yes," Jess said, deciding then and there to let her remaining stray awkwardness with words speak for her. "Out of town." *Definitely* out of town.

"Sometimes visitors aren't familiar with our rules. We try to be understanding, but the rules are there to protect the woods, and I'm afraid I'm going to have to ask you to leave the park."

Not a consequence that had occurred to her. To be separated from the others? And with no car, not even a horse to ride. The world shifted around her, and Jess wasn't sure if the effect was left over from the change or simply a matter of things happening too fast for her to keep up with. "But Mark—"

The naturalist eyed her again, head to toe. "I'll escort you to the nature center. It's the first place people come when they've gotten separated; you can wait for him there. It's out of the rain." She shook her head as her gaze landed on Jess's feet. "You sure you're all right? There's not anything you're not telling me, is there?"

Only everything. Jess felt it safer not to answer that one at all. She hugged her damp sweatshirt against herself and struck out for the nature center, determined not to wobble anymore until they reached it and she could sit. If she faltered, if she fell, then she'd only bring more park people here to help her . . . and she needed to clear this trail for Carey. Carey and Dayna and Suliya, and a resentful flaxen-haired man named Ramble.

❧❧❧

Things could be worse, Suliya thought. Jess had drawn the park naturalist—a peacekeeper of some sort, to judge by Dayna's reaction—away, and the palomino was under control.

For now, at least. His expression wasn't that of a man she'd trust to do anything but cause trouble at the first opportunity. She'd already caught him staring at her, his jaw dropped slightly with the same expression his horse-self wore when contemplating a bite—except he distracted himself, frowning, working his jaw, tilting his head . . . trying to sort out this new body.

"Burning hells," Carey said, contemplating the man. "That could have gone better in so many ways I've lost track."

"At least it's raining," Dayna said, but her voice held weary agreement, not argument. "Not hard enough to soak us, but it's enough to keep the casual visitors away. With any luck, we'll have this trail to ourselves until we reach the parking lot. And with *real* luck, Mark will be waiting for us."

Carey still eyed the palomino, his mouth twisted in disapproval. "He's never going to trust us now. Jess is our only chance."

Ramble gave an angry snort, as if he could have possibly understood. Suliya knew better . . . he was just expressing frustration over the way his jaw functioned. But she didn't disagree with Carey, either. The palomino—finally brought under control when Carey twisted his ear, a common enough tactic with a rank and dangerous horse—sat awkwardly on the ground, constantly shifting as though he might find a way to arrange his legs that felt natural. Carey'd slipped a rope around his neck, knotted so it wouldn't tighten, and hobbled his arms.

"Wouldn't using those on his *legs* do more good?" Suliya had asked at the time.

"He's used to wearing them on his front legs; he's not as smart a horse as Lady and I think he'll consider himself hobbled." And then he'd thrown her a wry look, rubbing a reddened spot on his cheek. "Besides, he can't hit us this way."

True enough. Though Suliya herself intended to remember that ear twist once they got under way and the man had the chance to figure out hobbled front legs in this form didn't mean he couldn't run as fast as ever.

Carey picked up Jess's harness and saddlebags, slipping them over his shoulder. His own bag was a travel-sling, as was Suliya's remaining bag. Dayna stuffed her own small shoulder-carry into Ramble's now empty bag and straightened her tunic; the rain beaded on it. Wizard's clothing, spelled against such inconveniences as rain. Suliya, too, had once taken such things for granted. "That's that, I suppose," Dayna said. "We need to get out of here before something else comes up."

"I doubt we've got much of a break where he's concerned—he'll try us out again soon," Carey said, coiling the end of the palomino's neck rope and closing his fingers around it. Where Suliya would have tugged, he just made a clucking noise. "Hup, Ramble. Let's go."

Ramble's evident doubt had more to do with his legs and their use; he was aware of the hobbles, aware of his earlier failure. He made a few hesitant attempts to rise, and then eyed Carey with what he thought was a sly look, waiting to see if Carey believed his inability to walk.

"Suliya," Carey said, most casually. "Find me a good switch, will you?"

"You're not really—" Dayna started, but stopped,

uncertain; she was already edging toward the trail, obviously eager to get moving, but—"He's human now . . ."

"A man who still thinks like a horse. Thinks he *is* a horse." Carey nodded at Suliya, who scanned the trees around them for a long and whippy limb . . . most of the brush bore short crooked branches, and the tree branches started way over her head. She finally found a sapling and tore off one of its lean branches; as she made her way back to the others, Carey again urged the palomino to his feet.

Same result. Suliya could have told him that. This horse—as horse *or* man—had his own ideas about what he would and wouldn't do. She stripped the leaves off the switch and handed it to Carey.

"Perfect," Carey said, making a show of examining it, tapping it against his leg. Ramble's nostrils flared in utter annoyance, and the next time Carey asked him to move out, he heaved himself to his feet, ungainly and uncertain, but this time really trying. "Thatta boy," Carey told him. "We can make this work, Ramble."

"You knew," Dayna said, background noise as far as Suliya was concerned; she was busy taking her first good look at the man. He was taller than any of them, thicker across the shoulders than Carey despite his overall rangy look, and the strong bones of his face suddenly seemed to suit him much better. Beside her, Dayna said, "You *knew* you wouldn't have to use it."

"I damn well hoped," Carey said. "I don't honestly know if I could have . . . And once he starts understanding things as a man, I doubt he would have forgiven it."

"And he won't give that rope around his neck a second thought, I suppose," Dayna said dryly.

Carey took a deep breath, one mixed with regret and frustration. "I don't think we can handle him without it. It's going to be a long walk out of here."

Dayna said, "It's *already* a long walk out of here. Let's just hope we find Mark at the end of it."

How casual they were. Roping this man, evading the peacekeepers of a foreign land, making plans to walk out to this *parking lot* thing Dayna kept mentioning . . .

Ramble followed Carey through the woods; Carey followed Dayna. And Suliya brought up the rear, hugging close the open-front sweater her younger sister had bought for her last year. At the time she'd agreed to come along; she'd thought it a certain way to gain Carey's attention, to earn his respect . . . and in turn, to regain her family's respect.

Now, watching Ramble, she felt the enormity of it nibbling away at the edges of her nonchalant self-confidence. The travel, her presence in this world that at once seemed familiar and alien . . . the irrevocable nature of this adventure she'd agreed to involve herself with . . . all represented in this horse so freshly turned to man that Carey led him away in hobbles, a neck rope, and a switch at the ready.

Chapter 13

Arlen eased off the livery horse with a groan, reminding himself—firmly—he'd been lucky to acquire the animal at all. Transportation of any kind was increasingly more difficult to arrange, and only the application of a wince-worthy amount of gold had allowed him to acquire this rough-gaited mount. *His*, now, though he had no illusions that the animal could carry him all the way to Anfeald.

Or that he'd survive the trip if it did.

A deeper part of him knew he'd do anything to get home. Anything.

It wasn't a part he could afford to show anyone else. So he eased off the horse and he groaned and he kept his inconvenienced businessman's face in place.

The gelding chomped placidly on its bit, preparing to spit it out entirely, perfectly reliant on his new owner—as Arlen was on him, as unexpected as it had been. He'd been surprised enough at the high price the livery owner named for the rental of this coarse, feather-legged creature.

"Not a rental," the man had said as they returned to the small boxy storefront that served as an office. It, too, smelled like a stall in need of cleaning. "Look around, why don't you. The only reason I've still got him is that the last couple of people through here got picky, and he's all that's left. The only reason you're *getting* him is that word spreads fast, and yon coacher"—he nodded in the direction of the road coach station—"is a friend of mine."

And Arlen, who'd trudged over to the livery ring from the overcrowded hotel with half a mind on the unprecedented devastation he'd seen the day before and the other half on picking the best path through the crusty, well-used snow that ought to have been cleared but wasn't, looked out the big front window of the livery ring office with several different kinds of surprise. He'd known people were getting restless with the service disruptions, but . . .

"Word?" he asked, looking at what he could see of the town—the main road, which in a small town like this should have been speckled with people going about their business with casual purpose. Instead they walked in clumps, their conversation full of emphatic gestures, their postures full of frustration. The road inns were full, with restaurants running out of shipped food items and their trapped occupants going from cranky to truly worried. Arlen, sitting at a breakfast table full of stranded travelers, had made do with monosyllabic responses and a good many shrugs at the speculation he heard.

Where's the Council? Why haven't they done anything about this situation? Why can't anyone tell us what's going on?

He wished he didn't know some of the answers . . . just as he simultaneously wished he knew them all.

"Mohi asked me," the man said, recapturing Arlen's attention and making his exaggerated patience as plain as the awkward features of his face, "if you came here, to make sure you got a horse."

"Did he?" Arlen murmured. "That was a kindness."

"Said you were a big help on the road yesterday." The man shrugged narrow shoulders. "So I held this one back a while. Not that I'll have any trouble getting rid of him if you don't want him. But it's going to be a while before the road coach crew scouts clear the road for the alternate route. You don't like the looks of the horse, you're free to wait."

"Not a luxury I have," Arlen said. "But I'd be glad to return him at the next livery ring instead of buying him outright."

The man laughed, a barking sound. "Think you can do better, do you? Didn't I just tell you to take a look around? The coachers're lucky they've held onto their harness horses—that horse won't make it back to me no matter what . . . so I'm selling him, not leasing him, and when all this is over people'll be dumping horses cheap. I'll stock up again easy enough."

So Arlen had his horse, complete with sale document, rough gaits, placid temperament, and distinctly gassy nature. And as he looped the reins over the animal's head and considered the narrow streets of the outlying area he approached—the first precinct city he'd come to and a river community that still had the reputation for the most finely ground flours in Camolen—he realized the blunt little man at the livery ring had told him the right of it. Even here, in Tyrla's precinct city— or what had *been* Tyrla's precinct—any number of people gave his horse furtive, covetous glances.

Arlen hesitated, ignoring his body's saddle aches and taking better stock of his surroundings . . . wishing Carey were here with him. Carey was the one used to taking note of every nuance of a journey; the one who had not only traversed Camolen in Arlen's stead, but another world as well. Arlen . . .

Arlen was more accustomed to traversing inner worlds, to tracking ideas and not strange city-ways. Now the close-set buildings loomed over him; long and narrow, they backed up to the river, each claiming a precious spot at the water's edge and the ability to launch a waterwheel. The buildings on the opposite side of the street took more width—warehouses, mostly— but jammed together just as tightly to take advantage of the prime river territory. Some of them still bore the muddy waterline of the most recent flood several years earlier, soaked into every crevice of the brick where even diligent scrubbing couldn't reach.

At the end of this street, if he'd been told right, was a road inn with a room or two left; barring that, he'd have to venture further into the city to find an independent city inn—and that, he didn't want to do. The people of a precinct city were accustomed to magic, to its uses . . . and to its users. Arlen's was not an unknown face, even without its mustache and accustomed length of hair. He'd been here often—Council business, with Council travel booths and preferential Council accommodations.

No, best to stay on the working edges of the city, even if his horse drew the envious eye of every stranded traveler here. Travelers who wouldn't recognize him—but who consequently wouldn't accord him the respect of a man with power at his disposal.

Including travelers desperate enough to pace alongside him as he headed for the road inn, too tired to care about the churned muck he walked through. Or perhaps they were just common thieves, knowing they could make good gold with the sale of his horse. Not far ahead, he spotted the livery ring building, where he went not to turn in the horse, but to seek a night's stabling—near the hotel as was the pattern of most cities. Not far from either would be a road coach station . . . probably closed.

One man to his left, one to his right, easing closer to him; they were husky, confident, hidden in clothes entirely without style . . . meant only to keep them warm through the winter and no more. Between their hats, scarves, and hair, Arlen could see little of their faces, nothing of their expressions.

But he saw people getting out of their way.

"The horse," he said casually—if plenty loud enough to be heard—"is spelled. Unless you want to be as gelded as he is, you won't try to take him from me."

One of the men snorted, making no effort to pretend he didn't know just what Arlen was talking about. Definitely after the horse, and bold in these disturbed and uneasy streets. "Never heard that one before."

"Bootin' nice try, though," his partner said from the other side, but closer than he'd been just an instant before. "Quick thinking. Think quicker, and you'll hurt less by giving him up to us."

Their skepticism came as no surprise. Arlen, precinct wizard, Council member, the most powerful remaining wizard in Camolen, had never heard of any such spell.

But if pressed, he thought he could come up with it.

He stopped, held out the hand through which he'd looped the reins—an offering. He said, "It makes no difference to me. You'll bleed badly, so be prepared."

They glanced at one another in wary surprise. Arlen could see their faces now—rough men, but not necessarily tough ones. Taking advantage of a crisis . . . as if people weren't having enough trouble without this kind of activity. And while *he* could take care of himself if he had to . . .

Grim temper, habitually slow to rise, made its way toward the surface. He'd gotten their attention; he'd gotten everyone's attention. He gestured with the outstretched hand and its rein, impatient. And though the men hesitated, one of them quickly made a sneeringly dismissive gesture, and they both took a step toward him, closing him in.

The inertia spell was a marvelous thing.

Just a subtle twitch of it, nothing like he'd used on the coach. Enough to use their own movement to send certain body parts opposite the direction of the rest of them.

Enough to hurt.

It got their attention.

They froze, horrified—afraid to move even to look down at themselves. The fear didn't stop their eyes from rolling in that direction, though in the next instant they looked to Arlen most beseechingly.

"Back up," he suggested gently, as if talking to idiots. At the moment, they probably were. "Back up, and go away."

Slowly, they did so. Carefully. One step, a pause, then another—until after three steps they simultaneously broke and ran.

Arlen watched them go with a wry and twisted smile, but quickly squelched it. A man less well-armed with magic than he would show more relief than that, and he'd already been memorable enough for a man trying to avoid notice. He walked briskly for the livery, knowing the story would probably reach it before he did. Already he spotted a well-bundled child sprinting along the building shadows, and a tense-looking pedestrian eased casually over to the other side of the street to avoid walking near the horse.

No doubt using the tiny spell had been a mistake. No doubt someone on this street knew the lanky traveler with no business in this section of the city had created the magic on the spot, and not simply been standing next to a triggered spell. No doubt he should have simply surrendered the horse.

Except he had to get to Anfeald. He had to reach Jaime; he had to reach the safety of his own hold, of his workroom and his trusted dispatch crew and his only chance to protect himself and the people he loved while he figured out what had happened to the Council . . . and what was happening to Camolen itself.

Moments later, with the horse tucked away and the livery ring owner's honesty secured by a combination of bribe and threat—unspoken threat, for the woman pedestrian had witnessed the thieves' flight and the wide-eyed boy at her side, cheeks still flushed with cold, matched the size of the child who'd run down the street ahead of Arlen—he stopped in front of the road inn. At first distracted by the scrawled placard in the inn's window that declared COMMON ROOM LODG-INGS ONLY, he noted only in passing that the street news carrier—one of throngs of young dispatch apprentices who relayed the most recent breaking news to those on the street—had climbed her short pedestal at the corner of the road inn. Since the interruption of services days earlier, the street news pedestals had gone abandoned, turning into bird perches and something for children to climb.

This girl, her coat flapping open and her expression too bright, a flush of fear and excitement instead of cold, didn't wait for a customer to approach her with precinct script, and didn't relay her news in discreet murmurs to select ears. Her voice, flung to the street, cracked in her effort to project . . . or maybe just with emotion. "Breaking news!" she cried, the traditional attention-getter, making Arlen realize that today, after days of painful wizardly static, he'd failed even to try the general dispatch service. Like everyone else, he turned to look at her, drawn by her urgency, drawn by her appearance after so long a silence.

"Breaking news!" she said again, and then hesitated; for a moment Arlen thought she would burst into tears rather than find the words to relay the news. Finally she blurted, "The Council of Wizards is dead! They're all dead!" Her voice steadied slightly, lowering as her audience moved in closer. "They've been dead for days. No one knows how."

Arlen thought she went on to mention the Secondary Council, to say that the disruption in services would be handled as quickly as possible, to mouth obviously crafted phrases of reassurance from the Secondary Council itself, to repeat that no one had survived the mysterious attack other than a palomino stallion, no one knew what had happened—other than the palomino stallion.

He couldn't truly have said for sure just *what* she relayed. For as much as he'd known from within that the Council had met with disaster, he'd been unprepared to hear it confirmed; he closed his eyes and turned away, twisting inside with the enormity of the loss. Personal loss. Tyrla. Darius. Zygia. How many years had they worked together? And Camolen's loss . . . the intensity of effort it would take to recover from this, the very real potential that the Secondary Council *couldn't*. That Camolen itself would collapse into a country of panic and violence. And while the other members of the gathering crowd shouted astonished disbelief, Arlen realized anew that Camolen and its Councils—both Wizard and Lander, with their respective supportive enforcement services of peace-keepers and precinct guards—had to do more than survive their loss.

They had to survive that which had caused it.

Melting, bubbling, distorted landscape. Distorted reality.

Oh, yes. He had to get to Anfeald.

Jaime stared out the huge window of Arlen's asymmetrical office, soaking in all the things about the room that spoke of him. As much as he liked to keep potpourri simmering, he regularly let it cook down enough to burn; she could smell the faint bitter odor of the black herbs glazing the bottom of the pot on his workbench without turning her head from the snow-covered fields visible through the window.

The wall held his favorite old needlework piece—not his best, but one he'd done years earlier as a distraction from his first major spell construction. The spell that had alerted the rest of the wizard community to his true potential for spell creation and theory exploration, and had set him on the path to the Council.

She'd asked him the nature of the spell, and he'd only laughed and tickled her neck with his mustache. Something boring and intricate in the checkspell category, she thought he'd said. She remembered the touch of his hands better than the words of his reply.

Cesna and Natt had been working in here so as to leave the dispatch wizards more room, and had moved Arlen's belongings to the side—his scribbled notes, his stones waiting for the spells he would impress upon them, the tall, carved stool that suited his lanky build. His current-projects cabinet—covered with tooled and dyed leather, filled with carefully organized papers—had been moved to make way for the apprentices' plainer, light-wood cabinet with small turquoise tiles marching around the drawers.

Arlen's workroom, so full of the feel of him and yet changing around her. Moving on, somehow.

Jaime turned away from the workbench and the view beyond, clenching her jaw in sudden anger. It was too *soon* to move on, dammit, even driven by crisis. This had been Arlen's private sanctuary, a place he had literally carved out of nothing—

That's it. Get mad. Stay mad.

Then maybe it wouldn't hurt so much.

Cesna's timid voice came from the doorway. "Jaime?"

"What?" Jaime snapped, deep from her exploration of mad. She looked up just in time to see Cesna flinch, and gave herself a mental kick, giving up the mad for now. It was already evident to her that Cesna had sustained an emotional injury the day the Council had been killed—contributing to it was her last intent. So she sighed and said to the girl, "Never mind, Cesna, I'm not upset with you . . . it's just . . . a bad moment. What can I do for you?"

Still warily timid, Cesna flipped her thin blond ponytail over her shoulder . . . and her expression shifted to puzzlement. "There're two people here to see you," she said. "They say they're here on behalf of Chesba"— the Lander of Sallatier—"and they want to talk to you."

"But . . . ?" Jaime said, voicing the doubt when Cesna did not.

Cesna frowned, shaking her head. "I don't know," she said, relaxing a little. "It's reasonable that Chesba might ask for advice; his precinct wizard is dead with the Council, and Forrett, his own hold wizard . . . well, Natt is more skilled. And everybody's couriers are running ragged, so he might have decided to send some advisors."

"But." This time Jaime said it with more certainty.

With a shrug, Cesna said, "They just don't seem like Chesba's type."

Jaime rolled this little nugget over in her thoughts a moment; it didn't seem like much, although Chesba was easy to characterize—a charismatic older gentleman who didn't hesitate to do what he considered right. Then again, Cesna was the sensitive among them. And Jaime herself, once she stepped out of Arlen's quarters or the stables, was far out of her league.

By the factor of an entire world, more or less.

"I'll meet them in the null room," she said, after an indecisive moment during which her brain fought the request to climb out of its foggy grief and think. "Have whatever refreshments you think are appropriate sent up as soon as possible. And I should change, don't you think?"

Cesna eyed Jaime's breeches and hay-flecked barn sweater and gave an unusually decisive shake of her head. "I don't know why they're here," she said, "but I think it's good to remind them that you're pitching in with the rest of us. That you care enough about what happens to Anfeald to do it."

Jaime blinked, taken by surprise . . . wondering briefly why anyone would expect else of her—she had, after all, already been involved in several adventures nearly the equivalent of dark ops on her own world, and gone far out of her way to testify at several hearings against Camolen criminals. And then, just as briefly, she wondered why it would be so important, here and now and with so much at stake around them.

Cesna gave her what—just as surprisingly—could have been called a pitying look. Then she ducked her head to stare steadfastly at the floor and said, "The precincts are assigned to Council wizards, Jaime. When new Council members are named, they have the option of using the existing hold."

It hadn't occurred to her. Arlen hadn't done so, after all; he'd chosen to build this place from scratch.

Now she found her mouth suddenly dry, her mind reeling from another blow. Now she understood Cesna all too well. She needed to show she had a place in this world, because she might well end up depending on the kindness of strangers.

Not a thought that had been anywhere near her mind when she'd made the decision to stay here.

"Son of a bitch," she said quietly, vehemently, and deeply felt. And then she brushed her hands over her hair in a habitual gesture to rid it of what hay she could, and stretched out the slump that had crept into her normally straight back. "I'm going down to the null room," she said. "Send them on up, and as I said, the refreshment. And I think it would be good to remind them—whoever they are, whatever they want—that along with pitching in, I'm also a guest here. A special guest of Arlen's, whom this hold is according the status to make decisions. Make sure I get one of the magically colored fancy glasses, will you? And have it already filled with ice water. And . . . you know how to listen in, don't you? Would you do that?"

Cesna allowed herself a small smile. "Gladly."

Jaime found herself with lips pressed together, face tense, shoulders bunching; she forced herself to relax. God, what had she gotten herself into? Not an intensely religious person, she still found herself sending out an honest prayer, here on this world where they didn't even know the word "God," but depended on afterworld guides she likened to angels.

On second thought, she sent an equally heartfelt prayer—*just let me get through all this*—to those guides. All the help she could get . . .

And then she headed for the null room.

She settled herself at the long table in this room

without windows, noting the brightness of its new lighting with absent thought. Mural-like stenciling decorated the wall and ceiling juncture, a new design since the last time she'd been here, and a more colorful one. But the chairs—padded table chairs—were the same, as was the flower-filled planter lining one end of the room. Pencil and paper lay on the table by the head chair . . . the one she took. Without warning, a pitcher, glasses, and Jaime's requested ice water appeared on the tray in the middle of the table; one of the spellcook's fancy magics.

As Jaime took her glass—etched in delicate iridescent colors only magic could provide—a man and a woman reached the doorway, hesitating there.

"Come in, landers," Jaime said, using the term she'd learned was the polite gender-neutral equivalent of *gentlemen* in Ohio—even when the people being addressed weren't landowners at all. They glanced at the room, hesitating; she said, "It's a null room. I couldn't imagine you'd have any objections."

"No, of course not," said the woman, stepping inside and making room for the man to follow. Both wore the longsuits that passed for business wear in Camolen, though in this case wrinkled by travel. Personal coach, Jaime thought; they hadn't ridden, not in those fine-sheened trousers and long-tailed coats buttoned from the breastbone on up to a high, collarless neck. No ties here—but they did wear decorative triangles of silk hanging on fine chains at their throats.

"Feel free to sit," Jaime said, gesturing at the five remaining chairs, "and please excuse my appearance. I wasn't expecting visitors, and as you know . . . things are a little chaotic right now."

"Please," said the man. "We're the ones who should be apologizing. Unfortunately, it's hard to send ahead an intent to visit these days."

"Unfortunately," Jaime said wryly as they flipped their coat tails out behind them and sat in what might have been an orchestrated movement. Used to working together. Both man and woman were of medium build and medium height and neutral coloring; her light brown hair showed highlights not found in his, but was cut in a similar style; he had faint freckles nearly lost in the tan of his skin tone and she did not.

Utterly unremarkable.

And at the same time . . . it made her uneasy that they should want to be that way. She suddenly understood entirely why Cesna had looked so puzzled and wary. She gave the tray and its contents a slight nudge toward them and said, "Given the effort you've made to get here, I won't waste any of your time. How can I help you?"

In words so light and smooth Jaime almost missed their import, the woman replied, "You can tell us where Arlen is."

At first she just blinked at them—and then her anger rose, overwhelming her sense of propriety. She scowled. "Have you come all this way just to be cruel? Because you can just turn around and go right back to Chesba with the news that I kicked you out on your—"

The man raised a hand, glancing at his companion. "Time is not so short that we can't do a better job of approaching the matter than *that*." He reached for the pitcher and poured himself a glass of what, by the color, was a bitter spice-bark tea to which Jaime had never grown accustomed but which seemed to be available at most business functions. "We have, of course, heard the recent dispatch news regarding the Council. The truth of the matter is that Chesba isn't sure it *is* the truth of the matter. It's one of the things we're here to find out."

"If it weren't true, what makes you think *I* would

know?" Jaime said, not as graciously as she might in light of the man's attempt to appease her. She lightly rubbed the side of her nose—her slightly crooked nose, a reminder of just how ruthless wizardly politics in this country could get. Until her first arrival in Camolen, it had been straight. Straight and high-bridged and as Gallic as her name, a reflection of her naivete.

The last two years had wrung that naivete right out of her. She knew what people could do to each other, the things they could justify to themselves if they even bothered to justify them at all. So she was less gracious than she might have been, and quite probably more suspicious than she should have been.

That they took it in stride bothered her as much as anything. "Who more than you *would*?" said the man, somewhat apologetically.

"When it comes to Council business, Arlen is just as discreet as he's supposed to be," Jaime said. "I'm not even *of* Camolen, as you must know. When it comes down to it, Cesna, Natt, and Carey know more about his work than I do." As soon as she said it, she knew she'd made a mistake; the woman's head lifted, her eyebrows raising ever so slightly over unremarkable hazel eyes.

"That's a point," she said. "Perhaps we could speak to Carey. Chesba mentioned him, also."

Jaime gave a firm shake of her head. "No," she said. "He's busier than I am, trying to hold things together, and so far you've done nothing but waste my time— I'm not about to let you waste his. I'm not sure what information you're digging for, but if the Council's not dead, they surely have a good reason for making us think they are." Offhand, she couldn't think of one, though a little voice in her head sang at the thought that someone else believed Arlen might yet live. "I'm not about to second-guess them, and if Chesba wants to pursue his suspicions, he'll have to do it somewhere other than Anfeald."

The woman regarded her coldly; the man less so. *Good cop, bad cop.* Except they weren't cops at all. *Then what, exactly?* This world might be alien to her, but she'd been here long enough to know that the Landers used their individual precinct guard for enforcement and investigations, just as the council looked to the country-wide organization of peacekeepers. Spies, then? The Camolen CIA and KGB?

If so, then she doubted she could take anything they'd said at face value.

Unless, of course, they were simply and truly assistants to Chesba, poking and prodding where they didn't quite belong. She supposed if she were a lander during this crisis, she'd want to get her information from somewhere other than the general news dispatch the new Council had used to announce Camolen's loss.

While the woman had continued her cold regard, the man relaxed in his seat somewhat, ran a hand over hair that didn't need rearranging, and said with casual precision, "We know someone's been working magic here. Magic beyond Arlen's apprentices."

Caught flatly astonished for the second time in this conversation, Jaime nonetheless found herself recovering more quickly. *Dayna's world-travel spell.* She hadn't realized that her friend's quirky brilliance had brought her so far, that the spell had been beyond Natt and Cesna. She kept her reaction on the inside, showing Chesba's people nothing more than a mild shrug. "Which has what to do with what? If it had been Arlen, you would have recognized his touch."

The man shrugged. "Signatures have been distorted before. We learned that last summer, as I know you're aware."

This time his outrageousness made her laugh out

loud. "You think Arlen would take mage lure to enhance his ability? The most powerful wizard in Camolen?"

"It might depend," the woman said, unaffected by Jaime's amusement, "on what he thought he was up against."

Jaime leaned her chin on her fist and looked at them both a moment. "You know," she said, "I've got things to do. I'm not sure what you're trying to accomplish, but I'm not interested in participating. I'll have someone escort you out." No doubt it was the ultimate rudeness to fail to offer them a night's lodging—winter roads with disrupted road crews, the day more than half gone, the travel booths non-functional . . .

Too bad.

Thanks to Cesna's eavesdropping, there was a burly man waiting outside the door by the time the two nondescript visitors gathered themselves and left the room. Jaime recognized him as one of the groundskeepers, but he acquitted himself well in his role as an unobtrusive bouncer. Cesna herself joined Jaime in the room a few moments later, offering her little more than a puzzled look.

"And to think," Jaime told her, "we were worried that they were here to scope the place out for a new wizard."

"Scope?" Cesna said, and then shook her head, apparently putting the word into context. "That may still come," she said. "I don't know *what* this was about. But I think you should know . . . while you were talking to them, one of the grooms came up to let me know they'd been seen coming out of the job room, and I could have sworn I heard someone upstairs. Nothing obvious was missing, but—"

"But our courier assignments are pretty much there for the world to see," Jaime said. "Well, so they know who we've got out on the road. They don't know what we're carrying—and even if they did, I can't think of anything *eyes only* out there today, anyway."

"They were asking about Carey," Cesna said. "There's enough information in that room for them to figure out he's not here . . . and we don't expect him to *be* here any time soon."

Jaime breathed a frustrated curse. "And can they really tell," she asked, not at all sure she wanted the answer, "just what kind of heavy-duty magic they felt?"

Cesna gave her head a quick shake, toying with the ends of her ponytail. "No," she said. But then she hesitated, mouth barely open.

"What?" Jaime said flatly.

"No one can pinpoint an exact spell," Cesna said reluctantly, "but they can identify things like the complexity and power involved in a spell. And there are only so many spells with the same combination of those elements as the world-travel spell."

Jaime felt suddenly tired; she closed her eyes, rubbing the lids gently with her fingers. She didn't know what her visitors had truly wanted, or what they'd walked away with . . . or even what they'd do with whatever they'd learned. But they hadn't been straight with her, and that was never a good sign. And—

Her head snapped up; she looked into Cesna's startled watery blue eyes. "They were in the stable," Jaime said. "They know the palomino's gone."

And like everyone else in Camolen, they knew that the palomino Ramble was the only living witness to what had happened.

"They could figure it out," she whispered. "Where Carey is . . . why he took the palomino . . ."

"Does it matter?" Cesna said, slowly sitting in a chair without taking her gaze from Jaime's.

She hoped not. But—

"Only," she said, "if they don't want anyone else to know what Ramble knows."

Chapter 14

Jess crouched along the outside wall of the squat, brown-painted nature center, not quite willing to sink down to the wet ground. Around her the park offered the very picture of happy nature—the rain stopped, the songbirds out in force, and just enough sunshine to make diamond sparks off the bright green leaves.

It'd been a long time since she'd been this miserable.

Even now, the park naturalist stood alongside the green Metroparks pickup truck in the small parking area before the nature center, talking to the ranger behind the wheel; both of them glanced her way with alarming frequency.

She knew they meant to be kind, that they were worried about her . . . a woeful woman waiting for her friend to show up, every word out her mouth making her seem odder than the one before, every passing moment increasing her worry . . . surely her friends would know to come look for her here. Surely they'd made it to the main parking lot safely once she'd distracted the ranger and they had had the wet nature trail to themselves. Surely they'd somehow gotten Ramble under control . . .

She shivered, trying to remember if she'd felt this sick after the first time the newly crafted world-travel spell had brought her here. Probably . . . she just hadn't known it. Hadn't known what this human form was *supposed* to feel like. That it shouldn't tremble like this, and that her vision shouldn't grey out when she stood up. That even weak human limbs shouldn't be rubbery beneath her.

With a tug to pull her sweatshirt sleeve down over her hand, she caught it in her fingers and rubbed the back of her covered wrist over her brow, trying to ease the ache there. When she looked up, the naturalist was heading toward her with purpose, and with the ranger on her heels.

"We've been talking," the woman said; her name tag, now that she'd removed her poncho, was readily visible. *Mary Carter.* Jess stared at it, strangely mesmerized, her thoughts foggy and drifting. Mary Carter crouched down to Jess's level; the ranger stood behind her, thumbs hooked into his belt, one moment too uncomfortable at the impending conversation to look directly at Jess, the next raking his gaze over the rain-darkened color of her hair, her larger-than-normal irises. The woman's skin around her eyes wrinkled more deeply, and she said, "We're not comfortable with the fact that you can't give us a contact number, and that you don't look well. We'd like to take you to a hospital."

Jess shook her head. "This is where my friends know to find me."

"It would be easier," the ranger said, "if you could tell us where to find *them*."

She could only shake her head again, trying not to let them see her shiver. Not shivers from being damp on this warm, humid spring day. Shivers from within, from a body too harshly wrenched from one state to another. If they thought she was truly sick, they'd never leave her alone. She said, "We are new to this spot. I don't know what road inn to use."

They exchanged a glance, and she wondered what she'd said that wasn't quite right this time, even knowing the way she formed her words alone might bring those expressions. "But this Mark fellow lives here," the ranger said. "That's what you told us. Don't you even have a last name? We'll look him up in the book."

She remembered the hugely thick book of thin pages and tiny print, and shook her head yet again. Caution, this time. If they found his name in the book once, they could find it again. They could find *him*. They might try to check up on her . . . they might tell someone else. They—the local peacekeepers and guards— might stumble across Ramble. And she knew from her early days here, from what had happened to the chestnut gelding turned red-headed man, what they'd do if they discovered Ramble.

They'd take him away. They'd put him in a small, closed-in space with no way to communicate with him, or to understand what he really needed. She shivered again, this time purely from memory. *The chestnut, dead in the street . . .*

"Jessie," said Mary Carter, "you aren't leaving us much of a choice. Your friends will know to check the hospitals when they don't find you here."

"No," Jess said, unable to hide a hint of panic this time. Her heartbeat pounded loudly in her ears, fast and uneven and somehow stealing the breath from her lungs.

The ranger reached down and took her upper arm,

not an unkind grip but enough to draw her to her feet. "It's best this way . . . Mary and the park volunteers will be here for the rest of the afternoon—if your friends come looking, they'll learn you're at Marion General."

They'd ask her questions she couldn't answer, they'd find all that was strange about her, they'd take her to that iron-barred place where they'd kept the chestnut—

"No!" she cried, trying to yank herself free, not caring that several people near their cars—locking doors, shucking raincoats, loading up with binoculars and water bottles—looked over to stare at her.

The woman said, "Bill, maybe we should let the police handle this—"

True panic gripped her even as she struggled to think through it, knowing if only her heart would stop racing and her legs didn't feel so weak she wouldn't be so scared and unable to stop herself from pulling against him—*just like the horse she was*, an astonishing revelation that made her laugh out loud with the absurdity of it all—something she shouldn't have done, she saw that right away. Saw the doubt flee from Mary Carter's face, and felt the ranger's fingers clamp more firmly on her arm. The laugh turned to a sob.

"Jess!"

A sweeter voice she'd never heard, instantly recognizable in spite of the time since she'd last heard it. Deep and easygoing and always sounding like there was a smile behind it. "Mark!"

She found him by following the gazes of the naturalist and ranger, too rattled to place him on her own. There, striding across the parking lot, more breadth to his shoulders than the last time she'd seen him but still with a carefree quality in his movement, even facing two uniformed park officials with a squirming handful of nearly hysterical—

"Jess!" he said again, not so loudly this time, just

making the point. He opened his arms slightly and the ranger looked at the naturalist; she gave the slightest of nods and Jess was free, sprinting gracelessly to throw herself at him with such force that he staggered, laughing.

But it was a quick laugh, and he ran a hand across her back and said, "Easy, there, Jess, everything's fine," in a way that told her everything *was*, that the others were safe—though he didn't neglect those two uniformed park officials, both of them coming across the brief strip of grass to join him. "I'm sorry," he said. "She's . . ." and he hesitated, finally adding, "a special child, if you know what I mean."

"She seems like more than that," Mary Carter said. "She seems ill. Not to mention *barefoot*."

"Lost the shoes again, eh?" Mark buffed the damp sweatshirt across Jess's back; she rested the side of her face against his windbreaker and—*just like the horse she was*—let herself rely upon his strength and confidence. "She's just scared," he told the naturalist. "She gets that way. I thought she was with a friend, or I never would have taken so long to get here."

"Mmm," said Mary Carter, not sounding entirely convinced.

But not arguing. Not talking about taking her to official places where people would ask questions and Jess wouldn't be able to answer them. Not stopping Mark as he guided her around in a clear intent to leave.

And as she let Mark lead her away, calling back thanks to the unconvinced naturalist and ranger, as she trusted in his feet to take them the right direction and his knowledge to reunite her with Carey and Dayna, some small part of her started thinking again.

Thinking about Ramble. That *he* had no one to trust, and no one to follow. He was here in this strange world at the behest of people he didn't even know . . . and he was truly alone.

Carey took an impatient glance inside the stall where Ramble slept off the effects of travel and changespell . . . not to mention a heavy dose of Valium. Unlike Jess, who had a sweetness in repose even when at her most horsey in nature, Ramble's strong-boned recalcitrance somehow came through despite his slack-jawed position in the fresh and deeply bedded stall. He lay as a horse on his side, twitching occasionally as though his fear and uneasiness had worked its way through the drug.

Thank the guides Mark had been able to bring the tranquilizer—and even that his mix-up in the timing between here and Camolen had made Dayna's some-what panicked phone call from the park a necessity so he could grab the old dental visit prescription on his way out. By then Ramble had become irritated and balky, and Carey had twice twisted his ear to bring him back into a state of better manners, feeling a supreme *wrongness* about the need to do so to another man. He very much doubted they'd have gotten Ramble into Mark's battered vehicle without the drug, which had hit Ramble's stressed system fast and hard.

Now they just needed for him to wake up, so they could start working with him . . . so Carey could get a sense of just how long it would take before Ramble could convey something of what had happened to him. Jess was using single words within days, he'd been told, and very simple sentences soon after. But along with whatever boost the changespell had given her, Jess had had the benefit of a human-intensive upbringing . . . and Carey had had the habit of talking to her on the trail.

He doubted very much this changed palomino had any such advantage. For a moment, looking at the long, ragged flaxen-and-orange-streaked hair of the man inside the stall, looking at his rugged frame and exotic skin tones—more of a golden tan than Jess's smooth toasted brown skin—he very much doubted they could overcome the disadvantages the palomino's basic training gave them.

For a moment, he believed Jess had been right from the start . . . their journey here was nothing but folly.

But it was a short moment, brought on by stress and worry . . . Jess, gone off somewhere with the park naturalist, sick from the change and no doubt frantic with worry. Mark hadn't even gotten out of the car as Carey and Suliya dragged Ramble out; he'd peeled back out of the driveway with the tires spitting gravel, on his way back to the park to try to find her.

Dayna came down the barn aisle—a wide, airy aisle built to Jaime's specifications, with the indoor ring attached on one end and huge double doors facing the old farmhouse on the other, ten stalls on each side with several of them a huge, double stall such as the one Ramble now occupied. Clean white paint made it bright, and hunter-green trim turned it cheery. The hayloft and storage stalls filled the place with the scent of hay, and even without cleaning spells, Mark and his crew of manure movers kept the place fresh. Jaime's pride and joy, whether she was in Camolen with Arlen or pursuing her career here in Ohio. Carey had once blown out all the windows and panicked the horses into shell shock with a bungled spell . . . a decision that kept Jaime from ever fully trusting his judgment again.

In retrospect, he couldn't blame her.

In retrospect, he'd do it again.

And maybe he just had.

Dayna glanced around, double-checking the hay bales stacked across the aisle to block Ramble's end stall from view; Mark had already pinned a cheery sign on the other side to waylay boarders' questions: HAY OVERSHIPMENT! Sliding double doors at the end of the aisle provided the only access to Ramble, and they'd already installed a chain and lock. She nodded satisfaction, then looked at the sleeping palomino. "Good thing Jaime has this thing about dentists—we'd never have gotten him here without that Valium." She sounded as wrung out as Carey felt. "God, I feel like I've run a marathon. Suliya is in the house sleeping it off. I don't see how Jaime does this so often."

"I don't think she does," Carey said. "The only time anyone used the first version of the spell was for the first travel here and back, and that first time out . . ." He trailed off, lost in the memories of the wild courier ride, the fall from the dry riverbed trail that had made him trigger the spell in the first place, wounded and already leaving Lady's saddle. No wonder he recalled little of his arrival here.

Dayna followed his thoughts. "Well, you were hardly in any shape to remember the details."

He gave her a look of exaggerated surprise at her understanding. "Better watch it. You're getting easy."

She rolled her eyes, entirely Dayna-like. "I'll have you know that phrase means something entirely different here, so I'll thank you not to use it when anyone else is around."

But Carey barely listened to her—focusing instead on the sound of tires crunching gravel. *Mark*. And— he fervently hoped—*Jess*. He headed for the open barn doors, wincing at the unusual complaint of his body at the sudden movement after standing too long, and the sudden realization that neither Ohio nor world travel had been kind to his permanently damaged body.

But after a few steps his movement smoothed out. And the important thing—yes, as he came around the corner of the barn to the curving horseshoe driveway, he spotted Mark's car—and two people inside. He broke into a jog, and when Jess spilled out the door of the passenger side, he was ready to catch her.

"Ramble," she said, at first making as if to barge past him and then looking from the barn to the house, uncertain which to head for. She gave him an anxious look, her hair in her face like a wild child and eyes to match. "Where is he? Did he calm? Did you all make it here all right? Is he well? I want to see him—"

He'd never seen her like this. Never.

"Jess," he said, barely garnering her attention before losing her again, her gaze going from house to barn to Carey himself, her hands gripping his arms with increasing urgency. He put his hands up, pushing her hair back and capturing her face in the same gesture—and holding her. "*Jess.*"

She fastened her gaze on him, looking from one eye to the other. Searching. For what, he didn't know. Firmly, he said, "Ramble is sleeping. He's fine. We're all fine. Suliya is sleeping. Dayna is in the barn watching Ramble. We're all safe, Jess—including you."

She whispered, "I thought they were going to take me away."

He hadn't known. He hadn't realized what he would put her through, bringing her back under these conditions.

No. He had. He just hadn't wanted to admit it.

He pulled her in close, wrapping his arms around her, rubbing her back. *Ninth Level fool.*

And still he wasn't so sure he wouldn't do it again. Jaime was right, he thought, to withhold from him that last bit of trust. "Easy, Jess," he said, automatically falling back to her words. "Easy, braveheart. We've got you now, and you're not going anywhere."

He wasn't sure which of them he was trying to comfort.

❧❧

By the time Ramble began to emerge from his drugged sleep, Jess was yawning herself awake from a short nap and Suliya had introduced herself to the wonders of the microwave while Mark flirted outrageously with her.

Dayna took the first chance to poke him in the arm, while Suliya retreated to the room she and Dayna shared to rummage through her bag for a lighter-weight shirt. "She's young enough to be your—"

"Kid sister?" Mark suggested. "I'm not exactly an old man, Dayna. You haven't been gone *that* long."

"Long enough," Dayna said, hearing the usual tones of asperity Mark brought out in her, even if—as Jaime had said—he'd grown into himself since she'd seen him nearly two years earlier. Sturdier, a little brawnier, holding down his responsibilities here at the Dancing Equine as well as part-timing at the LK hotel where they'd once worked together. "And she's *young* enough. If not in years, in mind."

"You used to say the same about me," he told her, as blithely untroubled by her comments as ever.

"If you don't watch it, she'll get a terrible crush on you and it'll just be a giant syrupy mess when we leave."

"Naw," Mark said. "Suliya's in this for Suliya. I can't give her anything worth a giant syrupy mess, and meanwhile, a good flirt is a helluva lot of fun. You're just ticked because I'm not flirting with *you*."

And then he grinned at her, irrepressibly Mark, until Dayna buried her face in her hands and groaned.

When she looked up, Jess stood in the arched opening between the kitchen and the living room, giving her a curious look—but all in all looking more like the woman she'd grown into, and not like Jess fresh from being a horse all her life. Dayna removed her hands and gave Jess a wan smile, making eyes at Mark—enough of an explanation for Jess, who no doubt took this kind of byplay between Mark and Dayna for granted. She switched her gaze to Mark and said, "Do you have soda? With bubbles?"

"For you," he said, "*extra* bubbles."

The slightest of wrinkles appeared between her eyes as she looked at him, the vaguely puzzled curiosity of someone not quite awake. Mark explained, "That's the new, improved, flirtier me."

"I liked you fine before," Jess said, but she thought about it a moment longer—watching Mark grab a glass from an upper cupboard, fill it with ice from the automatic ice dispenser in the refrigerator door, and pop the top on a cold Mountain Dew—and added, "This is nice, too."

He gave Dayna a triumphant grin, whereupon she threw up her hands, just as glad for the interruption when Carey came in from the barn, spotting Jess with relief.

"Jess," he said, stopping an arm's length away with an odd awkwardness as Jess took her first sip of soda and made her inevitable scrunchily pleased face at the carbonation. "Are you feeling better?"

She nodded. "Not right, but . . . not like my thoughts are flying apart anymore."

He gave what Dayna thought was a quiet sigh of relief. She wasn't sure; she couldn't tell what was going on in his head anymore. She'd always thought of him as the kind of guy who would do what was necessary, when it was necessary, and not look back . . . but it seemed to her that he was already looking back—and they hadn't even finished going forward yet.

Now he jabbed a thumb over his shoulder back in the direction of the barn. "He's just starting to move around. I thought you might like to be there when he wakes—what's that?" His gaze shifted from Jess's face to over her shoulder and beyond, where Mark emerged from a pantry with soda cans to restock the fridge. Dayna twisted around to see what had caught his attention, and found a wipe-off board on the back of the open door.

Mark didn't hesitate as he opened the refrigerator and shoved the new six-pack in place. "Jaime's message board."

"From Camolen?" Carey asked, moving a step behind Dayna as she headed for the board.

"Yep, that's the one." Mark straightened. "Looks just like a regular one, doesn't it? I've got a few spellstones left if you need to send anything her way."

"We brought more with us," Dayna said, giving the poorly cleaned board a critical eye. —*ame lo-king for Arle*— it said, as if written by a marker going dry or a message cleared with a single careless swipe of the hand.

"Came looking for Arlen?" Carey said from behind her. "When did she send that?"

"What?" Mark joined them, frowning at the board. "Wow, that looks bad. They usually come through a lot clearer than that."

"It's *new*, you mean?" Dayna looked from the board to Mark, and caught his absent nod.

"Strange one, too. Doesn't make a lot of sense. Why would she use a spellstone to tell us someone came looking for Arlen?"

Jess hiccuped over her carbonation, a desperately muffled sound, and followed it with a very practical, "Because she thought it was important."

Someone came looking for Arlen. Dayna frowned, caught Carey doing the same. He said, "I think we have to assume that it *is* important. Some aspect of it. There may be a lot more to the message than we see."

Quite matter-of-factly from her spot on the border of the conversation, Jess said, "It's not working right. That's why the travel was so hard, and my change. The magic's not well."

Dayna felt a little frisson of the *rightness* of it, and gave a sharp shake of her head anyway. "That's ridiculous."

"Dayna," Mark said, a reproving tone with an immediate effect on her. Startling enough in its own right, never mind that he'd done it at all, but when she saw the hurt on Jess's face she knew why.

It took a deep breath, a chance to get perspective, and then she was able to say, "I didn't mean *you* were ridiculous, Jess, it's just that magic is . . . *magic*."

"Not to mention," Carey added softly, "that we're in real trouble if she's right. *Camolen* is in real trouble."

"We *knew* that," Dayna said. "It's why we're here in the first place. But I don't think we should jump to conclusions based on two incomplete pieces of information."

"Three," Mark said, giving the board a long look before wiping it clean with the edge of his hand. "We could ask her to repeat."

"I think we'd better," Carey agreed.

"Better what?" Suliya said from, to judge by the sound of it, halfway down the hall and coming toward them. "It doesn't sound good by your voice."

"Just a garbled message from Jaime," Dayna said, not ready to alarm Suliya along with the rest of them.

"I'm going to Ramble," Jess said. "He shouldn't be alone."

Carey half-turned, looking back at the board with obvious reluctance.

"Go," Mark said. "Both of you. I'll be out when I'm done."

"He's awake?" Suliya said, appearing in the doorway

as she fastened her impossibly lively hair back with a fashionable latching comb from Camolen.

"Getting there," Carey said shortly. "Come on, then."

Jess left her half-finished soda on the counter and headed for the barn with long strides Dayna couldn't hope to match; she gave up and trailed behind, squinting in the bright sunlight as they passed briefly into the sunshine between house and barn. Carey paced her, apparently in no hurry . . . or, even with his longer legs, not willing to keep up with Jess? Dayna gave him a scrutinizing glance; she thought his misinterpretation of it was deliberate.

"She's worried," he said, nodding to where Jess had found and now peered between the bars of Ramble's assigned home. After a hesitation, he added, "I'm not sure she's not right to be. He's not doing well with the change so far."

"Don't wuss out on me now," Dayna muttered. Suliya, uncharacteristically wise, remained silent.

"Too late for that, isn't it?" Carey said dryly, easing to a stop just within sight of the stall—Dayna thought he could probably see the changed palomino over the height of the barred half-door, but she certainly couldn't. She started to move closer, but he put out a hand, shaking his head. "Give them some room. And no, I'm not *wussing*, to use your silly-sounding word. But I'd be foolish if I didn't have concerns after the way we had to drug him. This could take a lot longer than any of us counted on—and if we're right that something big is happening on Camolen, then that time could make a big difference."

"We'll do better with him than we did with Jess," Dayna muttered. "We *know* he's a horse . . . she didn't have that advantage, not until she'd practically become one of us. And we didn't have *Jess*."

Carey lifted his chin, a quiet gesture to draw her

attention to Jess herself, who had opened the door and slipped into the stall. With a great floundering stumble, Ramble came to his feet, finally visible to Dayna. Even so, she drew closer, and this time Carey came with her.

Jess waited inside the door. She didn't look directly at the palomino; she didn't even face him. She kept her body turned slightly while Ramble lifted his head, nostrils flaring, body stiff and tense.

He would clean up nicely, Dayna thought, realizing it for the first time. He'd been so difficult, so full of struggle . . . and then so crumpled by the drug—that she hadn't seen it. He wasn't her type, not with that hard look about him—head to toe, rugged and not quite crossing the line to coarse. But the hair alone would do it. Strikingly, stunningly blond.

Hair that was at the moment in his face. He shook his head in annoyance, and made a snorting noise, relaxing.

"That's what she was waiting for," Carey said, while Suliya nodded understanding. "An invitation."

If he said so.

He must have been right, for Jess moved slowly forward, keeping herself at an angle, hesitating once and receiving some invisible-to-Dayna signal that encouraged her to continue even as Ramble seemed to draw himself up into something bigger than he'd been, something more eloquent of line even with his rangy physique, his attention riveted on Jess.

It was a focus she returned, Dayna realized, noting Carey's sudden tension beside her. *Not worried for Jess.* Not with that look on his face, the glower in his eyes and that muscle twitching in his jaw. *Jealous. Guides, he's* jealous.

Jess eased right up to the palomino, and just when Dayna expected her to stop—*she* certainly wouldn't have gotten any closer to a man she didn't know—Jess

moved up until their faces were only a breath apart—
and stayed there.

"What?" Dayna whispered.

Tersely, Carey said, "All horses greet new herd
members this way. You've seen it. They take in each
other's breath. It just looks . . . different when human
faces try it."

"I'll say," Dayna muttered, taking a sideways glance
from him that silenced further words.

Ramble gave an unexpected bob of his head, startling Jess into lifting hers—an expression Dayna *did*
know . . . Jess uncertain, Jess tilting back ears that
wouldn't tilt in this form. And somehow he grew even
taller, and—Dayna glanced away in embarrassment—
obviously aroused. He did something then—she wasn't
sure what, whether it was another bob of his head or
if he actually nudged her with his shoulder, but it made
Jess stagger back slightly, either in surprise or from the
nudge itself. In an instant she whirled, ears definitely
back with that tilt of her head, and let go a kick that
missed completely.

Was *meant* to miss, Dayna realized, although Ramble
started back wildly just the same as if he'd been hit,
recovering to a much more subdued posture. Jess didn't
hesitate; she walked away, right out of the stall and
down the aisle to stand at the barn doorway, looking
out.

Dayna would have followed her, but Carey clamped
a hand on her arm. "No," he said, releasing her only
when she acquiesced. He slid home the latch Jess had
left undone and said, "Give her a moment."

And after a moment, Jess gave herself a little shake
and returned to them, a more casual walk than the
brusque strides that had taken her away. She looked
at Carey, and then she looked into the stall where
Ramble tugged at his clothing, doing a slow and

unself-conscious examination of his own body, his expression of such exaggerated puzzlement that Dayna felt her first stirrings of compassion, if not doubt.

Jess gave her head a little toss, a restless gesture left over from Lady. "He is as I said. He hasn't been brought up well. He's been stall-kept, not pasture-kept with mares, or even pasture-grown. He doesn't know his manners even when he's not trying to be rude. It's not his fault. But . . ." She trailed off, shrugged.

"But he'll be hard to deal with," Carey finished for her. "Suggestions?"

She didn't take her eyes from Ramble. "He needs to understand what has happened to him. He needs to know how to communicate. We need to understand his Words and Rules, so we can give him the support he is used to." She hesitated. "If he is like me . . . then he has been hearing language all his life. Some of it is there in his thoughts, waiting . . . now that he is human, it will begin to make sense."

"It didn't take you very long to get your meaning across," Dayna said, remembering the morning after Jess had arrived in her house and her first faltering attempts to tell her new friends that she was in fact a horse. That they hadn't understood or believed had been their failing, not hers.

Jess turned a dark look on her. "I was brought up to turn to humans for help. And I thought I could get what I needed from you."

Carey. Right from the start, she'd only wanted to be reunited with Carey; with all their misunderstandings, that had always been clear from the start. Dayna, too, turned her attention to Ramble; he was halfway out of his loose tunic and not the least bit interested in his audience. "I guess we'll have to find something he wants. Some incentive to learn."

"We *have* something he wants," Jess said bitterly. "To

be a horse again. It will be his first thought once he understands why he no longer has whiskers, or ears to point and a tail to flick. When he tries to run and can barely stir the breeze. And when he understands, he will hate you for what you've done."

Carey flinched. But as Dayna scowled at him, he gathered himself and said, "We'll just have to hope his desire to be a horse again is stronger than his hatred. Because cooperating with us is his only chance for that to happen."

Even Suliya looked unhappy, as if suddenly realizing in what she'd become involved. "It's not so bad, being human," she said in a low voice, not quite looking at Jess. "You spend most of your time that way now."

"Not so bad," Jess said. "Because I have a *choice*."

Carey rubbed the heel of his hand against the side of his thigh, his expression masked by fatigue. "Just see what you can do to help him along." The words sounded dragged out of him; Dayna realized anew that he hadn't rested after the rough transition between worlds. She'd haul him into the guest room to rest if she had to; they needed to be in top form to get through this. All of them. Ready for anything.

Jess answered by reentering the stall; the palomino instantly stopped his struggle with the tunic, letting it settle back into place. Having been chastised once, he didn't quite puff himself up as before, but watched her from the back of the stall with a certain wariness, clearly working up to redisplaying his magnificence for her.

She changed the angle of her head, turned, and lifted her leg just enough so only her toes touched the bedding. Instantly sulky, he subsided.

"Burnin' poot," Suliya said, wonder-struck tones

entirely at odds with her youthful slang. "It's just like watching two horses, clear as anything."

"That," Dayna said, looking at Carey, "is exactly the point."

Chapter 15

"*Ramble*," Jess said, getting a clear reaction to his name, then pointing at him and repeating it. He watched her—alert, as instantly aware of her true identity as she'd been with the changed animals the summer before and interested simply because she was a mare and he a stallion. She gestured to herself. "Dun Lady's Jess. Jess."

And so his learning started. Learning she rewarded with a less stern attitude on her part than on their initial encounter, less of a rebuff to his flirting, and on occasion an actual responsiveness—the willingness to admire him, to give him a throaty nicker of interest.

She wasn't in season. If he'd known her well, he wouldn't have attended her so. But he was alone, and she was a new mare, and—separated from his world, all he knew was to impress himself upon her.

She fell into it naturally. Thinking as he thought,

seeing his world through both his newly human eyes and her barely aged memories. Feeling his frustrations when he couldn't comfortably move about on four legs—he stubbornly tried it for a while—and understanding his sullen retreat into himself each time he discovered anew that he was indeed human.

But as she had, he learned quickly. He understood her words long before he played with forming his own. And no matter how she struggled to deal with her mixed feelings, her growing uncertainty about how her human friends and lover had handled their decisions, her anger at his situation, Ramble somehow knew how much she cared.

No one other than Jess went into his stall. He wouldn't allow it.

Jaime sat behind Carey's desk off the job room and let her face sink into her hands. Not despair, exactly . . .

Anticipation.

Rather than getting better, her attacks of mind-boggling misery had become distinctly worse. She never knew just when in the evening they'd hit; she'd taken to carrying a stoppered vial of medicated wine with her, and had learned to throw it back in a single swift gulp at the first sign of trouble. Simney understood the problem no better than ever, and Cesna made a project of digging up any and all reference books in Arlen's collection with the slimmest chance of providing clues; as far as Jaime knew, she was poring through one of them now.

Meanwhile, Jaime tried to reconcile the large number of pending messages with the much smaller number of Anfeald's couriers and the fact that she'd pulled a horse from the roster this evening. Too many ribs showing through his winter coat, and he'd stumbled with his rider today. No matter how many messages waited, she wasn't putting him on the roads tomorrow. At the same time, the messages funneling through Anfeald represented the best efforts of the precincts to keep their services running, the checkspells in place, the people safe . . . all things not to be taken lightly.

Still, it wasn't like any of the deliveries contained the answer to the mystery of what had happened to the Council, or why someone would come looking for Arlen, misrepresenting themselves as Chesba's people.

A quick run had confirmed that much. Imposters, come and gone without leaving any clues to their true nature and intent.

"Jaime."

She looked up toward the job room door and found Linton, the ranking courier and, as she thought of him, her co-conspirator in running the stables. He hadn't asked for the job; he hadn't ever wanted to do anything but ride. But he knew the horses and he knew the riders, and he was happy enough to offer his wisdom if she would be their mouthpiece.

Now he looked at her with concern, his face scratched and bruised at the leading edge of a thinning hairline, his thick wool shirt ripped, and something unidentifiable dangling from his hand. "Are you all right?"

She gave a slight snort. "Me? I'm fine. Just tired, like everyone else. And waiting. If I have to drug myself insensible, Gertli"—her erstwhile bouncer from several days earlier—"is ready to drag me back upstairs."

"With any luck it'll check for a bit," he said, and laid his unidentifiable something on the scarred wooden desktop. Long, muddy brown, writhing . . .

"It looks like giant freeze-dried earthworms in a mating dance," she observed. "And what happened to you? Looks like you got into a fight with a tree."

"Exactly that," he said, plucking ruefully at the tear in his sleeve. "I ran into something out on the trail."

"I would have thought the horses too tired to shy at *anything* by now."

He entered the room, slumping down in the single, plain wooden chair placed haphazardly at the corner of Carey's desk. A half-mended bridle hung over the back of it, and Linton sat unheeding on the thin saddle pad someone had dropped carelessly on the seat. "If she hadn't," he said, nodding at the earthworms, "I'd probably look something like that."

She stared again at the object, unable to make any sense of it, and shook her head. "I don't understand."

"Those are the ends of my reins, and see if I don't ride with shorter ones from now on."

She gave him an impatient frown. "Just *tell* me. What are you talking about?" But in the back of her mind, she thought she might know. She recalled Dayna and Jess's description of the meltdown area where the Council had died and she was very much afraid that she might know.

He shifted uneasily. "We weren't going very fast . . . just a sloppy little jog. Thank the guides—because this thing popped up on the edge of the trail between one blink and another." He shook his head. "It just . . . it almost looked like a giant fist squeezed the trees together, and what I saw was what oozed out between the fingers. Cammi booted right out of there—did a turnabout. The reins must've whipped out into that . . . spot."

"And your shirt?"

"Jagged edges of something that weren't there an instant earlier. Not a single instant." Linton shuddered. "Never much thought of myself as a coward, Jaime, but I'll tell you I never want to see the like again."

She didn't doubt it. Jess and Dayna had had the same reaction to the area where the Council died. But . . .

It was dark outside. Carey's personal job room was deep in the hold with no access to sunlight, but Jaime knew well enough what time it was; she had reason to keep track these days. It was dark now, and it had been dark for a while. "How'd you even see it?"

"I had a light with me—we all carry 'em now. Too easy to take a bad step in the dark when you're tired, no matter how well you know the trail." He rubbed a hand down his face, pulling his features long for a moment. "Guides saved me on that one. Had to have been more than luck, because I'm telling you—I hadn't triggered the light for more'n an instant before I came upon this mess."

"Damn good luck if that's all it was."

Linton, distracted, twisted to look over his shoulder. "Gertli's in the job room. You expecting him?"

Jaime shook her head. "I'm in here," she called; the evening misery was later than usual today; perhaps he'd gotten worried. "I'm still okay."

"That's not it," Gertli said, wearing a slightly puzzled expression—habitual of late—as he peered through the doorway at her. By dint of his size alone, he'd recently come to act as an unofficial peacekeeper for Jaime . . . a role for which his gentle personality left him ill-suited. But the precinct peacekeepers were currently as overworked and understaffed as the couriers, and Jaime'd had little choice but to recruit him.

Gertli frowned, an expression that made his harsh features—big-boned, with brows that met in the middle at the slightest excuse and a once-damaged nose slanting off to the side—downright fearsome. "Just had someone pop up in the travel chamber. She says . . ." and he glanced outside the job room and lowered his voice dramatically, "she says she's with the Council. The *new* one."

Jaime and Linton exchanged quick and equally

startled glances; then she looked down at herself, quickly assessing her appearance—not much better than when she'd welcomed the two "assistants" who hadn't been from Chesba at all. "Here?" she asked Linton. "Or in one of the meeting rooms? I suppose the null room would be an insult . . ."

Gertli cleared his throat. "She's waiting *here*." A roll of his eyes indicated the job room behind him.

"Guides," Linton sighed. He pulled his chin again and said, "Well, if she's that eager to talk to us"—with no warning, he meant, and the notable lack of courtesy to fail to stay in the comfortable chamber area until the unprepared hosts could be found and apprised of her arrival—"then by all means. Here is fine." He stood, removed the bridle and saddle pad from the chair, and looked around the room, at a loss.

"Here," Jaime said, taking the gear and dumping it behind the desk, along with the remains of the reins. Linton came around to stand by her side, and by then the woman had supplanted Gertli at the doorway.

She was no one Jaime had met before . . . or if Jaime *had* seen her, the woman simply hadn't made an impression. Too bland in nature and presentation, with a costly wizard-cloth longsuit in the most subdued of autumn colors that did nothing to bring out her small features or complement her olive complexion. She'd swept her hair back in a stern up-do too immobile to be anything but magically fixed in place.

Jaime did her best to keep dismay from her face, but Linton showed it for both of them. She couldn't blame him. Between the precipitous arrival of the wizard and her unyielding appearance, Jaime couldn't imagine this would turn into anything close to a social call.

"Welcome to Anfeald," she said, leaving out any excuses for the crude reception. Saying anything else would carry implicit criticism for the woman's failure to warn them. The dispatch was, after all, working well enough for *that*. She gestured at the seat and said to Gertli, who still hovered uncertainly in the job room beyond, "Let Natt and Cesna know we have a visitor, will you? And ask the kitchen to send some refreshments."

"That won't be necessary," the woman said, twitching the long tails of her suit aside as she sat. "I doubt I'll be here that long. Arlen may not have mentioned me to you; my name is Hon Chandrai." With title, no less, on a remarkably informal world that rarely used them. "While I was on the Secondary Council I did some work with him on the world-travel checkspells. Please . . . let me extend my condolences. These are far from the circumstances under which I wish I'd become a member of the Council. Arlen was an extraordinary wizard."

"He was," Jaime said, "an extraordinary *man*." The new Council, at least, didn't seem to think Arlen still lived, unlike her previous two visitors.

Jaime herself . . . knew she'd never quite believe, not until she saw the evidence with her own eyes. Or heard it from someone who had been there.

Like the palomino. Gone, now . . .

And this woman knew it. Jaime gave her a sudden sharp look, saw Chandrai watching her with hawk-like focus, her remarkably dark eyes cold but otherwise expressionless.

Of course they knew. Jaime should have been expecting this visit from the moment she'd ushered the falsely identified man and woman out of the null room, and even more so once Cesna mentioned how easily the invoked world-travel spell could be categorized as what it was by those with the skills to perceive it in the first place.

Like someone who'd actually worked with Arlen on the checkspell.

Linton stood at the side of the battered desk, watching the swift, unspoken byplay between them and looking utterly lost. Jaime felt for him . . . but he'd either catch up along the way or wait for an explanation.

Without preamble, Chandrai spoke—*Hon* Chandrai, and every gesture and expression seemed designed to remind them of the fact. Did she think she'd intimidate Jaime, who spent her time—her *personal* time—with Chandrai's superior in their field of magic? Who had testified against a rogue wizard and stood her ground against that wizard's sadistic apprentice? Who had twice helped Camolen avoid crises only slightly less threatening than the one they faced now? Chandrai said: "Unusual circumstances notwithstanding, I'm afraid you've got a lot to answer for."

"You said *what*?" Linton blurted, a borderline polite version of *I beg your pardon*.

Jaime knew what the woman was talking about . . . but she wasn't about to suggest it. So she raised her eyebrows in surprise and didn't commit herself to words. Chandrai might not intimidate her . . . but the truth was that Jaime had no idea just how much power the woman *did* have over her. Could Jaime be detained for her participation in the forbidden spell? Would the Council even bother, with everything else on their plates?

She thought not. But she wasn't sure.

Chandrai responded directly to Linton, pinning him with that cold gaze. Jaime winced. Poor Linton. He didn't have a clue. All he knew was that Carey was gone, trailing a hunch about the Council deaths. "Forbidden spells," Chandrai said, her words hard and precise, "are forbidden spells even if the checkspells have failed. We overlooked the illicit spellcasting here the first time—knowing what chaos Anfeald Hold must have been experiencing, and that someone here could have easily appropriated an old spellstone . . . frankly, we had other things on our minds. But while our situation is still every bit as dire as it was, we cannot overlook a second event."

What? Maybe Jaime *didn't* know what the woman was talking about. She gave a mute shake of her head. Certainly Dayna had cast that first spell, her signature not surprisingly obscure to the former Secondary Council. But the spell itself was beyond Cesna and Natt. "Maybe we should wait for Arlen's apprentices," Jaime suggested, when Chandrai offered no other information. "I think you're about to waste perfectly good intimidation over something we know nothing about."

"Frankly, it's annoying enough that I've expended the time and energy to travel here in the first place," Chandrai said. "I assure you, I would not be here without good reason—and my certain knowledge that both spells were triggered from the grounds of Anfeald leaves me less than willing to listen to naive denials."

"Oh, please," Jaime said, forgetting her wariness for a moment of utter irritation. "You won't even tell me exactly what you're talking about, probably *exactly* in case I don't already know—you don't want to spread the word about just *which* forbidden spell is now available to anyone who wants to try it. And we don't have walls around Anfeald, either the precinct or the hold grounds. I'm not denying that you detected whatever you detected, but I'm damned well saying I know nothing about it." And she didn't, she told herself silently. Not that second spell, anyway. Chandrai seemed to consider it one and the same as the first . . . which meant someone additional had cast the original world-travel spell.

For an instant she wondered who, and how they could have acquired it in the first place—and why they *would*, with so much going on around them. The answer came quite naturally.

The two who had visited her. They'd been in Carey's office; Cesna had been sure she'd heard something in Arlen's workroom. They, too, had felt the spell. They'd known Carey was gone.

They'd gone after him.

Time to do a more thorough check of Arlen's workroom—and to beef up the security spells.

Locking the barn door after the horse was gone.

Quite literally, in this case, with the palomino in Ohio. Jaime bit her lip to keep an inappropriate smile at bay.

Chandrai noticed anyway, damn her, frowning in an affronted manner. "There's hardly anything amusing about this situation. In case you haven't noticed, Camolen is in trouble, and it hardly behooves *any* of us for me to waste my time like this."

"Then don't," Jaime said simply. "Tell me enough so I can try to help, or leave me alone to help as best I can on my own." She lifted the twisting object that had once been trailing rein ends. "Do you think we don't know there's more going on than you've told *any* of us?"

In a flash, Chandrai lost her hard-edged composure. "Where did you get that? The site of the Council's death is off limits!"

Linton said dryly, "Those of us who travel by conventional means often run into strange things on the trail. Those *used* to be the ends of my reins."

"Have you told anyone else about it?"

"I'm more interested in what you can tell *us* about it," Jaime said. "Plenty of us have felt from the start that there's more to this than someone's decision to do away with the Council in a single, stand-alone incident. What Linton saw today pretty much confirms that."

"Plenty of us?" Chandrai said, the hint of unease on her face speaking volumes in one who had been so controlled. "Explain, please."

Jaime didn't need to say *Carey and Dayna and Arlen's apprentices*. No need to bring them into it at all. She jerked open a desk drawer, pulled out a thick pile of recent messages, and thumped them down on the desk. "Don't you think we talk to each other?" she said dryly. "Those of us who were left behind?"

Horains' daughter. Zygia's brother. Head couriers, lovers, family members, landers and those now trying to keep the bereft precinct wizard holds functioning.

"You must tell no one of your experience," Chandrai said. She nodded at the awkward twist of stiffened, distorted reins. "I'll take that."

"You must be kidding," Jaime said. "I've got couriers running these roads every day. Either what happened to the Council members was an attack and it's spreading, or they *did* something and *that's* spreading, or the whole thing is just some inexplicable event that the wizards went to check out and got killed, and *that's* spreading. As long as you're not talking, all the rest of us can do is guess. But I'm sure not sending my people out there without warning them to watch for this kind of phenomenon. I can't believe you'd even consider asking me!"

Chandrai winced slightly, and gave a single nod of her impeccably groomed head. "I suppose it's of no use in any event," she said. "If you've discovered corruption, then others are bound to do the same. Because," and she met Jaime's gaze evenly, "you're right. It's spreading. We don't know how it started, or how it was controlled to kill the Council, but the first known corrupted area is what they were investigating when they were killed. But most importantly . . . we don't know how to stop it." She offered Jaime and Linton the merest hint of a wry expression. "We've been trying to avoid widespread panic."

Linton said suddenly, "That's why the dispatch is barely working. It went down because of the Council's death, but you've kept it that way. To keep the word from reaching anyone who hasn't actually seen this . . . *corruption*."

"Essentially," Chandrai said, releasing a faint sigh. "Although that's simplifying matters considerably. Even were we not interfering, the dispatch would hardly be up to normal operations." But her companionable moment was over, and she pressed her lips—magically tinted to the most natural of been-kissed reds—firmly together before adding, "Perhaps now you understand why I'm here—"

"No," Jaime said, cutting off the admonishment she'd seen coming. "I only know that we'd still be utterly in the dark if someone hadn't triggered illicit magic in this area, and you hadn't come to scold me about it. And I think it's about time the other families knew at least this much—and the peacekeepers and precinct guards, while you're at it. *We* are not the problem here . . . but we're the ones who have to deal with it."

"You are entirely too certain of your place in this world," Chandrai said, annoyance stiffening her posture.

"Maybe," Jaime said, though it took effort to hide the fear she felt at those words. *Fear of being sent back, of never finding closure for Arlen's death. Never truly convincing herself he was gone, that he wasn't waiting somewhere for some*one *to find and help him. Her.*

"Or maybe," Jaime added, "it operates enough like mine that I know exactly my place in this world." She gave Chandrai her most matter-of-fact look, the one that meant *this is the way it is, and there's nothing you can do to change it*. "Doing my damndest to keep the people I care about as safe as they can be." She leaned back in Carey's chair, watching Chandrai try to decide how to deal with her unrepentant rebellion, well aware of Linton's impressed but alarmed regard. "Let me know," she said, "if you ever figure out what those spells were all about."

Chandrai gave her a tight smile. "Let me know," she said, "when you decide to tell us what *you* know."

Chapter 16

Jaime wasted no time after Chandrai left. With the day turned into evening, she knew she didn't have much time to waste . . . not if the evening ague came on her—and it hadn't missed a day yet.

She all but bolted from the office, calling back over her shoulder, "I've got to check Arlen's workroom . . . see if Natt and Cesna can tell if anything's missing—"

She didn't expect Linton to come with her; his concerns centered around the stable, and he'd only just come in from a long day of riding. But he did, and right on her heels as she headed away from the stables and into the hold proper, aiming for the stairs. "I can't believe you spoke to her like that," he said, and she couldn't decide if he was admiring or appalled. "Do you *know* how miserable she can make your life?"

"Other than kicking me out of the hold?" Jaime said, somewhat grimly. "I suppose she can probably blacklist me, but only unofficially. Just because she's a Council wizard doesn't mean she gets to do as she pleases."

"Guides, aren't you the calm one." He shook his head, took her arm, stopping them both at the base of the dark stairs. "If she convinces the others that you're involved in the use of a forbidden spell, you'll spend time in confinement." Jaime looked pointedly at his arm, but he didn't release her. If anything, his grip tightened slightly, even as his eyes narrowed. "Just exactly *where* did Carey go?"

Jaime hesitated, wondering about the laws here, and how much Linton could know before he, too, took on risk. "He's looking for answers."

After a moment, he released her, his otherwise benign features taking on a cast of distrust that the darkened stairwell only accentuated. "Answers," he repeated, and the suspicion was in his voice, too.

"Linton," Jaime said, "have you ever known Carey to back away from something that needed to be done? Even when everyone else says he's wrong?"

"I haven't known him as long as you," Linton said, but it was an admission of sorts.

"And you barely know me at all. But I've learned something about myself in these past few years . . . I'm not so different from him. We have different priorities, but somehow . . ." She thought about his comment that she could be confined for involvement with a forbidden spell. Deep down she'd known it; after her involvement in Calandre and Willand's hearings, she couldn't help but know it, even if she weren't familiar with the exact laws. She'd just avoided thinking about it so she wouldn't feel the fear she felt now. Confined. No horses, no chance to throw herself into the kind of riding that made her soul sing. Or possibly banished from this world. No Jess, no Dayna . . .

She already had *no Arlen.*

That was the thing to focus on. Doing something about that, even if it only meant finding out what had happened so she could dig her way out of the wondering. Find some sort of closure. And, if Dayna was as right as Jaime thought she was, keep it from happening to someone else.

She looked straight at Linton and said, "If I could tell Chandrai anything about that second spell, I would. Because I think *someone* needs to figure it out, and damn fast."

"You had no right," he said. "Either of you. You had no right to get me involved in something that could come crashing down on me. I've got a family here in the hold, a little girl—"

"Don't you *get* it?" Jaime said, cutting him off, her voice raised nearly to a shout. "You're *not* involved. And if you want to stay that way, you'll stop questioning me right *now*."

Linton stopped short, mouth still open, startled as he thought her words through.

She said, "Your best bet is to trust us. Trust Carey, because you know him. Trust me . . . because Arlen did, and Carey does."

She watched him think about it, going through hesitation, lingering at the impulse to dive in and be a part of it all—this time by choice. And then he gave the faintest of nods.

Jaime sighed with relief . . . and moved right on to other matters, figuratively sweeping the previous conversation under the rug. *It never happened.* How *Mission Impossible* could she get? "What I need is for you to talk to all the other couriers. Let them know what you saw, and if anyone else has seen anything like it, I want to know. All of us are on alert for it from now on. I want any sightings mapped and watched. If we have to, we cut our message load and spend more time scouting."

He winced. "No one'll like that." Not the landers, or the separated families, and especially not the peace-keepers and precinct guard.

"We'll play it by ear," she said, and at his puzzled expression, added, "Take it as we go. Make decisions as we get more information."

"Map it as we walk it," he said, understanding clearing his features.

"That's it." Jaime triggered the permalight in the lower stairwell and gave it a grateful glance. These days, she barely had enough concentration to maintain a glowspell the size of a firefly, not that she'd ever been any good at it.

"I'll post a meeting for tomorrow morning before the riders go out," he said. "I guess . . . it would be best if I just went back to the job room and made sure we've got all of tomorrow's outgoing accounted for."

"Everything but whatever you brought in with you." Jaime rubbed her forehead, suddenly aware that she'd had a distinct tingle of warning there for some moments, buried beneath the intensity of their conversation and the ramifications of Chandrai's visits. She fumbled for the flask by her side, barely hearing Linton's questioning comment, gulping it down just in time—

The evening ague rolled over her like a storm, crashing headlong into the magically enhanced dosage. She knew Linton caught her as she fell; she heard his bellow for Gertli.

And then she was gone until morning.

"Big bootin' whee," Suliya said, staring critically at Mark's computer monitor, her hand on the back of the chair Dayna occupied, scooted up just beside Mark's own desk chair. "Just the same as the dispatch, really."

Mark, heretofore congenial and hard to jostle from

his good mood, actually looked hurt. Dayna glanced over her shoulder with the kind of disapproval Suliya had learned to ignore a long time ago, and said, "Computers do a lot more than give people access to the Internet." She turned back to the big monitor with an interest that surprised Suliya. "I hadn't yet gotten one of these when I left. It almost seems like magic, now . . ."

"From what you've said," Mark told her, apparently willing to pretend Suliya hadn't snorted at his toy, "it's a *lot* like magic. The way a programmer builds a program doesn't sound all that different from the way a wizard builds a spell."

"Huh," Dayna said, looking entirely too thoughtful. If she got lost in playing with the computer, Suliya was going to get bored, fast . . . maybe she'd wander out and see what was on the entertainment device Mark called a TV. At first she'd thought she could learn a lot about this new world by watching it, but both Mark and Dayna had laughed when they found her at it. Game shows and soap operas, they'd said, had nothing to do with the real world. That's why people watched them in the first place.

Suliya said, "I think I'll go see how Jess is doing with Ramble."

In perfect unison—and without looking at her—Mark and Dayna said, "No!"

"Poot," Suliya said, sliding into a sulk. "You two sound like you have the same brain."

She wasn't sure why they both burst out laughing. As far as she was concerned, it only proved her point.

"Jess is having enough trouble with Ramble," Mark said, so reasonably. "Not to mention that he keeps taking off his clothes."

"You can't keep blankets on some horses," Suliya told him. "Bet he's one of them."

Dayna gave her a calculating look that put Suliya right on edge. "You want something to do?" Dayna asked. "Fine. Let's see about straightening your hair."

"What?" Aghast, Suliya clapped her hands to her head. "Not *my* hair!"

Mark grinned, and Dayna gave her a wicked smile. Teasing her, even as they meant it. "For as long as we're here, yes. You stand out far too much with that mop—can't afford anyone to take notice. Or we could cut it . . ."

Suliya gave a shriek of dismay. A small shriek, considering the circumstances, but Mark winced anyway. "Keep it down," he said. "I don't think Carey's feeling well."

"Not since we got here," Dayna said. "I don't think he knew how much help he was getting from the healers. The world travel messed him up, and there's no one here who can help. I sure can't pull off that kind of advanced healing magic."

"I gave him some ibuprofen." Mark gave an idle click of the mouse, and after a moment his machine muttered *you've got mail!* in a voice too cheery to be true.

Suliya didn't care about his mail. She glared at Dayna. "No one said anything about my hair when you talked to me about coming here, and no one's touching it now."

"No one knew we'd be here as long as it looks like we're going to be here," Dayna said. "And I was thinking you might like to get out and look around. Shop, maybe. You seem like you might enjoy shopping. Southland Mall isn't much, but it's more than you've seen so far. But you, in rural Ohio? You'll attract attention, all right."

Mark paged through several screens of text, faster than Suliya could follow; he made a snort of dismissal, got rid of the email somehow, and started the process

to shut down the computer, all as he nodded agreement with Dayna. "Gotta agree, you seem like a shopping kind of gal," he said. "And Dayna's right. We don't
want you looking memorable right now—and trust me,
even with straight hair, you'll be plenty memorable."
He glanced over his shoulder, tossing her a grin. "That's
a *good* thing, Suliya."

She eyed him warily. A compliment, then. But
still—!

"Besides," he added, "I thought you girls liked to
play beauty salon."

Dayna looked like she wanted to hit him, but didn't.
In a disgruntled way she said, "That's not very PC, you
jerk."

"Ha," he said, and grinned at her, leaning back in
his swivelling chair as the computer monitor went dark.
"I'm right, or you would have nailed me."

"It just so happens it's an easy spell to learn."

Suliya gave her a suspicious look. "And just how easy
is it to *un*-spell?"

"Easy enough, or I wouldn't have mentioned it,"
Dayna said, pushing back her own sandy, boringly
straight hair, cut in the currently popular multilayered
Camolen style at which those in Suliya's family would
have sneered. "Look, I'll just do a small little section,
okay? And I'll put it back, and you can see for yourself."

Still wary, Suliya agreed to that much . . .

Except Dayna couldn't. Her casual concentration
turned to quick consternation, and then to a flabber-
gasted string of curses. Suliya tried to hide her relief.

"A little spell like this should be a snap—we *know*
the spellstones work!" Dayna said, and tried a quick
series of additional spells, none of which had any effect
whatsoever. She went into an angry, scowling thoughtfulness, and Suliya sneaked away to the bathroom to

check her hair from all angles, making sure it was just as it had been.

She'd thought this would be an opportunity to prove herself invaluable to Carey ... but Carey barely noticed her, and her only contribution—boring, boring, boring, for days now—was to take watch outside Ramble's stall when Jess needed a nap or a meal. She'd *thought* she'd have been right in there with Jess, teaching the newly made man what he needed to know in order to tell Carey and Dayna what *they* needed to know.

Patting her hair back into place behind a headband borrowed from Jaime's bathroom drawer, she considered that given the expression on Ramble's face when he looked at her—when he looked at any of them, other than Jess—she might be better off outside the stall.

He didn't like being human. And he certainly understood who had made him that way—the other humans. That Suliya had been dragged along to Ohio just as much as he made no difference to him at all, if anyone had even mentioned it to him.

She peeked back into the office, a cramped little room with what could only be a man's touch—Mark, probably—in the browns and tans of the straightforward decor. The computer overwhelmed a desk that reminded her of the one in Carey's job room office, and the desk crowded up against unadorned bookshelves of some material that looked like wood but wasn't, chock full of books with the overflow shoved in every which way. The most remarkable object in the room was a strange little frame with five perfect silver balls hanging on clear string.

Which was to say, there was very little to remark upon in the room at all, and to Suliya's mind—considering she had crossed the barrier to another *world*—that made the room somewhat of a cheat. The kitchen was fun, and the house boasted any number of small oddities, but she'd seen nothing to—

Well, to take the curl out of her hair.

No one noticed her reappearance, or seemed to. Mark leaned back in his chair, nodded to something Dayna had said.

Dayna made a face, then seemed to find resolve. "That's that, then—I've got to hit the stores. If I can get the right kind of crystal, maybe I can invoke a spellstone, pause it, and suck up power through it to store in another stone."

"What's wrong with just using the spellstones you have?" Suliya said. "You brought plenty for all of us."

Dayna raised an eyebrow. "That's what you get for walking out of the conversation," she said, but almost immediately relented. "I'm a little concerned about how the trip over went. I think . . . Jess may be right; there's a problem with the magic. I'd like to have some extra power to feed into the stones for the way back."

Mark shook his head. "Sounds damned risky if you ask me. *Pausing* an invoked spellstone. Sheesh." But when Dayna turned on him, he held up placating hands. "Yeah, yeah, I'm not the wizard around here. Anyway, I know just the place. Kinda new, stuck off the end of Hocking Street. I'll take you."

"Me too," Suliya said quickly, and when they both looked at her skeptically—in a way her father's employees never would have dared to display even when she was a child—she added firmly, "I'm *coming*."

Dayna groaned. "I hate the fact that the phrase *burnin' poot* comes to mind," she said, and sighed. "At least *braid* the hair, will you?"

"We won't all fit in the truck if she doesn't," Mark said, and grinned, pleased with himself.

Suliya pretended he was a servant, tilted her chin in the air, and turned on her heel to return to the bathroom and such hair management tools as she'd been allowed to bring. But inside, she didn't truly mind. Inside, she had a little girl grin. *Time to explore.*

Arlen's travel slowed to an unbearable rate. *Too slow.* He took to packing supplies on the horse and buying them whenever he could get his hands on them. He was lucky to have found new foot gear, thoroughly waterproofed, and—tucked away in the back of a second-hand store—a ripped and crudely mended set of packs to sling over his saddle in lieu of himself.

On foot, his progress slowed considerably. Slowed further by the need to settle for a day now and then— getting the horse's hooves seen to, gathering what news he could. Nothing remarkable, past that first public revelation of the Council death.

If he wanted to, he could reach out and find the travel anchor in Anfeald, the one in his personal rooms. The rooms where he hoped Jaime still waited. *If only she'd been able to hear—*

But she hadn't; his nightly attempts to reach her had had no effect whatsoever, making him wonder if she were indeed gone. It didn't matter. He'd go after her if she'd left. It might well make him an outcast, but he knew how to kill the checkspell long enough to do it, sanctioned or not.

But he didn't hunt for the Anfeald anchor, and he didn't try mage travel. He didn't use any magic at all— aside from a few boughten spellstones to keep his feet warm as he trudged through the slowly diminishing snowpack and those undetectable, private attempts to reach Jaime. Between his gradual movement south and the rapidly changing season, he should find his feet on solid ground soon.

Or, he thought, clambering over a downed tree limb

just emerging from the snow with its dark smooth trunk shining slickly in the melt-off, he'd find his feet in *mud*.

He tugged the reins and the reluctant and rough-gaited horse made a big deal of stepping over the tree limb. "Grunt," Arlen said, more in encouragement than imprecation . . . for Grunt was what he'd finally named the creature.

He had no idea how many days—weeks—it would take him to reach Anfeald. He only knew he was determined to do it, and determined to stay out of trouble while he was at it—even if, as the only remaining member of an ambushed Council, he had a target of intent tattooed on his skin so deeply that he could all but feel the itch of it between his shoulder blades.

Even if despite the clues he'd gathered at the distorted, dangerous area his coach had nearly blundered through, he didn't yet know any more about the situation than the average man on the street.

Well. Perhaps not quite *that* little. And before he reached Anfeald, he intended to know more. "Come *on*, Grunt," he muttered in exasperation, reminded once more why he'd never taken to traveling on horseback when Grunt's wandering mind and random decision to stop in the middle of the road nearly yanked Arlen's shoulder out of place. "Quit fooling around and pretend to be heroic. Things will go a lot easier for both of us, I assure you."

Mostly, he thought, *easier for me.*

Then again, there wasn't going to be anything easy about this journey, about what waited for him at the end of it . . . about Camolen's recovery.

No matter what.

Jess leaned her forehead against the bars of Ramble's stall—his closed, locked stall—and breathed a sigh of relief.

She hadn't wanted the others here for this.

She hadn't told them she intended to ask him today. When they visited, hovering, trying to discern if he were ready for some real communication, she slid back into the easy work, the beginning work. The things Ramble understood but was bored with, so never did very eagerly no matter what.

And they trusted her. They expected her to let them know when he was ready to talk to them. Jess had moved through the morning in a strange haze of duplicity, knowing her own intent, knowing they expected to be told . . . and not telling. Not even Carey.

Never had she deliberately hidden anything from them before. From *any*one. She was by nature the most honest of horses, in her evasions and refusals as much as her willingness to try. She knew it had been one of Carey's favorite things about her as his top courier mount.

But he no longer rode Lady—not for courier jobs, not for pleasure. Some hidden piece of him had never accepted the horse part of her once he'd taken to the woman part of her.

It was that hidden piece of him that she no longer trusted. Certainly not to do right by Ramble, a horse already done immeasurable wrong. Carey *knew* it was wrong, he *knew* it—and he let it happen because Ramble was a horse. A tool. A member of a species to which Carey had devoted his life's work, becoming one of the best . . . but still an animal to be used, when all was said and done.

So she protected Ramble from him—from them *all*—and from the intensity of their questions. They'd push him. They'd upset him. They'd confuse him.

She wouldn't.

But somehow in the process she felt forced to betray her own honest nature.

She gave her forehead an unthinking scratch against the bars, horselike even in that, leaving her bangs in disarray. The rest of her thick, mane-textured hair felt tight against her head; Suliya, bored that morning, had sat Jess down for what she called girl-talk, weaving a complex braid while she was at it. "You hair's perfect for braiding," she said. "It'll hold anything!" She'd gone on to chatter endlessly about some of her early riding experiences, so that Jess decided the whole session was better described as *girl-listen*; she had the feeling Suliya was trying to communicate in some complex subtext, but that habit was one of the human things at which Jess had never become good.

So she went back to dealing with that at which she excelled. Ramble. Betraying him, betraying herself, betraying her friends and Carey, all in subtle little ways that distressed her even when she couldn't quite define them. She reached down to the second latch they'd installed at the base of the door—out of Ramble's reach, though he'd never tried to undo the upper latch, quite content to stay in surroundings that felt familiar and comfortable. He'd been waiting, interested, in the back of the stall as she'd taught him, eager for her arrival.

If he ever regained his horse form, he'd have much better manners than he'd started with.

Jess pulled a huge apple from the pocket of Mark's light jacket, buffed it against her stomach, and took a big bite before offering it to him; he accepted it, took a bite and, hesitating, offered it back to her.

He'd done the same thing the day before. It had been the moment she'd decided it was time to talk to him.

They ate the apple together, and she used the edge of the jacket sleeve to wipe the glint from his lip and chin. Some horses were like that with apples . . . more spit than there was apple. He let her tend him, nudging her only slightly with his shoulder. She'd been the same, once . . . expecting the humans to handle her. Expecting they had the right, no matter what form she was in.

"Ramble," she said, sitting cross-legged in the clean shavings of the stall, "I need to ask you some questions."

He sat beside her, reaching for the end of her braid and twisting it between his fingers. He'd been an exceptionally mouthy horse, and had turned into an exceptionally fidgety man—always touching something, feeling the textures . . . she'd taught him how to tie knots purely for the pleasure he got from it. "Ask," he said agreeably.

"You can ask, too, if you want," she said.

He fingered her hair, his mobile face twisting somewhat in conflict. He had the questions, she well knew . . . he just wasn't sure how to ask them. Like her, he understood speech much sooner than he was able to generate it.

"If you *want*," she repeated. "You don't have to."

He nodded, satisfied with that.

"Not long before we came here, when you were still horse," she said, watching to see that he understood, that he gave the tiny jerk of a nod he'd already acquired the habit of making as he took in information and processed it in his new human way, "you were out on a ride with Sherra."

"Sherra," he said. "Too . . ." and he made a serious face, a strict face. Trent, Jess was certain, had only laughed at half the things Ramble pulled . . . and Ramble had pulled half of them just to play the game.

"Yes, Sherra. She rode you, not far, and tied you while she talked to other people who came without horses. Do you remember?"

"No." He said it flatly; he didn't look at her. Lying.

Jess sighed and shifted slightly away from him, pretending to go off in her own thoughts. Pretending he wasn't there.

"Jess," he said, and started to nudge her; she turned a fast and furious look on him and he backed off, dropping her hair to thump against her back. "Jess . . ."

She didn't look. After a moment he gave a snort of pure exasperation, jerking his chin in a motion that would have been a curse of neck-wringing in his horse form.

If he'd said he was frightened, if he'd trembled, if he'd been honest in his reluctance . . .

But he wasn't. So she let him work through the dilemma of being ignored until he came around with honesty, as certain as anyone could be that he *would* . . . and that in itself spoke more of his recent journey than any of the others would ever understand.

Finally, he said in a low, half-sullen voice, "I don't *want* to remember."

She turned back to him, all her attention given up to him. He tossed his head, this time a precursor to showing off . . . except he knew better than to push it that far. "I'm sorry," she said. "I know it is a hard thing. But . . . an important thing. We need to know so we can try to make that place safe again."

He frowned; it turned his features harsh. "You . . . no." He looked away from her again, then back; it all but broke her heart to see how he struggled. For her. For her, when she was manipulating him as much as any of them.

"Tell me," she said softly. "All the things that happened in that place, before you broke away."

"Don't remember," he said, his chin hard and disapproving, his lower lip tight.

"You do." She pushed him this time. "You do

remember. We always remember." *We*, as in horses.
And *we*, as in the only two horses ever to discuss their
situation in human form.

He still didn't look at her. He didn't fidget or reach
out to her. But after a long moment, he said, "They
screamed. The trail ate them . . . they screamed. It came
to eat me. I ran."

A long speech. A hard one. "Attaboy," she murmured,
remembering Trent's use of the words as he'd come to
say good-bye to the horse when she, Dayna, and Suliya
left Second Siccawei. He flushed with pleasure and then
startled, felt the warmth of his own face, prodding the
flesh. But she wasn't done; she had to ask those things
Dayna and Carey would ask, or they would only be out
here to do it themselves. And while she might be
manipulating Ramble . . . she did it to make things easier
for him. They wouldn't know how much easier. Or Carey
would, if he stopped to think . . . but she didn't consider
him in a thinking mood of late.

They wouldn't be here in Ohio if he was.

"Did you see anyone else?" she asked Ramble.
"Besides the wizards. Anyone hidden?"

He shook his head; she didn't believe it.

"No one in the woods? Watching? Causing what
happened?"

"Magic happened," he said, a quick burst of matter-
of-fact words.

Dayna had said so, too.

"You felt the magic?" When he looked up, his surprise matching hers, she said, "Do you always feel
magic when it happens?"

"Always," he agreed. "Not . . . you?"

She hitched her shoulder up in a shrug. "Usually,
yes. Not everyone does, though." She eyed him. "Someone *made* the magic happen. You *did* see a person in
the woods."

He sighed hugely, letting it vibrate his lips a little. Giving up. "Yes," he said. "A person, a horse." Cautiously, watching her for permission, he touched her shoulder, her back. "This much. Stallion. With black mare. Pretty."

"Good," she said, and this time she thought she had it all. He wouldn't hold back much after that sigh. She had it all . . . and it was nothing. Someone had been in the woods; he or she had made magic happen, and the wizards had died screaming in a woods come alive with distorted reality.

Dayna had felt the magic. Everyone who had seen the spot knew how horribly the wizards had died. All they'd truly gained from their journey here, from Ramble's transformation, was the knowledge that a man had been there, bringing that unfocused magic into play . . . and presumably knowing the results. They now knew it hadn't been an accident.

But no one had ever truly thought it was.

Jess forgot where she was. She put her hands over her face and felt like crying, then felt Ramble's tentative touch on her arm. Trying to reach out; trying to follow the rules she'd set for him. It made her laugh, but the sound came out more like a sob. "Stupid," she said. "All for nothing. I *told* them . . ."

He made a sharp interrogative noise, as abruptly close to demand as he'd ever been with her. And for the first time responding as though he were a friend instead of a project, even a project she was training for his own protection, she looked at him, at his strong features and bright, beautiful hair, said simply, "They needed to know what you knew. That's why we're here."

"All for nothing," he repeated—another question.

She shrugged. "Mostly they already knew it."

"All for nothing!" His face darkened; this time the words were accusation, and Jess suddenly realized her error. He was a big man, stronger than Jess, stronger than any of them, and just as with a horse, their ability to control him depended on keeping him happy . . . and disillusioned about just which of them *was* stronger. Angered, endowed with enough intellect and spirit to direct that anger, and they could lose him . . .

"You can go back," she said. "*We* can go back." And they could, now that they knew what he knew.

"All for nothing!" He thumped his chest with his open hand. "This! Not *horse!*" And he gave a snort of utter disgust that left nothing of his feelings to her imagination. "They did this!"

"Yes," she said. "They did. What happened . . . many people need to be protected from what happened. They—*we*—needed to know. And now you can go back."

"Now."

It took her a moment to realize he wasn't just repeating her words, but was making a demand. *Now*.

"Soon," she whispered . . . both a correction and a plea for understanding.

This time, Ramble was the one to turn his back on her.

Chapter 17

Mark took them into Marion, an experience which delighted Suliya and made Dayna feel just plain strange. Looking at the small-town streets with their flat, midwestern flavor—carrying just a little more traffic than they'd been made for, offering a little less parking than needed—she felt like she'd been gone a lifetime. And oddly . . . like she'd never been gone at all.

They drove down Center Street, under a banner advertising the annual popcorn festival—"Popcorn," Suliya asked, "what's that?"—and past the imposing stone edifice of the courthouse, then city hall and the theater—right through town and almost out the other side, beyond the railroad tracks. Mark turned the truck down an alley with only inches to spare beyond the side-view mirrors, and just as Dayna gave him a skeptical look, the alley opened into a back parking area.

"Just *happened* to find this place?" she asked Mark as he took up most of the parking space with the truck.

He shrugged. "I dated a girl." An instant's unhappiness crossed his face. "She was too . . . interested. Asked too many questions. I think . . . I swear, I think she could tell. About Camolen. Just didn't want to deal with that."

"But you liked her," Suliya said, virtually unfiltered as usual, although in this case not without compassion.

Mark made a face, then nodded. "She works nights . . . she shouldn't be here." He led them between the buildings—just enough room there for a strip of concrete and a handful of struggling weeds; Mark himself had to turn sideways—and to the front entrance, beneath a fancifully lettered sign in purple and gold with the shop name STARLAND and a smattering of stars in the background.

"Mark . . ." Dayna muttered. Touchy-feely New Age, just what a Camolen wizard needed.

He stopped halfway through the door, leaving Suliya on Dayna's heels, eager to get a look inside. Incense-scented air swirled around them and escaped. "Lighten up. You want spellstones, right? This is your best bet, unless you want to hang around for a mineralogist show. I think there's one in a month or so in Columbus."

"What *is* this place?" Suliya said. "It looks like the stuff for magic shows. Not *real* magic, but those bootin' shows where people try to trick you without using it."

Mark gave her a hard look. "That's just the sort of thing you don't want to say once we get in here," he told her. "You'll insult everyone inside, not to mention drawing a lot of attention to yourself."

"Lips stitched," Suliya said cheerfully. She reached over Dayna's shoulder to give Mark a little push. "You'll let the flies in."

Inside, the tiny shop was decorated in the same vein as the sign, with plenty of purple velvet drapings and silken gold cords. Scratched glass display cases held jewelry and stones; a rotating rack offered card-mounted runes. Suliya went straight to the clothes lining the back wall—tie-dyed and batik and embroidered, all pretty much straight out of the seventies. Dayna dodged a small round table with a simple black cloth covering; a neatly stacked deck of tarot cards sat just off-center, wrapped in silk.

With a musical jingle, a woman ducked through the curtain of bells that separated the front of the store from the back. "Hi," she said. "Let me know if you have any questions. I won't pester you." She sat on a stool behind the cash register counter and display case, an incongruous sight among the plethora of New Age items in her jeans and plain polo top. After a moment, another woman emerged from the back, a clipboard in hand and much more the image of a proprietess for a shop named Starland. Short hair—short to the point of a crew cut, were it not for the longer fringes around her face and neck—jangling earings, and a filmy black top over a long purple skirt.

"Mark," she said, surprised.

"Hey, Rita," he responded, easily enough so Dayna figured this wasn't, in fact, the woman he'd dated. "Brought some out-of-town friends in. Dayna needs some stuff for a project."

"Stones," Dayna said. "Hard ones. Maybe some crystals . . . depends what you've got."

"I'll show you," the jeans-clad woman said, sliding off the stool and weaving expertly through several tight displays to reach the customer side of the counter. "We've got some token stuff up front here, but the best selection is in the back."

Suliya, having rejected all the clothing besides the

black baby-doll T-shirt she clutched, turned sideways to nudge past them in the opposite direction. "Look," she said to Mark, displaying the shirt. "A horse—with a *horn*."

Dayna sighed. And then her gaze fell upon the display case in the back corner, nearly behind the clothes, and she felt a greedy delight. In the background, the woman Rita rang up Suliya's purchase, her voice a little too casual as she said, "From where did you say you were visiting?"

"She didn't," Mark broke in, firmly.

"Maybe you'd like a free reading? As one of Mark's friends—"

"Nosy, Rita," Mark said, a tone of voice that told Dayna he really did know this woman . . . and also that he believed she was capable of discerning more than most. That she wanted to. Dayna looked over her shoulder, annoyed; he should have known better than to let Suliya come, if that were the case.

Clearly he was operating in pure Mark Mode . . . too laid back to notice things that really did matter.

Lighten up, Dayna. Mark's imagined voice in her head, his knee-jerk response to her need to control all the details. Of everything. Maybe this time he was right.

And meanwhile Suliya all but jumped up and down and clapped her hands. "Oh, yes!" she said. For a rich girl, sometimes she seemed astonishingly naive. Even Dayna had to hide a smile when Suliya added, "A reading of what?" in that same eager voice; the woman who'd shown her the stones didn't bother to hide her own amusement.

Dayna turned to the stones. Cut crystals, polished ovals . . . minerals and gems and a few that looked purely artificial. Satisfaction. It might take some hunting, the stones might not be quite right, but she'd find what she needed here. She hunted for the first pick, pushing her forefinger through the stones; touching them. Trying to get a feel for them, as she'd be able to do on Camolen and finding the power so faint she couldn't be sure.

Dayna couldn't help herself—looking at the plethora of stones before her, feeling her own spellstones in the pocket of her jeans . . . and wondering. A test, just a small test, just to see if it was worth buying the stones at all.

Saddened, Jess left Ramble with another apple and a few slices of melon; like her, he preferred many small meals instead of fewer large ones. And saddened, she almost missed the fact that there was a new message on the white board, even though they'd taken to leaving the pantry door open as they waited for Jaime's delayed reply.

Like the last, this one was full of what Dayna had eventually termed "static"; like the last, it was terse and to the point, even with the requested repetition. *Ha-visitors -ooking fo- Arlen b-cause of world-tra—l s-ell detectio-. Now think t-ey follo— -ou. B- c-reful.*

Staticky, but not unreadable. *Had visitors looking for Arlen because of world-travel spell detection.* That made more sense than the first time, then . . . very few people knew Dayna was willing to attempt magic of that complexity, or that because of her ability to mix raw magic and conventional magic, she could actually accomplish such spells.

Now think they followed you. Be careful.

She had to blink at that. Followed them? Why?

To stop us. Of course. But how could anyone understand enough of their goals here to *want* to stop them? And who would want to in the first place?

She couldn't think it through, not with the unhappy taste of Ramble's reaction clogging her mind.

Dayna was gone, in town with Mark and Suliya; Jess

had come in earlier to get Ramble's apple as they were preparing to leave. Carey had been asleep then—unused to the medicine Mark had given him, although Mark assured them it was commonly used and quite safe, this ibuprofen—and as far as she knew, he hadn't yet woken. She brushed hay and wood shavings off her clothes while she was still in the kitchen, and went to find him.

Yes, still asleep. On a bed for which Mark had apologized; all of the farmhouse's extra beds were narrow single-person beds, even the one that was Jaime's own. It didn't matter to Jess; hers was in the same room with Carey and she slept in either.

Now she watched him a moment, his back to her, crowded up against the wall as if it was all that kept him from tipping over. Even in his sleep he favored his sore leg, keeping it gingerly bent. Although the spring day was warm enough to keep Jess in a T-shirt, he'd drawn the worn navy bedspread over his arms, rumpling the covers into an impossible mess.

Jess eased into the bed, stretching out behind him, doing her best not to disturb him. Just considering him. Watching him, reaching out to touch his hair only when the urge became irresistible.

It woke him, but just barely. "It's me," she said, close enough to his ear to use the barest of murmurs. "I'm thinking."

"Is everything—"

"Fine." And it was, for the moment. Long enough for her to watch him and touch him and consider . . . things. His hair was so unlike hers, so fine in comparison—if not nearly as fine as Jaime's or Dayna's. Blond, but nothing like the palomino's . . . darkest gold, almost brown near the roots and the nape of his neck where he had it cut short. Mixed strands of ashy browns and deep blond on top, where he'd let it grow longer and the forelock often fell over his brow. Very human, all in all. "I need to think."

"And it helps to do *that* to me?" He was awake enough to put humor in his voice, and she knew exactly what she was doing to him, although for once that was not her intent.

"Yes," she said. "To be with you."

He gave her a wordless grumble and fell silent; she thought he dozed, though sometimes he leaned into her hand.

Very human. And he loved her. She had no doubt of it . . . day in and day out, just like any two humans. She sometimes caught him just looking at her . . . smiling. Or he touched her arm in the middle of a conversation about something else altogether, or ran his hand down her back, just the way she now traced a finger down his shoulder, found a knot of tension, and gently worked it out.

He loved her.

But there were things he hadn't faced, hadn't accepted. If he were truly at ease with the Lady part of her, he wouldn't avoid riding her. And he hadn't—not since he'd known her as Jess. He'd even changed the subject when she mentioned it.

Of late, she was beginning to believe he couldn't reconcile the fact that he felt one way about humans and another about horses. She wasn't even sure it was so wrong, intellectually . . . but it hurt her nonetheless. And now, when she saw what he'd been willing to do to Ramble—*for nothing*—it bothered her all the more.

He rolled back, half trapping her, and looked over his shoulder. "Jess," he said, half in amusement and half all-serious, "you're killing me."

"I just needed—"

"To think. I know." Still sleepy sounding, his voice

laced with affection, he said, "You keep doing that, and
I'm going to give you something to *think* about, all
right."

She smiled, but it felt small and sad. She said,
"Ramble doesn't know anything. Nothing to help *us*,
I mean." He knew well enough why he'd been brought
here, and how useless it had been. "And Jaime thinks
someone followed us here."

"Waitaminute, waitaminute." He twisted around in
the narrow space she'd left him, ending up propped
on one elbow and facing her. Carey. So human. So
driven . . . but not so driven he no longer failed to
understand the consequences.

This time, he'd accepted them for someone else. For
Ramble.

He said, "You talked to him? Really *talked* to him?"

She nodded, watching him, still half lost in her
thoughts. His was a face that could have come from
a horse. Not a rough-edged Ramble type of horse, but
something finely bred. Although he had not quite the
nose for it; not enough expression in his nostrils, and
too much in his forehead. She reached to smooth one
of the lines she'd just created there, and he gently but
firmly caught her hand.

"Why didn't you wait? What did he say? What
exactly did he say?"

Best not to answer that first question, not when the
answer was *I needed to protect him from you.* "He says
a man was there. He only saw a little. And he felt
magic from the man. Then he ran. That's all."

"That's something," Carey said . . . but he frowned.

Jess sank back down on the bed, looking up at him.
"Not new. Not if you believed Dayna. She felt the
magic . . . that means someone had to have been there.
We knew. We didn't *have* to bring Ramble here."

Gently—more gently than she wanted, she could tell

that by his preoccupied frown—he said, "We couldn't know without trying." He ran a hand over his face, still looking tired, and absently rotated the shoulder on which he wasn't leaning. "That can't be everything. He'll remember more, if we keep asking—"

"No," Jess said flatly. It was, she realized from the surprise on his face, a command. "He has said what he knows."

"Jess—"

She sat up suddenly; there wasn't enough room on the bed for both of them that way, so she slid off and stayed kneeling there where he could see her, could understand how serious she was. "*No*. He won't talk to you . . . he understands why he is here and he knows he can tell us nothing of worth. Carey," she said slowly, watching the surprise linger in his eyes, and close enough to mark the mixed brown and green of them, "if you try, I will take him away."

That shocked him; he flinched, though she doubted he knew it. Mingled with the shock was a sudden pain, and the draw of his brow against it.

"Yes," she said softly, and with perfect understanding. "It hurts. I know." She was beginning to think this was what being human was all about. Being capable of hurting the people about whom you cared the most.

He drew a deep breath, pushing himself upright and swinging his legs over the edge of the bed, making a half-hearted effort to pat the covers back into place. "All right," he said. "We'll talk about it later."

"We just talked about it." She sat back on her heels, not giving ground. Not this time. She could handle Ramble away from the barn; she was the only one. She had a spellstone to get back home; she would use it.

"And we may well talk about it again!" His voice rose, came out nearly as a shout, not a tone he'd ever used with her before.

She looked steadily back at him.

He threw his hands up. "We've got enough to deal with right now without getting stuck on this, all right? What about this message from Jaime?"

She frowned at him, not satisfied with the way he'd left things about Ramble . . . but realized she'd pushed hard, decided to give him the time to deal with it. "I left it on the board."

He didn't hesitate. He got to his feet and headed out the door. Jess followed more slowly, and found him contemplating Jaime's poorly transported words, frowning. As she came up beside him he shook his head. "Damn, I wish we could talk to her."

"Someone wants to stop us," Jess said. "I don't know why. You and Dayna did this to *help.*"

He gave her a wry look, his mouth twisted in a self-deprecating way. "Even if you think we're wrong."

"I think you're wrong," Jess said readily. "But I know you did it to try to help."

"For someone to want to stop us, they'd have to know what we were doing. Or *think* they knew." Carey shook his head again. "I can't put it together. Let's leave it here, see if the others have any glowbursts about it." He gave a sudden glance around the kitchen, the worn honey-pine cabinets and table and its markedly empty silence. No television in the background, no leftover snacks on the kitchen counter. "This isn't a good time to be separated. If someone's here and they came prepared, they could have finder spellstones."

"Mark took Dayna to look for spellstones," Jess told him. "Empty ones, for Dayna. She found out magic doesn't work from scratch here. She said something about doubling spellstones."

Carey winced.

"Is that bad?" Jess asked.

He said, "Not if it works."

Payys. Another small town, barely big enough for the livery. Arlen gave a sigh of relief as he spotted its sign, and then another when the woman wielding a stall fork was amiably willing to take on Grunt for the night.

The smaller towns. They were used to being bypassed by the rest of Camolen . . . and therefore much less disturbed by the disruptions that had everyone else scrambling to maintain themselves, running short on supplies anyway, and in general not behaving as the civilized folk of Camolen ought to. Not that life in the small towns seemed normal—people were worried, and conveniences had been unsettled. But for all of that, they seemed to go on with day-to-day life, wary and waiting for someone to tell them what was going on.

No one ever mentioned the kind of destruction Arlen had seen on the road . . . and seen again this very day, the smallest patch of oddness just off the road. He'd spent some time studying it, but when he'd given it a subtle prod of magic—just a dollop, not directed toward any kind of spell—it twisted itself inside out, doubled while he blinked, and drove him to retreat.

At least it had given him something to think about until the next time he found one—and he had no doubt that he would.

"Wantin' grain for the horse?" the woman said, barely pausing in her work with the fork. "I'm about to start feeding, but yours ought not get any for a while . . . I'll put it in a bucket here if you want, and start him on some hay."

"I'd be grateful," Arlen said, unloading the pack sacks and stripping the saddle from the gelding's back, letting the blanket sit there a while longer while the animal cooled.

Carey would be surprised at how much he'd learned about horses.

"Damn well better have the chance to tell him," Arlen muttered, earning a glance from the woman as she shoved her full wheelbarrow down the puddled, dirt-packed lane in front of the stall row. He gave her an embarrassed shrug and lugged his gear to the empty stall she'd pointed out to him. Grunt needed grooming, and then he'd need his grain—but Arlen wanted nothing more than to sit numbly and not move, here in his ugly-clothes persona and his upper lip that so keenly felt the cold . . . even his nose seemed colder without the mustache. Just sit and . . . sit. Exhausted in body and mind.

He found a wooden feed bucket with a broken handle, flipped it over, and plunked his cold posterior upon it. Just to sit.

And, he thought suddenly, to hunt for Jaime. He'd never reached for her at this time of day . . . always at night, when he was tired and presumably so was she. Elbows on knees, face in hands, he went looking. So easy, after all these nights, to fall right into it . . . *Jaime, I'm here. I'm alive. I'm coming.* Over and over again, never expecting an answer from someone with so little ability with magic, but hoping at least to feel the connection. *Jaime, I'm here. I'm alive. I—*

He startled at the suddenness of it. The brief clarity of *Jaime*, the shock of contact—

A voice of satisfaction, far too close to his ear. "Been looking for you, wizard. Should have kept your magic to yourself."

Jaime lifted her head from the message she penned to Chesba, gratitude for his cooperation and quick reply in confirming that the two representatives who had visited her were none of his, after all. On the stack of outgoing messages beside her elbow was another to the local peacekeeper station, asking about the two. But her pen—a nib pen, beautifully appointed and fit to the human hand, but a nib pen nonetheless—dripped a large blot of ink on the message, unheeded. The evening ague? Now? *Now?* It nibbled at her, swelling; she closed her eyes against it, unprepared.

But as it swelled, heading for unbearable—not *pain* so much as pressure—it popped, clearing for an instant of—

"Arlen?" she whispered.

Arlen jumped to his feet, stumbled over the bucket, and ended up standing there with it in his hand, feeling foolish on all counts. *Should have kept the magic to yourself, wizard.*

Even, apparently, the small spells. Spells that should have disappeared under the weight of daily magic use in Camolen without the application of intense scrutiny.

I've been looking for you.

Arlen eyed the man, found him far too close for comfort. Not a wizard—muscle. Hulking and obvious muscle, with shoulders that took a coat twice as wide as Arlen's and still it didn't close properly. He'd be highly protected from personal damage spells, then. No easy inertia spells, no spells that acted directly against him at all. And he'd be fast—at this distance, faster than a complicated spell. Faster than almost *any* spell, if the man was trained to the signs of a wizard's concentration.

Arlen would bet this particular man was trained in any number of things . . . none of them pleasant. "You must have been looking for some time, then," he said. *You must have known to look in the first place.* "The Council deaths were no accident. You had someone there. You *knew* I was still alive." He cocked his head, still thinking like a wizard going after puzzles. "Who are you with? What's this all about?"

"I don't think you need to know that."

Damn. Not an obliging villain, then. Not someone with an ego who could be prodded into verbosity. Someone with a job . . . who intended to do it.

"Get your horse," the man said, looking every bit like he was capable of doing this particular job. His flat nose attested to his experience; Arlen imagined he'd find scarred knuckles beneath the man's worn black leather gloves. The knuckles of those gloves were thickened, weighted. "You're about to have an accident on the road."

Arlen gave him a disbelieving stare. "You're not serious."

The man couldn't be. One more step toward Grunt and he'd be out of reach, and out of reach was far enough to accomplish whatever spell he wanted.

The man raised a finger as if in sudden discovery and, using a voice that let Arlen know he'd been played with, said, "Ay, right." He held out his hand, opened it . . . within his meaty palm lay a small vial. "Drink this first."

Arlen gave the vial a dubious look.

"I can kill you here," the man suggested. "I don't *want* to . . . the manure heap behind this place isn't big enough to hide a body. If you drink it, then you can delude yourself into believing you've bought yourself enough time to escape me somehow."

That made a certain amount of uncomfortable sense. "No doubt it's one of those mind-muddling doses meant to keep me from working magic."

"No doubt it's spelled to take effect immediately, too. Now take it, before I get bored and that manure heap starts looking bigger."

I am, Arlen thought, *more than my magic*.

At least, he hoped he was.

Cautiously, he held his hand out; the man tipped the vial into it. Arlen thumbed off the cap and poured the thick, honey-colored liquid onto his tongue. It tasted of honey as well . . . and by the time he'd swallowed, he felt his ability to concentrate fly away like so many bees. He gave the vial a respectful glance—what he suspected looked like a stupidly vapid respectful glance—and inanely returned it to the man.

"Now get your horse. Bring him here and saddle him." The man crossed his arms and spoke as though to a particularly dim three-year-old.

Arlen couldn't blame him. A dim three-year-old probably had quite an edge over him at the moment.

But physically, he was fine. No stumbling; no staggering. Nothing to draw anyone's attention. Run? He was headed in the right direction . . . *away* . . .

He thought the man could probably run just as well. Probably better. And that he'd only continue to follow Arlen.

"Get the horse," the man reminded him, patiently enough.

Arlen discovered he'd stopped halfway there. "Sorry," he mumbled without thinking.

Make that a dim *two*-year-old.

So stop trying to think.

Do.

He reached Grunt's stall, only a few doors down the equipment-littered aisle. Grunt gave him an eager greeting, stretching his coarse, winter-whiskered head over the door—no stall bars for this small establishment, although the stall sidewalls went to the low, slanting ceiling—in obvious expectation. Puzzled, Arlen followed the horse's gaze.

The bucket. He still had the bucket, hanging limply

from his grasp. Most carefully, he set it down beside the stall and reached for Grunt's halter and lead rope.

Grunt gave him a look of utter disbelief and fled to the back of the stall.

"Grunt," Arlen said in disappointment. "It's not a very big stall. Even I can see the inevitable outcome here, and I can't put two thoughts together." He opened the stall door; it swung out, effectively blocking the aisle leading outside and to escape. No, no running. But when he went into the stall after Grunt, he looked again at the blocked aisle, and several thoughts tried very hard to rub together and come up with an idea.

Stop trying to think.

Do.

Arlen whirled the end of the lead rope in a short circle and cracked it sharply against Grunt's haunches. Grunt quivered in astonished offense, not quite believing Arlen meant it.

"Put the halter on him and bring him here," the man said, not quite as patiently, unable to see through the sidewalls.

"Trying," Arlen said, even as he wound up for another smack.

Grunt saw it coming.

Grunt believed.

He dug his hind feet through the cheap straw bedding and into the dirt below, and he bolted from the stall in the only direction he could.

"Idiot!" the man exclaimed, high alarm building in his voice. "Whoa, whoa!"

He was a big man; Arlen looked out the stall to find him standing with his arms outstretched, enough to intimidate poor agreeable Grunt to a dancing halt.

Couldn't have that.

Don't try to think.

Do.

Arlen grabbed up the bucket, rolled it under Grunt's jigging feet, and charged down the aisle with a whoop, swinging the lead rope fast enough to make it sing through the air.

Grunt danced insanely atop the bucket for the merest instant before he broke, trampling over the man who would kill Arlen and leaving in his wake first a heartfelt curse of alarm and then involuntary cries of pain. As Arlen had long suspected, Grunt was not one of those nimble creatures who might have successfully avoided soft squishy things underfoot in tight spaces.

The liverykeep came charging out of the feed room, a metal scoop in one hand, a bucket in the other. "What the rootin'—" she started, but then words apparently failed her.

Words were failing Arlen, too, who had just enough presence of mind to note that Grunt had well and truly stopped at the other end of the stall row and that perhaps whoever had prepared the vial had overestimated Arlen's weight. Or had known his weight . . . but not the fact that he'd lost some of it while traveling. He swayed over the man, he with the unfortunate iron-shod hoofprint in the middle of his bleeding face, and said with much import, "He tried to take my horse."

"Guides damn him," the woman said, irritated, nudging the man's foot with her own and not even eliciting a groan. "Another one to haul to the poor-healers." She gave Arlen a narrow-eyed look. "You don't look so good. You got a problem, get to the healers before I have to drag *you*, too."

"Drugged me," Arlen announced importantly. "So I'd be too stupid to stop him. Ha. Too stupid *not* to . . ."

She waved irritably at him. "Then get to the road inn and sleep it off. I'll deal with the horse. Stupid fool." This to the badly injured man on the muddy, mucky floor. "I'm going to have to install a friend-foe detector with that new SpellForge perma-feature. Damned if that won't cost me some shine. Hey—you hear me? Get yourself to that road inn or—"

Arlen smiled, most beatifically, as the world spun a long, slow circle around him. Not at all alarming. That, too, had to be . . . the . . . "Too late," he told her, and slowly deflated into a remarkably boneless heap, his last thought that of what it would be like to be dragged all the way to the road inn.

Chapter 18

Carey hesitated at the screen door off the kitchen, staring out at the barn, glancing back over his shoulder to the kitchen. Empty now, although it bore signs of his lunch, a pan soaking in the sink from his rewarmed sloppy joes.

Sloppy joes. He could only imagine that Jaime, in coming to Camolen, had encountered food with equally idiosyncratic names. He looked into the living room where Jess read one of Jaime's old books, something about a black stallion. He supposed that to Jess and Ramble, the two worlds weren't so different. Both equally strange, and full of the strange ways that humans named and built and handled things.

Ramble. He needed to talk to Ramble. To see for himself that there was no little detail, no question Jess might have neglected to ask simply because she *did* look at the world through equine-tinted eyes.

From the sound of it, Ramble had only glimpsed the culprit . . . but what if that glimpse revealed a piece of clothing—a boot such as couriers often wore, the hooded half-cape favored over winter clothing by those in the northern regions of Camolen? When they had so little to work with, the details *mattered* . . .

But Jess . . .

She hadn't been bluffing. Short of physically restraining her—and keeping her that way—he wouldn't be able to stop her from taking Ramble away. From taking *herself* away.

Carey leaned his forehead against the worn white paint of the screen door frame, feeling the unaccustomed weight of this world settle around him. *On* him. A bone-deep fatigue he had no healer here to counteract, an awareness of his own unsoundness that brought back vivid memories of the days after he'd been hurt, when no one was sure just how well he'd recover from the spell Calandre had used on him— or even, for a while, if he'd recover at all.

Settling on top of that came Jaime's words. He didn't understand how or why someone would come after them, but he trusted that the threat was a real one . . . and that anyone with the resources and wherewithal to track them down would be smart enough to prepare finder spellstones. They wouldn't have to know this world; they wouldn't even have to know that Jaime's farm was called the Dancing Equine.

Although if it came down to it, he wasn't betting against that last. Plenty of people knew just a little bit about Jaime—Arlen's companion, the horsewoman from another world, and she who had spoken against both Calandre and Willand in a very public venue. Certainly anyone who took lessons from her at Anfeald knew the name of her farm.

They'd had a string of quiet days here. An opportunity to acclimate Ramble, to try to uncover his answers. Days in which they had no idea what was happening in Camolen, and during which their failing message system proved inadequate for true communication. *It was only ever meant for quick notes, not full manuscripts.* Thick, block letters, not fine script. And even at that, it faltered . . . the newest words had come through even more faintly than the previous ones.

For the first time he wondered if they could get back at all.

Any way he looked at it, the quiet days were over. As soon as Dayna finished with her spellstone hunt, they'd gather their things and go.

He lifted his head, looked at the barn. *Last chance,* it said to him. *Once he's back in Camolen with you, he's a horse again.*

Carey pushed the door open.

In Starland, in the wake of Dayna's surreptitious magic, the shop clerk's head jerked up, pinning Dayna with an astonished, dark-eyed stare. *"What—"* she started, and stopped, open-mouthed. Behind the counter, engrossed in some sort of reading with Suliya that had involved the flipping of cards, Rita gasped out loud.

Dayna came back from the concentration of doubling the lightest spellstone she carried—the friend-or-foe spell—and looked at the jeans-clad woman before her with a surprised embarrassment. The stones nestled snugly in her palm, one agate from Ohio with a typical cut-crystal shape, long and narrow and faceted. The other agate from Camolen—also long and narrow, but with unevenly rounded edges and a satin polish. Similar stones from different worlds, black with delicate white-lace patterns. Both now carrying the friend-or-foe spell.

She'd done it. She'd drawn Camolen's faltering energy through the existing spellstone to double it on the Ohio stone.

She just hadn't expected anyone to *feel* her do it.

"What," Rita said firmly, leaning over the counter with a deck of large cards in one hand, "are you doing?"

"Uh . . ." Dayna said, hunting for inspiration, still caught in her flush of success and very much caught out in the effort, "I—"

Mark leaned back against the cash register and raised an eyebrow, crossing his arms and suddenly, somehow, looking like the substantial and responsible one of the two of them. "What *are* you doing?" he asked. "Of all the places . . ."

"I didn't know anyone would *feel* it," Dayna blurted, now hunting for composure. Stupid, of course . . . there were plenty of people on this world who could no doubt detect and even manipulate magic, just as Dayna herself had been able. But she'd never realized her sensitivity before she'd reached Camolen, and it never occurred to her . . .

Of all the places. But that didn't mean she had to explain herself, or that she couldn't pretend she hadn't already effectively admitted she'd done anything at all. "Let me finish looking through these stones, and we can go."

"But did it work?" Suliya asked. "Weren't you going to—"

In unison, Mark and Dayna said, "Shut up, Suliya," except Dayna said it through her teeth. Mark only gave her a patient but implacable look.

"Burnin' poot," Suliya muttered. Dayna quickly picked out a tourmaline, a malachite, another agate, several nice onyx stones, and for kicks, a man-made deep blue egg of varying satin tones that the sales clerk muttered was fiber-optic material. Nothing here approaching the hard gems she'd have liked to use for the energy storage she had in mind, but then again even the gold they'd brought would only go so far.

Rita put the cards aside with a gesture of finality. "I'm afraid the energy here is too disrupted to focus on the reading any longer. Where *did* you say you were from?"

Again in unison, Mark and Dayna said, "She didn't." Then exchanged a wary glance, entirely unused to being of one mind.

The bells to the shop door jangled, and a fresh breeze blew through the incense-thick air.

"New deck of tarot cards," the new arrival said, as if they'd all been in whatever conversation he'd been carrying on in his own head. Dayna gave him no more than a glance—a medium-sized, duck-footed man with a shining dome of a forehead and the bright chip of an earring somehow out of place beside his soft features.

"Your third this week," Rita said, even as the woman with Dayna gave the man a look and sighed.

"The others just aren't *right*," he said. "They don't *feel* right. I was doing a reading for a friend last night, you know, and we both agreed. We don't think the—"

He's going to say "vibes," Dayna thought, and made herself look quickly at the shadowed industrial tan linoleum tiles at her feet, unable to stop her amusement. She'd never heard anyone in Camolen say *vibes*.

"—vibes are right."

Vibes. Not even the proprietors of little roadside healer shacks, offering fixes conventional healers could not with slick infomercial-like patter, said *vibes*.

"As they never will be, if you don't give them a chance," Rita said with some asperity, blissfully ignorant of Dayna's thoughts. "Not that I'm not glad to sell you another deck—"

The door was yanked open again, having never settled to a fully closed position. Busy little place, Dayna decided as the sales clerk moved to greet the new arrival; Dayna got only a glimpse of the tall, willowy woman who entered. Nondescript, aside from her bearing, with mousy coloring and mousy clothing. Although those clothes—

Mark cut off her view, dragging Suliya by the hand. "You almost done here?"

"Almost," Dayna said, adding to Suliya, "here, hold these," even as she dumped her cache of stones into Suliya's free hand.

"If this is your idea of shopping, I don't think much of it," Suliya grumbled, tilting her hand to shift and examine the stones.

Dayna gave an absent shake of her head. "No, this is hit and run."

"More like errands than shopping," Mark offered, pulling out his billfold, eyeing the price sign and estimating the cost to tug out a few fives.

"Wow, you must like crystals." The tarot-deck man edged in behind Dayna. Dismayed, she caught Mark's eye; he gave a tiny one-shoulder shrug. She knew the sound of someone wanting to make conversation so they could eventually talk about themselves. The man liked crystals. He liked the feel of them. He liked their . . .

Vibes.

Suliya got an impish look on her face, one Dayna didn't like at all, and said, "They're spellstones."

The brat. Dayna hastily scooped up a few more stones. "I'm done," she announced, and caught Rita's eye. "There's fifteen here in all."

With a clatter of keys on the old cash register, Rita rang them up; Mark eased through the clutter of the store to pay for them.

But Dayna was right; the man wanted to talk about

himself, not listen to Suliya's answer—to the point that he seemed not to notice she *had.* "I put them around the house, you know?" he said. "It makes a nice healing zone, you know? All my friends say so. That when you walk into the house, you can just feel the vi—"

Suliya said, "Here. Look at this one."

Guides. "Dammit, Suliya—"

And Suliya's glance said it all, written right there on the perfect sepia tones of her face. The face of a young woman used to having influence, who'd had enough of Suliya do this and Suliya do that and especially *Suliya, shut up.* As the man's finger reflexively touched the stone Suliya held out—the crystal-cut agate Dayna had doubled—Suliya triggered it. Both women from the shop jerked at the feel of magic, Rita's eyes narrowing as she dumped change in Mark's hand, her sales clerk pivoting around from the rune she showed the other customer—

Friend or foe. A blue aura surrounded the man, glowing far too brightly to have been mistaken for any trick of the light; he looked at his own hands, astonished and utterly wordless for perhaps the first time in a decade. Blue light surrounded Rita and the sales clerk as well, both of them clearly holding their breath, eyes wide and caught between wonder and fear.

"Oh," Suliya said, not looking at all pleased despite the perfect results of her prank. "Oh poot. Dayna—"

And Dayna looked where Suliya was staring. At the woman customer.

The woman customer limned in orange light. Fading now, but still unmistakable, as was the suddenly satisfied expression on her face as she gently pushed the sales clerk aside. "You made that so easy," she said.

Her clothes—mousy, but passing for funky post-hippie . . . and equally at home in Camolen as casual wear.

Dayna clutched her original friend-foe spellstone in one hand, her remaining selection of fresh stones in the other. Suliya gave her a panicked, apologetic glance, and Dayna gave a sharp shake of her head. "I don't know how she followed us here, but you didn't do it. She must have had a finder spellstone. Or known about—" *The Dancing Equine. Carey and Jess and Ramble . . .*

"The Dancing Equine. Yes. It's already being taken care of," the woman said. Annoyance crossed her face and she moved to the center of the store, stopping short when Mark straightened from the counter, stuffing his wallet back in his pocket and looking far more imposing than Dayna had ever expected of him. *Mark, grown up at last.* The woman touched her tunic just below the notch of her collarbone; no doubt the series of lumps there were her spellstones. She'd come prepared. She said, "You and your friends have a distressing habit of ignoring the rules and running off to do good."

Mark flexed his hands slightly, looking both ready and wary. "And the people who try to stop us have a convenient habit of failing."

"But *why* try to stop us?" Suliya blurted. "Maybe we're not supposed to be here, but we're only trying to find out what's gone wrong at home—"

"*What's gone wrong* is being attended. No one needs to know the details—"

"Get burnt," Dayna snarled at her. "The Council is dead. And I was *right*. A single tragic incident, my lovely ass. You know about the static, I'll bet. Whoever you are. And you don't want to accept responsibility—"

Behind the counter, Rita stealthily reached for the phone—911, that's all they'd need. "No!" Mark told her. "Rita, don't."

"Don't, *my* lovely ass." Rita glared at him, but drew her hand back. "I want you all out of here, right *now*."

"Exactly my intent," the woman said. "More or less."

Mark rolled his eyes, very much a *here we go again* expression.

Very low, Dayna said, "Get her spellstones."

The woman gave her a disapproving look as Mark hesitated, too aware of the woman's ability to invoke the stones as long as they touched her skin. "Don't ask me how you even made it this far," the woman said, and magic flared around them, strong magic. Rita and her sales clerk cried out; the clerk scrambled away, darting back behind the counter to leave Mark and Suliya and Dayna on the cluttered sales floor with the duck-footed man inching back to disappear between the hanging items of clothing.

Strong magic. Complicated magic. Enough to take them back to Camolen or imprison them for interrogation or simply turn them to ashes on the spot. Whatever she had on those spellstones . . .

But *only* what she had on those spellstones, whereas Dayna stood with all the magic of Camolen at her disposal if she could but somehow pause a spellstone in progress and draw on the connection. *Dangerous. Untried.*

Do it.

She flashed Mark a look, a warning. Closed her eyes, knowing he'd move to protect her if needed—if he could. And invoked the friend-foe spellstone, wishing she had something more complex, something that wouldn't be over so quickly—

She pounced. With the precision of a surgeon, she pounced. The invoked spell, released from the stone and still connected to it, stopped in mid-process, and hung there, the pressure of the magic beating within her like deep emotions threatening to explode.

And they would, if she couldn't control them. If she didn't guide them.

The obvious—a shield. They all carried shieldstones, but those were simple stones triggered by the use of magic against the wearer—not, say, against the building which could then fall upon the wearer.

She knew the shield spell well; she wove it in an instant—and then, in sudden inspiration, she called it up again, inverted it, and placed it over the woman. And then with Mark calling her name, grabbing her arm, the magic burgeoned around her, threatening to get out of hand. In borderline panic she siphoned it to the side, to the empty spellstones waiting in her hand, struggling to maintain control and suddenly aware that she didn't know how to stop the flow.

"Dayna!" Mark shook her this time, and hard. And then to Rita and her friend—"Stay put! She can't protect you if you don't *stay put*."

"Stop it!" Dayna snapped, gritting her teeth, trying to yank her arm from his grasp. "I'm—I can't—"

"Open your eyes, dammit!"

In the background, someone whimpered. *Suliya*. Or the man hiding in the clothing. Dayna couldn't be sure and didn't care. Panting with the effort, she slowed the influx of magic long enough to blindly grab a random fistful of stones from the display at her side—new, uncharged stones to soak up the magic and give her a moment to think.

She opened her eyes. She could see the shield; she didn't know if Mark could, or if he just assumed it, but clearly Rita saw something; she and her friend clutched each other, staring, ramrod stiff with the fear of making a wrong move. The air of the shield wavered—a shimmer here, a coruscating glitter there. Through it, Dayna found the woman—trapped in a bubble of Dayna's making with the furious energies of a discharged but unfulfilled spell beating against it, unable to turn back on the protected woman, unable to make its way out, and visible only through the violently sparking effect against the shield.

The woman within looked at her with both fury and horror. "You rife little idiot—what have you done?"

"What you couldn't." Dayna's words came out breathlessly, holding a myriad of feelings. Her own fear, her wonder at what she'd done. *Was doing.* And at the looming, surging threat she'd created. "You shouldn't have come. *You should have left us alone.*"

"Dayna, we need to talk to her," Mark said urgently—no longer tugging, but still gripping her upper arm. Not at all sure he had her attention.

"Guides alive!" Suliya said. "Look at—all the stones—"

All of them, not just the ones Dayna touched, but all the ones within her shield, still in their display tray . . . glowing.

The clothes rack moaned.

Mark, at her side, at her ear, insistent. "Dayna, don't do anything—"

She turned on him. "I don't have a choice!" Not as the magic built, the raw magic with which she was so good—except it now came at her like air whooshing into a vacuum. "I've got to plug it with something— and she's all I've got!"

"*What?* No! *No!*" The woman looked wildly around herself, her hand reaching for her spellstones. Her shieldstone. "You can't!"

She couldn't work a direct spell on the woman . . . but Dayna's inverted shield surrounded her, a bubble of insulation that she *could* affect with magic. "Relax," she muttered, pulling her wavering control back around her, biting her lower lip in utter concentration. "With any luck this won't hurt at all."

The world-travel spell. She'd memorized it for the spellstones; she'd never expected to invoke it on the spot. And she had no idea how the conflicting streams of magic would interact . . . the shieldstone, the inverted shield, the invoked magic swirling around inside . . . or what it might do to the woman within it all. So many forces battling each other in this small earthbound shop . . .

She shouldn't have come.

For a moment Dayna feared she'd lost the threads of the new spell amongst it all—so much magic! But—

"There!" She shouted triumph as the world-travel spell engulfed the inverted shield and snatched it away, along with an entire rack of rune jewelry.

Sudden silence. Maybe it had actually been silent already, the magic roaring only in Dayna's ears . . . but now, even for her, true silence reigned. The shop's stones no longer glowed, although Dayna thought she detected a suspicious glimmer winking out from among them. The blue fiber-optic egg she held sparked with definite energy, and she quickly tucked it in her pocket.

As if she could hide what had happened here . . .

"Burnt spellin' poot guides," Suliya said, apparently not willing to leave anything out. Dazed, she looked around the store, and then at herself. Checking herself for missing parts. *"Bootin'*, Dayna!"

Mark cleared his throat. "We'll, uh, pay for the missing stuff," he said, nodding to the one empty spot on the floor next to where the woman had been standing.

"Damned right you will," Rita said, the perspicacity returning to her tone, though a pale imitation of what it had been.

"What," said the sales clerk faintly, "did you do to her?"

"Theoretically, I sent her home," Dayna said.

"But . . ." *But, nothing.* That wasn't a sentence she needed to finish. *But I probably killed her in the process* wouldn't reassure anyone right now, not to mention the cold spot the possibility left in her own stomach.

Self-defense. It had been self-defense.

She'd seen people die before. She'd been involved in causing their deaths. But nothing like . . .

Not like this. One on one. Just Dayna, just the other woman. Now gone.

Self-defense, she told herself most firmly, as Mark cast a sympathetic glance her way. An empathetic glance. He'd been the first of all of them, armed with bow and arrows . . . self-defense. It still counted as killing.

The two Starland women stared at her. From the clothing rack, the male customer stared. Even Suliya stared. "Bootin'," she said again, this time only whispering to herself. "Just plain . . . bootin'."

Self-consciously, Dayna deposited the extra stones back into their container and smoothed her cutely flowered, cap-sleeved top—straight from the junior department at Sears only a few years earlier, and how much more innocuous could one small wizard look?—with her now empty hand. The awkward man had emerged just far enough from the clothing rack to watch her, wary, eyes wide and infinitely alarmed.

She smiled at him. "Now *those*," she said, "were *vibes*."

Curled up in the corner of the worn and comfortable living room couch, Jess stared at the pages of her book, no longer seeing the words . . . but thinking about them. About how the boy and the horse, stranded, learned to trust each other. To work together for survival. And then how hard the boy fought to keep them together, refusing to compromise when it came to the horse's well-being.

So she had once assumed of Carey.

Not that she now assumed otherwise . . . she just wasn't *certain* anymore. Decisions and reactions that had once come automatically now took thought . . . now brought worry.

She closed the book, gazing at the dramatic color and composition of the cover. *Nice stallion.* Chewed on a thumbnail a moment, wondering how much longer Dayna and Suliya would be in town and how long after that until Dayna and Carey agreed it was time to go home. And then she frowned, coming into alert, her thumb forgotten at the edge of her lip. *Magic.*

Significant, flaring magic.

She felt the implications of it in the very pit of her stomach, in the cold dark spot that suddenly appeared there; the fine hairs on her arms prickled up. Dayna would use such magic only if driven to it by dire circumstances . . . and if someone else wielded it, then Jaime's warning had come none too soon. *Or maybe not soon enough.*

"Carey?" she said, thinking him out in the kitchen, where he'd bumped around making himself something to eat and then settled, reading one of Jaime's horse magazines—she wasn't sure. Only when she lost herself in a book did she fail to track every aspect of her surroundings, and now she realized she'd truly let herself go; Carey didn't answer. After a few quick silent, barefooted steps to check the first-floor rooms, she realized he wasn't even in the house.

Not the barn.

Please, not the barn. Not doing the one thing she'd told him she wouldn't allow. *Couldn't* allow, not for Ramble's sake.

She fled the house, ignoring the ring of the

telephone behind her, and ran straight into the barn, where—

Where seeing Carey at Ramble's stall stopped her as surely as if she'd run into a wall. And hit her just as hard.

He glanced up at her. It was no consolation at all that he looked miserable, that he actually leaned against the stall bars with his back to Ramble, not trying to communicate at all. Having tried, and failed, given up— and leaving the path of it written on his face.

Jess forced herself to walk down the aisle, all the way to Ramble's stall. She glanced inside to find Ramble sitting cross-legged, facing the corner so stiff-backed he actually trembled a little. Angry stallion. Offended.

Carey wouldn't meet her gaze.

In a voice as stiff and trembling as Ramble's back, Jess said, "Was it worth it?"

Carey shook his head. "I don't know. I don't think so. But I don't think I could have not tried, either." He gave her a helpless look. "None of it makes any sense. Not the death of the Council, not the way Camolen's services collapsed so thoroughly, not Jaime's warning . . . *Guides*, how can Arlen be dead? Dead, just like that, with no one knowing why, and no one but a horse knowing *how*? My world is falling apart around me, and if I try hard enough, I'm supposed to be able to fix it. That's the way it always works . . . *if I try hard enough*." His voice cracked on the last words; he gave a despairing, sardonic cough of a laugh that might just as well have been a sob, and rubbed circles over his eyes with the flats of his fingers.

As if when he looked at her again, he might possibly see something different. Someone who was receptive to his self-deprecating little semblance of a smile.

Her heart broke for him.

It broke for herself, too.

In a low but remarkably even voice she said, "My world is falling apart around me, too, but as long as I could depend on you—*trust you*—I was all right. Now . . . all the rules have changed at once. Nothing is the same, not the world, not the people in it. Not you."

"Jess . . ."

She gave a sharp shake of her head. "I have only my own rules now. Only my own self to trust, and to make decisions. I will get my things, and then Ramble and I are going home. You should come back too. I don't think it's safe here anymore. But I think you'll do as you want, and not what matters to anyone else."

"Not what I *want*—" For a brief moment, he looked aghast. "Not what I *wanted*—I *had to try*. To fix—" He stopped, gave a short shake of his head. "It doesn't matter right now. What happens *next* matters. I'm not going to try to stop you from taking him."

"You should come too." She tipped her head at the house. "Get your things. Get everyone's things—be ready. Didn't you feel the magic?"

"Magic?" he said, looking suddenly haggard. *Giving up.* She'd never seen that in him. Never. "I should have . . . I must have been . . . distracted."

With Ramble. She didn't say it. She said, "From town. Maybe Dayna . . . maybe someone else. And Jaime said—"

"Just what the hells is going on?" he said, interrupting with utter frustration. "When is this going to start to make sense?"

"When it is too late," Jess said before she could stop herself . . . maybe because in her mind, it was already too late. Lives and patterns that could have—*should* have—withstood the changes were stretched out of shape, distorted past ever returning to what they'd been.

It wasn't something she'd ever comprehended as being possible. Rules were rules. You lived your life by them; she'd been trained and grown up by them, and respected them. She thought she'd learned the new human rules, and she'd been living by those, too.

Now she was learning that sometimes humans discarded all their rules, all their understandings between one another, and left even the most important people in their lives floundering. Not true to anyone, not even themselves.

Carey only looked at her, complete in his misery, and no longer attempted to explain himself. Finally, for once, accepting a thing as not possible. "Maybe," he said, after a heavy moment, "it's time to go—"

Jess lifted her head, drawn by the faint change in motor sound of an approaching vehicle. A downshift. A car preparing to turn.

Whatever Carey had done, he hadn't lost his ability to read her. "Not Mark's?" he asked in a low voice.

She gave the slightest shake of her head, listening hard.

He pushed himself away from the stall as tires crunched on the gravel driveway; two doors opened, then closed, and the vehicle moved away. "Charter coach," he said, a guess that nonetheless sounded confident. And grim. In this world, only those without cars used charters . . . older people.

Or those from out of town.

Even those from other worlds.

Think they followed you, Jaime had written. *Be careful.*

Touching a hand to his chest where his spellstones made a small lump under one of Mark's least garish T-shirts, Carey asked, "Do you have your shieldstone?"

"And Ramble's." In no-nonsense economy of movement, she went to Ramble's stall, shooting open both latches and yanking the door aside. "Ramble," she said, "I know you have anger. But this is danger, and I'm here to protect you. Will you wear the stones?"

He turned around just far enough to scowl at her. Like his clothing, the stones were something to take *off*; Jess had taken to carrying them herself.

She said, "They will protect you, too. From magic."

In a startlingly abrupt movement, he rose to his feet, shoved himself across the stall, and stopped before her, lowering his head slightly. She looped the stones around his neck, tucking them under his shirt so they touched skin, and the instant she finished, he whirled away and returned to his corner, his lips twitching in *want to bite* and his hard jaw made harder with tension.

Jess left him there, went to stand on tiptoe to peer out the wire-protected stall window. Two men hesitated before the barn; one wore what looked like new jeans, and the other a pair of fine cloth trousers, pleated, cut up the front to allow for ankle boots, and with a subtle shimmer Jess well recognized. Expensive cloth, spell-protected from tearing.

Camolen cloth. It went with their shortcoats, with the casual collarless shirts they wore beneath. In Camolen, unremarkable clothing in unremarkable colors, just as the men themselves were hardly likely to catch anyone's eye. Attractive but not striking, average in height and shape. One the color of light tea, the other of Carey's coloring. Nothing special.

If they hadn't been from another world.

"They are here for us," she said in a low voice as the men exchanged quick words, gesturing between house and barn, eventually deciding to stick together and to head for the barn first. "They're coming. They aren't big . . . but they could be strong." One touched his chest; the other dipped a hand into his pocket. "I think they must have magic."

"Maybe," Carey said, returning from the direction of the hay stall. "Depends on how prepared they are. We'd hoped Dayna could draw on magic from here— they may have done the same."

She turned from the window to find him standing in the open stall door, his back to it. Ready. He'd grabbed the dull old hunting knife Mark used to cut the hay twine and it hung from his hand, unobtrusive, half obscured . . . but like him, ready.

Run. They ought to run. Any sane horse would know it.

But not with Ramble . . . Ramble, who wouldn't understand, who would be as much of a problem as the men who'd come for them.

Jess watched out the window until the men entered the door in the middle of the length of the barn, the door that came through the tack room and that no one from the house ever bothered to use. Only visitors and owners. Then she moved to the middle of the stall, where she could still see beyond Carey but was closer to the door—feeling trapped, but not willing to leave Ramble—Ramble, who could comprehend none of this, who still sat in the corner with his back to the world. Alone.

Carey's fingers clenched and uncurled around the handle of the knife as they heard the men enter the aisle, unable to see them past the hay-bale barrier. Maybe the men would be as fooled as the horse owners who had been trooping in and out during the evenings, perfectly willing to accept that Mark had received a hay shipment big enough to fill the entire end of the aisle, never realizing the hay bales were only stacked two deep and Ramble lived in the stall beyond.

Maybe . . .

Jess found she'd stopped breathing to listen, and
forced herself to take in a deep and surprisingly shaky
breath. Ramble heard it, turned to look at her, his
mouth open—

"Shh," she said, barely making sound behind it, lifting a hand to stay him where he was—surprised to find
that shaking, too. *Not now, Ramble, oh not now*—

But Ramble didn't have to give them away. Not with
the voices coming close to the hay bales and one man
saying, "There's another stall beyond here; I saw it
outside. And there's plenty of light showing in the
window. I'll be burnt if those hay bales are stacked all
the way through."

Carey's fingers clenched then relaxed around the
knife, his posture stiff.

Afraid, Jess realized suddenly. Outmatched and
knowing it. He was a courier, not a warrior. A courier,
not a wizard. And one man against two, struggling with
his body's limits since his arrival here.

She moved up behind him and murmured in his ear,
"Two of us. And Ramble will not be taken. Three."

He cast her a grateful look—and in another instant
both of them jerked to attention as the top bale of hay
fell inward. Within moments the intruders had tossed
enough bales into the aisle behind them to walk
through, kicking the first bale out of the way.

The darker of them looked at Carey and Jess and
then took in Ramble beyond—Ramble, on his knees
and interested, now, in the new arrivals. Interested and
wary, but hardly alarmed in spite of Jess's warning, in
spite of her obvious concern.

No longer assuming they had the same interests.

"I hate it here," the man said. "Don't make this hard.
I'm not in a good mood."

"I feel for you," Carey said. "Neither am I."

"The question is," the lighter man said, nodding at Ramble so far, "what has he told you?"

Jess said in a low voice, "Nothing. He knows nothing. Leave him alone."

The man gave her a grin of what looked like true amusement. "*He's* safe. All we have to do is take him back and he's a horse again; he can't talk then."

"He can barely talk *now*," Carey said. "How the hells did you even know we were here, or that we had the palomino?"

Jess glanced at Ramble, who seemed more wary. Annoyed, even. She'd be, in his place. But he still had no idea—

"Here's how it's going to go," the light man said, ignoring Carey's question. "We're taking you back to Camolen. Once the situation there is settled enough that you can't interfere, you'll be released."

Nothing about Carey's body language made Jess believe the man, although when he spoke it was as if he wasn't concerned about the intruders in the least. As if they were in casual negotiation. "Interfere with what?"

The light man said, "That would be telling." He glanced at his partner, whose blandly pleasant features showed impatience. "See it, Carey. You're two couriers, and we . . . we're good at what we do. Shieldstones can be removed. You want things to turn out well, just come along."

"No," said Jess.

"Carey," the light man warned.

"He does not speak for me," Jess informed them.

"I *told* you," the darker man grumbled to the lighter. "Waste of time."

And Carey said, "But she speaks for me. We'll return on our own terms. Whoever you sent after Dayna failed—"

We don't know that. But Jess was silent.

"—and I'd like to be here when she gets back."

So casual. Though his stance was anything but, and Jess found herself easing back, and Ramble snorted and—

Someone moved first. She didn't see who and she couldn't even tell what, just that Carey doubled over and then he hit the stall bars, the knife falling from his hand, the light man grabbing his spellstones right through the T-shirt, yanking—

Jess scooped up the knife in a desperate furor with no strategy and no skill, but still with the astonishing quickness to slash the knife down the man's arm, leaving him hissing with surprise and pain, turning from Carey with a precision movement that disarmed her even as the darker man came in with brute force and slammed her against the stall, her head hitting the bars so the world turned black and distant, but not so distant she couldn't hear Ramble roar, "*Mine!*"

Something knocked her aside; she clutched at the bars and didn't go down, but wasn't on her feet . . . yet no one touched her. The world came back slowly, and even then she didn't understand what she saw. Carey, on his feet, sparring with the lighter man and taking the worst of it—but he had the knife again, and he had a grin on his face, a strange grin that Jess found frightening and reassuring at the same time though she barely had time to regard it as anything at all before she had to throw herself aside, stumbling into the stall. The *empty* stall.

Ramble. Ramble who didn't understand, but knew when another stallion touched his mare. Hurt her. *Mine.* And the darker man—not as fast as his partner, not as precise—didn't know how to defend himself against a man who fought not as a man, but a horse. Going for the throat. Hammering blows to chest and

sides in a strange overhand punch, quicker and stronger
and driven by more feral instincts than his thinking
opponent could hope to draw on. Bloodied, the man
went down, and should have stayed down—for as
horses did, Ramble drew back to let him admit
defeat—but gave no quarter when the man bulled back
to his feet, back into the fight. Ramble's grunts were
of rage; the man's of pain and not a little surprise.

And Carey held his own—a delicate balance with
which Jess, climbing to her feet, was loathe to interfere. Not until a chance shift in position allowed the
lighter man to see his partner's fate, and he muttered
a curse, flying into action—moving quickly, so quickly
Jess stood stunned as he danced around Carey in a
sinuous pattern, ending up behind him to place one
resounding blow to Carey's back, one so hard the very
sound of it made Jess hurt and Carey drop straight to
the ground.

"Stay down!" the man snapped, and she thought it
was to Carey but realized the man shouted at his
partner—and his partner, listening or else at last simply
unable to rise again, ceased to trigger Ramble's fury.

She thought about going for the lighter man, and
wasn't sure; she thought about yanking Ramble aside
and wasn't sure, and then she heard Carey make a
strange gasping noise and *knew*. She threw herself
between Carey and the lighter man, glaring him off—
but he wasn't attacking any more. He froze, looking
at her, assessing her, both of them caught in an instant
of hesitation to see what the other would do.

And then something eased within him; he backed
up, seeming more resigned than anything and dripping
blood from the cut she'd inflicted; blood from that cut
sprayed across the white boards of the stalls, painted
by the pattern of his own whirling movement. He gave
her the slightest of nods.

Disbelieving, distrusting, Jess risked a glance at Carey—he made a whooping noise, the sound of someone with all his breath knocked away struggling to take in that first deep gulp—and the lighter man didn't move. Didn't try to take her spellstones, didn't swoop in on Carey.

He doesn't think he has to.

She didn't understand it and didn't care. Ramble, uncertain now, retreated to the doorway of his stall. "Jess?" he asked.

"Attaboy, Ramble," she said without looking at him. "Good job. Whoa there a moment—" She eased a hand to Carey's shoulder, to where the warmth of his exertion dampened the thick cotton T-shirt, still not sure how long she could look away from the lighter man.

He said, "You stay down there, and we're on truce. Whoa, if you prefer it."

She gave him a quick glare, but didn't see any sarcasm much as she searched, automatically stroking Carey's back, too aware of the movement of muscle and rib playing beneath his skin as he worked through whatever the man had done to him.

"It didn't have to be this way," the man said.

"Yes," Carey said, still choking for breath but levering himself up on his arms to glare, to take in how things had sorted out. "It did." The darker man down, and hurt. Ramble in the stall doorway, now looking entirely to Jess for guidance and still ready to go after anyone who entered what he considered his personal territory. The lighter man bleeding, but . . . looking like someone who'd won.

Except that as he watched Carey recover, he frowned. The frown of a man expecting something else.

Carey said, "We're not going with you."

Exasperated, the man said, "My people just want you out of the way for a while. Not interfering."

Bitterly, Jess said, "How can you think we would trust you? Our friends are dead. The *Council* is dead."

His expression twitched and went oddly blank. "That was a mistake," he said. "They didn't understand what they were dealing with. None of them—my people, your people . . . wizards and their burnin' magic. Rife, all of them." He gave a disgusted shake of his head.

His partner, crumpled up against the wall where Ramble had left him, stirred. "*Just . . . kill . . . them.*"

"We can get the job done without that," the man said sharply, annoyed. "Things are under control here; they're not going anywhere. You take yourself back and have them send a replacement."

Jess flushed with sudden anger. Things *were* under control. This man had not been trying to hurt them, not even after she cut him; until that last moment when he'd turned on Carey with such speed and precision, he'd only been trying to control them. To take the shieldstones and return them to Camolen as he'd said from the start.

If he wanted to hurt them, any one of them, he could. Even Ramble.

"Ramble," she said, "I'm safe from this man. Do you understand? Even if he touches me, he does not possess me. If you go back in the stall, I'll come sit with you in a while."

"Yes?" he said doubtfully, looking at the man he'd hurt, and at the perfectly bland, bleeding stranger who seemed to understand what she was trying to do, for he took another step back, and Ramble's gaze left him and watched how she knelt by Carey, still rubbing his back with absent, soothing gestures.

Carey caught her eye, gestured minutely with his chin. *Move away.*

She felt like she was tearing something inside herself . . . but to her surprise, it was a wound already opened. A tear first made when she'd found Carey in here with Ramble in the first place, only—somehow—moments ago.

She stood. She moved away. "Yes," she told Ramble.

He flicked his head up with the internal conflict of it, and took a step back. "Come sit," he said.

"I will." She hesitated, not wanting to lie to him, not able to do as he wished . . . not wanting to draw him back out again by thwarting him directly. "I have to talk to this man. You can listen if you want. But we made a mess, and we have to clean it up. If you stay in there, we can clean it up faster."

He sighed hugely, gave his own tongue a thoughtful chew or two, and backed into the stall, sliding the door closed himself.

"Attaboy," she murmured. Beside her, Carey tried to climb to his feet, failed—and held up a hand to stay her when she would have gone back to him.

"I'll get there," he muttered. "Just knocked the wind out of me, that's all."

"Should have done more than that," the man said, without any particular heat behind it. He moved to the end of the barn, sliding closed the barn door Jess had left ajar, latching it, and then grabbing some of the baling twine Mark habitually looped around the bars of the hay stall to secure the inner handles. "You can open it," he told them, eyeing them as he tied a final knot, "but not before I reach you. So save us all some trouble and sit still a moment."

Carey gave a short laugh and threw himself into a fit of coughing, through which he said, "I'm the one who hasn't managed to get up yet, remember?"

"Or maybe you just haven't bothered." But the man didn't dwell on it; he shrugged out of his shortcoat as he walked down the aisle, passing between Carey and Jess with no apparent concern even as he took a quick look at his bleeding arm. The look he gave Jess was one of appraisal—almost, she thought, of approval. "Took me by surprise with that one. You're quick. But it won't happen again." Approval, but . . . warning. He completed the rip she'd made in his shirt sleeve and held the arm out to her. "Tie that off, will you?"

Numbly, she did.

No longer bleeding quite so freely, he crouched by his partner, fished around at the darker man's neck, and pulled out a chain of spellstones, quickly sorting through them to find the one he wanted before lifting the injured man's unresisting hand and pressing the stone into it, closing dark fingers around it. "I'm getting out of range," he said. "Trigger the burning thing, get yourself back. Have them send Lubri out. *Not* Mohi, you hear? You've seen where brute force is going to get us."

"Go root yourself," his partner said, not bothering to insert any malice, although Jess wasn't sure he had the energy to do so anyway. When the man stepped back—ending up between Carey and Jess and not, Jess thought, by any accident—his partner triggered the stone, sending a wash of magic over the aisle. The air rippled, a gentle current turned violent, and cleared.

"Reinforcements on the way." The man took another step or two back, so he could look at both Carey and Jess at the same time. "I understand your concerns, but I was told if you come back with me, you'll be safe, and released once you can no longer interfere."

"Dead people don't interfere," Carey said dryly. He no longer tried to rise, but sat back on his heels, looking better—as if it were a decision to stay down, and not a necessity. Still clearing his throat with a strange and puzzled expression, a flush came high on his cheeks to replace the utter paleness of shock.

Jess looked at the man from beneath a lowered brow and said, "What did you do to him?"

"I—"

A sudden blast of magic took the conversation away, surprising the remaining intruder as much as Jess and Carey—*not reinforcements then*—and he even pulled Carey to his feet, all of them moving back, squinting, trying to understand what they saw. "What?" Ramble demanded from the stall. "*What?*"

And then the magic faded and Jess did understand. She understood all too well. Although her memories from the site of the Council's death were from her equine eyes—colors severely washed out, focus entirely different—she had no trouble recognizing the same effect. Here. In the aisle of Jaime's barn.

What had once been the man's partner was now a lump of skin, jagged bloody bones, pulped and strangely extruded muscles mingled and entwined with what might have been painted flagstone.

And the smell . . .

Jess hadn't known there would be a smell when the magic-gone-awry was fresh. Not *this* smell . . . not so much of it.

Ramble made a choking noise and fled to the corner of the stall. Carey turned his head away, muttering a single faint curse. But the man walked a few steps closer, eyeing that which had been his partner. He even leaned down, broke off a piece of the unnaturally brittle flagstone, and studied the paint a moment before flicking the stone away to shatter against the wall.

When he faced them again, he dusted the touch of the stone off against his pants, for the first time favoring the arm Jess had cut. "My name is Wheeler," he said with a strange finality. "I think we're going to get to know each other a lot better than we expected."

Chapter 19

Arlen. She'd felt him earlier in the day . . . Jaime was sure of it.

Sure of it, or wishful thinking?

Total denial, Jaime told herself with finality. Stuck in limbo too long, no proof of his death other than a melted landscape where he might have been standing . . . too many other things going on to accept the grief.

Arlen.

The hope hurt.

Here it was well into evening, and she felt fine. No hint of the evening ague, long past any time she'd grown to expect it.

Although she had her dosing vial on hand. Close on hand.

Arlen, do it again. Touch me. Make me certain.

The hope . . . was a wonderful pain.

Jaime dropped the courier report she hadn't been looking at onto Carey's desk, letting it settle atop the others. Meltdown central, that's what they should call this place. Here where she mapped courier reports of the burgeoning dangers of the landscape. Not just Anfeald, either—not since word quickly spread about her undertaking, and now Camolen's couriers passed along sightings from their own precincts along with their message loads in a strange underground movement to deal with the dangers.

She wondered if the new Council even knew of the project, or understood the need for it—or if they were so tied up in the abstract hunt for answers that they'd lost track of the need for a practical response.

One thing Camolen sorely lacked, given its otherwise sophisticated nature: disaster site teams. No Red Cross on this side of the world-travel spell.

Jaime glanced up at the country map newly tacked up on the wall—the precincts of Camolen, from westmost Therand and Solvany to a few remote, sparsely populated eastern precincts whose precinct wizards didn't even make it onto the Council. She took no comfort in the fact that those territories remained unsullied by the red pencil she'd used to mark sightings; very little information came in and out, and the rugged mountains blocking them from neighboring lands outside Camolen—Jaime didn't even know their names—made for plenty of territory where meltdowns would go unnoticed. Therand and Solvany, too, were all but cut off from the rest of Camolen. Without travel booths, the Lorakan mountain range reduced travel to whatever managed to come through the two mountain passes.

This time of year, that wasn't much.

It didn't matter. There was enough red splotted over the main of Camolen to indicate how quickly the meltdowns were spreading. The more detailed map of Anfeald hung beside the job board, where the couriers could check their routes for danger spots.

And still none of them had any idea what was going on. She'd heard murmurings among the couriers, warnings to avoid invoking magic near one of the meltdowns—that magic seemed to irritate them and enlarge them. Thinking back to what Linton had said, it made sense . . . he'd had his narrow call after invoking a light.

Whatever else he'd wanted to say to her that evening had been lost . . . as well as her intent to have Arlen's workroom thoroughly inspected, although that task had since been done, with maddeningly nebulous results. Yes, the apprentices thought things had been disturbed. No, they couldn't be sure . . . right now, things were disturbed as a matter of course.

Jaime gave a gurgle of frustration and turned back to her paperwork. She'd already made assignments for the next day and put them aside for Linton to refine; now she'd moved on to what she considered optional in this triage situation. Topmost on the pile of Camolen's thicker, slightly textured paper sat a pale blue trifold addressed to Carey with a logo of magically stamped gold and bright turquoise. SpellForge Industries. One of Camolen's biggest commercial spellmaking companies.

Say what?

She fumbled with the seal, a general delivery seal that nonetheless required her to trigger it before it would release.

Jaime Cabot, not meant for magic. Consort of a wizard.

Maybe. If she'd been right about what she'd heard. Felt. Touched.

Arlen.

Finally the wax softened under her fingertips, and she was able to peel it off, wondering how long it would be before SpellForge came up with a reuseable sealer spell as she balled it up and tossed it in the low, square receptacle beside the desk.

The paper spilled open, releasing a smaller packet even as it rebounded to its original flat shape. She hadn't even known such spelled paper existed. *Fancy.* The embossed lettering at the top identified it as being from the desk of an executive at SpellForge; the exact nature of the man's position escaped her. Board member, she would have guessed.

I regret to bother you in this time of need and confusion, but find it necessary to make contact over a purely personal matter. Understanding that my estranged daughter may well have chosen not to inform Anfeald of her family affiliation, I ask you to keep this missive in closest confidence—for which reason it will disintegrate for your convenience, once you trigger the spell embedded at the bottom of the page.

Estranged as she is, my daughter Suliya has kept in touch with her younger sister, who now informs me there has been no contact from her of late, beyond any expected delay from the current crisis. Given the uncertain state of things, I would appreciate any word of her you might be able to provide. Enclosed also is a private letter for Suliya; among other things it expresses our wishes that she return home until Camolen stabilizes—a wish I reiterate to you and hope you will respect despite whatever employment agreement you have with Suliya.

"Like father, like daughter," she muttered, fingering the smaller packet and setting it aside. Suliya, a SpellForge child, struggling to be ordinary and yet still shaped by her foundation.

It explained a lot.

Given the uncertain state of things, I would appreciate any word of her you might be able to provide.

Jaime gave a short shake of her head. "I don't think so," she murmured.

Let someone else tell the board member of Camolen's most influential spell corporation that his daughter was off on another world, and that Jaime hadn't been able to contact that world despite her best efforts. She gave a wistful glance at the message board she'd brought down from Arlen's quarters and hung beside the map, using magicked sticky tape that released at a touch and would have been snapped up on Earth and turned into an industry bigger than Post-It notes.

Her last message had been desperate and to the point. *Can you hear me?*

Normally the messages disappeared once they were sent. This one waited, sad and scratchy-looking . . . and backwards. Bounced back at her.

Not enough power behind it, with all the disturbance within Camolen?

She hoped that was all it was.

Arlen. Carey, Dayna, and Jess . . .

So much hope, bundled up inside her, making her heart rush off into racing little dances when she least expected it.

"Please be right," she whispered to her heart, and set Suliya's unopened letter aside.

Dayna felt the magic even as Mark broke speed limits on rural Prospect-Mt. Vernon Road to reach the Dancing Equine. "Hurry," she told him, clutching the seatbelt that crossed her chest and all but bouncing on the truck's bench seat. The only thing that stopped her was that Suliya was already doing just that in the middle of the seat, a living example of just how annoying it could be.

Mark slewed the truck into the Dancing Equine's gravel driveway and Dayna shoved the door open, reaching for that very long step to the ground. "Stay here," she said.

"Not gonna happen," Mark told her, setting the parking brake and jumping out of the driver's side.

"Then stay *behind*," Dayna threw over her shoulder, already heading for the barn. "You may be the guy, but I'm the wizard."

She was sure she heard him mutter, "*In training*," but he did indeed hang back, and kept Suliya with him.

Dayna went to the end of the barn and yanked on the closed door—and succeeded in doing nothing but twinging something in her shoulder. How could it be locked from the inside? This was the only—

"Go around," Carey called from inside.

He didn't sound right. Strained. She exchanged a glance with Mark to see if he heard the same, and saw her own wariness reflected in his warm brown eyes. Eyes that weren't meant to be wary, but were born to be just what they were—goof-off guy eyes with a soft heart lurking beneath.

They went around. Through the central, people-size door into the tack room and beyond to the main aisle of the long facility, where they simultaneously stopped short at the sight of the hay bales haphazardly thrown about the aisle and the very obvious passage into Ramble's hidden area.

Dayna motioned for Mark to stay back, and when he hesitated she hissed, "I *mean it*." It took a renewed glare—and Suliya's hand on his arm—to get a nod from him.

She eased up to the hay bales, several storage stones in hand, and where Mark would have had to push his way through the gap, she slid through without so much as the whisper of hay against the flowered pattern of her shirt.

Jess was the first one she saw, and she regarded Dayna with such restrained tension that Dayna readied herself, bringing to mind the barrier spell she'd decided upon during the drive from town—going on the assumption that if everyone here had a shieldstone, a barrier spell was the only way to avoid physical confrontation. Her gaze skipped right over Carey, registering something not quite right but not hesitating there, and when she found the man slightly apart from them both, standing in the shadow of the closed doors, she knew she'd been right to prepare. Bland and attractive, like the woman in the New Age shop. Camolen clothing that at first glance passed for contemporary American style. Blood all over one arm; hell, blood tracking the walls and floor.

She didn't know why Jess and Carey were just standing there. She didn't have any idea where the terrible smell came from, and only a faint awareness of the strange blob against the wall by her side. Those were all things to figure out later. Now, without hesitation, with only the quick lip-biting expression of concentration she'd developed in the last year, she tapped the storage stones and threw the barrier around the stranger.

He flinched at the feel of magic, was visibly taken aback at the appearance of the barrier—not quite the same magic as the shields she'd so recently employed, but similar visuals. Enough so he'd know it was there. To the others she said sharply, "Do you still have your shieldstones?" and hoped the answer would be yes, or she'd have to come up with an inverted shield on top of the barrier.

Carey shook his head, glancing darkly at the stranger. But Jess, after a glance into the stall to check Ramble, nodded. Just one of them to protect, then. Dayna put the inverted shield spell uppermost in her thoughts and stepped into the blocked area, allowing Mark his first good view of the scene—and his first double take. Unlike Dayna, he zeroed right in on the blobby area.

"You guys have Salvatore Dali in to redecorate while we were out?" he asked, utterly bemused.

But Dayna, getting her first good look at it, felt the blood drain from her face. "That's the same meltdown effect we found in Camolen. Where the Council died," she said for Mark's benefit, and what little humor he had instantly faded.

"There was another man here," Jess said, her dark eyes flashing briefly at the blond man behind the barrier—he hadn't moved, he hadn't said anything, but by his stiffened posture he knew quite well what Dayna had done. "He tried to go home."

Suliya crowded up behind Mark and made a noise of utter disgust. "Ay, what's *this*?"

Dayna eyed the mess, suddenly and regretfully able to pick out several fingers clutching at air. "Guides," she said. "He must have hit a bad spot going in. I *knew* there was more to this than one incident. I *knew* it." She gave her prisoner a quick, angry eye. "I'll bet you know it, too."

"He's not talking about what he knows," Carey said. "Jaime did try to warn us, but it didn't come through well."

Dayna couldn't take her eyes away from the puddle of human and landscape melted right into the wall and floor; she barely heard Mark offer a quick explanation of the action in Starland. Her own inner words came much more loudly. *What happens when* we *try to return?*

And on the heels of that thought, the sharpest pang of homesickness she'd ever felt. *I want to go home.*

Camolen. Home. Still a home with many unexplored aspects; a home in which she was a virtual stranger. But *home*.

She gave herself an internal shake. She'd figure it out. They'd augment the spells with storage stones ... they'd send something on ahead to make sure the way was clear. She'd figure it out.

At the moment, she had to get a better idea of what was happening here and now. A glance at Jess gave her no clues; she stood between Carey and Ramble's stall like a stiff thing, all her natural grace gone, her expression deadened to everything except some secret internal conflict she didn't seem likely to share. Not with the way she didn't quite look at any of them.

Carey, on the other hand, was far from stiff. Rubber-kneed, she would have said. Bemused somehow. Dayna wasn't entirely sure he was truly focused on the conversation.

That left the man behind the shield, with his collarless casual exec shirt and exquisitely tailored trousers of tough, spelled material. Dayna narrowed her eyes, suddenly realizing that those trousers reminded her of nothing more than a stylish version of something a martial artist on this world would wear. Waist pleats along with the sharply pressed front leg creases, topping ankle boots of fine, soft leather that would make for the lightest of feet. "Who are you?" she said. "Your friend in the New Age store didn't have much of a chance to answer questions before she left."

Suliya eased through the gap in the hay, and Mark frowned at it. "Gotta fix that," he said, kicking the bottom hay bale into place and stepping over it to retrieve the rest. "Never mind me. I can hear." Dayna nodded, but no one else even seemed to notice. Not Jess with her inner struggle and Carey with his detachment or Suliya, who frowned thoughtfully as she moved closer to the prisoner, walking the border of the barrier to view him from all angles and then pressing her lips together to regard him with hands on hips.

"Like I said," Carey told Dayna. "He's not talking—other than to say his name is Wheeler. I think it's clear enough someone on the other side decided we're a threat, which means they believe Ramble knows something—"

Dayna scowled at no one in particular. "How would anyone even know the possibility existed?"

Absently, nibbling a fingernail as she stared at Wheeler, Suliya said, "Gossip. News. We knew he was the only survivor before we went to Second Siccawei, didn't we?"

"But no one even knew the Council was dead!"

She gave Dayna an impatient look. "Of course they did. We knew. Anyone at a Council wizard's hold knew. The Secondary Council knew. The landers found out next, you can be sure . . . and from there it probably went official. What juicier little bit to add along with it could you have? 'The only survivor was a horse'!"

Carey said, "That sounds like the voice of experience."

Suliya waved a negligent hand. "I know how secrets get out, if that's what you mean. Seen plenty of it." Abruptly, she pointed directly at Wheeler. "You. You've done work for SpellForge through FreeCast."

Wheeler gave her the barest of smiles. He'd tucked the hand of his wounded arm into his belt, and seemed not much discomfitted by his tenuous situation. "I'm surprised you remember. Then again, I'm surprised to see you here. I can assure you the SpellForge board has no idea you're involved."

"I don't answer to them," Suliya said, annoyed. "I never did. That was Papa's problem, wasn't it?"

"I think he considered his problem to be the fact

that you're a spoiled brat," Wheeler said. "It's open to individual interpretation, of course."

"Poot," she snarled at him, after just enough hesitation to reveal that his words had struck home. She turned her back on him and said in an offhand way, "There's a consortium of spell corps who like to push the limits; SpellForge is in it. They call themselves FreeCast. FreeCast maintains teams of what they like to call fieldworkers. Wizards, fistmen . . . they convince people not to make a loud fuss when something happens to go wrong. You'd be surprised what the Council doesn't know about." She jabbed a thumb at Wheeler over her shoulder. "He's done some bodyguard work for my family through FreeCast."

Dayna gave Wheeler a careful look, surprised to find him as casual as before—not angered by Suliya's words, and possibly even amused by her. Despite herself, Dayna was impressed. She, too, had been captured by what amounted to the enemy—or at the least, faced such opposition in desperate straits. She *knew* how she reacted.

Not like this.

"Tsk," he said. "Your father *would* be disappointed."

Suliya cast the most dismissive of glances over her shoulder. "I'm doing exactly what he wanted—standing up for something other than myself. For something I believe in. It just doesn't happen to be what *he* believes in."

Carey gave her a strange look—partly wary, Dayna thought . . . and partly disbelief. "Suliya, just who *is* your father?"

She waved him off. "He's on the board. It doesn't matter." But her mouth twisted in an embarrassed expression, and she said, "I never thought I'd be ashamed of him. I've always been *proud* of where I came from . . ."

Jess said suddenly, "You don't know he is part of this."

Suliya glanced at Wheeler; her face had gone a little sad. "I think I do."

Wheeler quite studiously didn't respond. Instead he looked at Dayna and said, "Where the hells did you come from, anyway? My recon calls you a 'second-year student who lacks the discipline to stay away from raw magic'—and you took out Argre in this world without magic."

"She started it," Dayna said, stung by the discipline remark. She held out her hand, showed him the stones. "I stored up some magic and I used it on her." Yeah, maybe it hadn't been quite *that* simple. "And you don't know squat about magic, do you? Your people are afraid of raw magic because it's *harder* to use, not easier. I just didn't happen to grow up with people telling me it was impossible, so I do it."

"You stored—" He stared at the stones, shook his head. "I've never heard of anyone even considering such a thing."

She shrugged. "So I like to color outside the lines."

But Carey, all too practical, said, "It's a brilliant idea . . . but not one Camolen wizards have any reason to come up with. I'm not surprised they didn't anticipate it."

"I'll bet Argre was," Wheeler said. "But then, she always went for the offensive magic too quickly. Foolish."

"Just like your pal who wanted to kill us instead of reason with us?" Carey said, absently rubbing his knuckles in a small circle against his chest. "And you wonder why we don't trust your word that we'd be safe if you took us back?"

For the first time, Wheeler lost his composure; his

face darkened. "If I'd taken you back on my word, I would have seen to your safety."

"Excuse us if we don't care to test you on that," Dayna said. She glanced at Carey, a significant look that he didn't miss. "The question is, what do we do with you *now*?"

Jess didn't care what they did with Wheeler. "I want to go home," she said, using her low voice, glancing up from beneath a quietly lowered brow because she'd been staring at the ground and didn't bother to raise her head all the way. Interrupting, completely, Dayna's train of thought. Carey looked away; he'd known this was coming.

She'd warned him, after all.

She said, "We know what Ramble couldn't tell us. We know FreeCast has something to do with the static and the meltdowns. People in Camolen need to know . . . the message board isn't working right. And I want to go home. Ramble wants to go home. He needs to be a horse again."

"But—" Mark turned from shoving the last hay bale back into place, turning to Jess in shock, looking from her to Carey.

"I want to go back," she said firmly.

"Jess, we don't even know if we *can* go back," Dayna said, as surprised as Mark. "And we need more time to pry information from this guy. Wheeler."

Jess looked at Wheeler; he returned her regard with the perfectly pleasant expression of someone unintimidated in spite of his situation. And she looked at Carey again, who'd turned back to her with a subtle plea in his face.

It tore her, made a clenched spot at the bottom of her throat that wanted to cry out loud. But she knew . . .

If she didn't do this for Ramble now, if she didn't do it for herself, respect her own feelings enough to act on them . . .

Either way, something ineffable would change. Something ineffable already *had*.

"You stay here then," she said. "I will not. I promised Ramble."

Tentatively, Mark said, "We could send something ahead, make sure the landing spot was safe. It'd be a different spot than the, um . . . than that guy used, wouldn't it?"

Wheeler sounded like a man who didn't want to remind anyone he was there. "The spell came from your wizard's records . . . but our people tweaked it for return location. You've got a chance."

"Hay," Jess said with finality. "Send hay. Then send us. We can have a good meal before we journey back to Anfeald." The original travel spell had dumped them a good day's journey from Anfeald the first and only time they'd used it.

"A whole travel spell for hay," Dayna said—but she was just being Dayna, and not truly objecting at all. From her resigned expression, she'd already thought of sending something ahead . . . and simply hadn't mentioned it, holding back with the hope that Jess herself wouldn't come up with it, and therefore wouldn't go.

Glancing between Carey and Jess, Mark said, "Jay *does* need to know what we've learned. All of Camolen needs to know it. Maybe you can turbocharge the spell with stored magic, like you did at Starland."

"I still can't guarantee it'll get through," Dayna told him, her expression speaking as loud as her words. *Whose side are you on?*

"But you think it will," Jess said. She knew Dayna that well. "Will you do it? Ramble and I can use his spellstone to send the hay first, and mine to get there, but . . ."

"But having a little turbocharge would be nice," Mark finished for her, having failed to shrink before Dayna's irritation as usual, his implacable expression making it quite clear he wasn't interested in taking sides one way or the other.

Dayna nodded at Wheeler, a jerk of her head. Angry. "And what about *him*? I can't do everything at once."

Wheeler leaned against the big aluminum door with his barrier. "You don't really need to worry about me. We *know* where my travel spell leads." He cast a regretful look at what was left of his former partner, then settled his frown on Suliya, long enough that she shifted uncomfortably. "Your father . . ." he said— stopped, shook his head, and started again—"I have the idea that SpellForge and FreeCast went dogleg on me with this one—told me to bring you all back and told the other two agents to . . ." he hesitated " . . . clean up."

Stricken, Suliya would look at no one. But Carey said, "Why would they?"

Wheeler shrugged. He'd been trapped long enough, still long enough, that Jess found he was not so bland as he'd first looked. That like Jaime, his nose showed signs of having once been broken, if not badly. That he had a scar through one eyebrow, and one on his chin—faint ones. Character marks. He said, "Because that's how I work, and they wouldn't have gotten me on the job otherwise."

"And they wanted you because you're the best," Carey said flatly.

Wheeler gave a faint grin. "If there wasn't something weakening the magic, you'd have good reason to know it." He shrugged. "My mistake. But it doesn't matter. If they broke faith . . . you've nothing to worry about from me. You tell me more about what's going on, you

might even find me on your side . . . because I have
to wonder how much *else* they didn't tell me."

Dayna snorted, planting her hands on boyish hips.
"Very convenient for you. So we just let you go, even
after what you've done here. What you *tried* to do."

"I'm not sure you have much choice," he said. "You
don't seem like the sort to kill in cold blood. None of
you. And I guarantee you that conventional means
won't hold me."

Carey scrubbed a hand through the short hair at the
back of his neck, suddenly looking tired of the whole
thing. "He's got a point, Dayna."

She gave him a furious glare. "You didn't learn
enough from Ernie? You let *him* go . . . and boy, didn't
that come back to haunt us!"

Jess understood Dayna's fear. She understood what
it was like to watch the world making decisions around
her, and in spite of her. But she said, "This man is not
Ernie."

"Guides, just use a burnin' spellstone on him," Suliya
said, her voice thin and a little thready. *Your father*,
Wheeler had started to say to her. Not *the SpellForge
board* or *FreeCast*—and if Jess understood that, so did
Suliya. Whatever was happening, her father had a direct
role. "It'll tell you where he stands, won't it? Or use
a liar spell. Just quit biting at each other about it!" And
she whirled to stomp off—and couldn't. Not with the
aisle once more blocked by a wall of hay, and Wheeler
himself behind a barrier against the double doors. With
a faint noise of despair, she turned against the hay bales
and hid her face, removing herself from the space in
the only way she could.

Jess felt a tug of compassion, an impulse to go rub
the young woman's back and tell her *easy* . . . but she
stayed where she was. If she was going to feel for
someone right now, it had to be Ramble.

And herself.

"That's a good idea," Mark said, giving Dayna a hopeful look. "You can do that, can't you?"

"Of course I can—but these storage stones aren't endless." Unexpectedly, she tossed him the one she'd just used, muttering in the most sardonic of tones, "Eat all you want. We'll make more." And almost immediately waved off Wheeler's frown, Carey's raised eyebrow, Jess's tilt of head. "Forget it. Old television commercial. Yes, I can do that. Yes, it's a good idea."

"Good," Jess said. "Then you can go back to thinking about sending Ramble back. With me."

"I think you should wait," Dayna said bluntly, although she hesitated as someone drove up to the barn—car door closing, tack room door opening and closing, a few moments of casual bumping around in the tack room itself, and then someone came into the aisle, evidently thinking herself alone to judge by her pointed comment about the odor she encountered.

"That's Caitlin," Mark said. "Her horse is at the other end of the aisle. Keep it down and we'll be fine."

"If you wait," Dayna persisted, barely seeming to notice the interruption, "I can be more certain of the magic, and take us all back at once. And we might have more information to give to Jaime."

Wheeler smiled. "I wouldn't count on that. I don't have details. I know someone went out to contain a situation with the Council and it went very wrong—the idiot used raw magic for an illusion spell, and triggered a mess. I know the initial problem involves magic—can't imagine you hadn't guessed that. I *believe* it somehow involves a SpellForge product, but that's common sense when you put the facts together. And I was told you were interfering—making the situation for SpellForge worse than it had to be, and that my job was to get you out of

the way so SpellForge could handle things its own
way."

Suliya jerked away from the hay, her face flushed
and crumpled with emotion. "I'll be spelled if that's
all! You know something about my father—you know
things he's done. You as much as said it!"

"I might," Wheeler told her, surprisingly gentle. "But
it's irrelevant to this conversation, and I have no reason to breach that faith."

"Tell me," she demanded, roughly wiping hay from
her damp cheek. "*Tell me*!"

Her reaction brought Ramble to the front of the
stall; he watched with a curious tilt to his head, ears
fully perked. Or they *would* have been.

They would be again, soon. When he was back in
Camolen. A horse again. Jess let Mark go to Suliya,
playing a role somewhere between big brother and
friend; she stayed in the conversation with Dayna. "You
see. Nothing to wait for."

Carey started, stricken. "You want to go *now*?"

"Now," she said.

From over Suliya's head and its trembling curls,
Mark said, "Look, I'm with you, Jess, but I think it's
worth an overnight. Dayna's already pulled off some
pretty serious magic today. And we should make one
last try to contact Jaime—even if we can't get all this
information through to her, maybe we can get some
sense of what's happening *there*. Try to prepare you
for it."

Jess looked at Dayna, trying to ignore Carey's pal-
pable relief, the way he leaned back against the wall,
the deep, trying-to-be-surreptitious breath he took.
Dayna, too, had sagged a little, as if she'd let some of
the air out of herself. "He's right about that," she said.
"I've done too much already. And this isn't exactly a
spell we want to go wrong . . ."

Jess felt the flare of her own nostrils, irritation made manifest. But she glanced at Ramble, who said, "Tomorrow," and nodded, and she gave a slight nod herself. "Tomorrow," she repeated. "But not beyond. Because today is already too late."

Chapter 20

Suliya sat cross-legged on the bed she'd come to call hers but in truth was borrowed space in a borrowed room that quite clearly belonged to someone else. Jaime's simple taste and style were nothing like her own; pleasant enough to the eye, it nonetheless lacked the expensive class to which Suliya had long been accustomed.

She stroked one of the shirts she'd brought. One of her favorites, cut perfectly to her measurements and well spelled against wear and tear; she could have worn it to clean the barn if she'd wanted.

She hadn't worn it at all. She'd brought it more for the comfort of having it than for the intent of wearing it. In truth, she *couldn't* wear it here, not without drawing attention—not with its Camolen cut, a very feminine version of Wheeler's professional attire, and the magical sheen of it. Smooth, slick material slid past her fingertips, and then the texture of color-on-color, satin-stitch embroidery. Gorgeous. Sensuous. A deep teal that was stunning against her dark skin, and usually reminded her of the sister who had given it to her.

Now it just reminded her of the family wealth and influence . . . and her sudden new insights into how those advantages had been acquired.

Out in the kitchen, Mark gave a low laugh at something Dayna said; those two pretended to quarrel more often than not, but beneath their words lay the easy byplay of long acquaintance . . . and a trust Suliya had never felt anyone offer to her.

Too much of her father, showing through? Or some other flaw?

She abruptly realized she had no idea of how the others viewed her. She knew only how she'd viewed herself, and suddenly that didn't seem like a reliable measure.

Mark laughed again; dishes clattered. They must be cleaning up after the evening meal. Normally Mark would be gone off to his night shift—at a small road inn, Suliya was given to understand—but he'd called in sick after the events of the day.

Suliya didn't blame him. She'd felt too sick to eat herself.

The pantry door squeaked open, and Dayna reported, "Nothing!" loud enough to be heard throughout the house—for Jess and Carey had retreated to their room immediately after the meal, but were no less anxious to hear a response from Jaime than anyone else.

Unfamiliar tones followed Dayna's announcement—Wheeler, asking a question Suliya couldn't make out. She'd be burnt if he hadn't passed Dayna's friend-or-foe test with bootin' ease—meaning his aura blazed just about the same mix of blue and orange light as his words would indicate, and that therefore he'd represented himself accurately enough that while they might not trust him, they could trust what he *told* them.

They'd just better ask all the right questions at the right time, Suliya thought darkly, still angered that while the man had said enough to cast doubt on everything she'd thought she'd known about her father, Wheeler then sealed his mouth against the questions he'd raised in her.

Well, maybe they'd go home soon. Maybe Suliya could just ask those questions herself. She'd already been shoved out to take the world on her own to prove herself . . . what more could he do?

With that intention determined, she quite abruptly snatched the shirt up and shoved it into her carrysack, not heeding the careless crumple of the material and pretending not to realize that the gesture was an empty one—this particular shirt could never wrinkle. For good measure, she kicked the carryall under the bed and headed for the hall and then the kitchen. If she couldn't pry any more information from Wheeler, maybe she could flirt with Mark. She liked the grin he gave her when she did, as if the two of them were sharing a secret joke of some sort . . . a joke on Dayna or just on the world in general, she wasn't sure, but right now it would be a rife distraction.

She didn't get that far. Jess's voice from behind the closed bedroom door distracted her, firm and yet carrying that sad note she'd had lately. Sad or frustrated . . . and as little as Suliya had known her before they'd come on this trip, she knew neither *sad* nor *frustrated* were words she'd have used to describe Jess with Carey.

"I trust Dayna," Jess said. "She won't send us unless it's safe."

"Dayna makes her trails as she goes along," Carey said. Also sad . . . working an argument he knew he was going to lose, but not willing to give it up. "She goes more on gut than experience."

"Inner feelings of what she believes is right, you mean," Jess said, the slightest hesitation there. Suliya drifted toward the door, all but putting her ear to the crack between door and wall. Even so, she couldn't hear Carey's response clearly, though he obviously confirmed the intent of his comment for Jess. She said, "She proves over and over that her inner feelings are to be trusted."

"She almost killed us with raw magic backlash," Carey said, more loudly this time. Frustrated, like Jess.

"Before she even knew what it was," Jess said, evidently unmoved. "I have inner feelings of what I think is right, too. Right for Ramble . . . and right for *me*. I told you so . . . over and over." Her voice got huskier than usual, her words a little clumsier. "No one listened. Even *I* didn't listen—until now I see I'm the only one left who can. Tomorrow Dayna will be rested . . . Jaime's message board will still be blank. I will take her the information about SpellForge, and Ramble will be himself again."

"You're really going," Carey said. Suliya held her breath, hearing the catch in his voice. Bold Carey. Do-what-it-takes Carey. Head courier, suddenly sounding like someone else altogether. Someone grieving and torn and full of sorrow . . . someone who's brought it upon himself and knows it, and maybe just a touch of surprise to realize so. "Jess," he said. "Jess, I—"

"I know," Jess said, sounding just the same—but not. No surprise. Just regret and sorrow. "Carey, you put me where I have no choice. Not unless I spurn who I am, and then neither of us would like me."

That wrung a groan from him, but no protest. "I

can't argue that," he said. "For someone who never used words until a few years ago, you have a way with them."

There was a pause, during which Suliya suddenly realized just how blatantly she'd eavesdropped, and how bad it would look if someone came this way to use the bathroom. She glanced around; not so much as a shadow darkening the hall entrance, or a skip in the rhythm of the conversation in the kitchen, which seemed to be about Mark's favorite tweak on Dayna right now—email versus the wizard dispatch.

Jess spoke again; she'd moved within the room, from one side to the other. Close to Carey, now. Sounding sadder than ever. "You never ride me as Lady anymore. You won't even talk about it."

Carey's silent scowl filled the air; Suliya might as well have been in there with them, seeing it. But it faded, and he said simply, "No. I don't." An answer to both statements . . . and to neither. There was another pause, one that puzzled her—until he spoke again, and this time his voice was rough with something other than sorrow, and slightly breathless as well. "This," he said, "is what I want you to think about right now. The way I love you. This is what I want you to take back with you when you're in Camolen without me."

And Jess murmured a response, but Suliya didn't catch it—and she was suddenly just as sure that neither had Carey, and that it was bootin' right timing to move away from the door.

Arlen woke.

For the moment, that was significant enough.

After his infringing awareness moved through dull perception of self to recognition of horse calling horse outside, the lumpy bed under his back, the bite of too-chill air against his nose and cheeks, and the truly wretched taste in his mouth, he finally put it all together.

The man. The road inn. Poor frightened Grunt. And the drug. Surely a miscalculated dose; his would-be abductor had wanted him pliable and unable to work magic, not dosed to insensibility. With a grimace, he worked his tongue around inside his mouth, and found not only did it fail to improve the situation, but that his mouth tasted equally bad in all parts of it.

It might, then, be time to open his eyes.

He did so cautiously, wincing at the alarming swirl of the canted ceiling—

No, wait. That was some previous generation's idea of style in textured ceiling presentation, not his perception. Offended but heartened, he lifted his head and discovered a tiny room with barely enough head room to stand. An attic room. His gear sat in an undignified pile by the door, clashing with the foil effect of the flower-dotted wallpaper; light streamed in a small round window with bright fuchsia drapings, and the bed covers someone had twitched over his clothed body were an astonishing yellow.

Arlen closed his eyes, put his arm over them, and muttered, "An exceptionally cruel awakening."

On the other hand, he was lucky to have woken up at all. And the sooner he forced his eyes open and got out of this bed, the sooner he could get out of this room. The sooner he would reach *home*.

The thought spurred him on, and he rolled out of bed, finding his limbs stiff and gawky but in working condition. After several attempts he draped his saddlebags and satchel over his person and stumbled out in desperate need of a bathroom.

When he finally found the road inn proprietor— bodily needs cared for, stomach full of the sideboard breakfast of vegetable bread and jams from the lobby—

he didn't ask about the circumstances of his arrival and the woman didn't mention them; he paid his bill and he headed for the livery, hoping to find Grunt in at least as good a condition as himself.

Grunt greeted him with suspicious surprise—*I know who threw that bucket*—and went back to eating what was left of his morning hay. Skirting the dark bloodstains on the dirt floor, Arlen found the rest of his gear where he'd left it and settled down on an upturned bucket—the same bucket, cracked and worse for wear—to study his map and rub his upper lip in absent search for the still-missing mustache.

He'd been doing this the easy way. Small but substantial towns, skip-hopping his way back to Anfeald. *Getting closer.* Always a road inn to be found, usually space in the livery rings, and people had been friendly without either nosiness or suspicion.

Things would have to change.

No more magic outside of life-and-death circumstances; someone had found him once, and they could do it again. No more reaching out to Jaime, no matter how subtle the magic—*I had her, burn it, I* know *I had her*—no more foot-warming spells, not unless he purchased them.

At least the passing days and passing territory had brought with them slightly warmer weather, although that in turn promised to bring on mud—and with his newly planned, deliberately obscure route and the disturbed service system within Camolen, he doubted the road crews would be as vigilant as usual.

For whoever last night's assailant had been, the people behind him could easily conclude Arlen was headed for home. And since he *was*—and unwilling to change that goal—his only option was to get there by the least likely route possible.

Side roads. Nights in barns. Zigzagging the small

trails and paths that made up ruralmost Camolen, varying his heading without varying his destination. "This," he told the map in complete disgruntlement, "is one of the reasons I became a wizard in the first place. To *avoid* such situations."

It wasn't entirely true. He was a wizard because he could hardly be else; he'd been spelling since he'd first learned how to lift his cousin's skirt in public at the age of three. Not, incidentally, when he also first learned that older and wiser minds could discern from just where a spell originated.

With a sigh, he folded the map and stuck it in the outermost pocket of his saddlebags, pried Grunt away from the faint wisps of remaining hay, and tacked the horse up, settling the bill as he led the horse out of the stable. He also paused to politely ask the attendant—not the same woman from the night before and thank the guides for that—where he might find Lilton Trail, after which he waited for the lad to duck back inside, and promptly headed in the opposite direction.

Walking fast.

By midday he found himself sitting on a rock—a dry rock, for which he counted himself lucky—staring at darkening slate clouds with the gloomy suspicion that they would bring not snow, but cold rain. He cut a round slab of spiced trail sausage from the long hunk he'd purchased at the edge of town, and when Grunt quit pawing the slush to uncover slumped winter grass to offer an inquiring huff, he let the horse take a good sniff.

Grunt wasted no time; he sucked the hard sausage into his mouth and chewed fast, as though he suspected Arlen might well go in after it; it was only after a few good hard chomps that the spice of it seemed to hit him, and he lifted his upper lip in a *flehmen* grimace of surprise.

But he never stopped chewing. And he took the second piece Arlen offered him, his nose twitching all the while.

"I have to give you this much credit," Arlen told him. "As a road partner, you do your share of the entertaining."

But Grunt, instantly aware of the moment he had no further chance for odd human food, went back to hunting out grass. Arlen fed himself, letting his gaze wander along the flattened landscape of north-central Camolen. Huge tracts of unclaimed land mixed with cultivated fields were still covered by traces of snow, though the peaks of the plow furrows were starting to poke through. Bright winter birds played along the edge of the road where the brush grew thick, scolding Arlen for daring to invade their sanctum. Big fat-footed hare tracks led across the field to his left, and the road stretched before him without a single recent track.

Perfectly normal. Perfectly quiet. If you didn't count the magic-hobbled wizard on the run and his rough-gaited, sausage-eating horse . . .

He hadn't ever been through this part of Camolen before. He'd been myopic, sequestered in Anfeald to push the edge of spell mastery, staying ahead of everyone else simply to protect everyone else.

Obviously, this time he'd failed. The whole Council had failed. Whatever had killed them, it was not something any one had anticipated. It may have even been related to something they'd approved—it wouldn't be the first time they missed a spell's side effect. Just before winter started, they'd approved that window-cleaning spell, unaware—as were the developers—that any building with enough sand content in its construction would become temporarily transparent as the spell was cast on its windows.

Too bad about that cheaply constructed brothel in

Kymmet. "Really," he said to Grunt, not sounding convincing even to his own ears. "A shame the way they lost their entire customer list on the spot."

Grunt lifted his head to give Arlen a solemn stare, perceived that *still* no more sausage was forthcoming, and eased away to tease a few brush twigs into his mouth.

But he stopped in mid chew, his ears pricking sharply forward, the end of a tender branch sticking out the side of his mouth and forgotten. Arlen shoved the last of his wafer bread into his mouth, climbing to stand on his rock at the same time—even as he supposed it was probably the wisest course to hide *under* the rock and leave Grunt to fend for himself.

Grunt snorted—a harsh, sharp noise with an extra *huff* of exhalation at the end. Arlen didn't have to be Carey to understand that one. *Alarm.* An equine demand of *who goes there.*

Except Arlen didn't see anything. Looking as hard as he could right where Grunt had riveted his gaze, he saw absolutely—

Oh, here now. What was *that*?

Just on the other side of the road, nearly hidden behind the brush . . . he left Grunt rustling happily within the brush by his rock and approached the heaving bit of spontaneous goo with caution. This was exactly the sort of thing the Council had gone to look at—just "a disturbance"; nothing more. Nothing violent, just something strange enough to gather them all in the same spot to examine it.

He felt nothing from the goo. No sense of magic. Just what his eyes saw—although that alone was quite enough. After a moment, it stopped heaving and oozing, becoming a melon-sized spot of crackling hard ground and brush and snow, all swirled together and intermingled.

He wanted to enclose it in a spelled case and study it—but that would mean using magic, pure folly this close to the town in which he'd been attacked. Pure folly almost anywhere, until he reached his defenses at Anfeald.

Raw magic leaves no signature.

The thought made him grimace and rub his upper lip. He might have cast his first spell at the age of three, but at two he'd tickled the family dog with raw magic, causing a backlash that put him in bed for a week, left him under supervision for a year, and left his parents wary for several more. Worst of all, the dog had never approached him again—a fact that molded Arlen's perception of raw magic as strongly as all the years of indoctrination to follow.

Which didn't mean he couldn't handle it.

And, because it was the only thing left to him, he called up the smallest tendrils of raw magic and gave the quiescent blob a little poke.

Suddenly he was two years old again, stumbling backward from what he'd done, watching the blob explode into a frenzy of activity and knowing he had utterly no idea how to stop it. Grunt snorted loudly from across the road and Arlen bounded over to him, jerking his lead rope loose and hauling him down the road with Grunt snorting and jigging sideways at every step.

By the time Arlen looked back, the blob was quiet again . . . but no longer did it seem quiescent. No, now it . . . lurked, like so much wizard bait.

What if someone in the Council had thrown raw magic around?

Not likely. He was the most adventurous of them, the most radical. If anyone had done it, it would have been him . . . as he'd so neatly just proven.

Then . . .

What if someone *else* had done so.

Someone allied with the same people who had sent the man in the stable.

Maybe, maybe not. *Supposition.* Arlen turned his back on the unsettling blob and led Grunt down the road at a more sedate pace while the horse snorted wetly and let him know he was not forgiven for his unseemly behavior. *All supposition.*

And the real question remained unanswered.

From where had the blob come in the first place?

Carey left Jess still sleeping, loathe to wake her on this day when he'd find himself saying good-bye. She slept hard in dawn time, only the faintest hint of a frown between her brows to indicate her disquiet. He crouched by the bed a moment, stroking the black stripe of her bangs in her dun hair, trying without success to smooth that frown away. *Braveheart.* She'd always been that to him; she always would be.

But before long he felt a faint tickle in his chest and he stood so he wouldn't clear his throat in Jess's ear. He blamed that tickle for keeping his sleep light, but he somehow doubted even a spell could have put him into a solid sleep. Not the night before Jess, still so obviously connected to him, nonetheless felt driven to leave under circumstances when they both knew they might never see each other again.

Not with the magic so quirky . . . and with things clearly going off-trail in Camolen.

He thought of Wheeler's dead partner and grimaced to himself in the dim light of the guest room. He thought of Wheeler, and the grimace turned to an outright scowl. They should *all* go back—except with Dayna's repeatedly expressed need to tweak the magic for such a large group, and the admittedly faint possibility of prying more information from Wheeler—not a man who would follow them tamely to Camolen for their convenience if he chose otherwise.

So Jess would go back alone. Or not alone enough, depending on how he thought of Ramble.

Carey grabbed the top T-shirt off the pile Mark had provided him and, slipping out the door, tugged it over his head as he walked blindly down the hallway. There was always something about being the first one up in a dwelling full of people. Something special about the rare quiet time as he momentarily put his thoughts aside and moved about the kitchen, setting up the coffee maker for Dayna and Mark and pouring himself a cola. And something startling about the protective feeling that surged up in him, the desire to make himself a shield from anything that might wake them on this day that promised to be so hard.

Hard on Dayna, who had to find it within herself to hold together fraying magic . . . with the responsibility of her friend's life in the balance. And hard on Mark, who adored Jess like a younger sister and who had introduced her to her first Dairy Queen, her first bologna sandwich . . . and at her own request, her first kiss.

Hard on Jess, who'd been pushed past the breaking point with their human behavior and decisions.

And hard on him, even though he deserved every minute of it and more.

Only Wheeler—ostensibly asleep on the living room couch, although Carey wouldn't be surprised if he'd woken the moment Carey left the guest room—had little to lose with the day's events. And Ramble, with much to lose, didn't seem to comprehend the stakes; he knew only that Jess intended to take him home, and back to his natural form.

A cough nudged at him, so he flicked the coffee maker on and took his cola outside with a small plateful of thinly sliced turkey meat, a morning combination at which Dayna routinely made derisive noises. He went out to the back perimeter of the yard, by the neat, white board horse fencing on which he balanced his plate; there he watched the sky prepare for sunrise.

He wasn't surprised when Wheeler joined him, his arm neatly bandaged in lieu of the medical treatment he needed but which would draw the attention of the authorities, and bare to the waist in those expensive slacks which spurned wrinkles despite being used as sleepwear. Thus exposed, it became obvious that Wheeler's expensive clothes had served as camouflage, hiding not an average, plain body but a whipcord physique in outstanding condition. Carey tipped the soda to his mouth to hide the dark humor of the revelation. He hadn't stood a chance the day before, and he hadn't even known it.

Wheeler greeted him with nothing more than a nod, and stood in a silence remarkably companionable given the events between them. Knuckling his chest, Carey said without rancor, "Just how the hells hard did you hit me yesterday?"

Wheeler said, "Harder than you know. Luck ran with you on that one."

"Yeah, I felt lucky," Carey said mildly but with ultimate sarcasm. After another moment during which the purpled clouds brightened to orange-red and the flat Ohio horizon made way for the sun, he added, "I was a little surprised to find you were still here this morning."

"The sleeping accommodations weren't *that* bad," Wheeler said, so low key it took Carey a moment to realize there'd been humor hidden in his words. But without prompting, Wheeler added, "There are things happening here . . . more than I've been told. I'm sure my employers—" he glanced at Carey, seemed to recall there was no point in being coy about that particular point any longer, and backtracked to say, "I'm sure FreeCast and SpellForge had a reason for failing to provide me with complete information. But that doesn't mean I won't try to fill in the gaps—or that they don't know it. The chance they took is whether the missing information is significant enough to change the way I see things."

Carey snorted, cleared his throat, and said, "Isn't it always? When people in power leave out the details?"

Wheeler gave a short shake of his head. "Not necessarily. Sometimes they just don't think it matters. Sometimes they just don't have the time. It's not always a matter of hiding things . . . just of dismissing them or losing track of them."

"Your faith in them is stronger than mine," Carey muttered.

"Maybe," Wheeler said, in a voice that indicated *or maybe not.*

"And when you find the details—*if* you do—and if they lead you to believe your orders were right, what then?" Carey set the green plastic soda glass on top of a fence post and turned to put the newly exposed disk of the sun at his back, not caring that Wheeler had to squint at him. "You'd better know right now—" But he had to stop, to work through a series of deep, rale-filled coughs that took him by surprise. "Damn," he said, shooting Wheeler a look of deepest annoyance.

"Give it a few days," Wheeler said, not unsympathetically.

"You'd better know," Carey repeated, picking up where he'd interrupted himself, "as pathetic a threat as it must sound right now, that you'd better not turn on my friends. All your working ethics be damned, if you so much as look wrong at any of us—"

"If I ultimately believe my orders were given in good faith? No. I won't turn on you. That's not my style," Wheeler said, utterly believable simply because he didn't bother to turn on the intensity. Matter of fact.

Which is what made Carey's spine chill when Wheeler added, "Not unless you try to return to Camolen before I'm ready."

Chapter 21

Jaime rode the perimeter of Anfeald Hold on a young mare too green for courier work, ostensibly getting in saddle time. In truth, she was preparing herself for the day when she could no longer think of these lands as even faintly hers by association.

Mostly, she'd been too busy to consider it. Mostly still holding out hope for Arlen, unable to accept the inevitable without the neat packaging of absolutes. She'd been like that about her mother's death, too. Her mother, young and pretty and with Mark's eyes—hers, too, Mark said—and killed in a tractor accident when Jaime was four and Mark not even old enough to have clear memories of her. The adults had whisked young Jaime away, of course . . . *protecting* her. They protected her all through the days that followed, not even considering her presence at the viewing and the funeral.

Until well into her teens, Jaime hadn't shaken the

feeling that her mother would walk through the door.
Never been able to trust those vague assurances that
her mother had indeed *gone away*. And since that time,
she'd always attended the burial of every horse under
her care who'd passed, of every pet she'd ever owned.
Of every friend's memorial viewing. And even then, if
the memorials were closed casket . . .

Not that anyone had ever come back. Not even her
mother.

"You're a grown woman now, Jaime Cabot," she told
herself, watching the flick of the mare's ears—overactive
ears, not as relaxed as they should be considering the
mare had grown up in the pasture Jaime now traversed.
The muddy ground made the going slick and while the
snow was slowly melting into spring, there were plenty
of remaining drifts to conceal horse-eating monsters.
"You're all grown up, and you need to face facts." She
patted the mare, gave her a little rein, and urged her
forward.

The fact was that despite today's news that the new
Council would stay in Kymmet until the crisis was
over—delaying new hold assignments and leaving the
staff and families of the recently deceased Council
wizards to run their holds as accustomed—sooner or
later she would have to leave this place. Probably to
return to Ohio, where the farm she loved somehow
didn't offset the loss of this vital, magic place . . .

And that of the equally vital wizard who lived here.

Carey had brought her grapes. Jess stared at them,
sitting in a bowl on top of an upturned bucket along
the outer wall of Ramble's stall, and her throat instantly
swelled shut with unexpressed emotion.

She knew it had been Carey. No one else would
have done it just like this. And only Carey, hunting
a bittersweet parting gesture, would know how truly

grapes were her weakness. Big red seedless grapes. She put her fingers firmly on her lower lip to stop the quiver there. Emotion or equine-like anticipation, she wasn't sure, but she wasn't about to have it seen. Especially not by Suliya, who seemed to crave companionship this morning as much as Jess craved solitude.

Neither of them got their wish. Jess was hardly companionable, but Suliya didn't give up and go away; they stayed in each other's orbit and annoyed one another.

"It's just no burnin' wonder," Suliya said, with no apparent care for whether Jess was actually listening. Jess fingered the duct-tape-wrapped film cannister Mark had rigged and then more or less competently sewn into a long braid made just for the purpose, one that would fall at Lady's withers instead of just behind her ear as her spellstones did. With no one available to attach Lady's courier harness, they'd each written a short message in the smallest readable font Mark's printer could manage; he'd then rolled the resulting page to fit in the cannister. Jaime's name was printed on the outside in Carey's sparse hand, although he'd had to struggle through the language adaptions inherent in the travel spell to remember the runes; that way if Lady lost track of things in the aftermath of the travel, whoever found her would be sure to get the cannister to Jaime.

Still, Jess wished there was a way to equip her with the courier harness. It bore Anfeald's mark on the breast collar, making it clear that Lady worked in an official capacity. Without it, if anyone saw her on the road, she was sure to lose time evading their well-meaning attempts to catch her.

But Suliya was still talking, even as Jess pulled a big juicy grape from the bunch and popped it into her mouth, savoring it. Savoring the gift. Suliya said, "I thought he just didn't think I could do it. Handle a position in one of the bigger stables, that is. And that he wanted me close to home for when I failed." She gave Jess quite a serious look. "Mum comes from Wyfeld, and that's why we settled there. It's pretty out of the way. But that hardly matters, does it, when there's a travel booth in the house?"

Sweet grape. Jess had another, and offered one to Ramble through the partially open door. He took it, and then he took her hand. Stroking it, examining it . . . and then just holding it.

Suliya said, "But that wasn't it at all. It wasn't *me* he was worried about, not really. He didn't want me around the big holds with the top wizards . . . people who might say things about SpellForge he didn't want me to hear. *SpellForge the wonderful*, making people's lives easier. *SpellForge the innovative*, providing services. What good is all that if you've got people like Wheeler running around behind the scenes like big bootin' bullies?"

Jess murmured, "Your father cares what you think."

"Ha!" Suliya said, and snorted, flipping her hair over her shoulder with an insouciance that only made her wounded expression more obvious in contrast. "He didn't want me talking to Arlen, I'll bet. Or other wizards."

"But you didn't know anything about people like Wheeler," Jess said, gently pulling her hand from Ramble's, unable to follow Suliya's logic and suspecting perhaps there wasn't any.

"I've been all through the halls of the SpellForge development area," Suliya said, sounding very much like the haughty Suliya of old. "Who knows what I could have said that Arlen would have found significant? I recognized Wheeler in the first place, didn't I?"

Ramble persisted, bringing Jess's hand back into the stall, leaning his brow against the bars to regard her. "Going home?" he asked, not for the first time that morning.

"Yes," Jess told him. "Soon." And to Suliya, "If he is the kind of man to send people like Wheeler after people like us, he is careful enough to make certain what you saw was not important. He cares what you think."

"Ay!" she said, offended. "As if you've spent so much time in spell corps facilities to know what is and isn't important."

Jess gave her a brief frown, a flattened ear; she traded her hand for a grape and moved away from the stall. After the day before, Ramble made no attempt to leave his safe area on his own; he spent a great deal of time making soft snorting noises at the remains of Wheeler's partner.

Suliya offered her own hand to Ramble, who wasn't interested. Pretending the rejection hadn't happened, she flung herself down on the hay bale that would precede Jess and Ramble to Camolen and plopped her chin in her hands, elbows on knees. "I just don't spell it," she said. "It *is* a company that makes people's lives easier and provides services. Why do they *need* someone like Wheeler?"

Jess shook her head. "I used to think I understood human things, but now I know I don't. And that was just small human things, like friendship and how you are with one another. I have no answers about big things like companies."

Suliya gave her a funny look, wrinkling her nose; all her excessive mannerisms dropped away for this moment to show the core Suliya. "Jess," she said, "friendship *is* the big thing. And you have that. You have all these friends looking out for you—all the couriers at Anfeald, that guy Ander who visits from

Kymmet and wants you bootin' bad, and Mark and
Jaime and, I swear, everyone who meets you. I hated
the way you had so many friends so soon after you got
to Anfeald, and I had none. And you have Carey. The
big friendship, if you trail my meaning."

Jess looked at Ramble—still leaning against the bars,
regarding her with clear possessiveness. Simple.
Unmistakable. "I know what you think to say," she said,
"but I'm not sure you are right. Or if you are, that I
can understand enough to be on the other side of those
things and . . . manage."

Suliya sunk back into herself. "Some people just
don't know when they have everything—"

But she broke off as one of the double doors slid
aside, filling the aisle with indirect sunlight that made
the overhead fluorescents pale in comparison. Dayna
entered, followed by Mark, who opened the door yet
further for his own larger self, and Wheeler,
and . . . Carey.

Of them all, only Wheeler looked largely unaffected
by recent events. The smile Dayna gave Jess came
across as wan and tired, as though the efforts of the
previous day had continued to drain her through the
night. Mark pulled off sunglasses to reveal worry that
didn't belong in those largely carefree eyes, his gaze
moving from Dayna to Carey to Wheeler to Jess as if
he couldn't decide which concern to settle on. And
Carey . . .

She couldn't look at him long enough to know just
what struck her as not-right. Then again, he didn't want
her to go. Didn't want there to be consequences to the
moment he'd walked out into this barn to interrogate
Ramble. Or the moment before that, when he'd taken
a palomino stallion and brought him to this world.

She didn't want there to be consequences, either.
But there were.

"I don't understand," Suliya said, "why we don't all just go home. Right now. Why should any of us stay in this place? We came to hear what Ramble could tell us, and we have—even if it amounted to nothing. Let's go back then, okay?" She added the American colloquialism awkwardly, but pleased with it.

Oddly, Carey glanced at Wheeler, a subtle reaction that made Jess glance at the man herself. Comfortable under the scrutiny, he said, "It's not a good idea. You're safer here right now."

"But Jess is going back. And Ramble."

"Horses," said Ramble unexpectedly, startling them all as he lurked uneasily by the stall door and prodding a little grin out of Mark.

And from Wheeler as well. "That's the crux of it," he said. "They'll be two horses in a disrupted land. Even if SpellForge sends out a FreeCast team to their arrival site—"

"They cannot catch us," Jess said scornfully. SpellForge had not been a consideration in her decision. She was taking Ramble back to go home, not to play a role in human games.

"Maybe," Wheeler said. "More likely, they won't think to try."

"They wouldn't think to try for me, either," Suliya said. "They don't know I'm here. And it's Dayna and Carey they really want, I'm spellin'."

Wheeler said nothing, but his light brown eyes glinted with mild amusement . . . as close to confirmation as he'd no doubt ever give.

"It doesn't matter anyway," Dayna said. "You guys seem to think I'm some sort of walking magic shop. *We need a spell, Dayna, pull off a miracle, Dayna.* Well, I'm not. I'm tired, I'm making things up, and the only reason I know half this stuff in the first place is because I jumped into the deep end—*without* water wings—

when I landed on Camolen. I'm not *supposed* to know it yet. I'm supposed to be playing with safe little spells to . . . to . . ." and she glared at Suliya, "straighten hair!"

"You keep the wrong company for that," Carey said, not a little ruefully.

Suliya's hand crept up to her shoulder-length curls in a protective gesture and she glared back at Dayna. "Are you saying you *can't* get us back?"

"That's right." Dayna crossed her arms, daring Suliya to challenge her word on it. "Can't. Not right now. Everything I've got is going into the spell for these two, and I have no idea when I'll feel ready to try siphoning magic into storage stones again. If you had any idea how close we came to—"

"It's all right, Dayna," Carey said. His voice was a little raggedy; he cleared his throat, shooting Wheeler a baleful look that only Wheeler seemed to understand. Jess certainly didn't. "Wheeler is right, I think. Best that we're not in Camolen right now. Jess will get what little we know to Jaime, and we'll all take a deep breath before we go back."

"I don't *need* a deep breath," Suliya muttered.

"Wheeler could probably do something about that," Carey muttered back, suppressing a cough that nonetheless made itself obvious. Jess watched Wheeler for a reaction, trying to understand . . . but the man gave no clues. No change of expression, no meaningful glances.

Instead he looked straight at Jess. "I should try to stop you."

"Why aren't you?" she asked him.

"Aside from the fact that creating another major scuffle right now will cause me more trouble than it'll save?"

"Aside from that." She, too, could use light human sarcasm when she chose . . . that she chose so rarely gave it all the more impact.

He shrugged—one-shouldered, the hand of his injured arm tucked into his waistband. He said evenly, bluntly, "Because I don't think you'll succeed. *Not getting caught* is a whole lot different from reaching Anfeald Hold. Especially for two horses."

She wanted to snap at him . . . but she had no answer to that. He was right. And all she could do was lay back her phantom ears, tilting her head at that certain angle and doing it unequivocally enough that both Carey and Mark reacted, shifting uneasily, and Ramble glared, not following the byplay enough to know why Jess had gone angry, but ready to respond to it.

Wheeler shrugged again. He looked like the arm hurt.

Jess felt not the slightest twinge of guilt.

They all held their breath, waiting for the hay to come back. All of them, eyes riveted to the spot where the bale had been sitting, where it had wavered and then winked away. They weren't, Jess was sure, aware of their collective reaction. But she was. Ramble was. Both of them, shifting uneasily, knowing that *holding breath* generally followed on the heels of *hearing something potentially threatening*, and when the whole herd did it at once, *run for your life!* often came next.

Jess couldn't blame Ramble; he hadn't had the chance to learn human habits. But she turned annoyance on herself, and she broke the moment that somehow seemed to hold them all. "It's gone," she said. "Now we'll go, too."

Dayna gave the slightest of sighs—the sound of relief, and also the sound of heavy responsibility. "I'm not sure where you'll end up, you know."

"I know." They'd talked about it the night before, briefly, before she and Carey had retreated to their privacy. Originally, the spell had dumped them out somewhere between Anfeald and Siccawei—Arlen's first attempt to bring someone back to Anfeald, off the mark. Dayna thought it might do the same, but since they were triggering it from a different location, she couldn't be sure. Dayna knew it held safeguards, that they wouldn't materialize inside a tree or rock . . . but that was all of which she was certain.

"We'll return. We'll recover. We'll eat. And we'll find Anfeald from wherever we are."

"You sound so certain," Mark said, a wistful note in his voice as he absently raised an arm to wipe the sweat off his cheek against the sleeve—the spring day, creeping past noon, had gone warm and humid, and the normally airy barn gave them no relief, not with hay bales blocking the airflow down the aisle.

"I am," Jess responded, aware of her own surprise. "For the first time in a while." She crossed her arms to grab the hem of her crop-top shirt, and Ramble took it as his cue, tugging at his own clothes in undisguised eagerness to be rid of them.

"This is where you leave," Carey said abruptly to Wheeler, even as Mark said, "Whoa, wait a minute Jess—give me a chance to say good-bye while you've still got some clothes on."

Jess tossed her head in mild irritation. "It doesn't matter."

But to them it did, and she knew it. And she did want to say good-bye to Mark. They hadn't spoken much about it, hadn't said *I might never see you again*, but they both knew it, just as Mark knew he might not see his own sister again. When he reached for Jess he did it in typical Mark fashion; arms open wide, he wrapped a big hug around her and lifted her right off her feet in spite of the fact they were nearly of the same height. "There," he said, and set her down to give her a kiss on the cheek. "That should last me until next

time." But when he stepped back to look at her he
faltered, and took her in for another, gentler embrace.
"Okay," he said in her ear. "I admit it. There's never
enough Jess until the next time."

"Never enough Mark," she said, knowing well
enough why he jammed his sunglasses back on the
moment he broke away. Men. She would teach him to
cry, sometime. The next time, if there was one. He took
another step back and turned on his heel, grabbing
Wheeler's good arm with none of the careful physical
respect they'd given the SpellForge agent up to that
point, literally dragging him the first few surprised steps
out of the barn.

But Wheeler followed the rest of the way without
resistance, only one backward glance at Carey and then
Jess. After that, Dayna pinned Suliya with an unwavering, sky-eyed gaze, until Suliya belatedly threw her
hands up and left, giving Ramble a reluctant glance
as she closed the door behind her.

Ramble by then was out of his clothes, the
spellstones sitting on top of the haphazard pile of
material while he hovered in the stall doorway, waiting for permission to leave.

If nothing else, he was returning to Camolen with
better manners than when he left.

Jess held out her hand and he came to her, though
her eyes never left Carey. They'd said their good-byes
the night before. The day before, when Carey had
made his choices. And possibly long days before that,
when he'd determined to bring Ramble here in the first
place. She wasn't sure, and she could see from his
expression as he moved up beside Dayna that neither
was he. "We'll make it back," he said. "Soon. I'll see
you in Anfeald."

Anfeald. Home to her, whether she was horse or
human. She wanted to say he might be safer if he

stayed here, with SpellForge agents after him and magic gone awry in Camolen. But he'd take it the wrong way, the way she didn't mean it, so she stayed silent, watching him. Hoping he could read her as well as ever, barring those times he refused to listen at all. That he could see she wasn't leaving him, but that she was returning to something else.

"Soon," was all she could say, and she could barely get it out at all. Quickly, unable to bear it any longer, she stripped off her clothes, threw them out of the spell area, and stood in the aisle with Ramble's warm broad hand in hers.

"Here goes," Dayna said. "See you on the other side, Jess."

"Thank you," Jess told her, removing her gaze from Carey just long enough to catch Dayna's eye, to make the words mean more than just two simple syllables.

Dayna nodded, closing her eyes to concentrate, her storage stones clenched in one hand and the magic rising around her. Rising around Jess and Ramble, percolating right through them. And Carey lifted his head, his eyes full of purpose, opening his mouth to call something, an offering. "*Braveheart*," he said, but—startled—bent over for a sudden fit of harsh, deep coughing.

When he straightened the magic had her, slower than a spellstone as Dayna pulled it together but just as strong, percolating up through her skin and bone and muscle with Ramble's scared and tightening grip on her hand the only counterpoint. When Carey straightened—

He stared at the bright red blood covering his palm, put fingers to the blood at his lips, lifted them to stare in disbelief. Looked over his hand to meet her eyes, a moment of shock and significance passing between them.

The magic took her away.

Chapter 22

She remembered this.

All of it.

The harsh change, the shock that came with it, not easing from one form into another, but being jerked out of one and crammed into the other. The dull ease with which she could simply continue to lie on the rough ground, rocks jabbing her skin and a damp drizzle leaking down from a featureless grey sky to bead upon her deep dun coat. The droplets collected, marking the time Lady spent stretched out on her side as they gathered, outgrew themselves, and rolled down her well-sprung barrel, leaving damp trails behind. Water beaded on her long black lashes, framing dull eyes. Water beaded on her whiskers and dribbled into her exposed nostril, inspiring not so much as a twitch.

Not at first.

Hampered by the rough transition, Lady floundered

in the leftover Jess-thoughts, the ones full of concepts and meanings too complex for her abilities. She needed an anchor, a single simple thought to start with. Something to build on.

Blood.

Wrongness.

Her legs flailed in a brief spurt of energy, hooves scraping against the rocky ground, churning up clots of lime mud and grey, wintering moss; she heaved herself up to rest on her chest, front legs stretched awkwardly before her. Beside her, a palomino, his gold coat deepened by blotches where water soaked through at hip and shoulder and the slabby curve of rib, lay motionless aside from shallow, eratic breathing.

Blood.

Wrongness.

Message for Anfeald.

She braced her front legs against the top-slick ground, digging down to a firmer base, and shoved herself to her feet to stand braced, head down, long mane and forelock obscuring her eyes and a coating of mud along one side turning her into a half-and-half horse—half dun with all the primitive markings a dun could carry, and half coated by light clay with gravelly little rocks sticking to her skin, smirching the boney features of her face above eye and cheek and jaw.

Lady again. A rough, hard slap from one form to another, but Lady again. Home.

Blood.

Carey, coughing so hard, looking at his own frothy bright blood with befuddled surprise. Back in what Lady vaguely thought of as the *other world*, knowing only that she couldn't reach it . . . knowing she'd chosen to leave and now feeling the pull of her fear for him.

She lifted her head slightly, snorting harshly to clear

her nose of water and mud—and as much as the memory-sight of Carey's blood worried her, the sight of the palomino relieved her. Ramble. Himself again. She took a step closer, running her whiskers along his hip, taking in the strong wet and musky scent of him. His ear flicked; he knew she was there. But his open eyes were as dull as hers had been, and he offered her no other response.

She nickered at him, barely making a sound. Question and request. *Get up. Get moving. Find yourself.*

The ear subsided; the eye closed.

She nuzzled his hip again—and when he didn't respond, she bit him.

His head jerked up; she bit him again. Hard enough to hurt, not hard enough to wound. He surged to his feet, a two-toned horse just as she, and stood with his head lowered to shake like a dog—orange-streaked mane flopping, small stones flying, freeing himself from the confines of what until so recently he'd been. And then he snorted—great big sneezy snorts, as wet as the drizzle around them, a whole series of them.

When he lifted his head, his eyes had brightened. He knew he'd come back to what he wanted to be, and unlike Lady, he'd hardly been human long enough even to consider taking on the form again. He was simply Ramble, a palomino stallion who had once been human and who for some time—a short while or maybe the rest of his life—might, if he chose, have a certain insight on human behavior.

Although it looked as though he might choose *not*. For he lowered his head again, bogging it, leaping into a back-arching buck and then another, squealing and grunting and charging a small circle with the pure physical expression of aggressive joy at shedding that human form. His second circle around he tried to entice Jess into the game, but she tucked her tail and haunches and tipped her head to warn him off with flattened ears; he veered away.

After a moment he approached her more courteously, waiting for permission to come all the way to her, to arch his neck over hers and most demurely nibble along the base of her mane. Flirting, but not strongly. Connecting.

Claiming.

It felt strange. Strange because Lady, sorting equine memory, could not remember a time since first becoming Jess that she'd had a simple, quiet social moment with a herd member. Strange because the Jess-voice in her head made mild protest, trying to draw her attention to Carey and to Jaime at Anfeald. But thinking of Carey made Lady think of blood and wrongness, and having Ramble's ministrations comforted her. And thinking of Jaime and Anfeald . . .

The hay bale beside them made a welcome distraction, and for a long while, that was as far as she got; she and Ramble fed together—she neatly, he by tearing away great chunks of hay and trying to work it into his mouth before he lost any of it to the mild wind. Lady ate until her stomach filled, twitching her withers against the irritating movement of a wet, unfamiliar braid and its burden, the round black thing Mark had attached to her. The courier pouch, as unfamiliar as it was.

The courier pouch. The one she had to take to Jaime. She wasn't ready to leave the hay yet, not for good, but she lifted her head to consider the trail to Anfeald.

The ground beneath them was sloped; that around them, rolling. The clay and limestone soil supported tough, scrubby bushes with stout thorns, faded brown to her eyes and with plenty of room to navigate between clumps. The bushes themselves reeked of goat and goat droppings; the damp, cool air told her about the copious hares that frequented the area, and brought her the fading scent of pursan—a predator cat not quite big enough to threaten a horse, but all the same not a creature Lady wanted to encounter. She eyed the trees on the opposite hill—stunted, bare-branched trees, just the thing for a medium-sized eater of things. She hoped, with the part of her that had learned to think more complexly since she'd added her human side to her makeup, to avoid that hill on the way to Anfeald. Beyond it, and who knows how many hills beyond that, mountains stabbed up at the sky like giant snow-capped teeth. She hoped, too, to avoid crossing such rough territory.

But she didn't know if they could.

Because she had no idea where they were, or how to reach Anfeald.

"I don't *know*," Dayna said, glaring at Carey, unable to dampen her annoyance even at his pale face and tormented expression, his features suddenly tight and a smear of blood on his shirt that led her glance to his hand. "You cut yourself," she said. "You'd better do something about it."

A cough rumbled in his chest. "I will," he told her.

"I don't *know*," Jaime said, glaring at Hon Chandrai. "I haven't authorized the use of any major magic, and Natt and Cesna are busy enough just keeping this hold secured and healthy. If you want to figure out who burst in on the eastern province, you're going to have to do it yourself."

Chandrai glared back at her. "We will," she told Jaime. "And you'd better hope we don't find you involved."

❧❧

"I don't know," Arlen said, staring with thoughtful but puzzled resignation at the hardened bloom of distortion by the edge of the narrow trail. Crowded by trees, darkened by shadow and early spring cloud-gloom, the spot had almost escaped his notice. "I think we're going to have to get involved. And sooner than I'd planned, at that."

Grunt bit the tender twiggy end off a tree branch and snorted wetly, not a comment Arlen found useful one way or the other.

Throughout Camolen, the meltdowns bloomed. Random blooms, some no larger than an apple, some big enough to flow across the horizon, engulfing all that stood in the way. Some met with old blooms, solidifying together in handshakes of startling vigor. Some made their own way. One small community became entirely circled, and immediately began rationing food while those within only hoped they lived long enough to starve to death.

Camolen knew.

Not the cause, not what to do about it, not how to stop it or in which direction they might run to escape it. But what had killed its wizards, what had left it without services, what had separated families and brought the daily life of its people to a terrifying standstill . . .

Camolen knew.

Chapter 23

Lady circled through the rolling hills, easing through the scrub, placing her feet carefully on the slick ground and keeping an eye out for the goats and their shepherd. The drizzle stopped; the clouds broke away into patches of sunshine. Bright, hot sunshine, a closer sky than she was used to. She stopped, closed her eyes, and let the warmth of it beat against her face, waiting for some internal signal, some tug that would tell her in which direction lay *home*.

Except a horse thrown from one world to another needed the chance to establish her sense of direction before she could call upon it. She knew which way lay east and west . . . but without an awareness of where she stood, not in which of those directions lay Anfeald.

Ramble followed along in her wake, never crowding her but never leaving much distance between them, happy to snatch at forming leaf buds, happy to be a horse again, happy simply to be with her. Now and then he came in close, resting his chin on her back before moving away.

She let him.

Eventually she led him back to the hay and they grazed at it like old pasture buddies, and then the sun was slipping down over the horizon opposite the toothy mountains. As darkness fell, she eased down to doze on her chest, legs curled cat-like to one side and her nose resting on the ground, upper lip drawn up just enough so her front teeth took the weight of her head.

Ramble moved in close, standing over her. Guarding for her.

She let him.

In the darkness, in her dozing state, she hunted for the Jess within her. For the human thinking that might sort out the details she'd noticed today and discern if not her actual location, the direction in which she ought to travel. Sometimes she could find that voice . . . sometimes it came to her in faint, simple directions. Now it was silent. Silent and grateful for the respite, imparting to Lady that this confused and wounded part of her wanted nothing but the solitude this form gave it.

Lady gave a resounding snort in response and climbed abruptly to her feet, shaking herself off and swishing her tail in brief annoyance. Ramble, startled awake, shied respectfully away; upon recovering, he arched his neck and nickered and came back to her all light on his feet, both proud and cautious. Reaching her, he touched his chin to her back, lips twitching; after a moment he lightly groomed her withers while she nibbled hay.

She let him.

Before the sun rose, they fell to the hay again, leaving only scattered remnants for the wayward goats, and when Lady lifted her head from the meal, she hesitated for only an instant . . . and then led them away from the mountains. She didn't know the mountains; she'd never seen them. As unfamiliar as the rest of the territory looked, the mountains were even more so . . . and horse-like, right or wrong, her decision was made. Soon enough she found a path, trodden more by petite cloven hooves than man or horse, softer ground to save their unshod feet. She took it, winding through the hills, heading down away from the sun, pausing every couple of hours to browse on what forage she could find, ever mindful that Ramble had never been a courier's horse, never been introduced to rough country.

She showed him the knack of tucking his quarters to go down steep hills, and of using crabbing sideways steps when steep ground got slick. She showed him river crossings, with slow careful movement against fast current and deep water—and once, how to swim without panic. She introduced him to the buddy system when the small black flies swarmed, he who had spent so much of his life in stalls and alone; they stood nose to tail and kept each other's faces clear of the pests as they dozed.

They bucked themselves awake in the cold mornings, rolled as day cooled into evening, and snatched burgeoning spring greenery along the way. And though Lady, standing with her head high as if she could see all the way to Anfeald, had disturbing flashes of *blood* and *Carey* and *urgency*, for the most part . . .

She was a horse. No human rules shaping her equine behavior, no human puzzlements deviling the Jess in her. Just she and Ramble and days on the hoof, steadily heading for more settled territory and roads she hoped would take her to Anfeald.

Ramble, for the first time in his life fulfilled with activity and interaction, ceased to aim his mouth at everything in sight, and had no chance to act up out of boredom. He stayed polite and respectful and even worshipful, and when Lady felt the first restless signs of her season coming on, he courted her.

She let him.

Every morning after Arlen ate whatever rude meal he had available—sometimes cold cheese and sausage, sometimes hot homemade mealcakes—he checked Grunt's back for tender spots and carefully saddled and loaded their gear. And every morning Grunt never failed to lift his head from whatever rude meal he had available—sometimes forage, sometimes hay—to cast Arlen the most reproachful look he could muster.

"It's not far now, Grunt," Arlen would tell him. "Not far at all."

It was always a lie. But he didn't think Grunt ever caught on.

"Give it time," Mark announced.

"That's all they said?" Dayna asked skeptically, eyeing Carey.

Carey himself said nothing, aside from a baleful glance at Wheeler—who very wisely refrained from the *I told you so* to which he might have laid claim. After a day at Marion General Hospital in an expensive health care system that Mark took for granted but Carey found foreign, offensive, and occasionally frightening, he was in no mood for *I told you so*. Especially when he hadn't wanted to go in the first place.

"Did they buy your story?"

"It would have helped if I had the faintest idea what flag football *is*," Carey said.

"A game—"

"You said. They wanted details. Concussive hemoptysis, they called it, and couldn't find any bruises, so they wanted details—they thought it might have been caused by some disease process and not a game."

Mark waved a dismissive hand. "I told them we'd gotten too manly and fire-snorting; they bought it. And the tests didn't show anything else."

"I would be astonished," Carey said with weary dignity, suppressing the now miserable ever-present impulse to cough simply because once he started, there'd be blood before he stopped, "if your health care tests could detect an expired composting spell."

"So they said give it time," Dayna repeated.

"And no more football, take it easy, report back if it gets worse or fails to get better, and follow up with my own doctor when I get back home," Carey said, adopting a dutiful tone.

Dayna gave him a dark look, blue eyes shadowed by her lowered brow and down-tilted head. "Home," she muttered. "I'm working on it."

They were two horses as if they'd never been anything else, and if Lady's message cannister hadn't rolled and bumped against her shoulder with her movement, she might have forgotten the complexity of her own nature.

A courier. On the job, and forging her way through remote, unfamiliar territory to reach her home stable. Avoiding hazards, avoiding people, letting Ramble claim her for his own—with Lady making their decisions and Ramble fully occupied making sure no other stallion had the chance to steal her away.

Given their isolation, he'd gotten a little desperate; she'd once seen him posturing to a baffled deer, and he filled the unfamiliar territory with ringing calls any time he scented a stray mining pony or a farmer's plow animal. He had no Jess-voice in his head, cautioning quiet— a voice that drove Lady to jog away at a ground-eating

pace no matter the terrain when he pulled such nonsense, until he had to choose between keeping his noise
and keeping up.

He always chose keeping up.

After a time the downhill travel leveled out, the
paths and trails turned to rutted roads—travelways
without anything but the most rudimentary spell protection, full of potholes and wheel ruts and blessed with
a centerline of thick, early-blooming wildflowers, most
of which were delicious. The trees grew taller and
thicker, and their tender tips tasted less acidic than
those over which Ramble had been making faces. Along
with the dried stems of the previous fall's grasses, they
began to find the first spears of new grass—and, by
now plagued by constant hunger, they slowed to search
out these greens. Once or twice upon passing farmland, Lady found ways to circumvent the fencing and
they snatched a clandestine meal among herds of cattle
which ignored them. Once or twice—more frequently,
now—they came upon areas of strange and contorted
landscape from which they bolted away with great
drama, returning to their original direction miles later
and with no ill effect.

After a time . . .

She lost her interest in Ramble's attentions, quite
abruptly no longer feeling the need. Ramble stopped
guarding her quite so jealously and began to treat her
more gently, more protectively—more warily, as well
he might any mare in foal.

And Lady was content. Despite the unending search
for enough food, the ribby look of her sides and the
ragged condition of her hooves, she was content.
Relentless travel aside, she was content. Content
enough that one day after too many days for a horse
to count, she looked at Ramble and looked at the
pleasant spring-fed glade through which they traveled

and she had the sudden impulse to stop. To stop traveling, to stay here and eat her fill day after day, swishing flies from Ramble's face and nibbling the itches at his withers, taking off into fits of sudden bucking play any time she pleased, and pretending not to notice when the small, battered, black cylinder taped and sewn to her mane finally fell off.

The horror of it hit her like a weighted quirt.

Blood. Carey. Arlen dead. Her friends in trouble. All of Camolen in trouble.

Depending on her.

She shied at nothing in the middle of the perfect glade, violently startling aside to race away with her tail clamped tight and her ears laid back. Ramble, sure they were under attack, startled in the opposite direction.

And Lady ran. Vaulting fallen branches and sudden dips, dodging thickets . . . she ran like a horse driven, unable to slow until finally she tired, failed to see a root hump, and tumbled, rolling over her shoulder and slamming up against a tree, her legs in the air like a bug on its back.

Noble courier mare.

Besieged by thoughts and emotions too complex for a horse to process or even outrun, she reacted instinctively to save her own sanity. She reached for the familiar touch of the spellstone braided into her upper mane and—

She changed.

So many days of living as a horse—for all practical purposes, a wild horse—had left its mark on her. Her skin stretched tightly over her ribs; her thick, coarse hair no longer hung evenly down her back but fell ragged, as when she'd first become Jess. Her tough feet felt worn and tired, her bare skin absurdly sensitive to the air and to the leaf mat beneath her back. And even human, she found herself so overcome with so many different emotions that she simply rolled over to her side, curled up, and cried. So much intensity to fit inside one frail human body . . . fury and fear and sorrow and worry and guilt, so much guilt . . .

And all the implications of the changes within herself. As Lady she'd known instinctively; even Ramble had known. As Jess she knew with both her heart and mind. She covered her low stomach with long fingers splayed out, found it as flat as ever. Too flat. But she knew what triggered that protective, possessive gesture.

That which she had wanted so badly. That which she'd thought to conceive as a woman, to carry as a woman, to bear as a woman.

The child she'd wanted—*they'd* wanted—but not of Carey. Never of Carey, never of any human.

She thought she'd known all along that this was the way it would have to be, and she'd been unable to face it. Unable to bear the conversation with Carey . . . just as she didn't know how she could tell Carey of this new life within her . . . this legacy of hers, and of the changespell that had brought her together with Ramble.

She wondered if he'd realize the irony of it . . . that this child, whatever form it took, had happened only because of Carey's own decision to change Ramble to a human for his own purposes—and then because of his inability to accept the limits she set when that change led to naught.

No answers. No easy new human life for Ramble. No understanding, not between Carey and Ramble, not between Carey and Jess.

Only between Jess and Ramble.

Exhausted, more so than she could ever remember, Jess slept. And when she woke, cold and stiff and cramped, she hunted through herself to find all her emotions drained for the moment, the storm faded down to something she could live with. More importantly, something *Lady* could live with. She studied the terrain, the types of trees, the soil, the roughly uneven ground, and put the observations in context with everything she'd seen since arriving so far from Anfeald. *Southeast.* Very east, to start with. And they'd traveled roughly west; time to add a northern slant, and see if she couldn't recognize the next main road they hit.

On the way to Anfeald. No more wavering, no more lingering in pleasantly perfect glades. Shivering now, Jess fixed her purpose in her mind, most firmly in her mind . . .

And triggered one of the changespells to take her back to Lady. To find Ramble . . . to find Anfeald. And maybe along the way to find herself.

Jaime lost track of the time—days and hours and weeks, all of which were subtly different from those of her own world.

She found it easier that way. Not because of the differences, but because it dulled the part within herself that noted the exact passage of time and tried to calculate the odds that Arlen was okay and yet had still not contacted anyone.

But Arlen wasn't stupid. If he—if *any*—of the Council wizards had survived, he could certainly figure just as well as she that his best chance of future survival—and of figuring out the mess in which Camolen found itself—was to hole up and play dead.

Just not this dead, Arlen. Not this long.

But then again, she wasn't paying attention to the time. She *wasn't*. She wasn't wondering why she hadn't heard anything from Carey, Dayna, and Jess, especially after the most recent arrival-magic over which she'd recently been questioned. She wasn't wondering why late winter had turned into spring and she still found herself alone here, running the hold with Natt and Cesna and Linton while the new Council—she'd never think of them as anything but the *new* Council—hid behind its secure walls in Kymmet and still, as far as anyone could tell, was no closer to understanding why the Council had died in the first place, or why even everyday spells now often went awry.

She didn't wonder about any of those things. She kept an eye on the pregnant mares, most of whom were so close to foaling they wore Camolen's spell equivalent of a foal monitor and spent their nights inside the foaling barn behind the hold while the year's maiden mare lived in the very stall from which Ramble and the others had left for Ohio. She tended her map, a project that—along with Anfeald's decently central location—had helped to turn the hold into a central courier hub of sorts. The place where people sent their news when they felt it was of general interest . . . and the place people came to get it. For Jaime with her map was the one to understand first that the new Council wasn't having any luck with understanding the meltdowns simply because they were never out and about with a chance to see one in process—and that they couldn't attempt a source trace until that happened.

Jaime was the one to realize that if the new Council *did* attempt a source trace, they probably wouldn't accomplish it anyway—not on a non-spell magical effect of such heretofore unknown properties. The people with those skills were dead.

She was one of the first to see the pattern when the communication and travel services problems changed from being a manpower problem—no one in place to run the upper levels of the dispatch and travel booth activity—to being a process problem—those who were now in place now encountered problems and

setbacks the system had evolved to avoid. Dependable
magic going wrong. People being blamed when magic
was the problem.

More was askew than just the meltdowns.

Most information, Jaime passed along freely. But
when she came to her own conclusions, when she saw
the patterns no one else had yet seen . . . those, she
kept to herself. Let it become general knowledge when
someone else figured it out—someone like a precinct
lander, whose job was to shepherd and protect the
people in the first place. Jaime, seeing what she saw,
had no desire to face the questions that would come
if she mentioned what seemed to her to be obvious.

So she watched the mares, tended the map, kept
copies of general messages for disbursement to anyone who wanted them, and—possibly most important
of all—kept Arlen's puzzled cats company. As much as
they adored Jess, as much as they slyly worshiped
Arlen, pretending it was coincidence that they ended
up wherever he did, they'd ever only disdainfully tolerated Jaime . . . until now.

Now they slept on her face.

Even when she came up to Arlen's quarters only
long enough to fling herself on the couch with her
booted legs hanging over the end, resting her eyes
against another round of message sorting and copying,
they managed to find their way to her, oozing along
the windowsill, creeping out from the bedroom. . . .

The older black-and-white cat had always been a
shy little thing; she merely sat on the back of the
couch and stared at Jaime. The jester of a calico
inevitably ended up on her chest, paws tucked, so
close to Jaime's face that his breath tickled the soft
spot under her chin.

And so he was when Jaime heard Cesna approaching
the open door to Arlen's rooms, quiet in her soft

slippers, hesitating at the entrance . . . taking in a soft breath, not bringing herself to interrupt, trying again—

The cats leapt from their self-appointed vigil over Jaime, hurrying to the entrance with no trace of stand-offish waffling; the calico tuned up his conversational voice and put it to good use.

Not Cesna.

Jaime's eyes flew open.

She couldn't say anything at first; she couldn't do anything but gape.

Jess.

Jess in hay-specked winter clothes from her changing stall, her feet bare and battered, her hair an unruly tangle, the bones of her face strong beneath gaunt features, her eyes carrying a touch of panic and uncertainty. Enough that Jaime didn't act on her rush of joy, didn't bound up from the couch to throw her arms around the friend whose reappearance meant Jaime herself was no longer so alone.

She levered herself upright on the couch, swinging her legs one by one from over its arm to a normal sitting position. And she said quietly, "Jess, it's so good to see you. Will you come in?"

Even in her first few days as a woman, Jess hadn't shown such hesitation, such wariness. She'd been full of curiosity and trust and frustration, desperate to find Carey and to make herself understood . . . but not this wildness. She took a step into the room, a single step, and held out a trembling hand—one of broken nails, bruises, and grime. It took Jaime a moment to realize what else she looked at within that hand—a film cannister. Black, but covered with worn silver duct tape to which stuck a proliferation of dark dun hairs.

Jaime stood and held out her own hand, making it simple; she would not chance a move that might scare this flighty version of Jess away; Jess would have to

come to her. And after a hesitation, Jess did. Enough
of a hesitation that Jaime worked a few swift facts into
place. Chandrai's latest visit provided the key—the
information that someone had worked Arlen's world-
travel spell in the eastern fringes of Camolen. And here
was Jess, as wild as a horse from the range, offering
a film cannister. A message cannister, battered and
worn and long carried.

It was all she could do to keep herself from burst-
ing into questions—when did you get back, why are you
alone, what happened to the others, what did you find
out—but she had no doubt they'd chase Jess off as
surely as any sudden movement. So she accepted the
cannister Jess tipped into her hand, worked the tape free
with the help of her pocket knife, and pulled out a
much-folded and rolled but well-preserved piece of
paper, printed on both sides in various fonts and then
covered with clear packing tape in crude lamination.

As Jess eased back a step, Jaime sat down and sorted
out what she had. Short comments from everyone
who'd gone to Ohio, each in a different tiny font—and
one from her brother. Hard enough to read in English
on this side of the travel spell, never mind such com-
pact, intense notes. Notes confirming that the message
board system no longer worked, that the farm was
doing fine and that Mark missed her and worried about
her, that Ramble had told them nothing of import—
but that Suliya recognized one of the men about whom
Jaime herself had managed to warn them, and he'd
come via SpellForge, provided by FreeCast. *Watch out
for them*, Carey had said. *Don't trust them.*

As if she hadn't figured that part out for herself,
even without a name to put on her odd visitors.

Still, it was something to pass along to Chandrai as
soon as she could. SpellForge, as unlikely as it seemed,
had some involvement in whatever was happening.

She smoothed the taped-up paper over her thigh, tasting bitter disappointment high in her throat and knowing she'd hoped for more. Had hoped, without admitting it even to herself, that Ramble had seen Arlen escape harm.

The wait wasn't over yet, then. Maybe it would never be over. Maybe she'd always lift her head, half expecting to see him whenever someone entered the room she occupied.

She took a steadying breath and turned her attention back to Jess. Wild Jess, still looking as if she might bolt at any moment. "Jess," Jaime said. "Are you all right?" She opened a hand in a welcoming gesture, one without any demand in it at all, just an invitation; Jess edged closer, not a direct approach—but when she made up her mind, she came all the way, kneeling by the couch as was her habit of old, a searching expression on her face as she hunted for words and didn't find them. Finally she just shook her head.

"It's okay," Jaime said. "We'll get things sorted out. It doesn't have to happen right this minute."

And to her surprise, Jess heaved a sigh—a very horse-like sigh with a flutter of noise at the back of her throat—put her head on the couch, and almost instantly fell asleep.

Jess woke to the gentle sensation of someone scratching between her shoulder blades, so like the congenial nibble of teeth at her withers that her first sleepy thought was *Ramble* until she startled herself by realizing that in thinking it at all, she'd shown herself human. Not Lady, as she'd been for so many days. Jess. Not Ramble beside her, but Jaime. As much as anyone, Jaime could read Jess's equine body language; as much as anyone, she could respond on that level.

And so she'd given Jess space, and not pushed her

when she was on the verge of bolting, so closed in by
stone and her own human body here in the hold. She'd
just made space for her, and Jess had moved into it,
all but ready to collapse with one of the fits of exhaustion that had dogged her recently. And now she made
the waking up easy.

"Better?" Jaime asked as Jess lifted her head, shoving
her hair out of her face. It didn't get lank and oily, not
as Carey's did if he failed to wash it, but it was grimy
and she was suddenly acutely aware of how well the
rest of her matched its condition.

"Better," she said, and she was. Not as shaky as when
she'd stood in the doorway, her equine companion of
the past days lurking in one of the far pastures, her
nerve threatening to desert her. Never had she stayed
so long as Lady since she'd become Jess. Never had
she been so long from people, not since Carey had first
watched her stand on shaky foal legs. And while her
world changed within her, she'd also watched it change
without. Watched the distorted areas grow more frequent, watched the strange patterns of activity on the
roads. Nothing was the same . . . not Camolen, not the
people she knew within it, not her own self.

As a creature who found solace in habit, Jess found
it all disturbing. Enough to shake her already rattled
confidence.

Enough so she almost hadn't made it up those stairs
to find Jaime at all.

But now . . . "Better," she said again, and nodded.

"Good," Jaime said. "Can we talk, then?" She waved
the taped-up paper gently through the air. "This leaves
me with a lot of questions."

Jess pulled herself up on the couch, delighted at the
immediate appearance of both cats. The calico turned
himself upside-down in her lap and gave her a look
of surprised annoyance when she didn't immediately

commence to roughing him up. The older cat, more demure, eased onto the back of the couch and purred. Occupied but not distracted by them, Jess said, "There are no answers to give you. The paper says everything we know."

"It doesn't say why you're here and they're not. Why you're the only one who came back."

"I'm not the only one," Jess said, wondering if she imagined the slight sting of accusation in Jaime's voice. "Ramble came back. I *brought* him back. They turned him human to learn what he knew, and he knew nothing. He suffered there. I brought him back."

"I can see why *you* came back," Jaime said, impatience on her face along with a certain ingrained weariness. Her carefree hairstyle had grown out in shiny, deep brown waves; now it merely looked shaggy, no longer spunky. But she didn't need to look spunky. She had a confidence in her place here that she hadn't carried when Jess had left. She was no longer a guest . . . she was a working part of this hold. One with authority—and she was trying not to use it on Jess, but she wanted those answers.

Jess didn't have them all. But she had some of them. She ignored the growl of her stomach to say, "Other people came from Camolen, like you warned. They tried to take us away." The notes she'd brought from Ohio had said that much, even mentioned Wheeler by name. "Wheeler said the others were safer to stay. And Dayna said she couldn't make the spells work for so many without more time. She had to use extra magic so Ramble and I could return. She didn't have enough."

"So they didn't come back. But they've had the chance—you've been here for—?" She scrunched her face slightly with the question.

"I don't know," Jess admitted. "Many days. The

magic was . . . skewed. It returned us to an edge part
of Camolen. Far away."

"No wonder you're so tired," Jaime said. Jess knew
there was another reason, but didn't speak
up . . . suddenly realized she wasn't sure she'd speak up
at all, not about that. Jaime picked the cannister up
from her lap and turned it over in her hand. "At least
you made it. We've got some parts of Camolen we can't
reach any more."

"What *is* it?" Jess asked. "All these days gone
by . . . doesn't anyone know what the bad spots are?
What happened to the Council?"

"The meltdowns," Jaime mused, and then shook her
head. "No, no one knows what's causing them. Thanks
to the information you brought, I've already initiated
a message to the Council, telling them SpellForge is
involved somehow. And I'll tell the peacekeepers—not
that they're not already maxed out just trying to keep
up with the riots that have started up along with
everything else."

Jess didn't know *maxed out*, but she got the gist of
it. And riots . . . "Things are bad enough already," she
said. "Why would people make them worse?"

Jaime shrugged. "Fear, mostly."

Jess couldn't help the frown at the grown-familiar
frustration within herself. The inability to understand
how people hurt each other. Frightened horses would
run. They'd band together for protection. They wouldn't
destroy things and strike out at each other. "I'm going,"
she said suddenly.

Jaime didn't hide her surprise, the widening of her
Mark-like eyes. "Going?"

"I left Ramble in one of the pastures. I told him
I'd come back."

"Jess, I don't . . ." Jaime hesitated, held out a hand
in what looked like supplication. "You just got here.

I've missed you, I've missed you *all*. We need you here. I don't understand—"

"Why I would go back to be with a horse? As a horse?" Anger seeped out, but it wasn't at Jaime, wasn't fair to make Jaime think it was. She watched Jaime closely, trying to gauge her expression and reaction. "I thought I understood some things about being human, but I didn't. I thought I understood some things about being friends . . . about being *lovers*—but I didn't. I can no longer be certain of my friends, and without that, I am not sure of the point in being human. In trying so hard to learn what it's all about." She shook her head; Jaime had gone from looking puzzled to frowning in a most unhappy way. "I need time," Jess said, then nodded at the cannister that had been bumping against her shoulder for so long and bore every sign of it. "I have done what I can. Now I will go do something for me. And for Ramble. *He* needs me, too. If you let us, we will use the furthest fields, the ones Carey was going to leave fallow this year. If not . . . we will find a place."

"Let you!" Jaime cried, comprehension beginning to dawn. She'd lost Arlen . . . in a way, she was about to lose Jess. "Of course I'll *let* you! I can't believe—I wish—" She stopped, clenching her hand around the film cannister, a hand that only moments ago would have reached for Jess instead, still wanted to reach for her now. But Jess had put distance between them with her words. Had removed Jaime's ability to take for granted their relationship, just as Carey and Dayna had removed Jess's ability to rely on their support and presence. Finally Jaime blurted, "But what about Carey?"

Jess didn't react. Or rather, she tried not to. But the calico was not to be fooled; he sensed her sudden tension and leapt lightly away, boxing the ears of the little black-and-white cat on the way. Carefully, Jess said, "Carey isn't here. And if he makes it back . . ." She stopped, took a considering breath, and wished the cat were still in her lap, giving her his warmth and affection. "There are some things he never accepted about who I am. He tried to pretend it wasn't so, but . . . I don't think he'll want anything to do with me now."

Jaime didn't understand. Not with that look on her face, the taken-aback, eyebrows drawn together over worried eyes. She might have been about to ask . . . but she hesitated on her words, and what eventually came out was, "Will you at least eat something? Rest again before you go? You look done in, Jess."

She *was* done in. But she was also through traveling, and could spend her days in a secure field that, not so far in the future, would hold more grass than she and Ramble could eat in a summer of grazing. She would be all right. *They* would be all right. Still, she gave Jaime a thoughtful, faraway look and said, "Eat something, yes. I have a sudden want for those spicy chicken parts you taught the cook to make."

She didn't think she could have startled Jaime any more . . . but without removing that startled gaze from Jess—expecting to be corrected at any time, no doubt, by this friend who eschewed meats and strong seasonings—Jaime contacted the kitchen and ordered the Buffalo chicken wings. Jess ate two servings.

And then she left, cantering out of the stable on worn black hooves, the cannister no longer bumping at her shoulder.

Chapter 24

Arlen stopped short in front of Grunt, who promptly ran up against his back, jamming his heavy shoulder into Arlen's kidney. Arlen gave an *oof* of both pain and surprise, and snapped, "Pay attention, Grunt."

Grunt whuffled the bemused noise of a horse who's been woken from a nap and nibbled absently at Arlen's uppermost arm. Even affectionately, one might say.

But Arlen was in no mood to notice, not with the landscape before him warped so sickeningly. He shook Grunt off and draped the lead rope around a tree branch, automatically taking the opportunity to scrape the mud from the sides and bottoms—and sometimes the tops—of his boots, using the nearest handy rock.

As an afterthought, he picked up the rock and hefted it into the distorted area before him. It landed with a hollow, mildly reverberating *thonk*—the wrong kind of noise altogether for a rock hitting soft spring ground—and rolled until it hit a jagged protrusion that Arlen didn't even try to identify. Maybe it had once been a tree; maybe a rabbit. For all he knew, maybe a chunk of cloud; there was no telling how high the damage rose.

Around him, the rest of the landscape didn't seem to notice anything amiss at all. A small flock of steel-grey birds fluttered in the brush to his left, the males flashing the brilliant orange of their underwing display in an attempt to impress the world in general. The air was still, the sun warm, and there were even sections of the trail—the edges and high points—that held firm beneath his feet. The woods around him had a familiar feel, with bud-studded branches in accustomed silhouettes and the bark patterns he was used to, as well as the varying but generally easy to navigate terrain—gulches he could easily avoid, shallow creeks that cut mild beds through soft soil and stopped at hard bedrock, glittering in miniature rapids over a profusion of water-rounded stones.

Anfeald Woods, or coming close.

But such normality was becoming harder and harder to find. The damage before him loomed large and impressive, but he'd realized only this morning that it was possible to stop at any random point along the trail, scan the woods, and find a spot of distortion. Small ones, barely discernible against the cheerful disorder of the woods . . . but they were there. And the large areas were becoming harder and harder to circumvent, forcing him to take Grunt far out of their way . . . although if he'd had a better sense of direction, he might well have wasted less time finding the trail again.

More than once he'd wondered if he'd be able to reach Anfeald at all. Not because of the hardship— he was tougher and leaner than he'd ever been, and if the oft-mucky footing of early spring slowed him, the warming days made up for the annoyance—or because he'd been accosted by many more men of the same ilk as the ill-fated fellow who'd found him so many small towns ago.

No, it was as he pondered the distressed pockets of landscape, as he skirted the edges of them, now sometimes running into two or three obviously separate occurrences with overlapping borders, that he wondered if he'd make it home. Sooner or later, he'd find himself trapped. And sooner or later, upon finding an actively distorting area, he'd have to try to follow the instigating energy to its source . . . thus giving himself away to whoever wanted him out of the way.

Supposing they were still looking at all.

Were they smart, they'd be turning their attention to the distortions, as was all of Camolen. But somehow he doubted they'd see it that way. "Too convenient for me," he said to Grunt, who paused from his browsing to give Arlen a doubtful look. Arlen turned his attention back to this latest roadblock and felt common sense give way before a sudden surge of anger. *I want to go* home, *burn it!* Home to Jaime if she still somehow waited for him, home to his familiar workshop and his defenses, where he could throw himself into solving this problem whose solution so obviously eluded whoever now ran the Council. Home to his frequent and good-natured arguments with Carey over matters between landers and wizards, home to Jess's natural ebullience, her touchingly open nature, the amusing sly looks she cast at Arlen whenever she meant to tease Carey.

Home to the familiar—which none of *this* was. Not the travel, the vulnerability, the inability to use the magic that had long ago become second nature—

Damn whoever's behind this. "Damn them all to the

lowest hell!" he said with such abrupt vehemence that
Grunt stopped chewing altogether and Arlen realized
how loud he'd been in the otherwise pleasant activity
of the woods. He gave the gelding a pat, and thus
reassured, Grunt went back to wrapping his flexible lips
around the stubbiest of sprouting greens. Ruefully,
Arlen told him, "If I do enough shouting, I won't have
to use magic for them to find us. Whoever *they* are
in the first place."

He knew the look of an enforcement agent when
he saw one. He just didn't know who'd sent his. Too
bad Grunt had trampled the man so thoroughly.

Or, remembering the helplessness of being drugged—
over drugged—and the intent in the big man's eye,
maybe not too bad at all. Maybe . . . just right.

It still left him in this mess. It left Camolen in this
mess, with only Arlen remaining as a Council-level
wizard, and unable to use his skills to help either
himself or his people. Although . . .

He reached through his open coat front and dug
around in the deep baggy pockets of the horrible
orange tunic he'd acquired way back near Amses—he
fervently hoped to wear the thing to shreds before
anyone he knew actually saw him in it—and pulled out
a handful of cheap spellstones. He'd intended to get
closer to home—perhaps to *be* at home—when he
experimented with these, but now he thought perhaps
he had a better chance of getting there if he did a little
poking around on the spot.

He already knew that raw magic incited the distur-
bances, even once they seemed to have solidified and
gone dormant. He couldn't use his own signature-
ridden magic to experiment with small spells, but . . .

He picked out a spellstone he thought he recalled
as being designed to enhance one's sexuality—utter
nonsense, since those kinds of spells had to be

customized for the recipient, but people did ever
hope—and triggered it.

The stone produced a small wash of token magic—
thin magic to Arlen's magical sense, with a tinny one-
note feel to a man accustomed to producing orchestral
magic himself. Grunt, too, felt it, and regarded Arlen
with a sudden hopeful interest that alarmed Arlen
enough so he took a few steps aside. "One of the
reasons I like cats," he said pointedly to Grunt, "is that
they seldom hump your leg."

But he didn't lose track of the purpose of the
experiment, even as Grunt briefly pawed the ground
in his frustration, gave up, and returned to his favorite pastime of pulling food into his mouth.

Arlen could have pawed the ground in frustration,
too, for as the spellstone went dark, the disturbed area
didn't so much as ripple. "Not that anything else has
made sense lately," he said, ignoring the frequency with
which he'd been offering asides to the gelding. Wizards were supposed to be eccentric, especially theoretical specialists like himself. Everyone said so.

Then again, only a theoretical wizard was likely to
have the ability to do what he tried next. Choosing a
spellstone he believed was meant to offer a hokey
greeting appropriate to new parents, he tossed it at the
disturbed area and invoked it in mid-flight.

An image appeared above its travel arc, glowing with
purples for congratulations and gold for luck but looking subtly *wrong* somehow; he couldn't read the words
against the backdrop of melted reality, and then when
the active spellstone landed, he didn't have the chance
to try—for the melted reality spasmed in reaction,
reaching for the stone, enfolding it, warping the colors into the swirl of mixed landscape hues.

Arlen tensed, taking a few steps back and ready to
run, but once the spellstone had been engulfed, the

warping activity ceased, leaving the distortion with new splots and globs of bright color that should have faded as soon as the spellstone discharged . . . and didn't.

Arlen frowned at the mess, rubbed a finger down the mustache he didn't have, and muttered, "Well, *that* wasn't right." He searched the spellstones piled in his hand, poking them aside with his finger until he found a similar one—meant for the newly partnered, but close enough. Same gaudy colors, same bright message . . . he triggered it, this time knowing it wouldn't affect the disturbed area from here and giving all his attention to the spell itself.

Words hung in the air, incomplete and sagging, the colors uneven and the pithy message hard to read. On a quick hunch—this was his strength, this troubleshooting process—he moved a step closer to the disturbed area, and watched the cheery greeting fall apart completely, scattering into illegible lumps of quickly fading color.

No wonder the new Council hadn't been able to get anything but the most basic of services up and running again. Whatever this effect was, wherever it came from, it gobbled up raw magic like candy, thriving on it; it grabbed conventional magic only with the most direct of contact. But even in disdaining conventional magic, it interfered with it, breaking down spell structures and distorting the results. Arlen looked askance at Grunt, realizing he was perhaps luckier than he'd first suspected at the benign results of that sexual enhancement spell.

And then the questions crowded in. What if he ran all these experiments on an actively warping area, what then? That, too, was something he could try without revealing himself to those who watched for his magical signature; following the activity to its source was not, and would have to wait as long as possible—

although initiating either experiment depended on finding an area of actively warping reality.

Arlen dumped the spellstones back into his unpleas-
antly orange pocket and closed the coat around himself, fastening the toggles in the cooling afternoon.
Ahead of him lay the huge area of disturbance, one
he wanted to skirt before sundown. A glance behind
showed two other easily identified areas of nastiness,
small enough to wrap his arms around if he'd had any
such desire. To the side he found a fist-sized spot, a
blackish blot on which one of the male birds perched,
flashing his underwings for all to see.

He came to the grim realization that he'd have much
less trouble finding an active warp than he liked to
admit.

Home.

"I'm trying," he said to Jaime. But only Grunt heard
him.

"I'm *trying*," Dayna said, fighting an overwhelming
load of guilt and pressure as she faced the impatience
of her friends. Well, minus Mark, who was at work,
and plus Wheeler, whom she'd come to appreciate
more and more in a visual sense—not quite so bland
as he'd seemed upon first glance—but whom she would
never call a friend.

At least they always knew just where he stood.
Repeated friend-or-foe spells yielded just the same
results as the first, convincing her that while he was
hardly on their side, when he intended to work against
them, they'd know it.

"I'm trying," she repeated, with less vehemence and
more despair. "If *you'd* ever tried to deconstruct a
spellstone—"

How many days had passed, and still they sat here
in Ohio? Wheeler was the only one who seemed at ease

with it, seemed to think it was the best course. Safest for them. He'd pitched in as they opened up the end of the barn after Ramble's departure, standing by with Carey and the hose while Mark charred the remains of his partner with a propane torch and then passed the otherwise inexplicable mess off as fire damage.

Watching them had given Dayna the cold grue; Mark's face had been pasty and tense, displaying all his awareness that the inexplicable mess itself had once been a human being. Carey had been in grim and determined mode, and Wheeler . . .

It was impossible to tell what Wheeler was feeling. They might know his intent, they might know his truthfulness . . . they never knew his feelings.

Even now, with Carey chafing to go home on one side and Suliya in a distinctly resentful mood on the other, Wheeler sat on the couch with his ankle crossed over his knee, his hands laced together over his belt, as serene as if they discussed plans for a trip into Columbus and not across worlds to their Camolen home.

Home. For she was homesick as she'd never been upon leaving her snug little house between Waldo and Marion, the musty, buttoned-up house that was still in her name but which she knew she'd soon sell. Unlike Jaime—who had a life she loved here and a man she loved there—Dayna had no great conflict, nothing pulling her back to the life with which she'd started.

And now she wanted to go home.

She pulled her legs up to sit cross-legged in the half-open recliner, the only one of them small enough to do so without overlapping the confines of the chair, and buried her face in her hands, momentarily overwhelmed with the situation. The things she'd have to accomplish . . . the odds against her ability to do so. The people counting on her . . .

Especially the people counting on her.

"I don't understand," Carey said. Of all of them, he needed to get back to Camolen—back where Anfeald's healers understood his needs and could deal with the new problem. As Marion General's doctors had promised, he'd stopped coughing up blood; the concussive hemoptysis was healing on its own . . . but never quite all the way. Even now Carey gave his little undertone of a cough before continuing. "Why are you deconstructing Jaime's spare travel spellstone at all?"

"Bootin' good question," Suliya said, casting Dayna a resentful glance. "I've had about enough of this— you won't let me go exploring, you won't let me go home—and I *know* you've made new storage stones. Those egg things glow enough to keep me up at night."

"The fiber-optic stones. They're great—they hold a hell of a lot more magic than the crystal-cut stones," Dayna said, lifting her head with brief enthusiasm at that accidental find. If she thought they could get back into the New Age shop without being chased out with brooms and fire extinguishers, she'd grab up half a dozen more of the things. But then again . . . storage space wasn't the problem. She had enough stones. She had enough magic siphoned into them, and no wish to struggle through the process again.

The problem was what she'd learned as she was doing it.

The increasing static.

Her increasing concern about spelling them into unknown territory.

"Great," Carey said flatly, echoing Dayna's word. "Then we have the magic to boost the spells we came with."

"I—" Dayna looked at them all—the impatience, the sulk, and the cool distraction, and finally said it out loud. "I'm not sure it's safe to use those spells.

Whatever's happening in Camolen . . . it's getting worse. It took me three sessions to fill the storage stones, and I could feel the difference each time. I really think we should try to arrive at Anfeald. And the only way I know to do that is to pick apart the spell Arlen gave Jaime that would take her there."

Suliya gave her a narrow-eyed look. "Ay," she said, "you saying we might be *stuck* here?"

Unexpectedly, Wheeler let his crossed ankle fall to the ground, leaning forward a little to join the conversation. "What's spelling in Camolen will pass."

"You *believe*," Carey said, his voice pointed.

Wheeler shrugged. "Yes. I believe."

"I don't want to end up stuck here because you believe *wrong*," Suliya said. She pushed herself out of the couch, quite obviously distancing herself from Wheeler, and paced the living room to frown at the black fireplace insert, even giving it a little kick. "If things are getting worse, we should try to go back *now*." She turned around to glare at Dayna. "I want to go back *now*."

"Before it's too late," Carey said, but his words didn't hold the conviction they might have. He exchanged a glance with Dayna, gauging her reaction, and then looked away. He'd seen it—she didn't know if it might already be too late.

Suliya knew them both well enough by now; she read the exchange and her sepia-toned skin flushed darker. "You burnin' well ought to have said something before things got this bad!"

Miserably, defensively, Dayna said, "I only filled the last of the stones yesterday—it's terrifying work, in case you hadn't noticed. And our friend Wheeler has made plenty of noise about taking it slow. As soon as I realized how bad it'd gotten, I started working on the deconstruction. And I wanted to have an idea of how it was going before I talked to you all!"

"I still believe you should go slow," Wheeler said. "But now . . . I won't stop you if you try to go back. It's been long enough."

The others hardly paid any attention to him. Suliya crossed her arms and kept her glare on Dayna. "If it's so rootin' hard to deconstruct this thing, make up your own!"

Wheeler gave her a look that might have been impressed . . . or it might have been disapproving. Hard to tell. He said, "I'm really surprised your father let that mouth come out of his household."

"Burn off," Suliya told him, sparing him only the merest of glances. "I wouldn't be here if I wasn't a disappointment to him in more ways than you can count. Then again, he's turned out to be a real rootin' disappointment to me, too, so I guess we're even."

Dayna was glad for the respite of their exchange; it gave her the chance to come up with words in response to Suliya's demand instead of her initial gape-mouthed astonishment and anger, although Carey's brow was still slightly raised from his own reaction. *Make up a spell.* Right. "Suliya," she said, unable to stop the words from coming out between clenched teeth, "Arlen is Camolen's best theoretical wizard. I can cast a spell I've learned from his work, I can put it into a spellstone, but I damn sure can't come up with the same thing on my own. And raw magic—that's sure not something I want to count on for world travel. We'd probably get there—and we'd *probably* look like Wheeler's ex-partner."

"Raw magic," Wheeler said, looking distinctly uncomfortable. *A first.* But whatever was on his mind, he didn't say it.

Probably just as scared as everyone else on Camolen when it came to using the spell technique. Dayna made a little face at him, too distracted to do it right, too aware of Suliya's anger turning to true dismay and fear.

"That's it, then," Suliya said, her voice hardly more than a whisper; she sank back onto the stove. "Here's where we stay."

"Unless I'm right about the interference passing," Wheeler said.

But Carey just looked at Dayna. Full of understanding, of comprehension about the race they ran—to deconstruct the spell and reconfigure Dayna's spells to land them within Anfeald Hold before the magical static grew so bad it was foolish to try even that much. He said, "If there's anyone in this room more stubborn than I am, it's you. You'll get us there."

Dayna said, "I'm trying."

Jaime finished crosshatching an area of her Camolen map and cast a glance back at Linton, who consulted his list. "North of Kymmet," he said, standing on the other side of Carey's desk where he could keep an eye out for incoming riders in the job room. "Where the Kymmet-Dryden Road splits to loop around Dryden Lake. The whole intersection is out, and it takes in that little jut of the lake, plus seven acres south and ten east. The report is two days old."

Jaime made careful notations in erasable pencil, then picked up the red penstick and marked in the area, noting the date of the sighting along its border. "That does it for Dryden," she said, all too familiar with the hard knot of dread in her stomach. "Anyone who knows the territory can still get in or out, but the roads are gone."

Natt's voice held the slightest tremble of despair. "That does it for a lot of communities. Look west to Gioncanna—it's been surrounded for days. For all we know, it's been *engulfed*."

Jaime took a step back, taking in the patchwork of red overlaying the map, seeing the results of this session . . . the steadily shrinking clear areas. The detailed map of Anfeald in the job room looked no better. Suddenly overwhelmed, she gave the pencil a flippant toss into the air; it landed on the floor and broke with a snap. "For all we know, *most* of Camolen is engulfed. None of these reports is more recent than two days, and the dispatch is useless." She hadn't even attempted to return the static-filled missive from Suliya's family, a peremptory demand for a response on their wayward daughter's status. Plenty of people were wondering about their families right now, and Jaime had no answers to offer, not even if the wording of the message had left her with an uneasy feeling that it had actually been a threat. It didn't matter; even their considerable influence couldn't overcome a magical natural disaster. "The only reason Chandrai hasn't been here to yell at me recently is because she can't *get* here."

"Jaime—"

"No." Jaime cut Natt off with a slash of her hand through the air. "That's enough. I'm not sending any more of our people out there." God, she didn't want Jess-as-Lady out there, either, running at liberty with the furthest fallow pasture as home base. But Lady knew to avoid the meltdowns . . . and from the state she'd been in when she'd delivered the notes from Ohio, the worst thing Jaime could do would be to close her in that pasture.

Besides, who knew. *That pasture* might be the very next place to be hit.

"They know not to use magic on the road," Linton started, bringing her attention back to their couriers— but subsided at the sharp shake of Jaime's head.

"*Everyone* knows not to use magic near the

meltdowns by now," she said. "But they keep cropping up, and they keep growing. I don't want any of our couriers caught out there, away from home and circled by meltdowns. Everyone who's in Anfeald stays in Anfeald." She gave the two men a look—a challenge, really—to check for resistance, for signs they'd fight this turning-point decision.

There were none.

Linton's long features, recently set in perpetual grimness, looked only grimmer. And Natt—eating under the stress and plumper than he'd been even a handful of days earlier—rubbed a hand over the balding area of his head and said tentatively, "If I may suggest—"

"Please," she said, and meant it. The more ideas other people offered her, the less she had to come up with on her own.

Not that any of her own ideas had done them any good. Not really. Made things easier, in a way—kept them informed, kept them feeling like they were doing something right up until this point when it became clear that nothing they'd done or *could* do would make any difference at all—but in the end, had not a whit of effect on the end results.

He said, "We're taking for granted that because *we* know not to use magic next to a meltdown, and that *we* know only the simplest spells are reliable anymore, *everyone* does. But not everyone uses magic as often as those of us here, or couriers who routinely rely on map lights and night glows. If we're going to draw our people back, then I think we should use them within Anfeald for as long as we can. Spread the word to people who lost dispatch access and never regained it, and who might never have heard any of the warnings at all."

Linton looked at Jaime, his interest piqued. "That's

a good one, Jaime. All the couriers know Anfeald well enough to have a good fallback if they find their way blocked."

Jaime knuckled her lip, and wondered in a strangely remote aside when on earth she'd picked up that habit. Natt was right. They'd made assumptions; they'd been forced to make assumptions, with all their manpower committed to carrying information on the large scale, dealing with Camolen's macrostructure.

Camolen didn't *have* a macrostructure. Not anymore.

"Good call," she said finally. "No one goes out without at least a day's worth of food and water, though. And we'll revisit the decision twice a day." She rubbed a hand over her hair, scrubbing it into complete disarray and not caring; the edge of Carey's desk seemed to come up and meet her rump. "I don't know who we're kidding," she said. "No one knows what's happening. No one knows how to stop it. No one knows how many people have died . . . or whether we'll *all* die before this is over. We're not doing anything but keeping ourselves busy until then."

From somewhere, Natt mustered a reassuring firmness . . . or what was meant to be one. The newly habitual uncertainty in his voice diluted his own effectiveness. "We have to trust that the Council has made breakthroughs since the last time we had contact," he said. "Even now, they may be spelling a solution . . . they may have even started clearing up some of the damage. This is *their* job, not ours. We have to trust them to do it."

Jaime bent from the waist, scooping up the broken pencil without lifting her weight from the desk. "The thing is," she said heavily, "I don't." Not without Arlen.

"It's all we have left," Linton said. "We do our best to get the people through. We do what we *can* do. And we trust the Council to do the rest."

Jaime said, "I'll try."

Chapter 25

Lady ran the far pasture with Ramble, making no effort other than that of being a horse. No messages to deliver, no responsibilities other than that to herself and the tiny being growing within her who as of yet made few demands and offered no restrictions. Almost a year before Lady the mare would foal, and her Jess part kept her muted reaction to herself.

Ramble ran by her side, content with his herd of one, still exploring this new existence—one neither he nor Lady had ever had before. Two horses following their own rhythms, unimpeded by human rules—even if the human rules were ever in the background, an ineffable but permanent part of Lady's nature. Where Ramble had learned fewer rules and learned them badly, she woke from naps with the phantom feel of Carey's hand on her withers, his whispered *good job* in her ear. She flashed on her memories of his white-faced astonishment, staring at his own blood.

Then Jess would come to the fore, fretting and worrying and wanting to *do*. To *fix*. To change, and let the human side of herself somehow make things better.

But Carey was nowhere in Camolen, and Lady knew it. She left the Jess part behind by charging over the rolling hills, inciting Ramble to bucking spurts that carried them away from Anfeald.

When they visited the pasture, they had food—early grass, hay, and daily grain. When they left, no one tried to stop them. Not even the unknown humans they saw along the paths they trotted; everyone seemed too busy, too distracted, to care about two loose horses. Lady watched the couriers come and go, and knew she could be part of it if she wanted.

She didn't.

But their freedom shrank anyway. The bad spots, the ones that had killed Arlen and terrified Ramble . . . the meltdowns Lady had seen multiply during their long journey home to Anfeald . . . they'd followed her here. They'd settled in for good, and spread themselves so thickly over the land that she and Ramble were forced into ever more circuitous routes to reach their favorite places—the point of land jutting out over an old creek bed where they could look over the countryside, standing in the ever-present breeze and thus free of the spring gnats. The deep pool down in the creek itself, where Ramble shoved his head in up over his eyeballs to snort bubbles in the water and where Lady established a ritual roll, splashing and churning and rising up wickedly pleased with herself. The deer path that gave them the excuse to tuck and jump fallen trees in perfect form simply for the brief moment of flight . . .

They'd lost the pool a day or two earlier, discovering

in its place a hardened dome full of twisted fish and crawdads and smelling only as dead water creatures can smell . . . an odor that kept them back a goodly distance, snorting and dancing and lowering and raising their heads in an attempt to find some focus point that made sense of it all.

And now, as Lady led Ramble in a brisk trot down the human-made trail from the gnat-free vantage point—her mind on the pleasant twitter of birds, the smell of rain in the air, and the shifting shadows of late afternoon—she rounded a canted angle of trail and nearly ran head-on into an active meltdown. She stopped short, scrabbling backwards while Ramble, unprepared, slammed into her hindquarters and then whirled to get out of the way, more alarmed at the prospect of her ire than at the meltdown he hadn't quite noticed yet.

Freed of his interference, Lady jigged a tight circle and raised her head high to give the meltdown a blasting snort, one that got Ramble's riveted attention as he realized what she already knew.

Their only way home was blocked.

It got someone else's attention as well, a crouching figure tucked in by the edge of the meltdown, one which stirred at the great fuss they'd made and turned to face them, startling Ramble so much he took off down the trail at gallop speed, leaving only the sound of his hoof falls behind him.

And Arlen said, "I'm hungry, but not *that* hungry."

Arlen.

ARLEN.

Lady stood stock-still and stared at him while the Jess-voice clamored in wordless excitement within her, generating such astonished delight that Lady finally broke into a series of bucking leaps, snorting with high drama, twisting and dancing in midair. Blowing hard with the sudden burst of exertion, she finally came to a standstill back before him, examining every inch of him with first one nostril and then the other, up and down the length of his body while he stood there with amusement on his face and his hands spread open so she could check those, too. In the back of her mind she was quite aware of a strange horse in the woods, calling to her and evidently tied and unable to reach her. The Jess in her *knew* this was Arlen . . . but still she had to examine him, blowing soft breaths at him, tickling his face as she discovered the missing mustache and his neck as she found the collar to a shirt that still faintly bore someone else's smell.

At that he laughed and gently moved her nose away. "Please," he said. "I've been alone on the road for a long time, Lady. There's only so much attention my neck can take."

Lady didn't understand, but a bubble of amusement from within told her that her Jess-self did; the amusement came out in a sneezy snort and she suddenly had the need to talk to him, to throw question after question that this self couldn't even begin to formulate, never mind convey. Something in her demeanor must have changed . . . must have alerted him. As she reached for the trigger of her change spellstone, he put a sudden hand on the strong, flat bones of her face and said with alarm, "No! Don't do that!"

She took a step back, moving out from under his hand and tossing her head in annoyance and defiance. She made her own decisions now.

"You can't use magic, not next to *this*," he said. "You'll drive it crazy. Even if it was through churning— and it's not, or I wouldn't have been able to trace it just now—the changespell is far too complex to trust right now." He shook his head, frustration on his face as he read annoyance in the wrinkle of her nostrils.

"I'm sorry. I'll keep it simple. I know when you do turn back to Jess, you'll understand. Lady, the spell won't work. It might seem to work, but it'll go wrong. It'll hurt you. There's no telling *how* it'll end up."

Hurt her.

Hurt her baby.

She flattened her ears in a comment that would have crisped Arlen's hair had he heard it in human terms. And she left the spellstone alone.

It had been a close thing, close enough to leave Arlen shaken even as he rejoiced to find Lady here . . . and puzzled over the circumstances. He didn't know the orange-marked palomino with whom she traveled, didn't know why she would be out with another horse and without her courier harness. For the moment, he was simply relieved to have caught the distant look of concentration in her eye, and to have forestalled the use of the spell—for her reaction had made it clear enough she'd intended to change, all right.

If only she could. If only they could talk to one another, filling in the considerable gaps of each other's knowledge. He could tell her where he'd been, and why he'd taken so long to return . . . in essence, why he wasn't dead. He could tell her what he'd just learned, following the vague magic to its roots in an effort that had taken every bit of his skill. And she could tell him about Jaime, how the hold fared, what they knew about the Council deaths.

All the same, he was glad for the company.

Especially with the new knowledge weighing heavily upon him, the realization that the Council could have stopped this crisis had they been just a little more thorough, that they had in some small way been responsible for their own deaths, and in a large way, for the crisis gripping the land.

SpellForge.

He should have at least realized that the spell consortium was involved when he'd seen that man at the stable so many small towns and four-corner settlements ago, he *should* have. So carefully cultivated to blend in despite his large size, so prepared. Classic characteristics of a FreeCast agent. Usually those agents worked to protect spellmaker products during development, or to protect spellmaker wizards or even managers' families. "Your Council is like a humanitarian think tank," Jaime had once said, "and those spellmaking companies are just big computer software moguls."

"They're cutthroat," he'd agreed, but in reality knew little about them other than the spells he approved. That . . . and all the big spellmakers worked with FreeCast.

And of the spellmakers, who else but SpellForge had only recently released the biggest leap in commercial spell technology since mass-produced spellstones? A technology that had been vetted and admired by the Council, Arlen included. Technology that even Arlen had embraced, immediately installing it in his own hold for the convenience of those who struggled with daily amenity spells.

For Jaime.

And how he'd anticipated the look on her face when she discovered a light she could turn on and off as easily as the lights in her own world.

"Stupid," he muttered viciously at himself, earning a nudge from Lady. He did what he'd never done— what he'd never had a reason or chance to do. He threw an arm around her sturdy neck and took comfort in her solid presence, the reassuring touch of her muzzle curving around to whisper against his back. He'd seen Carey do the same many a time . . . though never after Lady had first become Jess.

He still didn't know just why the permalight spell distorted Camolen's magic . . . he needed his workroom, a ream of notations, and a month of quiet to figure that out. But there must have been something in the spell, some hint or clue of trouble that the Council missed. Some indication of this resulting environmental damage.

There *must* have been.

And now they were dead, Camolen was literally falling apart around him, and he and Lady—and Grunt—were trapped here with FreeCast agents on his trail.

He had no doubt about that last. They'd have placed agents in this area, hoping to intercept him on the way to Anfeald. And those agents would certainly be skilled enough to recognize his signature . . . the one he'd revealed when he'd grabbed the faintest tingle of a recognizable trail from the eruption now settling beside him and followed it to its source. One source, and also many . . . multiple invocations of a spell he'd barely been able to remember. A spell to which no one other than himself and the other original Council members had ever been exposed in the first place, and a trail so faint and diffuse that no one else still alive would ever be able to trace it.

No wonder SpellForge wanted him out of the way— no wonder they'd turned to FreeCast agents to get the job done.

"We could have trouble," he told Lady, standing back to rest his hand on her withers. She curled her neck around to look at him, ears at attention. "Maybe not now . . . it's getting a little late, and even these people won't want to navigate the woods in the dark. Too easy to stumble onto one of these bits of nastiness."

Except he heard hoofbeats—

But hesitant ones. Faltering ones. When Lady raised

her head to nicker a welcome, he knew her companion had returned; in a moment the palomino came into sight, a travel-muscled creature of no great grace but inimitable strength and a hard kind of beauty. A stallion, Arlen noted, and gave Lady a questioning glance—but as it became evident the palomino intended to stop and hover at the edge of true contact, she more or less dismissed him, leaving him only one ear's worth of attention with the other ear back on Arlen.

Then again, what did Arlen know about horses and their relationships? As long as the stallion didn't cause him any trouble—Arlen had trouble enough already—then he could be ignored. There were plenty of other things to occupy him now that he'd gained some idea of the forces tearing Camolen apart.

"We've got to stop it," he said to Lady, a little unnerved by the way she truly seemed to follow the conversation. Horse . . . but now more than horse. He held up his hand and ticked off his fingers. "We've got to stop it; we've got to get those spelled lights in peacekeeper hands. Until then, we need some kind of protection from it, for everyone." He hesitated there, his thoughts drifting away long enough to sketch the basic protection spell premise—since the distortions happened in reaction to magic, creating intrinsically magical damage, any shield would have to create a vacuum of magic. Something he had never actually experienced, and thus something he hardly knew how to reproduce. He shook his head, short and sharp, and left the details for later. "We've got to heal what's been done. And, burn it, we need to find some way through to Anfeald so I can tell Jaime I'm still alive. Unless she knows?" And he looked hopefully at Lady's fine-boned face, the soft brown eye gazing back at him from beneath a long thick fall of forelock.

More than horse . . . but still horse. She didn't

perform tricks, use her hoof to scratch runes in the mucky ground, or otherwise answer his question. But she looked at him with understanding and nuzzled his arm, lipping at the material of his jacket in affectionate sympathy.

"We've got to stop it," he muttered yet again, as Grunt whickered anxiously from the woods, rustling branches and snapping twigs in exploration of his lead rope limits. Feeling left out. "In a moment," Arlen told him, raising his voice with some annoyance and never stopping to think that Grunt could hardly understand. Not with other things on his mind, like the sudden realization that stopping the damage meant stopping the light spells meant reaching the peacekeepers meant going in the opposite direction from Anfeald Hold altogether. Anfeald, the goal he'd held fixed in his mind for so long, the one thing that had kept him putting one cold mud-covered foot in front of the other. The thought of turning away gave him a physical wrench, a frantic twisting within.

Unexpectedly, Lady gave him a solid nudge; he took a step to regain his balance, and she crowded him until he took another. Away from the wounded trail. Away from Anfeald.

Lady, at least, knew which was the right decision.

"All right," Arlen said crossly. Besides, maybe if he backtracked to the peacekeepers, he could find an open trail to Anfeald from there. "I have to get Grunt before he starts bleeding from the ears. We'll put some distance in before we settle in for the night. No point in being anywhere near when the FreeCast agents descend here tomorrow."

He pulled Grunt back out of the woods, watching as the gelding became instantly besotted with Lady, going so far as to duck his head and make a foal-mouthing gesture at her while Lady gave the gelding no more than a polite sniff. "Poor old Grunt," Arlen murmured. "*I* appreciate you even if you *are* missing your manly parts."

But he had no real thought behind his words, and no real appreciation of their odd little caravan—two horses at complete liberty, one of which kept his distance and the other of which led the way, followed by an obsequious gelding of roughest breeding and his person-by-default, a lanky wizard with an unusually developed road gait and the precinct's ugliest shirt, its tattered condition and impending doom a mercy. His thoughts—and his heart—were at Anfeald, making every step he took in the opposite direction a trial in determination. "We'll stop it," he said, and startled them all by suddenly whirling around to walk backward, pointing a warning finger at the glob of distorted woods as his voice raised to a shout, "and then we'll be *back*!"

Three pairs of equine eyes riveted to his strange behavior; three sets of ears pointed his way in concern. Arlen tugged his ugly orange tunic back into place, then snatched his jacket from atop Grunt's pack to ward himself against the evening cold, all the while pretending he didn't feel foolish under the scrutiny and muttering to himself, "Well, we *will*."

Stop the damage. Create protection. Return to Anfeald . . . in that order.

With a hand on Lady's withers as they walked, Arlen retreated into his thoughts. Shield theories. *Protection.*

Without it, he didn't think he—or anyone else— would ever make it home.

Carey returned Jaime's old schoolmaster mount, JayDee, to her stall, glancing at Sabre's expectant look on the way by. He'd never presume to ride Jaime's Grand Prix dressage mount—no one rode Sabre but Jaime, and Carey's less theoretical, more intuitive style of riding would make him a poor match for any upper-level dressage horse—but he'd taken to longeing the horse in a variety of careful exercise programs gleaned from Jaime's books, hoping to keep him decently fit during this long and unplanned layoff.

JayDee he presumed to ride, keeping himself fit—working through the bad days of gulping ibuprofen and surreptitious coughing—and more to the point, occupied. Out of Dayna's way, she who would not be nagged. Just as well; from the constant expression of worry she'd taken to wearing, she nagged herself enough for all of them. Even so, as he encountered her at work—first in the solitude of the little office room and more recently in the middle of the airy indoor ring, a lap desk and lawn chair as her furnishings and plenty of space for experimental magics—he invariably fought the urge to question her. *How much longer*, that's all he wanted to know. Simple enough, wasn't it?

How much longer.

"I'll be back," he told Sabre, who'd been returned to the stall that had so recently housed Ramble. Finding himself unable, this once, to leave Dayna alone. Suliya he left cleaning stalls, fresh from her own ride on the lower-level lesson horse during which she'd copied the warm-up exercises Carey employed.

More power to her. Maybe by the time they got back, she'd truly be ready to learn those things she'd thought she already knew.

Dayna stood in front of the chair, the wood-topped lap desk set carefully to the side on a square of plywood that kept the arena dirt from crawling into her papers. Her closed eyes held a slight squint at the corners; her mouth moved in a soundless mumble—and as ever, she looked incongruously slight compared to the power she could wield . . . *was* wielding.

Wheeler leaned against the kickboard rail nearest to her—just under the ring letter H. If his arm still pained him, it wasn't evident. Then again, with Wheeler, who could tell? Watchful but relaxed, he lounged in the startling combination of his expensive Camolen trousers and one of Mark's colorful country-themed shirts, a thing of blocky red-and-black color and pearl-front snaps, rolled at the cuffs and untucked at the waist . . . and he did it with such insouciance that no one would ever guess he was stranded in a strange world and watching someone he'd intended to abduct and now suddenly depended upon.

Carey, well versed in the folly of interrupting an uncertain wizard in mid-spell, stopped at the entrance to the indoor ring and waited. Within a few moments Dayna's concentration was replaced by satisfaction, and she opened her eyes. She spotted him immediately. "Couldn't be good any longer, huh?" she asked, but not without understanding.

He shrugged, and then had to ask. "How's it going?"

"I fixed the shield," she said, her satisfaction fore-most again.

"What shield?" Startled, he didn't sound nearly as appreciative as he knew he ought to be; he caught a glimpse of Wheeler's faint amusement as Dayna wrinkled her nose at him. Undeterred by any of it, he headed out into the ring.

"The one I've got up around me right now," she said, with perfect timing; her smile said she knew it.

That stopped him, feeling a little foolish but not so foolish as if he'd run right into it and bounced off. A quick scan showed no sign of it; he frowned. What *was* she up to?

"You won't see it." She pushed back her sandy hair, recently trimmed from its shaggy Camolen cut to the wedge-like style she'd had when they'd first met. It suited her—short, sharp, and no-nonsense. "The problem with using magic here is that it disperses so quickly—quickly enough that I figure at least half of the storage stones went to waste when I sent Jess out. So I've been playing with that inverted shield spell I pulled on the goon-lady at Starland." She glanced at Wheeler. "You would be the goon-guy," she informed him. "One of them, anyway."

"Yes," he said, amusement intact. "I understood that."

"The *remaining* goon-guy," she said, in case he hadn't gotten *that*. Threats, Dayna-style . . . but Carey wasn't sure how much she meant it anymore. If anything, Wheeler's friend-foe spell tests were now more friend than foe, and he certainly seemed to consider that Dayna and Carey had been stalled here long enough to let his employers do . . .

Whatever it was they'd intended to do. For good or for bad.

Although recently, Carey had seen the faintest hint of anxiety in Wheeler . . . a doubt, and an increased attentiveness to Dayna's efforts. Never a nag . . . never getting in the way . . .

But the man wanted to go home. Was ready to go home.

Carey didn't like Wheeler; knew he'd turn on them if necessary. But in an odd way he also fully trusted the FreeCast agent to indicate *if necessary* came to pass. Enough so he didn't add to Dayna's not-so-subtle threats. He said, "So you've got a shield, something we can't see. And it keeps magic in . . ."

"But doesn't mess with anything else," Dayna said, back to being satisfied. "We can go in and out, we can maintain a certain density of magic, and Suliya can run back and use the bathroom at the last minute before we spell out of here, because you know she'll forget."

"I heard that!" Suliya shouted. A moment later a forkful of fresh manure flew from the aisle into the arena, making Carey duck but missing Dayna completely.

"Good," Dayna said, deadpan enough so Carey knew she was teasing. "Maybe you'll remember to pee *before* you join the rest of us this time."

"Guides," Suliya said, still out of sight—within a stall and working, from the varied and muffled sound of it. "Did I *know* we were going to a shopping place where the bathrooms would be hard to find? Did I *know* this place was so uncivilized? Just that *one* time—"

"So is that it?" Carey said, deciding to ignore their byplay . . . especially since he hadn't taken a hit from the contents of Suliya's badly aimed fork. "The shield, the travel spell . . . you have what we need? We can go home?"

"I'm not sure how much like home it'll be," Dayna said, suddenly sober. "I've made contact a few times through the spellstones Ramble left behind, and things feel really . . . wrong." She glanced at Wheeler. "It'll pass, you said. I hope you're right."

Being Wheeler, he didn't respond with token words of reassurance. "They've had more than enough time," he said. "I wouldn't take anything for granted. I'm not."

She turned on him with accusation. "You *were*."

He nodded, unaffected by her anger, by the sudden sharp look Carey turned on him. "I was," he agreed. "Now I'm not. Now . . . now I don't like the sound of what you've told me about the magic, and I think we need to get back."

"Great," Dayna said. "Just great."

Right. The man who'd kept them here for the sake of his once-removed employers, so sure that SpellForge would resolve its—and Camolen's—problems—now felt just as sure that SpellForge *hadn't*. Meaning that

perhaps Carey and Dayna could have done some
good—

Except—

"We couldn't have returned before you were ready,
anyway," Carey said, realizing it anew. "What's there
when we go back . . . is what's there when we go back."
And let's go back now. Just as soon as they could haul
Mark from the farm's financial work over which he
struggled to say his farewells, just as soon as they could
make themselves ready . . .

Carey was ready *now*.

"Try it," Dayna suggested, nodding at the nothing-
ness between them. "If it works like I think it will, I'll
just hold onto this spell and we'll go."

Carey gave her a doubtful glance, thinking for an
instant that he would indeed run right into and then
bounce off the shield, much to Dayna's not-so-innocent
amusement. But a glance at her face—just a trace of
worry, but more excitement than anything—convinced
him otherwise. As Suliya drifted to the edge of the
aisle, watching with fork in hand, Carey took careful
steps forward, not entirely sure he'd know when he
passed the invisible boundary into magic.

One moment he was waiting for that first tingle of
magic . . . and the next something seemed to burst
within him, an agony of heat exploding in his chest—
so he could barely see Dayna's alarm, so when he
started to say *I'm in trouble* all he got out was a dazed,
"I—" as something inside him gurgled the words and
he clutched at the front of his shirt, pulling it as if that
would pull off the pain. Dayna rushed in to grab at
him, trying to slow his descent as his knees gave way,
and by then he was coughing. Deep, wet coughs and
when the blood splattered his hands, he only stared,
stupefied, unable to think beyond that which somehow
tore him apart from the inside.

By then Wheeler joined them and not only kept Carey upright but snapped a few nonsense words over him, roughly hauling him away from Dayna's magic. "I'm sorry," he said, just as roughly. "I thought I'd botched the spell—I didn't know it was just dormant—"

Carey couldn't hear him; Carey couldn't spare the thought to hear any of them, to see any of them. He tore mindlessly at his blood-soaked shirt with his blood-covered hands, clawing at his own chest, bright crimson fluid streaming down his chin as Wheeler finally lowered him to the ground with an entirely unWheeler-like curse and the faintest hint of panic.

Cool Wheeler, upset.

Calm Wheeler, panicked.

Nothing could have scared Carey more.

Chapter 26

He's dead, Suliya thought, not even knowing why. Just seeing the blood, astonishingly bright, hearing Carey gasp and cough and choke.

He's dead.

She ran a few steps into the indoor ring where Dayna bent fervently over Carey in his throes of . . . whatever had happened, and where Wheeler knelt, trying to say something to Dayna, totally ignored until Dayna whipped her head up to shout at him, "What did you *do*? I know it was you, I *know* it!"

Suliya stopped short at that, hesitating where she could still see all of them, not yet part of them . . . and suddenly certain she had nothing to offer. Her fingers wrapped around the long wood handle of the stall fork, clenched tightly; she discovered it in her grip and threw it away. Somewhere. She didn't know, didn't care.

"Remoblade," Wheeler said, answering Dayna in a

single clipped word as he turned Carey on his side with
efficient ease. Suliya felt a chill hit her spine.
Remoblade. Remote blade. So unlawful it wasn't funny,
but the checkspells interfered with surgeon's spells and
couldn't be employed.

"Remo *what*?" Dayna said, not of much help with
whatever Wheeler was trying to do. "I swear, Wheeler,
you start talking or I'll find some way to turn you inside
out!"

"Keep him on his side," Wheeler ordered her as
Carey fought them, a drowning man searching for air
and operating on instinct; flailing, beyond intellectual
thought, he made it almost to his knees before Wheeler
carefully but capably took him down again. "His *bad*
side. He's bleeding in his lung; we need to keep the
other one clear. It won't be so bad after that first hit."

Dayna threw her weight on Carey's hip, got a
glimpse of Suliya, and snapped, "Get Mark. Get him
now."

Suliya ran. She left an aisle of startled horses, heads
lifted and ears pricked, in her wake, and she stopped
short at the double doors to bellow at the house, at
the open window of the room in which he sat. "Mark!
Mark, boot the poot out here!"

She saw a shadow approach the window, crouching
down to peer between the open dark curtains; she
gestured frantically at him, her arm windmilling her
urgency. Immediately, the shadow retreated; Suliya ran
back to the arena, right up to the struggle in the dirt.

Or not so much of a struggle, for Carey had subsided somewhat, and though she hadn't intended it,
she'd come to a stop right in front of his face, close
enough to see his lids half closed and his eyes glazed
over in pain and shock. Blood dribbled from his mouth
and soaked into the dirt beneath it, but not so copi-
ously as that first horrifying glimpse she'd gotten.

"—remote blade," Wheeler was saying to Dayna. "Doesn't leave a mark on the outside, acts on the inside. This one was more like a vibrating burr than a blade— bigger initial shock value, and then more damage—" He suddenly cut himself off as he seemed to hear his own words, and realized to whom he said them.

Too late. As Mark pounded up behind Suliya, cursing his own intensely muttered alarm, Dayna lost control. "Oh my *God*," she said. "Do you even *think* about what you're saying? Do you even think about what you *do*? What kind of a—" But she, too, managed to cut herself short, to leave room to snap, "Get it out of him. Get it out *right now*."

Wheeler shifted, kneeling behind Carey to let his own thighs act as a bolster, keeping Carey right where he wanted him. Looking at Carey's pale face, Suliya felt a sudden sting of renewed horror.

"Ay!" She crouched down and poked him. Poked him hard, on a collarbone where she figured it would hurt but not mess with whatever Wheeler had done. Hazel eyes sparked, showing more awareness . . . smarter awareness. "Yeh," she said. "You just hang around. I still want that promotion—"

Wheeler said, "It *is* out. That mnemonic I used . . . I'm not good with spells. Or I might have realized—"

"You did this that first fight," Mark said suddenly, his posture changing from tense and startled to *looming*, and making Suliya wish he wasn't behind her. "Didn't you? And he ended up at the hospital and you didn't *say* anything."

"I thought the spell failed!" Wheeler lost his composure and started to rise; Dayna snatched his sleeve and he caught himself, stopping Carey as he threatened to roll onto his back. "I *thought* the interference had nullified it, that it ran its course with little damage. I had no idea it was waiting for an infusion of magic!"

"It doesn't matter right now," Dayna said grimly. "Look at him." For that instant, they quieted, leaving space for the harsh, liquid sound of Carey's breathing, the groan that came with every breath. The long muscles of his neck stood out in stark relief with the effort of it. But his eyes . . . his eyes were coming back to them, helped along by Suliya and her poking, definitely following the conversation.

But when he tried to add something, the effort turned into a liquid cough; he rose to his elbow to spit blood into the dirt.

"Nine one one," Mark said with some certainty, as if that should mean something to the rest of them.

To Dayna it did. "Can they treat him at that hospital?"

Wheeler said, "It's just an injury now. The magic is gone."

"We were about to leave. We could still do it. The healers—" Dayna hesitated, looking at Carey. "God, Carey, you always get yourself in such a mess. First a compost spell, now an internal eggbeater—I *swear*—" Her hands, resting on his leg, tightened briefly.

He jerked in a single cough of wry laughter. *Compost?* Suliya thought, considering him. Was that the spell Calandre had thrown at him, the one no one talked about but that had left him half a courier?

She supposed she'd want it kept quiet if someone tried to compost her like garbage, too.

Wheeler bypassed all of it for the practical. "You're the one who's so concerned over the magic's changes, maybe the healers *can't*—" He hesitated, leaving Dayna room to snap at him.

"Then we *won't* go back. We'll call an ambulance—but we've got to decide!"

Suliya had never seen such conflict on Wheeler's face as the agent said, "If he goes to your hospital, we'll have to leave him behind. SpellForge—"

Carey's eyes widened at that; he gave an ineffective push against the ground as if he might rise further, choking on words that never made it past his throat; Wheeler restrained him without even seeming to think about it. They argued about him, above him . . . while Suliya watched him.

"Yes, and what about SpellForge?" Mark said, distinctly menacing in posture and stare considering how easily Wheeler could have put him down. "First you don't want anyone going anywhere. Now you say you can't wait. Too bad for you, buddy, that Carey's more important than what you do and don't want—"

"SpellForge," said Wheeler, unaffected by Mark's threat, raising his voice for those first few words and then dropping down to dark, dry certainty, "seems to have failed. And they haven't done what's right when it was necessary—when their failure became obvious—or the magical interference would be *improving*, not getting worse by the day."

"By the hour," Dayna interposed in a mutter, watching Wheeler with eyes narrowed, her hands a total contrast where they rested on Carey's leg by the knee, patting him in an absent but comforting way. No longer so panicked, she had taken Wheeler's cue that the worst of it was over; despite what Suliya had thought upon first seeing Carey, he had more than a few moments to live.

Though not many.

"So you—what?" Dayna asked. "Think we need to rush back and save the day? And you couldn't have said this earlier?"

"To what end? Before now, this moment, did we have a way to return?" He gave her a bitter look. "And would you have believed me if I had?"

"Yes," she said, a sharp gleam in her eye. "I'm the one feeling the changes in the magic, remember?"

"Then use the spell now! If we *can* go back, we *must* go back! No one else knows what's happening—"

"None of the other agents?" Suliya said in surprise, the only one accustomed to FreeCast ways.

Wheeler gave an impatient shake of his head. "They were never told. *I* was never told." At their simultaneous stare of response he said, "I believe I mentioned that I find out what I need to know whether or *not* I'm told."

They looked at each other a moment, a moment in which Carey actually did manage to push himself half upright, still struggling to breathe but fully intent on the conversation. Especially intent on Mark's next words, a murmur of an aside with all the threat gone from his stance, "With the magic going gonzo, if you don't leave soon, you could be stranded here forever. Dayna, it all makes a certain amount of sense . . ."

"The hell it does! I'm not making that decision without details. Not when it means leaving Carey behind."

They weren't paying attention to Carey himself, none of them were. No one but Suliya, who saw the way his eyes widened, the way his blood-rimmed lips soundlessly formed a single word. *Jess.*

Wheeler looked at Dayna and said simply, "The permalight spell came with an unexpected price."

She jerked as though in response to a physical blow. "Guides, those things are *everywhere*—" And cut herself off with a shake of her head. "It's just an environmental side effect? They'll figure it out. If it's that obvious, they'll—"

"How?" he asked. "The Council is dead. They're not supposed to be—some fool panicked and drew up raw magic when he tried to conceal his spying, and in the process killed every single wizard skilled enough to follow the casting trail to the permalight spells." He opened his mouth as if he might have something else to add, and then didn't.

"*I've* followed trails—" Dayna started, not appearing to notice his hesitation—but slumped instead of finishing. "But always a very strong spell, to a single spellcaster . . . not a diffuse effect to a multitude of sources." She glanced at Mark. "He's right. It's different. I would have said it couldn't be done."

"If SpellForge had told the new Council as they should have, the light spell would be forbidden by now. There might not yet be a checkspell, and the Council might not have spread the news to every single household in Camolen all at once, but they'd have put a cap on the worst of it—and the interference wouldn't have escalated. Not the way it has."

"You're guessing," Dayna said. But she looked down at her hands, no longer resting on Carey's leg but fingers clenching each other. "I hate this . . . but I think it's a good guess."

"It might not matter," Wheeler said. "It might be too late already. We could go back and it could be too late to stop the destruction." He narrowed his eyes, tightly gauging Dayna's response, and after a moment added, "Do what you want. But I want to go back now. Here and now."

Dayna looked a Carey, a beseeching gaze from unusually vulnerable blue eyes. "Normally I'd go for Camolen's magic over hospital care any day, but there's no predicting—I'll come back for you, Carey, if it's at all possible, I'll come back—"

"No!" he said, forcing out the ragged but emphatic word and then paying for it with a round of coughing and spitting. He looked at Suliya, just as beseeching as Dayna had been an instant earlier.

She knew what he wanted, even through her surprise that it was she to whom he turned. She found her voice surprisingly firm. "No. He needs to go back. He has to try to make things right with Jess."

Wheeler looked at Carey and said flatly, "You could die. You could die without ever getting the chance to see her."

Carey took the most careful of breaths, spoke in the most cautious of whispers, words that were still as strong as anything he'd ever said. "Death," he said, "would be living *here* without ever seeing her again, and knowing I didn't even try."

Wheeler and Dayna exchanged a glance, brought Mark in on it. A silent round of decision-making, and one that burned up anger in Suliya. "Ay!" she said. "You heard him. If we go back, *he* goes back."

Dayna let out a long breath that could only be acquiescence. But when Carey turned a grateful gaze to Suliya, mouthing a thank you, she didn't know whether to be relieved for what she'd done for him, or frightened of what she might have done *to* him.

Jaime opened bleary eyes to diffuse dawn light, instantly alarmed but taking another moment to realize why.

Natt, waking her. Natt's anxious face, looking as ungroomed as she'd ever seen him, with the light, fine shadow of his beard creating a hard line on his usually soft face and his eyes still a little gummy even by candlelight. He wore a thick, layered silk dressing gown she'd never seen, and carried the scent of a woman's perfume. The chill of the unwarded spring night surrounded them both.

"The meltdowns," Jaime said, as soon as she found her tongue, her fingers clutching the dark green linens that in this world weren't linens at all, but some other natural fiber she could never remember. "Do we have one here?"

"Grace of the guides, no," Natt said, an instant of horror crossing his face. "But something's shown up in the travel booth. There's an arrival alarm—"

"I thought we'd deactivated all unnecessary spells," Jaime said, swinging her legs out of the futon-like bed and groping beneath the bed frame for the canvas slip-ons she often wore around the hold. Like the covers weren't linen, the canvas wasn't exactly canvas, but in her mind they were close enough.

"How often do we use that one? No one thought of it."

"So who is it?" She stood, impatiently finger-combed her hair back from her face, and decided that under the circumstances—and with the addition of a sweater—her current attire of ankle-length sleep-shirt was just fine.

"It's not *who*. It's *what*. And I think you can answer that question better than any of us."

"Do I like the sound of that?" Jaime grabbed a mint from the bowl by the door on the way out, wishing for mouthwash.

Natt, holding the candle so it would light her way as well as his as they entered the dimmer areas of the hold, said, "No one's sure."

She followed too close on his heels, too impatient to do otherwise, and then surged ahead when the ground-floor travel booth came into sight. Cesna waited there with her own candle, one of the old thick stumps under severe rationing. Camolen had gone years . . . *generations* . . . without any significant loss of lighting ability. No rolling blackouts for them, no sudden wink-out of lights because someone somewhere hit a power pole with his car. The candles were old, stashed away in the back corners of drawers and cupboards, and precious.

Not that they offered enough light for Jaime to believe what she thought she saw in the travel booth, folded and neatly centered in the enclosed stone space.

Sabre's blanket.

With a wordless exclamation of surprise, she pushed into the booth and snatched up the fine wool cooler, a dark teal blanket banded in black with a ropy net lining, tailored to be slung loosely over a hot horse. Over Sabre, *her* horse—she knew it as soon as she felt the familiar material, and before her searching fingers came across the embroidered name and logo. *The Dancing Equine*.

"It's Dayna," she said. "Dayna and Carey. They're at the farm, and they're coming back."

"Here?" Natt scoffed. "Not according to the spells you say they had with them, they're not. When they return, they'll end up—"

"Here," Jaime said firmly. She left the chamber, thrusting the cooler at Natt's midsection so he had no choice but to take it. "This belongs to my horse. It came from my farm. Who else do you think would send it?"

"Why send it at all?" Cesna said, a softer protest. Unlike Jaime, she'd taken time to dress, but her fine, light brown hair hung limply about her shoulders and pillow blotches still marked her young face.

"We haven't been able to talk for nearly a month," Jaime said. "Maybe longer. I've lost track, between your calendar and mine. The point is, they know we're having trouble with magic. This could be a heads-up; it could be a test. It could be both. With any luck, in a few moments we'll know."

Cesna lifted her head slightly, a listening attitude. "Yes," she said. "Here it comes."

"Guides." Natt's soft voice took on a new kind of horror. "What's that kind of magic going to do to the area?"

"It's Dayna," Cesna said, her eyes big and hollow in the obtuse light of the candle she held. "The new Council said . . . that is, she's so careless with raw magic—"

Jaime wanted to protest, to tell them Dayna was hardly *careless* at all—she just employed that which they would not. But it didn't matter, because the end result would be the same. When the Council's message—the final dispatch message from *anyone*, as it turned out—came through warning them to avoid using magic in an affected area, and to avoid raw magic under any circumstances, they'd all immediately recalled Dayna's claim to have felt raw magic before the old Council died.

"We'll let her know," Jaime said firmly. "And we'll just have to hope—" *that the sudden burst of travel magic doesn't cause a meltdown on the spot,* but she didn't finish the thought out loud.

She didn't need to. They all knew. And she didn't have the time, because the air inside the travel chamber rippled, an effect she'd never seen from this side of the spell. Rippled, wavered, and—somewhere between one blink and another—figures appeared within the ripples and quickly stabilized, a pond of matter recovering from disturbance, crowded into a space meant for one, maybe two . . . not four.

Four?

Those figures hardly seemed to be aware of their welcoming party—and Jaime hardly knew what to make of what she saw. *Carey's down, there's a stranger—*

"Dayna!" she said, but Dayna only gave a sharp shake of her head, going to her knees where Carey struggled to rise, to say something—and failed.

The stranger spoke to Dayna, a few quick, hard words from a lowered head, and she came to her feet. "We need a healer," she said, looking out at Jaime and barely acknowledging Natt and Cesna. "He should have stayed, the fool! The travel—" She scowled, targeting Cesna. "We need a healer *now*."

"Go," Natt murmured to Cesna. And to Dayna, a gesture at the stranger—a stranger in Mark's bold shirt and a pair of Camolen-cut pants—and a no-nonsense question. "Who's that?"

Dayna went back to Carey, tossing the answer over her shoulder. "Name's Wheeler. Came to abduct us, changed his mind. More or less. It's a long story and Carey's—" She closed her eyes, thinking, and Jaime abruptly knew she was hunting spells, hunting for something that might help—and that if she couldn't find one, she'd be just as likely to make it up on the spot with raw magic.

"No!" she cried, getting everyone's startled attention; Suliya's wide-eyed face, Wheeler's unsettling gaze, Dayna's blink of surprise. Carey lifted his head, his eyes glazed and unfocused; for the first time Jaime saw the blood. *Oh guides, that can't be good.* The blood, and the gurgle, and the blue tinge of his lips, the grey of his skin barely noticeable in the candlelight.

Natt closed in on them, coming down hard on the heels of Jaime's command. "No magic," he said. "No *raw* magic, Dayna."

"I knew that," Dayna said, surprisingly mild. She knelt by Carey. "But—"

"Dayna," Jaime said, "We're using *candles* for light."

She looked, showing the shock of it; they all did. Suliya's lip trembled slightly, and then she glanced away, to Carey—and then right through him, assessing a burden Jaime couldn't see.

"Those bastards," Wheeler said. "They said they'd do the right thing."

"What bastards?" Jaime asked. "No, wait—I don't care." She entered the crowded chamber, pushing in beside Dayna and crouching for a closer look at Carey, checking his torso, looking for a wound to cause the bright frothy blood she saw. "*This* is what I want to know—what happened?"

"Another long story. He should have *stayed*, dammit—Mark would have had him to a hospital by now—"

Suliya whispered, "He had to—Jess—you *know* he had to—"

On sudden impulse, Jaime leaned over and said, "She's here, Carey." Not saying where, or in what form, but— "She's here. She's well. She brought me your notes, and I told the peacekeepers."

The corner of his mouth twitched. "Good job," he said, almost soundlessly. Jaime stood, dragging Dayna up with her and right out of the booth.

"Jaime—!" Dayna yanked her arm away, rubbing it, hating to have her size so used against her.

"We're in trouble here, Dayna," Jaime said, her voice low and intense, welcoming Natt and his candle into the conversation with the slightest lift of her chin. "Real trouble. I wish you'd *all* stayed in Ohio, if you want to know, but Carey—"

"Even if we wanted to use magic, the spells aren't reliable," Natt said, not giving Dayna any time for protest. "Cesna's getting the healer, but she's stuck with physical remedies and the vaguest of healing spells, and you know damn well it won't be good enough for *this*." He gestured roughly toward the travel booth, more upset than he'd first seemed, and Jaime reminded herself that he and Carey had worked together with Arlen for some time now.

"We didn't know," Dayna said, her voice as low as Jaime's, the words coming out with difficulty. "We knew it was bad, but—"

"We've got a lot to catch up on," Jaime said. "I just

wish I could send you right back, but there's no way. For all I know that last shout of magic gave us a meltdown outside the front door, or even within the hold. We just *can't*. His only chance is to stop the meltdowns, and no one even knows what's causing them."

Dayna gave them a grimly triumphant little smile. "*We* do."

Lady browsed beside Ramble and Grunt, three horses moving slowly deeper into the woods with the leftover drizzle from the dawn rain dampening their coats and the giant splashes from disturbed branches soaking through to the skin. Ramble tolerated the gelding, disdainful, having been warned off more than once by Lady and leaving Grunt delighted to have friends and delighted to browse untied, as unknowingly fettered to his companions as to any tree.

Lady kept them close to where Arlen chewed—and chewed—some tough trail fruit leather. To judge by his expression, he enjoyed it no more than he enjoyed the rain; his shapeless floppy hat still drooped over his eyes, leaving her only a view of his bristly jaw. No more depilatory spells, and he'd run out of safety-spelled razor blades—or so he'd told her as he made brief and brisk toilet that morning, apparently in quite the habit of talking to anything that might perk an ear.

He was not meant for being on the trail, not as Lady was or even Lady-as-Jess. It had not suited him, for though he'd grown tougher, handling Grunt's saddle and pack equipment with ease, walking the uncertain footing with practiced resignation, judging trails and short-cuts and skirting small blots of destruction with efficient skill, he'd also lost weight, going from lean to thin in a way that showed even under his layers of clothing. Unlike Carey, who'd always found a meditative peace on the trails, Arlen wore a constant expression of longing, as though his mind were ever elsewhere. And though he maintained a cheerful dialogue with the horses, keeping his touch gentle and attentive when they interacted, Lady could well feel his underlying discontent.

If she'd been human, she might have rationalized it as the circumstances—the damage and danger all around them. But she was equine, so she simply recognized it for what it was.

Homesickness. Longing. A certain conflict of purpose with needs.

Things she felt herself. Felt and couldn't understand and dismissed . . . or tried to.

At that she realized she'd moved too deeply into the woods, with a tiny spot of corruption to the left of her and a larger spot just ahead, still as difficult to focus on as any of them had ever been. She snorted gently and reversed course, a deliberately thoughtful move that ever set her apart from other horses.

Lady, once touched by Jess, had never again been only a horse. No matter how desperately she'd tried, no matter how she'd depended on her time with Ramble to take her there.

And Lady, more than only a horse, knew well that the new scent of approaching strangers meant no good for Arlen. They were still out of sight but closing, separated slightly in course. *They meant to box him in—*

She called to him, strident and loud enough to startle Grunt and Ramble—both of whom knew of the strangers, neither of whom attached significance to their presence; they started slightly, rustling, and she glanced back with her ears flat, unable to hush them to silence.

Arlen hastily rewrapped what was left of his breakfast and shoved it into his coat pocket, glancing first at Lady—she called again, making sure he knew it was no coincidence—and then at the woods and trail. He seemed to consider his gear, as though he wondered how fast he could slap it on Grunt's back and be away from here—but in the end he backed up against a tree in a posture that Lady well recognized.

He was taking a stand.

She'd fought beside Carey and Jaime, but never Arlen. She eased closer, watching him, her neck raised and arched, her prancing steps infused with the intent of a war mare ready to protect her own.

He stopped her with a gesture, and although her legs resented it, she made herself wait, backed by Ramble—ready to protect *her* if not Arlen—and Grunt, who watched them all with an innocent curiosity, moist greens drooping from the corner of his mouth. Lady bobbed her head, the only thing left for her to do, impatience in stark contrast to Arlen's quiet readiness.

The agents closing in on them cast aside their stealth. Two came from the woods and one from the trail, all reminding Lady of peacekeepers in their movement and attitude, even though one of the men carried a barrel stomach under his barrel chest and the other had plenty of grey in his hair and lines in his face. The woman, too, was stocky, filling out her muddy-colored lightweight jacket to the seams. All of them confident.

Lady did not underestimate them; the Jess within her provided enough narrow-eyed alarm to keep it from happening. But she stood where she'd been told—stock-still, now, intensely attentive—and Ramble, taking his cues from her, did the same.

When the agents were close enough, Arlen crossed his arms, leaned back against the tree, and said, "You people are just amazing—the sky is falling and you're trying to kill the one person who can stop it."

They exchanged a glance among themselves and came on.

Arlen flicked a spellstone out onto the trail, invoking it in midair. Garish colors blazed to life, words Lady couldn't read and what seemed to be a distorted image of a man and woman exchanging sappy looks. The agents flinched, stopping several arms' lengths away. At their discomfort, Arlen smiled happily. "The sky is falling," he repeated. "You won't recognize the phrase— learned it from a friend of mine—but you ought to get the gist of it. You certainly seem to know the implications of throwing silly little spells around. We were lucky with that one. Imagine what would happen, for instance, if I decided to spell-shave? I really need one, you know." He rubbed a hand over his jaw and frowned.

"You couldn't be so stupid," the woman said, her voice ragged by nature rather than fear.

"Stupid would be to let you get any closer. Stupid would be if I were you, and I was after *me*." Arlen tilted his head, a faintly derisive gesture. "Or has SpellForge got you convinced that things are under control?"

"There's already a permalight checkspell in place," the woman said. "Things *are* under control."

"Don't *talk* to him," the older man said, disgusted. "Just—"

Arlen overrode him without a glance. "You think so?" he said. "I don't. There's been no sign of stabilization. Of course, we don't have to take my enlightened word for it." He held out his hand; nestled in the palm was a single stone. "We can give it a try." He tossed the stone at her; she caught it without thinking, displaying the reflexes Lady had feared she would possess.

The woman gave Arlen a startled look; he said, "Don't worry, I can trigger it from here."

The older man scoffed. "No one can do that."

"You think not?" Arlen said. "I just did it with the calling-stone. Of course, it's your life to risk. I'm not the one holding the stone."

"It's one of the permalight stones, all right," the woman said, sounding less certain. Abruptly, she flung it away; it fell into the woods with a plopping sound no louder than the rain from the branches it disturbed.

Arlen recrossed his arms. "Of course," he said, "the good thing about being a wizard is that you don't *need* spellstones. They're handy little tools, but sometimes it's nice to customize things." He rubbed his jaw again, gave a thoughtful frown . . .

Lady felt the flicker of magic; quite obviously the woman and the barrel-shaped man did as well. They backed a few steps, looking around with alarm . . . waiting for the woods to spring to life around them, stirring them into a forge pot of deathly reaction.

Arlen calmly rubbed his fingers across his cheeks, leaving them clear of stubble. "Much better," he said. "Shall we see if we get a reaction to the next one?"

"Clever," the older man said. "They told us you would be. That's why they sent a good number of us. Do you know how many people are converging on that little display of magic? Sooner or later, we'll catch you off-guard."

"I doubt that," Arlen said, giving a small smile as he glanced in Lady's direction. "It does amaze me that you're willing to keep trying. All I want to do is stop the damage . . . and find a way to fix it."

"Our people can do that without you," the agent said. "Your interference will only make it harder for them."

Arlen snorted gently. "You mean, my intention to reveal the nature of the problem to the rest of Camolen. That *would* be inconvenient for SpellForge, wouldn't it? You tried to stop me from figuring it out and couldn't; you've tried to stop me from doing something about what I learned and won't. You *killed my friends*—and the world will know it. I suggest you go back and warn SpellForge to get ready for it."

The quiet one, the bigger man, gave a sudden jerk of his head that looked more like an order than a suggestion: retreat. He said to Arlen, "You're only putting off the inevitable," and simply turned and walked away.

With reluctance, the older man did the same . . . and then the woman, although she looked over her shoulder once or twice while she was at it, showing reluctance of a different nature. She'd been convinced . . . and she was afraid.

But not of Arlen. Not anymore.

Chapter 27

The magic hit Dayna like a blow. Not from the strength of it—it came through as a scant trickle, distorted and warped as were all the spells she'd felt since returning. But she gasped at the impact of it—a noise of surprise beyond mere surprise.

Distorted it might be, but she knew that signature when she felt it. The signature of a dead man.

In the turmoil of the hold, no one immediately noticed her reaction. Like Wheeler and Suliya, she sat in the back of the job room, behind the common-use desk and out of the way of the discussion in the middle of the room; the couriers moving in and out and around them, wincing over the meltdown-riddled map. Carey had been installed in what Dayna couldn't help but call the school nurse's office—the courier first-aid room—although the healer tending him was most assuredly the equivalent of an experienced doctor. There they would have stayed, had they been allowed ... but they were not. Wheeler left easily, Dayna with more difficulty, and Suliya had to be dragged away despite Simney's assurances that they would be fetched as soon as it was appropriate, for good or bad.

Somewhere along the line Suliya seemed to have acquired loyalty to someone other than herself.

Jaime hadn't even considered staying; she didn't have the choice. She and Linton were already in deep discussion when Dayna and her entourage returned to the job room, a conversation into which Wheeler was all too happy to insinuate himself. Dayna, numbed by the turn of events—unprepared for Camolen's dire state, unprepared for Carey's further collapse and the prospect that no one here could help him, full of self-repercussions for both—sat behind the desk and numbly watched the bustle as couriers responded to the alert, preparing their horses before they even knew their assignments.

Assignments still under discussion.

"These are *couriers*," Wheeler said as Dayna realized her mouth had dropped in reaction to Arlen's magic; she forced herself to close it, her mind and heart racing, barely able to follow along as Wheeler, incongruous in the red-and-black western shirt, made his point. "They don't have the kind of training it takes to work with the public in a crisis situation. Especially not if they're going to demand that people give up their property."

Natt gave him a withering look—more, Dayna thought through her daze, because Wheeler the outsider dared to speak up than because his comment held no sense. "Gathering the permalight stones is the only certain way to stop their use."

"We can spread the word," Jaime agreed, "but Natt's right—there will always be people who think they're the exception. That it won't matter if they use just one little spellstone. Or that we're wrong. We can't leave the stones out there where they *can* be used."

Linton crossed his arms, looking tense. "You're right. But Wheeler's right, too. Some of our couriers are burning good at dealing with difficult customers—but this goes beyond."

"Spell it back a level," Wheeler said, his mildly annoyed expression speaking volumes to someone who knew him. "I didn't mean gathering the spellstones was a bad idea. But the couriers should have a backup plan for people who won't cooperate, rather than waste their time trying to *make* those people cooperate when they aren't trained for it."

"You should know what it takes," Suliya said under her breath, garnering no one's notice but Dayna's— Dayna who smiled wryly in agreement while she frantically and silently hunted for another sign of Arlen's signature, just a small clue to prove to herself that she hadn't imagined his magic . . . or allowed the distortion of Camolen's power to trick her. She had to know for sure—*had* to—before she said anything in front of Jaime.

"What, then, do you suggest?" Still stiff, Natt leaned over the end of the desk, weight resting on splayed fingers.

Wheeler sat at the other end, one hip hitched over the edge of the desk, a relaxed contrast. Restrained, under the circumstances—here in what could be considered enemy territory. The corner of his mouth crooked aside; he gave the smallest of shrugs. "First of all, make things easy for the couriers, so they can move fast today. They should simply ask everyone to spread the word, and assign each community a spot to turn in the spellstones and receive chits of surrender. That's first wave. Second wave—that's tomorrow—the couriers go home to home, checking chits and asking for stones. Have them make a list of those people who won't cooperate—and keep in mind some people won't have chits because they didn't have spellstones in the first place. Third wave, send someone with more authority around with the list."

"And eventually, send someone like you?" Natt said, openly antagonistic and earning a worried look from Cesna—a Cesna whom Dayna found changed, never fully recovered from experiencing the Council's death.

But Wheeler only nodded. "Eventually. Until then, accept that you won't get *all* the spellstones. Their early distribution surpassed any commercial spell up until this point. The goal is to spread the word as widely as possible and make it easy for people to comply."

Jaime gave him a skeptical look. "That kind of thinking isn't exactly what your colleagues led me to expect when they came to visit."

"Force is a last resort, and leads to the poorest possible result."

"Which doesn't mean you're not prepared to use it, as Carey can burnin' well tell you," Suliya said, louder this time.

Wheeler gave her a gentle smile; only in retrospect did Dayna give him a double take, looking for the not-at-all-nice undertone she thought she'd seen. By then it was gone. By then, they'd gone on to discussing details. *The ride of the Paul Reveres*, Jaime called it, making Dayna snort even in her distraction, her dismay at the complete silence from Arlen. She'd been so certain . . . Maybe it was time to go looking.

Distancing herself from the clamor of the job room, she gently reached for the feel of *Arlen*, casting her direct communication spell toward the magic she'd felt and keeping the effort to the lowest possible trickle of magic.

His response was so strong, so clear—a whisper

zinging straight to her mind like a skillfully shot arrow. *Who?* Dayna jerked, startled, not expecting it in spite of her hope. "Arlen!"

Silence fell around her; she opened her eyes just in time to see Jaime descend upon her, taking her upper arms in a punishing grip—wild-eyed Jaime, and not someone Dayna thought she knew. "What about Arlen?" she demanded, only inches from Dayna's face.

"Whoa, Jaime—" Linton said, uncertainty on his long features.

"What about Arlen?"

"I—he—"

Wheeler somehow came between them. "Maybe if you stop shaking her," he suggested in a way that wasn't a suggestion at all.

"Dayna!" Jaime said, pleading now.

Dayna knew she should have been reacting to such treatment, defending herself as she was wont, throwing her *keep off* signs up in Jaime's face. Instead she searched Jaime's bay-brown eyes in wonder and whispered, "He's alive. I just . . . I just *spoke* to him."

"Magic?" said Wheeler in disapproving alarm.

They all turned on him at once, all of Arlen's colleagues and friends and his lover, all snapping a quick "Shut up!" before turning back to Dayna, a tight semicircle of anxious faces that made her want to run.

"Back off, guys," she said, gaining strength in her tone. "I felt a spell with his signature and I went looking—" She glanced at Wheeler and added, "Don't worry, we're whispering. It may not be smart, but *not* talking to him would be even stupider. Of anyone, who do you think needs to know about SpellForge? Who do you think can help us out of this mess?"

"Is he okay? Where is he? Where has he been? What's happening?" Questions tumbled out of Jaime; she looked as though she could barely restrain herself from grabbing Dayna again. "Are you *sure*? Are you really *sure*? God, Dayna, if you're wrong about this, if you make me *believe*—" She stopped short, gulping an uncontrollable but silent sob, and spun away from them all, hiding her face in her hands. Linton, Natt, Cesna—all took a step toward her, reaching for her, stopping short with the uncertainty of such strong emotion, of further exposing such vulnerability.

It was Dayna who rose and gently touched Jaime's back from behind, talking to the bowed head, the obscuring fall of sienna-touched brown hair, and the self-striped maroon tunic stretched over her bent shoulders, typical Camolen style. "I'm sure," she said gently. "He's not far from here, that's all I know. He's not far, and he sounded strong. I should go talk to him, don't you think?"

Jaime nodded most emphatically without lifting her head from her hands, drawing a short laugh from Natt; a glance showed him red-eyed, but with hope in his face for the first time Dayna had seen since her return. Cesna, damaged Cesna, had withdrawn to the corner, gripping her elbows tightly enough to whiten her knuckles . . . unable to believe.

"Okay, then." Still gentle, Dayna said as reassuringly as possible, "I'll find out what I can," although already her thoughts were racing ahead to the overwhelming desire not to ask questions of Arlen, but make demands—*where the hells have you been* foremost among them.

If ever she used restraint . . .

"Ask him—" Natt started, and then the others were all talking at once, suggesting their own questions, hemming her in with noise.

"I can't ask him anything if you don't give me some peace!" she snapped, and they drew back slightly so she could return to her seat—everyone but Wheeler,

who had never moved from the edge of the desk in
the first place. She sat, glared them all back another
step, and closed her eyes to concentrate more easily
on the conversation within, easing the spell into place
with as little magic behind it as she dared. *Arlen?*

A long moment passed, long enough that fear tightened her chest—and then she felt his responding ten-
dril of magic, his clear, clear voice. *Thought I'd scared
you off.*

Voices from beyond the grave can do that, she told
him, not sparing the sardonic tone. *We've thought you
were dead—where the hells—*

But no. She wouldn't say that.

At least, not quite.

Arlen, never offended by Dayna's blunt outbursts,
didn't need to hear the rest of it. He said only, *I know.
I'm sorry. I had no choice, and beyond that it's a long
story.*

Where are you?

She got a brief image of woods, random meltdowns,
three horses. *Lady. Ramble.* And an ugly dark gelding.

He said, *Not far from Anfeald, but blocked off. On
my way to the peacekeepers if I can make it. Dayna,
you have to pass the word; the corruptions are
caused—*

SpellForge! Dayna said, talking right over him. *The
permalight spells!*

Ah. Looks like you've done fairly well without me.

Hardly. She made a face, not even considering what
it would look like to those watching her so closely. And
quickly, she sketched for him their trip to Ohio, their
failure   with   Ramble,   their   encounter   with
Wheeler . . . and the grave condition of his head courier.

He didn't interrupt . . . and then he didn't respond
right away. After a moment—just long enough to make

her anxious—she felt the faint gust of a sigh. *"Carey's
got a knack for putting results above survival,"* he said,
and she could tell by the faint echo that he'd said it
aloud. *Oh, hells, that was a mistake— "Lady, no—no
changespell! We already talked about this—no, whoa.
Whoa!"*

For another long moment Dayna heard nothing but
internal silence with a background of faint static, magic
with enough wrongness to it that she began to feel
queasy. In her physical ear, only faintly, a voice became
insistent—she didn't even know whose it was. "Dayna,
what's going on? Are you all right?" She held up a hand
to forestall the interruption, just in time for Arlen's
return. Harried-sounding, he said, *I've only got a
moment, I've got to deal with Lady—my big
mouth . . . listen, Dayna, you've got to take steps to get
those light spells under control.*

We are.

*And you've got to send someone to the peacekeep-
ers, in case I don't make it.*

She grimaced, but had to acknowledge the sense
behind that move. *We will.*

*And here's the big thing. We've got to come up with
some kind of shield to protect people from the—what
did you say Jaime called them? Meltdowns? Yes, good
name. I've been working on it—*

Inverted shields! Dayna blurted without thinking.
With the magic on the outside!

You have *done well without me,* he said, but his
inner voice was dry enough to cause her chagrin. *I've
been working on it. Don't you even try—we can't have
raw magic in play.* None. *You understand that, right?*

She nodded, knowing he'd perceive it.

*My problem is in making the shield interior free of
magic,* he told her. *I've visited Jaime on your magic-
free earth, but I always had a connection to Camolen.*

I don't know what no magic *feels like. In truth*—and now she could hear his chagrin—*I haven't the faintest idea. And until I do*—

There was silence between them, but only for a moment. Only long enough for Dayna to consider and discard the ramifications of letting him go deeper, beyond the surface of her thoughts. *You want to borrow a memory?* she asked him.

She felt his slow grin.

"*I'll be right back,*" Arlen told Dayna, out loud as well as through the finest pinpoint of targeted message he could send—and even then he examined the woods around them uneasily as he opened his eyes, trying to take in the enormity of the things he'd learned—of Jaime, here and waiting for him and never giving up hope despite all evidence; of Dayna and Carey and Jess gone to Ohio with the stallion who'd seen the ambush, a decision that drove a wedge between Carey and Jess . . . of Carey, now barely hanging on.

And again of Jaime. *Never giving up hope . . .* What he'd done to her with his attempts to communicate, sickening her every evening as he'd pushed himself into her unskilled mind across such a distance.

Too much to encompass emotionally; intellectually he gently put it all aside and applied himself to the present. *Dayna.* He should have thought of it as soon as they'd connected—Dayna had lived most of her life in the absence of magic, and now she wielded it freely; she'd even recently developed a mirror spell for use in Ohio. If anyone knew how the opposing states felt . . .

But first he had to deal with that before him, a mare about to burst into changespell and lacking the human reasoning that would prevent it. Although as he eyed her—looming over where he sat on his heels at the base of the tree, its deeply furrowed bark digging into his back through the threadbare coat and the roots framing his feet—he had to admit even human reasoning wasn't always enough to overcome human emotion.

Lady pawed the ground, dangerously close to his toes; she snorted on him.

He wiped off the side of his shave-spell tender cheek and said, "You know you can't. Not until we get this meltdown situation sorted out—and I think we're on the way to doing it. If you want something to distract you, think about getting us to the peacekeepers. That's our first step. Changing here will kill you, and you'll be no closer to Carey."

She shook her head in a snakey threat, flattening her ears.

"You are," he said, "more opinionated in this form than I remember."

She pawed the ground. Damp dirt scattered across his worn buttercorn-colored boots.

"Don't be rude. Do you think I'll change my mind?" He stood abruptly and she whipped her head up to eye him from an eye held high, her nose pulled to a long, very prissy looking expression and crowding him. Unimpressed, he waved a hand at her; she shied wildly away as though expecting to be struck and he was unimpressed by that, too. "Look at me," he said, pointing at his own face. It still burned from the shave-spell, though he hadn't noticed it while spell-talking to Dayna; he forbore to actually touch his sandpapered skin. "*Smell* it if your eyes aren't up to the job. That little shaving trick of mine may not have triggered any meltdowns, but even a little spell like that is hardly reliable." Unconvinced but warily responsive, she eased up to him and ran her whiskers over his face, whiffing hot breath on painful skin as she took in the odor of blood and serum. "One hell of a brush burn, and I'm lucky it's only that. Never mind the meltdowns—you damn well won't be around to see them if you try to change right now."

She backed a step, snorted hard, and pawed at the ground . . . but this time he felt a difference in the movement. Not Lady being pushy . . . Lady unable to communicate. Bobbing her head at the tree, giving her nose a little flip. Frustrated.

Realization bloomed. "Talking to Dayna is a very minor spell. It takes hardly any magic at all once the connection is made . . . and if it fails, there's not much it can do to us. Besides, if you're settled down enough that I can go back and talk to her, I can get the information I need to build a shield against the meltdowns. And trust me, that's something I need to do. It's something I've been *failing* to do for some time now." He cocked his head at her. "Let me talk to Dayna, and then we'll head for the peacekeepers. You think you can give a smooth enough ride to keep even me on board without a saddle?"

He couldn't tell if she'd understood; she stood quietly, suddenly looking like nothing more than the average horse—which to judge from Carey's stories, she'd never been. Always his favorite . . . always doing something about which he could brag. With perfect timing, she sidled up to him, lipping his jacket in a coquettish manner, shyly and gently rubbing her brow against his chest. He laughed. "Aren't you just the charmer. No wonder Carey—*oof*!"

She did it again, bumping hard against him.

"Carey," he said cautiously, following a hunch—and then warded off another shove. Then again, what other way did she have of inquiring? "He came back with Dayna," Arlen told her, waiting for another shove, knowing he'd found the right question to answer when none was forthcoming. "I gather there was some kind of fight—"

Up down, up down; her head bobbed fast enough to make her thick black mane fly. She knew that much, then.

"You know he's been hurt? A remoblade."

She knew. This time she stood quite still, watching him intently, waiting for his next words.

He gave her the truth. "The only way to save him is to stop these meltdowns so the healers can use magic. And that means getting to the peacekeepers. Frankly, when it comes to that . . . you're of more use to me as a horse. If you'll take me there, that is. It's up to you, Lady . . . you can try to change back to Jess, die in the process, and leave Carey to die after you . . . or you can get me to the peacekeepers and help me save him."

Even with her equine comprehension, with her limited ability to follow the arguments he'd made, he was sure she understood the gist of it.

And that meant she had no choice at all.

Jaime hesitated just inside the doorway of the darkened first-floor room, her hand still trailing on the ornate metal door latch; after a moment her eyes adjusted enough to find the cot-sized bed in the back corner of the small room and to convince herself she saw a hint of Carey's dark blond hair on the pillow. She said in a voice that couldn't begin to express her rampaging joy, "Arlen's alive, Carey."

The sheets rustled; she opened the door just a little wider so the light from the window at the end of the hall—a window no longer protected by spells, making them all grateful the weather was warming while the worst of the spring insects hadn't yet appeared—eased

into the room along with her, bringing dawn to its
simple furnishings without inflicting harsh light on
Carey himself.

He gave the undertone of a cough she'd already
come to expect from him, a throat-clearing reaching
deep, trying to avoid the true cough that would come
anyway.

And did.

She went and sat in the chair by the bed, hesitating to reach out to him and doing it anyway, a simple
hand on his shoulder. They'd almost always been allies,
but they'd never been friends. They understood one
another . . . but kept it at that, intersecting mostly
because of Jess and Arlen and satisfied to leave it that
way.

Satisfied except for moments like this, when she
wished she knew just the right words for him. Simney
had been blunt enough. Without magic—more than the
simple generalized healing spell they'd used to bring
him out of shock—

Well. Carey knew it. According to Dayna, he'd
known this might happen when he chose to return
rather than risk permanent exile on earth. Permanent
separation from the one person he'd somehow managed to drive away, and with whom he now needed to
try to make things right.

"Arlen," he said, coming up on his elbow to look
at her, keeping his voice low, keeping his words short.

"Dayna felt his magic. He's not far from here. He's
worked up a shield against the meltdowns." She hunted
for the easiest way to sum it all up, the facts he would
want to know versus those that would just fill out the
story. "We've got couriers spreading the news about the
permalight spells." She hesitated. "If you hadn't come
back—you and Dayna and Suliya and even that goon
Wheeler—we'd never have known in time. Arlen knew,

but we couldn't make contact with him without Dayna—and he wouldn't have been able to complete the shield spell without her."

"I'm baggage . . . on that part," he said, the wry tone somehow coming through in his altered voice and interrupted words.

Jaime shook her head, and though she'd never before considered the matter, she felt not a trickle of doubt when she said, "You're the one who always holds everyone together. The nexus. No matter whose idea it seems to be . . . I don't know that we'd be bold enough to come up with our ideas if we didn't know you were there to charge off with them." She wrinkled her nose. "Even if we're usually just heading into trouble."

He snorted, then brought the back of his hand across his lower lip; blood looked black in the low light. Jaime offered him a damp cloth from the small table at the head of the bed. "Anyway," she said, looking away as he wiped his lip and frowned at the cloth, the wood chair creaking under the shift of her weight, "we're heading for the peacekeepers. Arlen wants us backing him up— there are agents after him. I don't entirely understand it, but I gather SpellForge has some goons available through this organization called FreeCast. Like Wheeler, before you lured him to the good side of the Force. And they *really* don't want him reaching the peacekeepers. They think SpellForge has everything under control. *I* think SpellForge has its collective heads up its collective butts. And they obviously don't know Arlen isn't their only problem. So we'll make a run for the peacekeepers—at last word, there's a clean patch of woods we can cut through—and I fully intend for all of us to make it." She glanced at him. "You too, by the way. Your job is to hang in until we get things stabilized enough that Simney can use some serious magic on you."

He nodded, but from his expression, he didn't think

he was fooling anyone. *Sooner or later*, Simney had said, *that lung's going to fill. That's assuming he doesn't just plain stress out his system before then*.

Simney didn't use terms like *falling blood pressure* or *spiking heart rate* or any of the medical jargon Jaime would have heard on the cable health channel at home. Then again, she didn't have to. The grey of Carey's face, even in this poor light . . . the blue of his lips. They told enough of the story, along with a struggle for breath so profound he paused between almost every word if he managed to string more than two together in the first place.

Now he took a few quick stuttering breaths and said all at once, "Tell Jess I'm sorry."

Tell her yourself would have been the standard sidekick's reaction, but Jaime was no sidekick and Carey wouldn't have asked if he hadn't needed to know she would do it. Just like Arlen. Just in case. She murmured it out loud. "Just in case."

He gave her a twisted smile. "Just tell her."

Jaime shrugged, gripped by the sudden sadness of the moment, trying to keep it from showing. "It won't hurt her to hear it twice." And then winced, because that had been a sidekick's line and it would only serve to drive home how dire things truly were.

He grinned, real humor, and said, "Bet that hurt. To say."

She scowled at him. "Get better so I can hit you."

"Good," he said, settling back down on the bed like a collapsing feather pillow, sinking in smaller and further than she thought he ought to. "Now I know . . . you're ready to go kick . . . some SpellForge butt."

"You watched too much TV while you were at my place," she told him. But he was right.

She was ready.

Chapter 28

Keeping Arlen on her black-spined back turned into more of a challenge than Lady had expected—or had ever even experienced. The bareback rides with Carey and Jaime—those had been partnerships, and if a rider's unmitigated seatbones grew hard against her back after a while, the increased communication was worth it.

Arlen had the sharp seatbones, all right . . . but none of the communication, and none of the balance. He wound his fingers in her mane, letting her choose the trail and letting her choose the pace—she mostly gave him a sloppy little jog, something to which he could easily sit but which also kept them moving; she slipped into an easy canter only on the sections of trail she knew to be smooth and level. Not many of those on the shortcuts she took to reach the peacekeepers.

Ramble followed her, back and to the side, and Grunt trailed behind them both—loaded up and wearing his halter, but on his own since immediately after the first time he'd jerked Arlen off Lady's back with his slow response time.

Exhausting, trying to shove herself back under Arlen when his balance wavered. Numbing, to carry someone with so little talk between them, and so many accidental signals—the second time Arlen fell, he'd inadvertently cued Lady to canter and she'd automatically done it.

And at the same time . . . exhilarating, to be the one in charge. No gentle acquiescence to the bit, no soft response to someone else's choices . . . human choices, that Lady now understood would always put human needs above equine needs. Perhaps that was just the natural order of things. Lady—on her own—put equine needs first; as Jess she tried to balance them. Lady under saddle and under halter had always given over her choices to humans. To Carey.

That it even occurred to her to do otherwise made her want to buck and squeal and leap, too full of freedom to keep it inside.

But she didn't. She kept Arlen on her back, she dodged meltdowns in the trail, she picked her way through off-trail detours, and she headed for the peacekeepers' hold. By choice. Because to do otherwise meant Carey's death, and the desire to make her own decisions had nothing to do with her feelings of loyalty as Lady and the almost unbearable worry of the Jess sublimated inside her.

Horse scent tingled in the breeze as they approached the trail fork from Anfeald Hold; she lifted her head, hunting the source. Behind her, Ramble called out his challenge, a great deep bell of a voice with grunts of punctuation no other horse could mistake for anything but a stallion. Several horses answered, and then Lady's ears pricked to Jaime's faint and anxious call. "Arlen!"

Without thinking, Lady picked up her speed, moving into an extended trot that sent Arlen bouncing on her back; reflexively, he clamped his legs to her sides.

With the trail juncture in sight, full of milling horses, bordered by a fading meltdown, Lady broke into a startled canter, a choppy gait full of the contradictions she felt. "O-oh no," Arlen said, his teeth clicking as he bounced; he yanked on her mane, the only thing at hand. "Whoa!"

And then she caught wind of *others*, her equine senses geared more toward intensity of odor than finesse of identification but still she instantly thought *human*. In the woods around them, closing on them, but she couldn't *think* with Arlen thumping and bouncing and grabbing at her. With the sudden downwind rustle of brush, a figure emerged from the camouflage of leaves and dull brush almost at her feet; it was all she could do to keep from shying out from under him.

"Whoa!" Arlen cried, completely unaware of those *others*, clenching her barrel with his long legs and hauling on her mane. Metal gleamed dully along an astonishingly long blade, and quite abruptly Lady did just as she'd been told, tucking her butt and dropping her head so Arlen flew neatly over her withers, rolling onward and out of reach. The blade flashed down to score her shoulder and she kicked out wildly, catching only the edge of a sleeve as the blade descended again.

Ramble screamed, a stallion's challenge, and knocked her aside, knocked her *down*—

She wrenched herself aside, trying to avoid Arlen's sprawling figure, trying to avoid the meltdown in progress, well aware that more agents converged upon them.

Armed men and women, ready to turn the hunt into a kill.

"Arlen!" Jaime screamed, her cry of greeting turning to one of horror as the woods seemed to boil with brown-clad agents—only a handful, but how many did it take to kill a man gone head-over-heels off his horse? Lady had saved him with that very tumble, but now he lifted his head from the dirt with a dazed slowness, unable to defend himself; Lady herself hit the ground hard just behind him, legs splayed and thrashing the air as she fought to right herself. Ramble screamed again, this time with pain, and then the man he'd engaged screamed as well—but only for an instant.

"Burnin' poot!" Suliya cried from behind her, almost masking Dayna's equally emphatic curse.

Jaime didn't waste time or breath on curses; she jammed startling heels into her mount's sides and headed across the intersection of trails to Arlen. In the next moment a blur of dark bay movement—*Wheeler's horse*—blocked her way, shoving her gelding aside with such force that the horse almost went down; Jaime pushed her hands forward to give rein, clutching mane and urging the horse to keep its feet as Wheeler surged ahead into the melee.

"Close up!" Dayna shouted behind her. "Close up, we can use the shield—"

Closing up was just what Jaime had in mind—but now she hesitated, confused by the action as a pack-loaded dark brown gelding trotted by with choppy, anxious steps. Lady struggled back to her feet, blood splashed on her deep sand coat, black mane and tail flying; she spotted an agent heading for Arlen and lunged for him while behind her Ramble struggled to rise, hamstrung so badly one hind leg flopped uselessly with his efforts. Wheeler jammed his horse between Arlen and yet another agent, and would have flung himself off to join the fray if something hadn't hit him in the chest and stuck there, stunning him and stopping him utterly short, a motionless figure in the middle of chaos.

But he'd given Arlen the time to get to his knees, to find Jaime and Dayna and Suliya and shout, "The shield! Get over here!"

"Close up!" Dayna repeated, running her horse into the back of Jaime's.

"But the shield lets people *through*—" Jaime said, bewildered, still trying to see how many of the enemy were left, if even now someone charged up behind Arlen—

No. They'd have to get through Lady first.

She drove her horse right up to Wheeler's mount, aware he was trying to say something and couldn't, that he didn't look right, and she did a flying dismount, kicking free of the stirrups and flipping out of the saddle to land on her feet, already running to Ramble. The stallion who'd been there at the start of it all, and now couldn't even rise . . . she snatched his flaxen mane and pulled. Pulled hard. "Up, up, *up*," she cried, giving him something to throw his head against, a counterbalance for his malfunctioning leg. Up he came, stumbling forward, stopping only when she threw her arms around his neck and told him "Whoa, whoa," in the calmest voice she could muster. *Close up*—

She left him by Wheeler's horse and whirled to find Lady holding off an agent who would have come up on Arlen's back—lightning-fast front leg strikes from a perfect warhorse levade, snaking neck threats, as of yet untouched by the woman with the long knife who looked determined to get past but somewhat taken aback at facing a horse determined to stop her.

Front leg strikes. Jaime blinked, realizing this was a Lady she didn't know . . . a Lady gone on the offensive, not merely defending herself or Arlen. Aggressive. Ears flattened, eyes squinting and focused and

hard. Before Jaime could do so much as suggest that
the woman back off, the agent lost the considerable
odds against her; Lady's hoof hit her collarbone with
a crack; the blade hit the ground. And Lady reached
out and took that broken shoulder in her teeth to shake
the woman like a rag doll and throw her aside.

Then Jaime spotted someone else beyond the
woman, a man wisely breaking off his sprint to Arlen,
calculating whether he could reach Arlen before Lady
reached *him*.

Jaime knew the answer. So did Lady, who snaked
her neck down and trembled with readiness.

The man took an abrupt step backward.

To Jaime's astonishment, Lady leapt for him. "Lady,
no!" she cried, lunging forward as if there were something she could actually do to stop the mare.

Lady whirled, as fast, *faster*, than anything Jaime had
ever seen. Poised for action, resenting interference, she
turned on Jaime. Appalled at the trickle of fear she
felt—fear of *Lady*—Jaime somehow knew *not* to order
the mare around, *not* to tell her she was wrong.

To appeal to her as an equal.

"Please," Jaime said. "Please don't, Lady. He's backing off—" And then in desperation she blurted, "We're
going to shield; we need you with us—"

Her nostrils flared to their utmost and ears still half-
flattened, Lady gave Jaime a hard stare . . . a long stare.
When she came out of her fighting stance she did it
with such deliberation that Jaime realized it wasn't
acquiescence in the least. It was *decision*.

She found herself shaking in the aftermath.

Lady went straight to Ramble, meeting him nose to
nose across the tail of Wheeler's horse and blocking
Jaime between Ramble and Wheeler. Unable to reach
Arlen, Jaime stood on her tiptoes a few futile times
and finally subsided. Arlen was there, somewhere

beyond the quarters of Wheeler's horse and the back of Dayna's; he was safe. She shifted to call under the horse's neck. "We're all here!"

"Grunt?" Arlen called back, evoking a moment of utter, baffled silence that even the forest seemed to respect. "Grunt!" Arlen repeated impatiently. "My horse! Does someone have my horse?"

"I have a packhorse," Suliya called back from the other side of the horse-human huddle.

"That's Grunt," Arlen said with relief, and then to Dayna, "Here we go, then—"

The magic flared and stuttered, so strained that even Jaime felt something amiss; she fought to get past Ramble and found herself squeezed up against Wheeler's horse, her hands almost immediately covered in something wet and slick and soaking into the bay's dark coat. Blood. Startled, she glanced up at the slumping agent, finding him lolling much closer to her face than she expected and—catching his gaze—she gasped at his stark complexion and the exquisitely wry look in his eye. Held there, she opened her mouth to say something, except nothing came out. Nothing at all, until Arlen said, "Good job!" in the background and she glanced up to find the shield had stabilized, leaving them inside a bubble with a shifting, oily sheen.

The agents—three of them now—hesitated across the wide intersection of trails, looking to one another as if one of them should be able to identify the effect . . . but no one could.

Of course not, Jaime thought, smugly proud. It was Arlen's magic in test flight and working just as it should.

At least, as far as she could tell.

"Ay!" said Suliya from the other side of Wheeler and the loaded packhorse and Dayna's horse. "Ay!" And she suddenly popped up from under the belly of the packhorse, bumping the nose of Wheeler's bay, quickly soothing the animal as it shifted away, pinning Jaime more firmly between Ramble and the bay. Suliya ended up just inside the bubble, hands on hips, staring out at the men. "Time to get bootin', you think?"

Several of the agents offered an immediate curse at the sight of her; only one of them voiced what they all knew. "Suliya?" It was a stocky woman, and she stepped forward with a long, curving knife in hand but out of guard position. Lady snorted at her; Jaime took it for displeased recognition. The woman said, "Do you know how hard your father's been looking for you?"

"I've been . . . away." Suliya smiled slightly . . . not pleasantly. "Now I'm back. And I'm telling you to go away. Unless you want to *harm* the daughter the SpellForge head chair has been hunting so hard?"

One of the men gestured roughly at the clump of people and horses behind her; Jaime, soothing Ramble—he trembled with pain, now, and still bled freely—eased her hip free of Wheeler's jabbing dead-weight toe and turned so she could see the man's expression more clearly.

Uncertain. And . . . frightened. A big man, a capable man . . . full of muscle and strength. Frightened. With the inflexibility born of that fear, he said, "They can't stop the mangles until we stop everyone who's inter-fering with their efforts."

"Interfering!" From the center of the clump—and to judge by his voice, still on the ground—Arlen said, "You pliable idiots! How could I have been interfer-ing back when your people accosted me in Payys? That's just an excuse! If they had a fix, they'd have used it already!"

"You *planned* to interfere," the man said stolidly. "You're *here*."

"Damn," Arlen muttered, low enough so Jaime could barely hear him. "He's got me pinned on that one."

Suliya, cocking one hip and crossing her arms, said, "My father's had plenty of time to fix the meltdowns. The *mangles*. It's our turn, now. And did I mention how my father will react if you hurt me?"

"I can burnin' well tell you how he'll react if we fail!"

"*Guides*," said Suliya, and threw her hands in the air. "I tried," she added over her shoulder. "All right then, here's what's spellin'. This shield protects us from the . . . er, mangles. No magic in here, none at all. We can go right through an active meltdown." She scowled at them, looking every inch the head chair's daughter despite her rumpled condition. "If you won't go away, we'll *have* to."

"How're you—" the man started.

"Spellstones," said the woman. "I saw him do it before. He'll toss one right into that dying mangle over there and trigger it from where he is. He can do it, he really can—"

"Actually," Arlen said, quite modestly and still totally obscured from Jaime's sight, "I have a whole handful. Twelve or so—"

"More like twenty," Dayna said.

"There's another thing," Jaime said, startling them all; she didn't think they'd even noticed her until this moment. "Anfeald couriers are already spreading the word about the permalight spells. SpellForge doesn't have any secrets anymore."

Wheeler spat blood between the horses and pushed himself upright enough that Jaime could clearly see the knife hilt emerging from his chest, quivering with every movement he made, every word he formed. "I wouldn't be here if SpellForge was running us true," he said, barely loud enough to be heard. "My partner died for their lies. You will, too."

"Wheeler," said the man flatly, the threat inherent. "I thought that was you. If you weren't already—"

"Shut up!" Suliya cried, so fiercely that Jaime made an instinctive movement to grab her arm—and realized she was still trapped behind Ramble's trembling, drooping form, one she'd duck under if she weren't afraid he might actually fall on her.

But Suliya stayed within the shield on her own, coming up short at its boundary—though her back tightened at Wheeler's harsh, short laugh.

"Whatever happens to me, I dealt true," he said. "And I didn't close my eyes to SpellForge lies just because I was afraid of the head chair or FreeCast."

Lady snorted, her alarm drawing Jaime from the male agent's anger; she thought at first one of the other agents might be closing on them, creeping along the edge of the meltdown at their backs to come through a shield that was meant to keep only magic out. But the woman agent's eyes widened. "Mangle!" she said, turning on them with fury. "You didn't need to—we haven't—"

"I *didn't*," Arlen said, trepidation filling his voice.

Jaime jerked around to see it coming, a roil of movement like a tidal wave through the woods; without thinking, she clutched Wheeler's leg, terrified beyond thought in spite of their shield—their untried shield—

exploding trees and screaming rocks and twisted birds and the smell—

She closed her eyes and covered her head and screamed, unheard even to her own ears. Ramble staggered and went down; Wheeler's horse took a hit of some kind, jostling Jaime to her knees and making her suddenly aware there was as much danger within the shield as out if the horses panicked. She crawled blindly up against Ramble's side, using his bulk for protection—cracking her eyes open once but only for an instant, unable to bear the turmoil of warping reality and still—she knew only because she felt it in her throat—screaming. So caught up in the here and now of the horror that *here* meant everywhere and *now* meant forever.

Except eventually it stopped, or at least died away to near completion, with little roiling meltdowns still active in the main body of the destruction around them. She'd run out of scream; she crouched panting by Ramble, her face up against his golden coat; when he groaned she felt it through the skin of her cheek. *Stop it*, she told herself when she realized her teeth were chattering.

They didn't.

She looked anyway . . . she found they'd all gone down, all but the horses, although Lady, too, was on her knees. Dayna's horse was gone; Wheeler's stood crowded up against the edge of the bubble with Grunt and the others, crouched and quivering, ready to explode into flight at the first excuse. Wheeler himself had fallen off and lay twisted on the ground at Ramble's head, the knife jutting obscenely into the air from his chest. Suliya, her wet cheeks marked with fear, crawled toward him. Arlen raised his head, still wearing his ridiculous floppy hat; he'd thrown himself over Dayna, as if it would have done any good had the shield failed.

And behind Jaime was the woman agent, the one Lady had recognized. She'd dropped her weapon along the way, but she'd somehow made it into the bubble of safety before the meltdown rolled over them.

Still on her knees, Lady saw the woman, gave a startled huff. An offended huff. Her ears flattened; she heaved herself to all fours and as the woman looked up, as dazed as any of them, she still knew well enough to be alarmed.

"Lady, *no*," Suliya said, her voice full of impatience,

the reprimand of human to horse; she held Wheeler's hand, and she glanced at Lady in only a peremptory way.

"Don't do that," Jaime said sharply. "None of you. I don't know what happened between you all in Ohio, but I know what I saw when she finally made it back to Anfeald. She's not the same—not as Jess *or* Lady."

Dayna said nothing. Dayna knew what had happened. And so did Suliya, to judge by her face.

"She may not know all of our words, she may not think like us . . . but you'd best speak to her as though she does. She's got opinions and rights. Give her the courtesy you'd give anyone else."

"It worked for me," Arlen said. "But then, I talk to Grunt the same way. Which, come to think of it, didn't work nearly as well. Poor old Grunt."

And Lady's ears had come up. She ignored the woman; she came to Jaime instead, snuffling her face, running her whiskers along Jaime's skin and in the end, lipping at her hair, her expression suddenly soft.

"You're welcome," Jaime said quietly. And then, since no one else had done it, she turned to the newcomer, finding her as still and quiet as one substantially sturdy woman could be among the enemy. "Too late," Jaime told her. "We know you're there. Now come over here and stop this horse from bleeding. I don't care if you use every item of clothing on your body—get it done."

The woman glanced out on the meltdown, and then at the perfectly normal ground beneath them . . . and then at those she had called *enemy* only short moments before.

She began to undress.

She removed her jacket and then the knit fiber plainshirt—as close as Camolen clothing got to the T-shirt—below, replacing the jacket over the under-clothes that remained. "It's an action shirt," she said.

"It's got some healing properties. Dunno if they'll work again once we get out of this shield—"

They had better. Jaime didn't know how they handled horses in Camolen who had only three legs. She glanced at Wheeler and then Arlen and then back, finding Lady had taken up a watch over the woman. Good. Out of her hands for now. But Wheeler . . .

Thanks to Suliya, Wheeler wasn't quite as twisted as he had been, but he was just as dying. Again he caught Jaime's eye; again she found herself snared there, unable to look away until he did, and when he *did*, she followed his gaze. Out to the unsettled meltdown that surrounded them—and then back to her.

She followed his thought just as easily. No magic in here, in the shield . . . but they couldn't afford to drop it, and it would be suicide to take him out of it and attempt a spell in the middle of the biggest meltdown she'd ever seen.

There was nothing they could do for him.

"I'm sorry," Jaime said.

"Me too," he said, barely getting the words out; she moved closer, shoulder to shoulder with Suliya, who still held his hand.

She said fiercely, "I'll make sure my father knows it was *you* who saved Arlen."

Faint as it was, his grin held dark amusement. "All I could ask for," he said, not much in the way of sound behind his words.

Jaime closed her eyes a moment, overwhelmed, and when she opened them, Wheeler's sharply perceptive gaze had gone distant and still. Suliya placed his hand on his chest, but continued to stroke his hair, confusion laced into her somber expression. He'd been her enemy, her father's tool . . . and he'd ended up a hero.

Nothing Jaime could do.

But there, finally getting up to his knees, *still*

wearing that hat, was Arlen. Someone she wanted *in* her hands, and badly. Someone she'd never quite believed to be dead even if events and circumstances and the people around her had hammered her with the fact over and over and over again. "Arlen," she said, and he gave her a grin. Somewhat chagrined, a little embarrassed, and a lot more little boy delight than she'd seen in a long time.

At that she couldn't stop herself. "Arlen!" she said, and launched herself behind Suliya's back with such zeal that they both tumbled back to the ground, where she kissed him with enough enthusiasm that Dayna eventually started clapping, her droll tone somehow coming through in the calculated timing of the clap . . . clap . . . clap.

"Shut up!" Jaime said, tearing herself away for just an instant. "I'm not through!"

"She's not *through*," Arlen said with mock irritation.

"But—what happened to your face?" Jaime asked, suddenly aware of his reddened skin. "And where's your mustache? And where'd you get that *hat*?"

Arlen propped himself up on his elbows, giving Dayna a sorrowful look. "You let her get distracted. I'll remember that."

"I'll *never* be distracted," Jaime said. "You came *back*. Every time someone walked through the workroom door, I expected it to be you. Every time I heard a footstep in the hall, I thought it would be *you*. I *knew*—"

"And you were right." He pulled her in for a satisfied kiss, but she pulled right back away.

"You don't understand." She shook her head, put a hand over the empty spot that had lurked inside her since she'd started her very first vigil for someone who could *never* come back. An empty spot . . . empty no more. "*You came back*."

"I'll show you what I understand," he said.

After a moment, Dayna started clapping again, and when they both turned to glare at her, she said, "Ahem. Meltdowns? Light spells? Peacekeepers?"

"We can't all make it to the peacekeepers," Suliya said, still staring down at Wheeler. "Not Ramble . . . and we're missing your horse."

With utmost reluctance, Jaime put a few more inches between Arlen and herself. She said, "You're right. We need to get Ramble back to the hold—and whoever goes to handle him will need a wizard along for the shielding."

"Look!" Dayna said, pointing at the ground. She moved the shield boundary a few inches, out onto warped ground with arrow-sharp crystals extruding sideways from what might have been rock. Within the shield, the crystals crumbled into the finest dust, a confectioner's powder of metallic earth. "Reclamation!"

"That's a start," Jaime said, smiling at Dayna's excitement.

"I'll go back," Suliya said abruptly.

They all looked at her, all but Arlen, who'd taken to gazing at the destruction around them. The peacekeeper run was the glory mission, not taking wounded heros home.

She shrugged. "Arlen should be with the peacekeeper group. If I go with him, then Jaime's got to take Ramble with Dayna. Doesn't seem too bootin' right, does it? Splitting you two up again so soon. Don't suppose I'd impress *anyone* if I insisted on that."

Jaime gave her an uncontrollably big grin. "No," she said, reaching out for Arlen's hand.

But the glance he gave her was distracted, and an instant later he was looking out at the meltdown again.

"I keep seeing what it looked like, when it rolled over us," he said. "The last thing the rest of the Council—"

"Don't think of it," she said fiercely.

He gave her a look of mild surprise. "I'll always think of it."

Chapter 29

Impatience welled up inside Lady, pushing her into movement—an uneasy shift of her weight, an unnecessary flicking of her ears; she raised her head from her scrutiny of Ramble's care and inspected the meltdown around them, switching her attention from one spot to another with jerky exaggeration. The smell faded, but the remaining strength of it still triggered all her instincts to run. Strong smells meant large predators, no matter what she knew to the contrary; the smell of Ramble's blood and Wheeler's death did nothing to dissuade her instinctive urges. Not when she had the protection of her yet unapparent offspring to consider.

But neither instinct nor fear created her impatience. The people around her did that, slowly recovering from the attack and the meltdown, checking each other over, speaking in tones that meant relief and accomplishment.

Except they hadn't accomplished anything yet. All they'd done so far was survive.

Carey still waited for healing, healing that couldn't happen until Camolen's magic stabilized. Jaime may have started the stabilization process with Anfeald's couriers, but even Anfeald was only one precinct among many; only the peacekeepers had the authority to go to the source of the problem.

Peacekeepers!

She thought it loudly on the inside and snorted her emphasis on the outside, gaining the startled attention of everyone within the bubble. She pawed the ground, making it as clear as she could that the snort was no random thing. That her agitation was of significance.

"She's right," Arlen said. "We need to get moving—the sooner the peacekeepers have this information, the sooner Camolen can begin recovery. The sooner *Carey* can begin recovery, eh Lady?"

Jaime gave him a blank look as Lady stopped her pawing to snort more gently at Arlen, a rolling snort. "How did you—"

He grinned at her. "I can't suddenly read her mind, Jay. It's a continuation of a conversation we had not so long ago." He started to replace his hat on his head, gave it a second look, and sent it winging into the mangled forest, where it caught on a jagged protrusion and swung. "No more of *that*," he said. "And this shirt—it goes, at the first opportunity."

"You cannot imagine our relief," Dayna told him, checking the cinch on Wheeler's horse. Arlen smiled—but sobered quickly enough as he helped Suliya to her feet on his way past Wheeler, not pausing with the effort; his gaze stayed on Lady and when he stopped before her, she gave his shirt an affectionate nudge.

"You've got a choice," he told her. "You can go back to Anfeald and take the chance to see Carey, or you can help us get to the peacekeepers. If you wait to see Carey . . . you might miss him."

His meaning was clear enough to a horse with Jess in her mind. In an instant, she pricked her ears toward Anfeald. *Carey*. Her life had always been about Carey, one way or the other. She could not abandon him now.

And that meant that despite her yearning, despite her fears, despite her intense need to resolve that which had come between them, she had to go to the peacekeepers. With the rest of the horses shaky and upset, Lady was the one who could lead them swiftly to the peacekeeper hold, finding the shortest detours around meltdowns once they reached the trail again, taking the lead with the confidence to keep the others from faltering.

She knew one thing for certain—it would be Jaime she carried. She loved Arlen dearly, but if he never found his way to her back again it would be too soon for her; the next time, she'd dump him sooner and with much more purpose. She moved the short distance across the crowded bubble to Jaime, carefully stepping over Ramble's tail and hind legs. Jaime watched her uncertainly, a roundly athletic woman with flyaway hair and a few more lines by the edges of her mouth than not so long ago, and when Lady dipped her head, the gesture of a horse politely reaching for her bridle, Jaime said, "Are you sure? I mean, hells *yes*, Lady, I would be honored, but you know . . . he might not be there when we get back."

In the background, Arlen offered, "Simney will go to work as soon as Anfeald stabilizes. And the sooner we reach the peacekeepers—"

Neither Jaime nor Lady responded to him; Lady only dipped her head to Jaime again. Jaime reached out to stroke Lady's arched neck, running her fingers over the spellstones braided into her mane. "I'm supposed to tell you . . ." she said, and hesitated, but in the end got the words out. "He's sorry. Whatever happened . . . he's sorry."

Lady blinked; she ducked her nose and rubbed it along the inside of her front pastern, full of feeling and self-knowledge a horse wasn't meant to have, and wondering if the bittersweet pain of it would hurt any less if horses could cry.

Chapter 30

Carey never got enough air. His heart raced to make it happen, faltered when nothing helped. He sat propped up in his own bed, alternating between utter terror and a more comfortable haze of disbelief, no longer strong enough to do so much as wipe his own chin clean of the blood that came up with every cough and gurgle. Maybe he simply no longer saw the point.

Or maybe he was lost in other things. More important things. *Jess, I'm sorry. Jess, I did my best . . . and we both know it wasn't enough.*

He wouldn't have said it out loud if he could; he was never alone. Simney or Cesna or even Gertli; someone always sat by his bedside, sometimes in pairs. Sometimes they cried. Sometimes they murmured things they thought would comfort him, and sometimes Simney chanced using a simple pain relief spell—he recognized that one—or other spells, basic things nonetheless risky in Camolen's spell-twisted environment but which seemed to help make the breathing easier. They argued over it when they thought he wasn't listening, so Simney chanced to murmur fiercely, "I *know* it might go wrong and kill him! Do you think I'd do it if he weren't about to—" and then cut off, but her words had been obvious enough.

It didn't matter; they were right. And he wasn't listening, not really.

Jess, I'm sorry.

Until that hour after endless hours when Cesna sat holding his hand and said brokenly, softly, "It's all right, Carey. You've waited it out longer than any of us thought you could . . . but the basic spells aren't enough anymore, and we don't—we can't—" a hesitation, one entirely filled by the somehow still astonishing sensation of taking a breath and getting no air with it, over and over and he knew what she meant to say and he knew he was tired and he knew . . .

No more *I'm sorry.* Now, perhaps, time for *good-bye.* Exhausted and grieving and so full of regret that it welled up to trickle down the side of his face, mixing with blood. Gently, Cesna wiped it clean . . . but her hand trembled. He barely felt it. He felt his heart race, he felt his breathing hitch . . . slow . . .

"Carey!"

He was beyond recognizing voices, or knowing how many heartbeats had passed since Cesna stopped talking and started crying. This new voice came right to his ear, fierce and earnest. "We're cleared to work *real* magic, Carey—Linton just came in with the biggest collection of spellstones you'd ever hope to see, and Arlen's contacted Natt from the peacekeepers—he said things are stable enough that if we want to take the chance—"

She stopped, pulled herself together, and said simply, "It's going to be all right, Carey. Give me a few more moments, and we'll get you eased. It'll take awhile, but you're going to be all right. You have to be. I just promised Jess."

Jess . . . one more chance . . .

Awakening.

A long time coming, and slow.

Vague awareness came first, a sensation of warmth and then vague soreness. A healing kind of soreness, the kind that comes after exertion. He opened his eyes to the familiar view of his own ceiling, the unique patterns of carved stone over the bed. No one hailed the flicker of his eyelids; after a long moment of consideration, he turned his head to confirm that he was alone in his own bed, in his own bedroom. An unfamiliar table sat in the middle of the room; someone, until recently, had been keeping enough of a watch to take their meals here. On the short, tile-topped bedside table sat a glass pitcher and tumbler; cool moisture glinted on the outside of the pitcher, revealing the water's freshness. The room held the diffuse light of either dawn or twilight; he wasn't sure which. The room contained neither permalight nor normal glowspell, although a stubby candle sat on the bedside table.

Eventually, he sat up. Discovered he didn't tremble; he didn't cough. He didn't bleed. The dull ache remained. Healing left to go.

He slid out of bed, found himself clad in light sleeper bottoms, and wondered who'd had the honors. He gulped a tumbler of water, then half of another, and padded barefoot over old and comfortable rugs to the window. A touch confirmed what he thought he perceived—the window spells back in place. Anfeald couriers had spread the word . . . lights out in Camolen. Back to the glowspells that had served them so ably, so long.

Outside, light still filled the sky, more so than he would have guessed from the dim nature of the room; the stretching shadow of the hold across the road confirmed twilight. In the distance, two riders emerged from the woods, skirting the small blot of a meltdown and cantering easily for the hold.

He'd know that movement anywhere. Not the choppy nature of the dark bay's gaits, but the collected ease of the dun, and the quiet seat of her rider. After a moment he picked out the lanky frame and uneasy, elbow-flapping style of the second rider, and gave a short laugh. *Arlen*. Jaime had said he was alive, but somehow until this moment . . .

Eventually he'd learn how and why. For now it was enough to know it was true. Arlen was alive, and he'd come back—from the peacekeepers, most likely, and with Jaime and Lady at his side.

Lady. His stomach tightened suddenly, a frisson of unexpected emotion. He hadn't been sure he'd have this chance . . . that he'd live to try for it, or that she'd be here if he did. He needed to grab some pants, throw on a shirt, test his legs on a slow trip down the stairs to greet her—

But something kept him at the window. As the light faded, shadows disappearing into true twilight, he stood straight-armed against the sill, swaying just enough to remind himself it had been a close thing after all. And in the twilight, a lone horse cantered out again, stripped of her gear, scrubbed clean of her sweat and saddle marks. Cantered out in a leisurely fashion, carrying herself just as beautifully as under the guidance of Jaime's expert riding. His fingers tightened on the stone sill, struck by her beauty and by the fact—

She was leaving.

But not far out, she came to a light stop, and she raised her finely-molded head to look back over her shoulder. Not at the door to the barn from which she'd come, but higher. To this window.

For a moment, he stopped breathing, thinking—hoping—she might turn around.

She gave a little flip of her head—a challenge—and cantered on.

But he'd gotten the message.

His place, this time, to go to her.

Chapter 31

Lady grazed alone. Ramble, newly and permanently crippled, had a spot of honor in the sick stall within the hold stables as the wound closed, and from Jaime's daily reports, did well enough with the confinement, newly mannered and newly adored. Suliya cared for him, Jaime said. Suliya who'd turned down her family's urgent pleas to return home, who took lessons without argument, and who still cried over a man who'd had so much integrity he'd died for someone he'd once taken orders to kill.

Pleased as she was for Suliya, Lady knew how to snort in all the right places so Jaime knew that the young woman nonetheless had next to no chance of ever riding her again. And Jaime only laughed and said, "Good for you." After that, on occasion, Lady changed to Jess when she saw Jaime coming.

The first time, she was startled at the changes in

her body—her exquisitely tender breasts, her propensity
for the hiccups, and her odd wish for potatoes fried
in hot spices. Jaime, too, must have noticed something,
for after that someone came to the open pasture every
day with an offering of light grains mixed with the
drooling-good supplement Lady had never before
needed. Otherwise Jaime didn't mention the changes;
neither did Jess. They talked about Jaime's decision to
move to Camolen permanently, and her plans to bring
Sabre along and start a new school here in Anfeald.
They talked about Camolen's excruciatingly slow
recovery—for although the magic had stabilized, the
services infrastructure remained down and the landscape ravaged—and of Arlen's intense amusement at
the new Council's delirious relief at his reappearance.
Jaime brushed out the snarled tangles of Jess's dun and
black hair, expressing mild sorrow at its wild-horse rag-
gedness.

As Lady, Jess spent considerable time staring at the
dark spot along the hold's face that had once been her
bedroom window—hers and Carey's. As Lady she
missed him; as Jess she hurt beyond words, and so only
became Jess for Jaime. She knew from Jaime that he'd
healed well, worked hard, and spent as least as much
time as she staring back out that window.

But there was a rightness in her time here. Enjoy-
ing her gallops, her dozing, the pleasure of a good roll,
the increasing awareness of new life within her even
so early in its growth. She accepted food but no one's
touch; she kept her manners but made her own rules.

Finally, he came. With the insects buzzing a summer morning symphony in the rolling, horse-dotted
fields around the hold, he walked the long path to her
far pasture and paused by the always-open gate, a soft
blanket tucked over his arm, an apple bulging out of

one hip pocket, and uncharacteristic uncertainty
shadowing his eyes and making worry lines in his forehead.

In his free hand he held not a bridle, but a bitless
sidepull.

He, who had never ridden Lady once she'd been
Jess. Never talked about it. Never faced the physical
reality of who she was.

She came to the gate and dropped her head for the
sidepull, a simple headstall with reins attached to a soft
cavesson. And then she moved next to the old tree
stump by the gate, used by years' worth of riders for
just this reason. Carey left the blanket over the gate,
stirring gently in the breeze, and the apple by the gate
post. He stood on the tree stump for a moment, facing her sturdy dun back with its thick black stripe, the
one he'd traced so often in its fainter iteration down
her human spine.

Patience.

The very patience he'd given her in her early training, in her struggles with balance and the restraint of
her natural exuberance and acceptance of rules, she
now gave back to him. Sweeping her long tail at the
flies, flicking an ear at the squeaky twitter of birds, she
waited.

Finally, his weight settled onto her back, as gently
as ever.

How she'd missed it!

After a moment he relaxed, giving her the faint lift
of seat that once meant *move off* and now meant he
was ready if she was.

She took him out into the woods, letting him ease into
the habit of working with her—of supporting her when
she needed it, of reminding her and pointing things out
to her instead of commanding and ordering.

In truth, it was all he'd ever done once she'd come

into her own as a courier horse; all he'd ever needed to do. He had somehow forgotten that along the way.

They returned home at a passage, an airy floating trot that Jaime had taught her and Carey had never felt, and he laughed out loud when she offered it. She stopped at the gate, a perfect square halt, neck arched and high, reins loose on her neck. He hesitated, much as he had when mounting—a reluctance of a different nature. But he slid off, and when she swung her head around for removal of the sidepull, he scratched the itchy spots behind her ears just like he always had, running a wistful hand along her spellstones.

Not many of them left.

She gave a good shake, the summer breeze cool on her back where he'd been sitting, and eased into the pasture, realizing for the first time that the rest of the hold had limited today's activities to the nearer pastures. Horses going in and out, grooms spreading wheelbarrows of stall pickings, the daily round of fence inspections . . . no one came near.

Carey lifted the blanket and settled it over her withers, a soft fold of material that came to her elbows and smelled of their rooms even though she'd never seen it before. And then, astonishingly—awkward as ever after he'd been riding and his body started to stiffen—he sat before her.

"I almost didn't have the chance to say this." He hesitated, struggling with the words even now, his face full of the death he'd touched. "I almost died, not having you, and it was worse than the dying itself. I had to think about that. A lot."

She bobbed her head. She knew.

"Once," he said, "you came and sat at my feet, newly human and still willing to give yourself up to me."

She stood stock-still, hoping too hard to move.

Carey buried his face in his hands, then scrubbed

those hands over his lean features and through his hair, leaving it entirely mussed, a warm, dark-rooted blond in the sunlight. "It's got to go both ways, Jess. It's taken me far too long to realize it."

She gave a huge sigh of relief, of hope fulfilled and heart overflowing. She changed for him. The blanket was wonderful about her human shoulders, soft and caressing and full of bright colors her horse's eye hadn't been able to appreciate. But it did nothing to hide the swell of the child within her, the early months of the long equine gestation translated into a shorter human term.

Carey froze, taken completely by surprise; struggling. He knew where she'd been, who she'd been with, in those days of running from easternmost Camolen to Anfeald. He knew her mare's seasons. He floundered, muscles stark as a clenched jaw—and then he glanced up to the window she'd watched for so long, looking at that room where he'd almost died. And he let out a long, slow breath and he said softly, "Hey, Braveheart."

She sat in the grass next to him, surprised by her own awkwardness and of the instant opinion it was best to be a horse if pregnant. She said simply, "We were horses. We did horse things."

"Mm," he said thoughtfully. He touched her long, ragged hair; he smoothed the thin healing scar on her shoulder, his outward calm belied by the unsteady nature of his touch. "Maybe that's the way it had to be."

She thought of the moments she'd sat beside the tree and cried, coming to accept this very thing. She looked away from him. "Yes. I think so."

He startled her with a playful poke to the same leg he'd been stroking. "Ay," he said, a clear imitation of Suliya. "How about you come stay with me for a while, and we'll do human things?"

She said, "Yes."
For Carey—finally—*awakening*.
For Dun Lady's Jess . . .
Legacy fulfilled.

Doranna's Backstory . . .

After obtaining a degree in wildlife illustration and environmental education, Doranna spent a number of years deep in the Appalachian Mountains, riding the trails and writing SF and fantasy books. She's moved on to living in the Northern Arizona mountains, where she still rides and writes and now dabbles in building websites for other authors. There's an Arabian and a Lipizzan in her backyard, a mountain looming outside her office window, a pack of dogs running around the house, and a laptop sitting on her desk—and that's just the way she likes it.

You can contact her at:

dmd@doranna.net

or

PO Box 31123
Flagstaff, AZ 86003-1123
(SASE please)

or visit *http://www.doranna.net/*

DORANNA DURGIN's
Fantasy

"Doranna Durgin envelops her appealing characters with a rare, shimmering aura of mystic legend."

—*Romantic Times*

"Durgin has a remarkable gift for inventing unusual characters doing incredible things."   —*Booklist*

Changespell   87765-8 $5.99   ☐

"Durgin tells this deeply insightful and touching tale with a deft clarity. Her eye for detail will delight and astonish you ..."

—*Hypatia's Hoard*

Barrenlands   87872-7 $5.99   ☐

"Ms. Durgin knows full well the value of pacing as she exquisitely choreographs action and character development into a pleasing whole."

—*Romantic Times*

Wolf Justice   87891-3 $5.99   ☐

"Wolf Justice will delight fans ... Well-rounded and widely appealing, this one comes highly recommended."   —*Hypatia's Hoard*

Wolverine's Daughter   57847-2 $6.99   ☐

"Move over, Xena! The adventures of Kelyn the Wolverine's daughter are a pure joy to read. ..."   —*A.C. Crispin*

Seer's Blood   57877-4 $6.99   ☐

A Feral Darkness   31994-9 $6.99   ☐

TIME SCOUTS CAN DO

In the early part of the 21st century disaster struck—an experiment went wrong, bad wrong. The Accident almost destroyed the universe, and ripples in time washed over the Earth. Soon, the people of the depopulated post-disaster Earth learned that things were going to be a little different.... They'd be able to travel into the past, utilizing remnant time strings. It took brave pioneers to map the time gates: you can zap yourself out of existence with a careless jump, to say nothing of getting killed by some rowdy downtimer who doesn't like people who can't speak his language. So elaborate rules are evolved and Time Travel stations become big business.

But wild and wooly pioneers aren't the most likely people to follow rules... Which makes for great adventures as Time Scouts Kit Carson, Skeeter Jackson, and Margo Carson explore Jack the Ripper's London, the Wild West of the '49 Gold Rush, Edo Japan, the Roman Empire and more.

❦❧

"Engaging, fast moving, historically literate, and filled with Asprin's expertise on the techniques and philosophy of personal combat, this is first-class action SF."   —*Booklist*

"The characters ... are appealing and their adventures exciting ..."   —*Science Fiction Chronicle*

❦❧

The Time Scout series
by Robert Asprin & Linda Evans

Time Scout	87698-8	$5.99	___
Wagers of Sin	87730-5	$5.99	___
Ripping Time	57867-7	$6.99	___
The House that Jack Built	31965-5	$6.99	___

THE SHIP WHO SANG IS NOT ALONE!

Anne McCaffrey, with Mercedes Lackey, S.M. Stirling, and Jody Lynn Nye, explores the universe she created with her ground-breaking novel, The Ship Who Sang.

THE SHIP WHO SEARCHED
by Anne McCaffrey & Mercedes Lackey

Tia, a bright and spunky seven-year-old accompanying her exo-archaeologist parents on a dig, is afflicted by a paralyzing alien virus. Tia won't be satisfied to glide through life like a ghost in a machine. Like her predecessor Helva, *The Ship Who Sang*, she would rather strap on a spaceship!

THE CITY WHO FOUGHT
by Anne McCaffrey & S.M. Stirling

Simeon was the "brain" running a peaceful space station—but when the invaders arrived, his only hope of protecting his crew and himself was to become *The City Who Fought*.

THE SHIP WHO WON
by Anne McCaffrey & Jody Lynn Nye

"The brainship Carialle and her brawn, Keff, find a habitable planet inhabited by an apparent mix of races and cultures and dominated by an elite of apparent magicians. Appearances are deceiving, however... a brisk, well-told often amusing tale.... Fans of either author, or both, will have fun with this book."
—*Booklist*